D0394707

# The Best American Mystery Stories 2015

GUEST EDITORS OF
THE BEST AMERICAN MYSTERY STORIES

1997 ROBERT B. PARKER
1998 SUE GRAFTON
1999 ED MCBAIN
2000 DONALD E. WESTLAKE
2001 LAWRENCE BLOCK
2002 JAMES ELLROY
2003 MICHAEL CONNELLY
2004 NELSON DEMILLE
2005 JOYCE CAROL OATES
2006 SCOTT TUROW
2007 CARL HIAASEN
2008 GEORGE PELECANOS
2009 JEFFERY DEAVER
2010 LEE CHILD
2011 HARLAN COBEN
2012 ROBERT CRAIS
2013 LISA SCOTTOLINE
2014 LAURA LIPPMAN
2015 JAMES PATTERSON

# The Best American Mystery Stories™ 2015

Edited and with an Introduction
by **James Patterson**

Otto Penzler, *Series Editor*

HOUGHTON MIFFLIN HARCOURT

BOSTON • NEW YORK 2015

Copyright © 2015 by Houghton Mifflin Harcourt Publishing Company
Introduction copyright © 2015 James Patterson

ALL RIGHTS RESERVED

The Best American Series® is a registered trademark of Houghton Mifflin Harcourt Publishing Company. *The Best American Mystery Stories*™ is a trademark of Houghton Mifflin Harcourt Publishing Company.

No part of this work may be reproduced or transmitted in any form or by any means, electronic or mechanical, including photocopying and recording, or by any information storage or retrieval system without the proper written permission of the copyright owner unless such copying is expressly permitted by federal copyright law. With the exception of nonprofit transcription in Braille, Houghton Mifflin Harcourt is not authorized to grant permission for further uses of copyrighted selections reprinted in this book without the permission of their owners. Permission must be obtained from the individual copyright owners as identified herein. Address requests for permission to make copies of Houghton Mifflin Harcourt material to Permissions, Houghton Mifflin Harcourt Publishing Company, 215 Park Avenue South, New York 10003.

www.hmhco.com

ISSN 1094-8384
ISBN 978-0-544-63874-7
ISBN 978-0-544-52675-4 (pbk.)

Printed in the United States of America
DOC 10 9 8 7 6 5 4 3 2 1

These stories are works of fiction. Names, characters, places, and incidents are products of the authors' imagination or are used fictitiously. Any resemblance to actual events, locales, or persons, living or dead, is entirely coincidental.

"The Snow Angel" by Doug Allyn. First published in *Ellery Queen's Mystery Magazine,* January 2014. Copyright © 2014 by Doug Allyn. Reprinted by permission of Doug Allyn.

"Cowboy Justice" by Andrew D. Bourelle. First published in *Law and Disorder: Stories of Conflict & Crime.* Copyright © 2014 by Andrew D. Bourelle. Reprinted by permission of Andrew D. Bourelle.

"Rosalee Carrasco" by Tomiko M. Breland. First published in *Ploughshares,* Winter 2014. Copyright © 2014 by Tomiko M. Breland. Reprinted by permission of Tomiko M. Breland.

"Wet with Rain" by Lee Child. First published in *Belfast Noir.* Copyright © 2014 by Lee Child. Reprinted by permission of Lee Child.

"Red Eye: Patrick Kenzie vs. Harry Bosch: An Original Short Story" by Dennis Lehane and Michael Connelly. First published in *FaceOff,* edited by David Baldacci. Copyright © 2014 by Dennis Lehane and Michael Connelly. Reprinted by permission of Dennis Lehane and Michael Connelly.

"Harm and Hammer" by Joseph D'Agnese. First published in *Alfred Hitchcock's*

*Mystery Magazine,* October 2014. Copyright © 2014 by Joseph D'Agnese. Reprinted by permission of Joseph D'Agnese.

"The Adventure of the Laughing Fisherman" by Jeffery Deaver. First published in *In the Company of Sherlock Holmes.* Copyright © 2014 by Gunner Publications, LLC. Reprinted by permission of Jeffery Deaver, Manager.

"Crush Depth" by Brendan DuBois. First published in *Ice Cold,* edited by Jeffery Deaver and Raymond Benson. Copyright © 2014 by Brendan DuBois. Reprinted by permission of Brendan DuBois.

"Molly's Plan" by John M. Floyd. First published in the *Strand Magazine,* Issue XLIII, June–Sept 2014. Copyright © 2014 by John M. Floyd. Reprinted by permission of John M. Floyd.

"A Bottle of Scotch and a Sharp Buck Knife" by Scott Grand. First published in *Thuglit,* Issue 11. Copyright © 2014 by Zach Basnett. Reprinted by permission of Zach Basnett.

"Shared Room on Union" by Steven Heighton. First published in *The Dead Are More Visible* by Steven Heighton. Copyright © 2012 by Steven Heighton. Reprinted by permission of Alfred A. Knopf Canada, a division of Penguin Random House Canada Limited, a Penguin Random House Company, and Steven Heighton.

"Afterlife of a Stolen Child" by Janette Turner Hospital. First published in the *Georgia Review,* vol. LXVIII, no. 3, Fall 2014. Copyright © 2014 by Janette Turner Hospital. Reprinted by permission of the *Georgia Review.*

"Apocrypha" by Richard Lange. First published in *Bull Men's Fiction, Bull #4.* Copyright © 2014 by Richard Lange. Reprinted by permission of the author.

"Staircase to the Moon" by Theresa E. Lehr. First published in *Alfred Hitchcock's Mystery Magazine,* September 2014. Copyright © 2014 by Theresa E. Lehr. Reprinted by permission of Theresa E. Lehr.

"A Man Looking for Trouble" by Lee Martin. First published in *Glimmer Train Stories,* Issue 90, Spring/Summer 2014. Copyright © 2014 by Lee Martin. Reprinted by permission of Lee Martin.

"Many Dogs Have Died Here" by James Mathews. First published in *Iron Horse Literary Review* 16.3, 2014. Copyright © 2014 by James Mathews. Reprinted by permission of James Mathews.

"Motherlode" by Thomas McGuane. First published in *The New Yorker,* September 8, 2014. From *Crow Fair: Stories by Thomas McGuane,* copyright © 2015 by Thomas McGuane. Used by permission of Alfred A. Knopf, an imprint of the Knopf Doubleday Publishing Group, a division of Penguin Random House LLC. All rights reserved. Any third party use of this material, outside of this publication, is prohibited. Interested parties must apply directly to Penguin Random House LLC for permission.

"A Kidnapping in Koulèv-Ville" by Kyle Minor. First published in *The Normal School,* Spring 2014. Copyright © 2014 by Kyle Minor. Reprinted by permission of Kyle Minor.

"The Home at Craigmillnar" by Joyce Carol Oates. First published in the *Kenyon Review,* Winter 2014. Copyright © 2014 by The Ontario Review, Inc. Reprinted by permission of The Ontario Review, Inc.

"The Shot" by Eric Rutter. First published in *Alfred Hitchcock's Mystery Magazine,* November 2014. Copyright © 2014 by Eric Rutter. Reprinted by permission of Eric Rutter.

# Contents

# Foreword

AUTHORS ARE SELDOM cultural icons in America. A vast number of young people cannot identify a photo of Joe Biden or Mitt Romney, have never heard of *The New Yorker* or *The Atlantic,* think Abraham Lincoln is the president of the United States (yes, a survey taken last year showed that 4 percent of Americans were confident that this was the case), and guess that Stephen Hawking is, like, um, a quarterback. Yet they can instantly recognize a photo of Katy Perry or Beyoncé and, in all likelihood, provide a comprehensive discography in relatively accurate chronology. But an author? Someone who writes the books from which their favorite films are so frequently adapted? No.

Publishers spend small fortunes advertising and marketing their star authors, and legions of writers work their fingers bloody tweeting, blogging, posting, and whatever else it's possible to do on various social media. Authors make personal appearances at bookshops, libraries, universities, and whatever organizations will have them, and they give scads of interviews for newspapers, magazines, websites, radio programs, podcasts, and television shows. Nonetheless, most may as well be laboring in the Witness Protection Program for all the recognition they receive, while their books seemingly are released as documents that only those classified with top-level security clearance may locate.

Having made that (perhaps) hyperbolic statement, I should note that there are occasional exceptions to the anonymity of authors, and there is no greater refutation of the concept of anonymity than James Patterson, the guest editor of *The Best American Mystery Stories 2015*.

Several factors contribute to the recognizability of Patterson's name and, more recently, likeness. First, predictably, is the enormous popularity of his books, largely instigated by his creation of Alex Cross, the African-American psychologist who works as a homicide detective in the Washington, D.C., police department. While most mystery writers struggle with the expectation of writing a book every year, the prolific Patterson increased his presence by writing multiple books every year, ultimately producing so many different series that he hired other authors to collaborate with him. When he began to add books for young readers to his opera, his output reached a book a month—every one of which sold enormous quantities (the *New York Times* reported that one out of every seventeen hardcover novels published in the United States since 2006 has been written by Patterson).

As books are being published with such regularity and in such impressive numbers, there is always a Patterson book on the bestseller list and in the front of the store, so it is impossible to avoid being reminded of his work and his name. He is now a "brand." Also, and this is extremely unusual in the world of publishing, his books are advertised on television, frequently with the author on-screen, enticing potential readers while warning them of the scary stuff that awaits them.

Finally, Patterson has become a highly visible spokesman for literacy programs, to which he offers more than his name and image. He has initiated several programs to which he has contributed millions of dollars, most recently in the form of stipends to independent booksellers.

How he found the time to be the guest editor for this book is anyone's guess. Why he agreed to do it is more complex. Trust me—it's not for the money, which would be a rounding error for his monthly income. It's not because he needs another book on the shelf to prove he works hard. I confess that I didn't ask the question, lest he pause for a moment to ask himself what in the world he was doing.

Most likely Patterson has an affection for this important series and liked the idea of being part of it. I helped him assemble a library of great fiction (titles that he chose), reflecting his eclectic but elevated taste (he loves *War and Peace, Ulysses, One Hundred*

*Years of Solitude*). It is evident that literature means a great deal to him, and let's face it, having his involvement with this book will help sales (Houghton Mifflin Harcourt is even releasing a hardcover edition this year). A lot of contributors who are not household names will receive exposure that they would have been unlikely to have had otherwise.

As has been true every year (and this is the nineteenth volume in the series), this is a wonderful collection of original fiction about extremes of human behavior caused by despair, hate, greed, fear, envy, insanity, or love—sometimes in combination. Desperate people may consider desperate acts, and desperation is a fertile ground for poor choices. Many of the authors in this cornucopia of crime have described how antisocial solutions to difficult situations may occur, and why perpetrators feel that their violent responses to conflicts seem appropriate.

The psychology of crime has become the dominant form of mystery fiction in recent years, while the classic detective tale of observation and deduction has faded further into the background. Those tales of pure deduction may be the most difficult mystery stories to write, as it has become increasingly difficult to find original motivations for murder, or a new murder method, or an original way to hide a vital clue until the detective unearths it. The working definition of a mystery story for this series is any work of fiction in which a crime, or the threat of a crime, is central to the theme or the plot. The detective story is merely one subgenre in the literary form known as the mystery, just as are romantic suspense, espionage, legal legerdemain, medical thriller, political duplicity, and stories told from the point of view of the villain.

To find the best of these stories is a yearlong quest, largely enabled by Nat Sobel, the best literary agent in the world, and by my invaluable colleague, Michele Slung, who culls the mystery magazines, both printed and electronic, for suitable stories, just as she does short story collections (works by a single author) and anthologies (works by a variety of authors), popular magazines, and, perhaps the richest trove to be mined, literary journals. As the fastest and smartest reader I have ever known, she looks at somewhere between 3,000 and 5,000 stories a year, largely to determine if they are mysteries (you can't tell a story by its title) and then to determine if they are worth serious consideration. I then read the harvested crop, passing along the best fifty (or at least those I liked best) to the guest editor, who selects the twenty that are then reprinted, the other thirty being listed in an honor roll as "Other Distinguished Mystery Stories."

A word of thanks is more than appropriate for the previous eighteen guest editors (listed at the front of the book), who gave so much of their time and energy to help make this such a distinguished and successful series.

The search has already begun for suitable stories for next year's edition. To qualify, a story must be—duh—a mystery, must be written by an American or a Canadian, and must have had its first publication in the calendar year 2015 in an American or Canadian publication. If you are the author of such a work, or its editor, or any interested party (your credentials will not be reviewed), please feel free to submit it. Every word of *Ellery Queen's Mystery Magazine, Alfred Hitchcock's Mystery Magazine,* and *The Strand* is read, so there's no need to waste postage on sending a story from them. If the story was first published online, only hard copies will be read; these must include the name of the e-zine, the date on which it was published, and contact information. No unpublished stories are eligible, for what should be obvious reasons. Submitted material will not be returned. If you do not trust the U.S. Postal Service to deliver the book, magazine, or tearsheets, please enclose a self-addressed postcard to receive confirmation.

The earlier submissions are received, the less hurriedly will they be read. Please send submissions to Otto Penzler, The Mysterious Bookshop, 58 Warren Street, New York, NY 10007. If your story is one of the fifty or sixty or more customarily delivered by thoughtless dunderheads during Christmas week, it may not receive quite the same respectful reading as those submitted in less crowded months. If the story is published during the last week of the year, okay, fair enough. But if it was published in the spring and you just got around to sending it, I will view it as a personal affront and an attempt to ruin my Christmas celebrations; you will have had to write an extraordinary story for me to forgive you. Because of the unforgiving deadlines necessarily imposed on a work of this nature, the absolute final date for receiving material is December 31. This is neither an arrogant nor a whimsical decision, but is essential in order for production schedules to be met. If it arrives on January 2, it will not be read. Yes, really.

O.P.

# Introduction

A few years ago, I dug up some short stories to share with my son, Jack. I got him the world's greatest (and funniest) story of workplace dysfunction, "The Catbird Seat" by James Thurber. I dusted off the classic that some say inspired *The Hunger Games*—"The Lottery" by Shirley Jackson. I got him the not terribly short but unforgettable Hemingway classic, "The Short, Happy Life of Francis Macomber." I passed him the heartbreaking "All Summer in a Day" by Ray Bradbury. And several others.

They included laugh-out-louders, cry-in-your-handers, heart-in-your-throaters, and shake-your-fist-at-the-worlders. All, to my mind, were profound and provocative. It's no wonder these stories have endured through the years. Each one manages to say something more profound and provocative in a few pages than some novels manage to say over the course of several hundred pages.

These days, Americans tend to think about short stories in a, well, shortsighted way. How many short stories can the average person name off the top of his head? Probably a few here and there by Edgar Allan Poe, sure. But how about ones that were written in the last year? The last five years? The last ten? I think you'd be hard-pressed to find even a handful of people who could do it.

It's a simple fact of modern life that short stories are not very popular. Which is bizarre when one considers what one hears about our attention spans. My personal theory is not that they don't work for us any longer but rather that we (except when we're trying to inspire our kids with the things that inspired us when we were their age) have largely forgotten about them. And, perhaps, that they haven't been very well published lately, given the changes in the magazine world.

The short story is also one of the most fertile mediums for adaptations. Movies, TV shows, and plays are often adapted from short stories, and it's not hard to see why. With such a limited amount of space, authors bring to life a world created through the painstaking selection of every single word, leaving a lasting, highly visual impression in the minds of readers.

Think of some iconic films, ones that have made a cultural impact in our world — *The Birds, The Curious Case of Benjamin Button, Brokeback Mountain, The Shawshank Redemption, Minority Report, Million Dollar Baby.* Did you know they were based on short stories? Does the typical moviegoing American know? People love short stories, and often they don't even realize it.

When I think about the batch of short stories you're about to read, it makes me wish more people would read these imaginative, rich, complex tales before (if?) they get the big-screen treatment. I often hear people lamenting the state of Hollywood, how they're hungry for original, dynamic, surprising stories rather than another middling popcorn one. If that's the case, I've got one thing to say: read these short stories. You can thank me later.

One such story, "Molly's Plan" by John M. Floyd, details the formation and execution of a bank heist so real and intense that I find it impossible to believe the tale took up only a few pages. "Branch manager Donald Ramsey was fond of saying that no one on earth was brave enough or foolish enough to attempt to rob his bank. He was mistaken," writes Floyd. And just a few paragraphs later? Not to give too much away, but we learn that to get people to follow a bank robber's instructions, "A little blood is a fantastic incentive . . ." An imaginative twist at the end of the story makes it a truly satisfying read.

Jeffery Deaver's "The Adventure of the Laughing Fisherman" delivers a walloping blow to the head with its big number of unexpected turns. A modern send-up of Sherlock Holmes, the story introduces us to Paul Winslow, whose affinity with the famous sleuth isn't quite what it seems. I was so enamored with the originality and creativity of this story that by the time I read the last word, I found myself cursing the format of the short story, because I wanted to read so much more about this imaginative character

Deaver has created. This one could easily be a major Hollywood franchise.

Another of the things I love about short stories is how they can make fresh voices accessible to readers. I'd bet people are more willing to read a few pages of a short story by an unknown author than they are to read an entire book. Take "Rosalee Carrasco" by Tomiko M. Breland, an up-and-coming writer whose fiction placed in the 2014 Writer's Digest Popular Fiction Contest. This story about a high school tragedy blew me away with its simplicity and power. As you'll soon discover, it's what Breland chooses *not* to say that packs the biggest punch.

There are also glimpses into the lives of intriguing characters, as is the case with Kyle Minor's "A Kidnapping in Koulèv-Ville" and Lee Martin's "A Man Looking for Trouble." The former examines the choices of a privileged young woman living in Haiti, while the latter explores the devastating effects of infidelity and war on a small-town family. These are unfamiliar characters living through very familiar circumstances. The reader is innately drawn in—who didn't rebel against their parents during those wonderfully arrogant teenage years of life? And what person hasn't had the realization that their parents, once so heroic and infallible in their childhood eyes, are just normal people perfectly capable of making their own bad choices? "That night, I couldn't say I loved my mother, or Bill, or my father, who had gone without saying a word to me," writes Martin. "I could only say that I felt sorry for them—sorry for all the trouble they'd found—and I felt sorry for Connie, who didn't deserve to be on the other side of that trouble. It would be a while before I'd be able to say that I didn't deserve it either." These stories offer real, poignant portraits without ever veering into the maudlin or melodramatic.

I'm confident that you'll enjoy reading these stories (and so will Jack), and I have no doubt we'll be seeing a few of them adapted for the big screen in years to come. Of course, it would be nice for as many people as possible to read these stories before that happens, but there's a bright side to Hollywood's hunger for short stories. It means that as long as authors keep writing with such vividness and ingenuity, we'll reap the benefits of having fantastic stories available to us both on screen and on paper.

JAMES PATTERSON

# The Best American
# Mystery Stories 2015

DOUG ALLYN

# The Snow Angel

FROM *Ellery Queen's Mystery Magazine*

I SMILED WHEN I saw the dead girl. Just for a moment. Reflex, I suppose.

In Kabul, I once clawed through a busload of bodies after a bomb blast, desperately seeking any sign of life. Didn't find it.

As a Detroit cop, I saw victims almost daily, and even after transferring home to Valhalla, on Michigan's North Shore, I've seen more corpses than I care to.

But never one like this.

The teenager was sprawled on the snow-covered lawn, her honey-blond hair wreathing her face like a halo. She was surrounded by lighted holiday figures, a laughing Santa in his sleigh, eight wire-framed reindeer, gaily winking and blinking. The girl's white satin gown was dusted with ice crystals that reflected the flickering LEDs, making her glitter like the display's centerpiece.

A snow angel.

The scene was so perfect, it almost looked posed, like the girl had dozed off in the middle of a photo shoot for a Hallmark card.

She hadn't, though.

Her face and lips were a pale pastel blue, her brows and lashes rimed with frost.

In her last moments, she'd thrashed about, striving to rise. To live. But the bone-deep cold sapped her strength. She slipped into an icy coma and then away, leaving her body centered in the image her struggles had created.

A perfect snow angel.

And at first glance, I couldn't help smiling. Instinctively reacting to the scene. Who doesn't love a snow angel?

My partner, Zina Redfern, caught my smile and gave me an odd look. I turned away, trying to morph my grin into a wince. I doubt she bought it. Zina is short, squared-off, and intense. All business. Raven-haired, with dark eyes and a copper complexion, she favors Johnny Cash black on the job. Slacks, boots, and nylon jackets. If she owns a dress, I've never seen it. Her heritage is First Nation. Anishnabeg. But she's a sidewalk Indian, grew up tough in Flint's east-side gangland. She's a solid partner, but not an easy read.

"Who called this in?" I asked.

"Mail lady," Zina said. "She dropped a package at the house around eight this morning. Spotted the girl on her way in, took a closer look on the way out. Called 911. Van Duzen caught the squeal, found the girl. He pounded on the front door but nobody answered. He thought he'd better wait for us. Mail lady didn't know anything, so he sent her on her way."

"Okay." I nodded, then I turned in a slow circle, scanning the crime scene.

We were in Sugar Hill, the richest enclave in Valhalla. Homes here don't have addresses, they have names. This one, Champlin Hall, was an honest-to-God nineteenth-century mansion. A sprawling brick Beaux Arts estate with ornate stonework, towering Gothic windows.

Built by one of the old lumber barons, the estate had been updated over the years. The carriage house became a six-car garage, servants' quarters now housed exchange students from the Sudan, Serbia, or Ontario, depending on which sports they specialized in.

A half-dozen cars were parked in the circular drive, all of them dusted lightly by last night's snowfall. No one had come or gone. The only fresh tire tracks were from the mail truck, my Jeep, and Van Duzen's prowlie, still idling in the driveway, its exhaust rising white in the icy air.

A pristine, snowy Saturday morning. The kind they put on magazine covers.

Except our star attraction wasn't breathing.

Joni Cohen, Valhalla PD's intern tech, was kneeling beside the girl, collecting her nonexistent vitals.

Tall, gawky, and permanently perky, Joni's a junior at Michigan State majoring in forensic anthropology. Her class schedule keeps her in constant transit between Valhalla and the capital down in Lansing. Somehow she pulls a 3.9 GPA and still does a first-rate job as a crime-scene tech.

Ordinarily, Joni's totally absorbed by her work. Whistles softly to herself amid the carnage of a five-car pileup. No tunes today, though. With Santa and his reindeer beaming over her shoulder, she couldn't even fake "Jingle Bells."

"So?" I prompted.

"First impression, it's pretty much what it looks like," Joni said, frowning down at the angel. "Hypothermia. There are no tracks but hers, no signs of violence. It looks like she took a shortcut across the lawn, headed for a car in the driveway. Maybe felt woozy, sat down to rest a minute? It was eighteen degrees last night and she wasn't wearing a coat. She nodded out and . . . well. She froze to death."

"Are you all right?" Zina asked.

"No," Joni said flatly. "I know this girl. Not personally, but I've seen her around the Vale Junior College campus. A freshman, I think."

"Whoa, take a break, Joni," I said. "The state police Forensics Unit will be here in a few minutes—"

"No, I'm okay. Really," she said, taking a ragged breath. "My uncle warned me if I did my internship in Vale County, sooner or later I'd be working on people I knew. At least this girl wasn't mashed by a road grader. Let's just—get on with it."

"Okay," I said. "Time frame?"

"Her body temp's twenty-one degrees above ambient. I'd estimate she walked out here around eleven. Actual time of death was probably between one-thirty and three A.M. We may get tighter numbers after the autopsy. There's no scent of alcohol. If she'd been drinking, it wasn't much."

"Wasn't legal either," Zina said. "I found her purse in the snow beside the driveway. Her driver's license says she's Julie Novak. Seventeen. Poletown address, north of the river. But her student ID is from Valhalla High, not the college."

"Vale Junior College offers advanced courses for gifted kids," Joni said.

"I'm not sure how bright this girl was, considering," Zina said. "Do you think her dress is odd?"

"Odd?" I echoed, but she wasn't asking me.

"Definitely off," Joni agreed. "It's more like a prom dress than something you'd wear to a house party. She looks like . . ."

"A snow angel," I finished. "What are we now, the fashion police?"

"Nope, we're Major Crimes," Zina conceded. "And a lot more went wrong for this girl than her taste in clothes. It was seriously freakin' cold last night. What was she doing out here without a coat?"

"Let's ask," I said.

The front porch was the size of a veranda, three stories tall, supported by *Gone With the Wind* columns. I hit the buzzer beside the massive front door. No response. Leaning closer, I could hear the faint sounds of tinny TV laughter, somebody yelling for somebody to get the goddamn door. No one came. I tried the knob. It wasn't locked.

Stepping inside, I felt an instant jolt. Time travel. Frat party funk, the morning after. The aroma of stale beer, cold pizza, reefer, and sex hanging in the air.

Smelled like teen spirit.

I started down the hall toward the TV room.

"Where are you going?" Zee asked, hurrying after me.

"They'll be in the game room."

"Who will?"

"Everybody who's ambulatory."

"You've been here before?"

"Once or twice."

The end of the hall opened into a giant playroom. Pinball machines, foosball, and pool tables lined the walls. In the center, a long, curved leather couch faced a jumbo flat-screen TV.

None of the pool tables was in use, unless you counted a moose-sized lineman who'd wrapped himself in his Val High letterman's jacket and conked out amid the cue sticks.

Several college-age kids were sprawled across the couch in various states of disarray, bleary-eyed and hungover. Four young guys, three girls, watching a soccer game on the big screen.

"Hey, guys," I said, holding up my badge. "I'm Sergeant La-Crosse, Valhalla PD. Who's in charge here?"

They looked at each other, then back at me. A few shook their heads, no one answered. They weren't belligerent, just baffled and groggy.

"Okaay," I said, "easier question. Are the Champlins at home? Parents, I mean?"

"I'm Sissy Champlin," one of the girls said, nestling deeper in the arms of her bull-necked boyfriend. She had a nose ring, spiky blond hair with blue highlights. "My folks are in . . . Toronto, for the weekend. We had a little bash last night. We're the survivors."

Her boyfriend was staring at me. Sloped shoulders, head the size of a watermelon. U of M sweatshirt. "I know you," he said slowly. "You played hockey for Val High back in the day, right? Defense?"

"Have we met?"

"Nah," he grinned, "I've seen you on game film. Mark shows that scrap in the playoffs when you and your cousin wiped out Traverse City's front line. The refs tossed everybody out. Awesome, man."

"What's your name?"

"Laslo. Metyavich. I'm goalie for the Vale Vikings."

With his dark hair buzzed down to fuzz, he looked more like a Cossack warrior in pajamas from The Gap. He was wide enough to be a goalie, though. "Were you here last night, Laslo?"

"I live here, man. We all do," he added, gesturing at his bleary comrades on the couch. "Exchange students."

"A girl left your party last night and—got into some trouble. Julie Novak? Does anybody know her? Or who she was with?"

Again, baffled looks.

"Wait a sec," Sissy Champlin said, frowning. "Julie? A young chick? Wearing a white formal, like a freakin' bridesmaid?"

"You know her?"

"I know she came to the wrong party," Sissy sniffed. "That Indian kid brought her. What's his name, hon? The geek who tutors the basketball players?"

"Derek, you mean?" Laslo offered.

"Last name?" Zina prompted.

"Some foreign name," Laslo said, without irony. "Patel, I think. Derek Patel."

"Any idea where we could find Mr. Patel?"

"He crapped out early." Laslo shrugged. "Lot of guys did. I

think some wiseass spiked the punch. Derek's probably crashed in one of the guest rooms. I'll show you." He started to rise, wobbled, then quickly sat back down. "Whoa," he said, looking a little green.

"Stay put," I said. "I know the way." Laslo slumped back on the couch. Sissy brushed his arm away. She was on her cell phone, frantically texting.

Zina and I headed into the guest wing, an eight-room addition added back in the fifties. Working opposite sides of the hall, we rapped once, then stuck our heads in, scaring the bejesus out of various young lovers. On my third knock, I found an Indian kid conked out atop one of the twin beds, fully dressed in a dark suit and tie. Tall, slender, skin the color of café au lait, thick curly blue-black hair. He sat up slowly, blinking, dazed and confused.

"Derek Patel?"

"I . . . yes?" He shook his head, then knuckled his eyes. Trying to remember his name. I totally sympathized. Been there, done that.

"Do you know a girl named Julie Novak?"

"Julie? Ah . . . sure. She was my date last night. Is she okay?"

"Why shouldn't she be?"

"She ditched me and went home. Said she wasn't dressed right. I was in no shape to drive, so I gave her my keys and . . . oh damn! Did she wreck my car? My God, my dad's gonna kill me—"

"She didn't wreck your car, Derek. Were you two drinking a little last night?"

"Just the virgin punch," he said. "Julie's underage."

"If you were drinking nonalcoholic punch, how'd you get wrecked?" Zina asked.

"I did a few Jell-O shots with some of the guys. I'm not a big drinker."

"What about Julie? Did she do a few shots too?"

"No! Only the punch, like I said. I promised her dad—oh God, her old man's gonna be totally pissed. He hates me anyway. He's prejudiced, I think. Is he here?"

"No. Put your shoes on, Derek. We have to go."

"Are you arresting me?"

I didn't answer, hoping he wouldn't push it. He didn't. Glumly slipped into his tassel loafers instead. I sent Zee off to scout the rest of the house while I walked Derek out.

Outside, the scene had gone from Christmas-card quiet to

crime-scene chaotic. Valhalla PD prowl cars had sealed off both ends of the circular driveway, their emergency strobes flashing in the gentle snowfall, blocking in the half-dozen cars parked in front of the house. A third prowlie was sitting astride the rear drive that led back to the garage.

The snow angel was blocked from view by the state police CSI van, and the area around her had been taped off with yellow police lines. Techs in black nylon state police CSI jackets were crouched over the vic while Joni looked on. She still wasn't whistling.

I marched Derek to the nearest prowl car. Joe Van Duzen, VPD's greenest patrolman, hurried to meet us, six foot, with a blond crew cut. In khaki slacks and his bulky brown VPD jacket, he's a recruiter's dream.

"What's up, sarge?"

"This is Derek Patel, Duze. He's a material witness. Park him in your prowlie, keep him on ice. He doesn't leave and nobody talks to him, understand?"

"Copy that. What the hell's going on in there, Dylan?"

"The morning after the night before, Duze. Don't lose this kid, okay?"

"You got it." Duze eased Derek into the prowlie's back seat and closed the door.

Zina was waiting for me at the front door, her mood darker than before.

"We've got problems, Dylan," she said. "C'mon."

"What's up?" I asked, falling into step.

"I found the famous virgin punchbowl," she said. "In the living room. There are two of them, actually. One with fruit punch, one with margaritas."

"Sounds right."

"I also found these," she said, holding out her open palm. Three small red capsules.

"Oh hell," I said, feeling my stomach drop like a freight elevator. "Roofies?"

She nodded. "Date-rape drug. Found 'em on the floor near the punchbowls. Both concoctions are murky, but you can see the remains of some caps on the bottom. I think somebody laced both bowls with GHB—" She broke off as I tapped my collar mike.

"Barden? Is your prowlie blocking the driveway?"

"Yes, sarge."

"Take a walk, check the parked cars in the drive, make sure no-body's asleep in one. I don't want any more angels."

"Angels?" he asked.

"Check the damn cars, Tommy."

"Copy that."

"You said you've been here before?" Zina asked, as I switched off.

"Right. To parties, back in high school. Mark Champlin was older than we were, but he'd been a three-sport all-star back in the day, and his folks were big athletic boosters. This place was jock central. Parties almost every weekend, free beer, groupies, and Mr. Champlin was good for a few bucks if a player was short. From the looks of this crew, things haven't changed much."

"Ever go upstairs?"

"No, it was off-limits. Why?"

"C'mon," Zee said. "You're gonna love this."

She was right. The second-floor rooms were larger, plusher, complete with en suites and walk-in closets. And at the end of the corridor, a single door stood wide open. Its latch was shattered. It had been kicked in.

I rested my hand on my weapon as I eased through, but there was no need. None at all.

"Wow," I said, turning in a slow circle, taking in the room. "What have we here?"

The bedroom looked like the honeymoon suite at a Vegas bor-dello. Mirrored ceiling, angled mirrors on the walls, king-size beds in each corner. A larger, circular bed occupied the center of the room, all five of them close enough for easy hopping, covered in what looked like faux ermine.

A large-screen TV loomed over one corner. On a shelf beneath it, a Sony video recorder was flanked by a long row of DVDs. Half of them were clearly commercial porn, garishly labeled. The other half weren't labeled at all, only numbered. I opened one. No labels inside either, just a handwritten number on the disc that matched the jacket.

"What do you think?" I asked.

"I think this room's wired up," Zee said, pointing out nearly invisible lenses mounted in the mirrored ceiling. "If they've been making home movies, I see my future on a beach in Bimini. Check out the gear on the nightstands."

Against the wall, between the beds, small bedside tables held a selection of lubricants, massage oils, and sex toys. Some had obvious purposes, a few I could only guess at.

"Okay," I said, still taking in the room. "We've got a party going on downstairs, somebody kicks open the door to this playroom, but does no other damage I can see."

"The beds aren't even mussed," Zina agreed. "Maybe somebody was hoping to get lucky later?"

"It doesn't matter why. The drugs flip this thing from a teenage tragedy to something a lot messier." I pressed the eject button on the recorder, removed the DVD, and slid it into an evidence bag. "C'mon, let's round up the usual sus—"

"Hey! You guys can't be in here!" a kid said. "You know the rules. Second floor's family only. No guests!" The boy in the doorway was maybe fifteen, wearing a green Michigan State sweater, but I doubt he was college bound.

His heavy-framed glasses housed twin hearing aids. His eyes were wide apart and guileless, with the slight Asian cast of Down syndrome. I guessed his emotional age at ten or twelve.

"It's okay," I said, showing him my shield. He glanced at it, but didn't react. I doubt he knew what it was. "What's your name?"

"I'm Joey Champlin. You can't be up here. My dad doesn't allow it."

"Do you know how the door got broken, Joey?"

His face fell, and the look in his eyes was as good as a signed statement.

"You—still have to leave," he repeated.

"Sure," I agreed. "Whatever you say." We already had what we needed, and in a house with an all-star dad and an army of jocks, I doubt many folks paid attention to this kid.

So we did as he asked. When I glanced back, he was gone.

The next hour flew by in a fury. I had patrolmen seal off the house and herd the kids into separate rooms. We took names, ages, and vital stats. No talking. No breathalyzers either. They were of age, in a private home. How they partied was their business.

All we wanted was info about the girl on the lawn.

What we got was doodley squat.

A few kids knew Derek Patel from school. Nobody seemed to know his angel date at all. Time to change tactics. Maybe Derek had sobered enough for a conversation.

Leaving Zina to finish questioning the final few, I headed out the front door. And went from hangover central into a grab-ass free-for-all.

Derek Patel was sprawled on his back in the driveway, his face a bloody mess. Van Duzen was wrestling with a big guy in a flannel shirt, who was clearly trying to break free to have another go at the kid on the ground.

I came on the run. Crashing into Van Duzen's opponent from behind, I snaked an arm around his throat in a crude chokehold. I managed to haul him off Duze, but he was bull-strong and enraged. He kept kicking wildly at Derek on the ground. It was all I could do to hold him back.

I drove a quick body shot into his rib cage, but he was so wired he didn't even feel it. I had no idea who he was or what the hell was up, and it didn't matter. We had to shut him down.

Throwing my weight backward, I hauled him down on top of me, still locked in a stranglehold. I tried scissoring my legs around his knees to immobilize him, but it was like wrestling a bear. Couldn't hold him.

Patrolman Tommy Barden came charging up with his nightstick drawn. He slammed it down hard across the big guy's midsection, driving his wind out, locking him up for an instant. Barden was drawing back for another swing when Van Duzen shouldered him aside.

"Don't hurt him, damn it! He's the girl's father!"

Duze and Barden piled on, each seizing one of the big guy's arms, pinning him down with sheer bulk. The four of us lay entangled in a squirming rugby pileup in the snow, straining, struggling.

"Mr. Novak," I panted, trying to keep my tone level. "Stop fighting us, please. I'm going to ease my hold to let you breathe, but I need you to calm down."

He didn't reply. For a moment, we lay frozen in a tableau, a violent counterpoint to the holiday display on the lawn.

I released my hold a little. Novak gasped in a quick breath. And then he broke, sagging back against me. Sobbing like a child.

I had Duze drive Carl Novak into Hauser Center, the "house" shared by Valhalla PD, the state police, and the Vale County sheriff's department. No handcuffs. Novak wasn't under arrest, but he wasn't going anyplace either.

I ran Derek Patel into the emergency room in my Jeep, pedal to the metal, with lights and sirens. Derek didn't say a word. Probably couldn't. His nose was flattened, clearly broken. I guessed his jaw was dislocated as well. I turned him over to the ER staff, and was pacing the crowded waiting room like an expectant dad when my partner rolled in. We stepped out to the corridor, away from the others.

"What the hell happened?" Zina demanded.

"Derek felt woozy, so Duze let him walk around to get some air. Carl Novak showed up, saw his daughter dead on the ground. When Derek tried to talk to him, Novak lost it. Laid him out, broke his nose, maybe his jaw. I warned the ER staff Derek might be high, so they'll have to run a tox screen before they can work on him. He won't be talking for a while. Your turn," I said. "What did you get from the interviews?"

"Short version? Julie Novak left the party early," Zina said. "Only a few kids noticed and they're pretty vague on the time. Pretty vague on everything, actually. Half of them are still hammered, the other half are so hungover they wish they were dead."

"One of them is," I said. "Any luck with their smartphones?"

"I collected a half dozen. Joni's downloading them now. She thinks she can patch together a highlight reel of last night's action—"

"What in the devil's going on here!" An Indian doctor in a white lab coat bulled between us, grabbing my shoulder, jerking me around. "The staff says you people brought my son into emergency. Beaten! What have you done to him?"

"Yo! Calm down!" I said, backing him off, flashing my shield. "I'm Detective LaCrosse. Who are you?"

"I'm Dr. Patel—"

"Derek's father?"

"Yes, I—"

"You need to cool down and listen up, doctor," Zee said, stepping between us. "Your son was assaulted. The man who attacked him is in custody. So is Derek. A girl he took to a party last night is dead, possibly of a drug overdose. Does Derek have access to GHB or similar drugs in your home, doctor? Or your office?"

Patel stared at her, stunned. "Drugs?" he stammered. "Derek? Are you out of your mind?"

"GHB, specifically," I pressed, keeping him off balance.

"Dear God." Patel looked away, swallowing. "The, ah, the party Derek attended? It was held at the Champlin home?"

"That's right."

"Then I have a—conflict. The Champlins are my patients. By law, I can't disclose any information—"

"Then you'd better hire your son a good lawyer, sir," Zina said.

"Wait! Please," Patel pleaded. "I can't discuss my patients, but I *can* tell you that my son did not take GHB nor any other drug to that party. He would never do such a thing. And there would be . . . no need to."

"Because . . . the pills were already there?" Zina pressed. "Are you saying someone in the family has a prescription for them?"

"I can't comment on that, detective," Patel said. "But in good conscience, I cannot *deny* it either. Do you understand what I'm *not* telling you?"

"Got it," Zina nodded.

"Without a release from the Champlins, that's all I'm free to say. I'm—sorry about before. May I get back to my son?"

"Go ahead," I said. "But if I were you, doc, I'd get that release. We'll be talking again."

As Patel stalked off, my cell phone hummed. I turned away to take the message. Listened, and frowned. "Okay," I said. "I'm on my way."

"Is something wrong?" Zina asked.

"That was the district attorney. The Champlins' lawyer wants a meet-up, at the Jury's Inn."

"Looking for a deal?" she said, surprised. "The case just opened."

"He doesn't want a deal," I said. "He says he can close it for us."

I left Zina at the hospital. She'd get Derek Patel's statement as soon as he could talk.

I headed into Valhalla, a quaint, shoreline resort that's exploded from a small town into a small city in the past dozen years. Internet money, mostly. Yuppies from Detroit, Flint, and Chicago fleeing the cities to get away from it all. And bringing a lot of it with them.

As a boy, raised in the backcountry, I couldn't wait to get out of here. But after two tours as an MP in Afghanistan, then police work in Detroit, I'm happy to be back. Most of the time.

The Jury's Inn is a convenient hangout for cops, lawyers, and media people, catty-cornered from the county courthouse, just up the block from police headquarters. You can order a burger or a beer, cut a plea deal, or nose out a headline without leaving your barstool.

On a snowy Saturday morning, the place was half empty, the jukebox murmuring Motown oldies while three deputies coming off the mid shift swapped fibs and a pair of lawyers huddled over cocktails, dealing their clients' rights away like penny-ante poker. Our criminal justice system at work.

At the rear corner of the dining room, a massive octagonal table sits apart from the others, ensuring privacy for anyone who chooses it.

Today it was Todd Girard, prosecuting attorney for the five northern counties. Tall, blond, and male-model handsome, Todd is North Shore royalty. Lumber money, a Yale grad. A local legend.

Three years ahead of me in Valhalla High, Todd was a deadeye shooting guard in basketball. Our sports shared part of the same seasons, so we passed in the locker room and hit some of the same parties, including a few at the Champlin estate. We weren't pals at the time, but I knew who he was. Everybody knew who Todd was.

The Girards own lumber mills, paper mills, and pieces of everything else. Their homes are estates in gated enclaves. A hundred-plus years ago, they rode the timber trains into Vale County and logged off the northern forest like fields of wheat.

My mother's people, the Métis, mixed-blood descendents of the original French *voyageurs* and the First Nation, arrived around the same time, fleeing a failed rebellion against the Canadian government. In Canada we'd been woodsmen, trappers, and traders. And, finally, rebels on the run.

In Michigan we became loggers, ax-men, sawyers, top men. The LaCrosses and our kin did the grueling, dangerous work that made the lumber barons rich. After the timber played out, the Girards stayed on in their Main Street mansions, to manage banks and businesses and wield the local reins of power. Shrewdly, for the most part.

The Métis stayed on too, doing whatever work came to hand. Lumbermen, merchants, mechanics, and carpenters. A few outlaws.

And one cop.

Todd Girard is Old Money, but doesn't flaunt it. His lambskin sport coat was comfortably distressed and his jeans were faded. A blue chambray shirt, open at the throat. No tie. Business casual for the north.

In school he was a party animal, but his National Guard unit served a hitch in Afghanistan. He came back changed. We all did. He takes Vale County crime personally now, which keeps his conviction rate in the high nineties.

His number two, Assistant DA Harvey Bemis, was beside him. Suited up in his usual three-piece pinstripe and a U of M tie, Harvey is an eager beaver who looks a bit like one, protruding front teeth, anxious eyes. He's an attack dog in court, a guy you want on your side. But I've never had a beer with him afterward. I think he wears his tie to bed.

The third man at the table was plump and sleek, casually dressed in a tweed jacket over a golf shirt. Jason Avery is the most expensive mouthpiece north of Detroit. His silvery mane was a bit disheveled and he hadn't shaved. I guessed his Saturdays rarely started this early.

"Detective Dylan LaCrosse," Avery said. "Thanks for coming."

"Counselors." I nodded, dropping into the chair facing them. "I'm here as a courtesy to the prosecutor, but I'm in the middle of a homicide case so I'm short on time. What's this about?"

"The Champlin case," Todd said. "I've known Mark Champlin for years. To avoid any appearance of impropriety, I'm stepping away from this one. Harvey Bemis will take it to trial if it comes to that."

"Which I hope to avoid," Avery interjected smoothly. "We need to resolve this mess before it becomes a disaster for the whole North Shore."

"What kind of a disaster?" I asked.

"Before I get to that, I'll need a guarantee," Avery said. "I'm willing to reveal information damaging to my clients, but this conversation will remain confidential."

"We're all gentlemen here, with the possible exception of Dylan," Todd said drily. "Okay, we're officially off the record, Jason. What's your big secret?"

"The Novak girl, for openers. I can close that case."

I stiffened; so did Todd. He had our full attention now.

"I'm listening," I said.

"It's my understanding that the girl drank nonalcoholic punch, passed out on the lawn, and . . . succumbed to the cold. In fact, a tox screen will reveal the presence of a drug. GHB. You have Julie's date, young Derek Patel, in custody, I believe. As a suspect?"

"He's one possibility," I admitted.

"The wrong one," Avery said flatly. "The punch was spiked. GHB, commonly referred to as a date-rape drug, was added to it."

"By whom?" Todd asked.

"I'm coming to that," Avery said. "For the record, the drug was legally prescribed and properly secured under lock and key—"

"It was locked in the playroom, wasn't it?" I said, getting it.

Avery nodded. "Quite so. GHB is a legal sleeping pill, but on occasion the drug is used by my clients to enhance . . . well. Recreational sex. All those involved are consenting adults. I can supply their names, if necessary."

"Skip that for now," I said. "What happened to the girl?"

"Her date, Derek Patel, brought her to the house party. The elder Champlins were away for the weekend, and such parties aren't uncommon. Their daughter, Sara, was present, as well as a number of exchange students, all of whom are of age—"

"What exchange students?" Harvey Bemis asked.

"Jocks, Harvey," I explained. "They attend Vale Junior College on sports scholarships."

"They keep the school competitive and give Mark a new audience for his highlight reel every year," Todd added. "Cut to the chase, Jason. Who doped the punch?"

"Joey Champlin," Avery said simply.

The room went dead still. No one spoke for a moment.

"The . . . handicapped kid?" I said at last.

"I'm afraid so. Last evening Joey was watching TV with the exchange students when his older sister ordered him to bed. The boy took offense. He has a history of difficulty with impulse control. He broke into the playroom, grabbed a fistful of pills, and dropped them in the punch as a prank."

"Sweet Jesus," Todd said, looking away.

"The boy had no idea what the pills were, or what the consequences might be," Avery continued. "Joey confessed to his sister this morning. He's very sorry, but . . ." He opened his hands expansively. "I doubt the boy's capable of comprehending the damage he's done."

"How old is this boy?" Harvey asked.

"Sixteen," Avery said. "His IQ is in the mid-sixties, which places him in legal limbo between juvenile court and adult incapacity. I doubt he can be tried."

"He can't just walk either," Todd said grimly. "What are you offering, Jason?"

"There's a bit more to it," Avery said. "Vale Junior College is being vetted at the state level to become a fully accredited four-year institution. I don't have to tell you what a blessing this would be for the North Shore. Kids who lack the resources to pursue a higher education downstate could live at home, attend school here." He glanced pointedly at me.

"That's good news," I conceded. "How is it relevant?"

"Mark Champlin is heavily involved in those negotiations. A scandal at this time could derail the process, perhaps permanently."

"The snow angel isn't a scandal," I said. "She's a homicide victim."

"Snow angel?" Bemis echoed, frowning.

"Julie Novak," I said. "When we found her in the snow, that's how she appeared."

"By whatever name, her death was inadvertent," Avery said. "A regrettable accident."

"Or negligent homicide," Bemis countered. "A mentally challenged kid made an awful mistake. Fine. He can plead to it, the judge will place him in a state institution for evaluation—"

"And any hope for his future will disappear," Avery shot back.

"Joey Champlin's record will clear at twenty-one," I pointed out. "Julie Novak isn't going to *see* twenty-one."

"The point is moot," Avery said. "The Champlins are unwilling to ruin the boy's life for what was, in every sense, a juvenile mistake."

"We *might* be open to a compromise," Bemis said, glancing at Todd. "If one of the parents pleads to negligence—"

"To be held up to public ridicule and shame?" Avery asked.

"*Somebody* damn well should be ashamed!" I snapped.

"Dylan's right, counselor," Todd said. "My office can't just write this off. Especially since Mark and I are friends. You have to give me something, Jason."

"I've been authorized to offer a hundred thousand dollars," Avery said.

No one spoke for a moment.

"A hundred for what?" I asked.

"Joey's a mentally challenged minor, with emotional problems," Avery said quickly. "No good purpose will be served by trying him. The Champlins offer fair compensation instead. Joey will be placed in a secure facility, for appropriate treatment. The Champlins will issue a public statement of regret for the incident and, *privately*, will proffer a financial settlement to the girl's family. One hundred thousand."

Bemis glanced nervously at Todd. The prosecutor's face showed nothing.

"If, on the other hand, formal charges are brought," Avery continued, "my admission of Joey's involvement and the offer of compensation will vanish. The Champlins will resist any attempt to incarcerate the boy, and they have formidable resources. We're dealing with a tragedy, not a crime."

"That's for the courts to decide," I said.

"You can pursue legal action, of course," Avery nodded. "But what can you win? Joey will most likely be remanded to counseling and the Novak family will get nothing. Are you willing to risk that, Todd?"

"As a friend of the family, I can't be a party to this," Todd said. "It's your call, Harvey."

"I . . . sympathize with the Novak family, of course," Bemis said, reading Todd's eyes as he spoke. "But there's not much point in convicting a mentally handicapped minor of a charge he'll barely comprehend. And a court fight could be disastrous for the college."

Bemis paused, waiting for his boss to comment. Todd didn't.

"Let's make it two hundred thousand," Avery said. "That's my final offer and it expires in sixty seconds."

Bemis glanced at Todd, who gave a barely perceptible nod.

"All right," Bemis nodded. "We can live with that."

I wasn't sure who "we" were, but he didn't speak for me.

"Slow down," I said. "Before we agree to a settlement, shouldn't we consult the Novak family?"

"Sorry, but that's out. They can't know about Joey," Avery said.

"And an offer of compensation could be interpreted as an admission of guilt. Any approach must be made unofficially, without revealing any part of this discussion. Mr. Novak works as a logger. He might be more receptive if the offer came from one of his own." He glanced pointedly at me.

"You're kidding," I said. "You want me to sell this to Novak? Without telling him anything?"

"He's free to decline, of course," Avery said. Taking a checkbook out of his vest pocket, he jotted in a few figures, then slid the check to me.

"This is drawn on my personal account, detective. Two hundred thousand dollars. When Mr. Novak cashes it, he'll be given a release to sign, acknowledging it as a final settlement."

"This is a mistake," I said. "At least let me tell Novak the truth about what happened."

"Unfortunately, that's not an option," Avery said. "It would violate privilege and open the Champlin family to litigation. I can't allow it."

"Novak could be facing felony charges for assaulting the Patel boy," Harvey Bemis added. "Remind him of that, Dylan. Given a choice between a paycheck and jail time, he'll do the right thing."

"Right for who?" I asked. "Novak's a wood-smoke stud. He's used to getting up off the deck to come back at you. He won't take this."

But I was wrong.

By the time I got back to Hauser Justice Center, Carl Novak had been cooling off in an interview room for over an hour.

Locked up alone in a ten-by-ten concrete box, he had time to absorb the death of his daughter. And to consider a future that could include months, even years, locked in rooms like this one.

He was seated at a small steel table bolted to the floor in the center of the room. I took the chair facing him. It was just us. Off the record. No one observing from the other side of the two-way mirror, no recorders, no video cams.

Novak was dressed for work, in a faded flannel shirt, bib overalls, and cork-soled boots. His shoulder-length shaggy hair was shot with gray, his face seamed and weathered by the wind. His knuckles were oversized, scarred from rough labor.

Red-eyed, coldly furious, he listened with folded arms as I offered my sympathies on the death of his daughter, then outlined Avery's offer of compensation. His eyes widened at the figure. Cocking his head, he eyed me curiously.

"Two hundred grand?" he echoed. "For real? Jesus. Do you know how many cords I'd have to drop to make that much?"

I nodded. "My dad was a logger."

"I know. I worked with your old man years ago, on Moose's crew, cuttin' pulpwood in the Comstock. He's dead now, right? Car crash?"

"Killed by a drunk driver," I said.

"Tough break. Anybody offer you two hundred thousand for him?"

I didn't answer.

"Nah, of course not," he said. "I liked Dolph, he was steady, a good worker. But your old man wasn't worth no two hundred grand, dead or alive. But that's what them people figure my Julie's worth, eh?"

"Mr. Novak—"

"Save it, LaCrosse," he said, waving me off. "This ain't on you, I know that. And it sure ain't on Julie. It's on me, and I ain't even got enough put aside to bury her decent. Been working two jobs just to keep her in school, and I got three more kids to think of. I—" He looked away, swallowing hard. "I'll take the money. Got no choice."

"You realize if you do, it's over. You can't sue later."

"Never figured to. But off the record? Just two wood-smoke boys sittin' in a room? Who done this, Dylan? Who killed my girl?"

"It's an open case, Mr. Novak. I truly can't comment. But I can tell you this much. Nobody meant Julie harm. It was an accident, or close to it. Hard as it might be, it's best to accept that, and move on."

"Is that what you'd do?"

"I don't know what I'd do, Mr. Novak."

"My Uncle Matt was killed in Vietnam," he said absently. "My ma's only brother. Know what his wife got? Ten thousand. And a flag to lay on his coffin. Ten grand for his life. I'm getting a lot more for Julie. Maybe I should be grateful."

He waited for a comment. I didn't have one.

"Hell, maybe you're right," he sighed. "There's no help for a thing like this. No way to set it right. Tell your people I'll take the deal."

"They aren't my people," I said.

He met my eyes dead-on. Cold as the big lakes in January.

"Sure they are," he said.

I didn't attend the snow angel's funeral. I wasn't sure how the Novaks would react and I didn't want to intrude.

A week passed, and then another. Christmas was in the air, and as an early present, Vale Junior College won state approval to become a fully accredited, four-year institution.

Good for us.

I began to think Jason Avery had been right. We'd salvaged a positive outcome from a god-awful situation. Won the greatest good for the greatest number.

I thought that right up until the night Derek Patel disappeared.

Ten days after Julie Novak's funeral, Derek Patel vanished from the campus of Vale Junior College. His folks weren't overly concerned when he didn't show for dinner; the boy often stayed after class on lab nights. But when he wasn't home at ten, his mother called the school.

A security guard answered. The school was locked down, but Derek's VW Bug was still parked in the lot. The guard found it unlocked, with the driver's door slightly ajar. Odd, but not necessarily ominous.

Until he noticed Derek's keys in the snow beside the car.

And the bloodstains on the headrest.

The crime occurred on school grounds so jurisdiction initially fell to the state police. But when my chief informed their post commander the missing kid was part of an open case, they kicked it to us.

Not that it made any difference.

We had nothing. CODIS, the combined DNA index system run by U.S. and Canadian crime labs, identified the blood spattered in the car as belonging to Derek Patel. Violence had obviously been done, but in the swirling snow and the bustle of the busy parking lot, nobody had noticed anything out of the ordinary.

A few students mentioned a rust-bucket white pickup truck parked near Derek's V-dub around the time he vanished, but nobody got a good look at the driver, caught a plate, or could even swear to the make of the truck.

Maybe a Ford. Maybe a Chevy. White. Rusted out around the wheel wells. Big guy behind the wheel. A working stiff, not a student.

Why a working stiff?

"You know. Tractor cap, canvas vest, wild hair? A wood-smoke boy. Cedar savage. You know the type."

I knew. Which narrowed my list of potential suspects down to the sixty thousand blue-collar folks who didn't live in Sugar Hill or the condos along the lakeshore strip.

Rusty white pickups? That slimmed our suspect list down to a thousand or so. But I didn't need a thousand names. I already knew the name.

I questioned Carl Novak, of course. Spoke to him on the porch of his double-wide in Poletown, a Slavic enclave in the smokestack shadows of the Deveraux hardboard plant. Novak didn't invite me to step in out of the weather, a deliberate breach of etiquette in the north.

His alibi was rock solid, though. Novak could account for every minute of the day Derek Patel disappeared. Witnesses could vouch for his whereabouts the entire time.

Which proved beyond a doubt that he was involved. Nobody keeps total track of a day, unless they expect to answer questions about it. Innocents don't need alibis.

Still, on the face of it, Novak was as pure as the new-fallen snow. Probably felt ten feet tall and bulletproof. He was sure that he'd won, and he wanted me to know it.

And I did. But there wasn't a damn thing I could do about it.

Dr. Patel and his family were out of their minds with worry. The state police assigned an electronic intercept team to their home to deal with a possible ransom demand.

They tapped their landline home phone and their cells, ready to identify the relay tower as soon as the call came, then triangulate the signal and home in on it.

But there was no call. No ransom demand. No threats.

As the shopping days before Christmas dwindled down to the final few, there was no word at all.

Derek Patel had vanished as though he'd never been.

And when the dreaded phone call finally came, it didn't ring at the Patels' home. Or even at my office. It came to Bowie Cadarette, a conservation officer with the DNRE.

A farmer named Pete DeNoux capped a coyote that had been killing piglets. Pete hurried his shot, didn't nail the rogue cleanly. Gut-shot him, he thought.

That would have been sufficient for some folks. The wound would likely prove fatal. The predator would crawl off into the brush and bleed out. Even if he survived, he'd be minus his taste for bacon.

But DeNoux was a wood-smoke boy, born in the north. Raised on some unwritten rules. If you shoot something, you damn well put it down. You never leave a wounded animal to suffer. Ever. Not even a thieving coyote.

Pete had no trouble following the blood spoor through the snow. Trailed the rogue male back to the farthest corner of his land, near his fence line.

He found what was left of the animal near its den at the base of a toppled pine. The poor bastard had made it home, only to have his own pack turn on him. Maddened by the blood scent, they ripped him to pieces.

The deep-woods wild has countless graces, but mercy isn't one of them. It's a human concept, and not all that common with us.

Satisfied, if a bit dismayed, Pete turned to leave, then hesitated. There were a lot of bloody bones around that den. Too many for a rogue coyote. The pack had been working over another carcass. DeNoux took a closer look, expecting to find the remains of his piglets. The bones weren't from a shoat, though. Nor a deer, nor anything else he recognized.

At first.

Pete was no biologist, but he'd butchered enough game to know the basics of bone structure.

Even so, it took a good twenty minutes for his mind to accept what his eyes were seeing. Even then he harbored some doubts.

Until he found the remains of a torn tennis shoe . . .

DeNoux was so shaken, he wasn't sure who to call. So he rang up the conservation department. And they called me.

*

Ordinarily the district attorney would check out a crime scene personally, but Derek Patel's skeletal remains were tied to a case Todd Girard had stepped away from. I guessed he'd be stepping away even farther now. Faster than a buck on the run.

ADA Harvey Bemis arrived at the coyote den dressed for heavy weather. In his L.L. Bean down-filled parka, with matching tanker cap and furred earmuffs, he looked ready for a trek across the polar ice cap. I was wearing my usual leather car coat and jeans. In the shelter of the tall pines, twenty degrees doesn't seem that cold. Especially when you're seething.

"Is there any question the remains are the Patel boy's?" Harvey demanded.

"Not much," I said. "We haven't found the skull yet, but the shoe is the brand and size described by the family and the blood type's a match."

"Why haven't you . . . found the skull?" Harvey asked, glancing around the savaged ground as though my officers and the state police CSI team had overlooked it somehow.

"This isn't the original dump site," I explained. "My partner and a conservation officer are backtracking it now. Most likely the body was ditched out near the shore highway. The coyote pack found it there, tore it apart, then carried the pieces back to the den."

"I thought coyotes were afraid of people," Harvey said.

"That was before the Internet boom, when folks realized they could do business anyplace you can plug in a laptop. The population along the north is exploding, Harve. We're crowding onto their habitat, and coyotes don't read Darwin. As they get used to seeing us around, they lose their fear. If they find us dead on their turf, we're lunch. Like roadkill, chickens in a coop, or a fawn frozen in the snow."

"Coyotes didn't kill this boy," Bemis said grimly. "We both know who did this."

"Actually, we don't. Whatever the time frame for the killing turns out to be, I guarantee you Carl Novak's going to have an alibi the KGB couldn't break. A family reunion, a christening? He was there, surrounded by fifty witnesses."

"Then he hired it done!"

"You're exactly right. He did. And we helped him."

"Helped him? What—?"

"Novak was working two jobs just to keep his daughter Julie in school, Harvey. He didn't have two nickels to rub together. Then she was killed and Avery wrote him a check. Tipped him like a bellhop. Two hundred thou for his daughter's life. And now?" I gestured at the savage clearing. "Look what a backwoods boy can accomplish with a few bucks."

"He's not going to get away with this," Bemis said furiously. "Alibi or no alibi, I want that sonofabitch arrested! I want him hauled into the House in cuffs—"

"No," I said.

"What do you mean, no?"

"I mean I'm not going to bust him, Harvey. He'll just lawyer up, and we'll get nothing. Novak's not the one I want anyway."

"Of course he is! What are you talking about?"

"His daughter died in the snow, and nobody was held accountable. And now we've got another dead kid, or what's left of one. We gave Novak money instead of justice. So he used our cash to buy his own justice."

"He bought *murder!*"

"Damn right. And that's the guy I want. The sonofabitch who killed this boy for money. And Novak is going to give me his name. Because he's angry and hurting, but most of all, because he feels *justified!* He thinks he bought retribution. When I tell him the truth, that he killed the wrong boy, he'll unravel like a cheap suit."

"But you can't tell him! It was revealed in confidence!"

I almost decked him. It was a near thing. I snatched up a piece of Derek Patel's shattered femur instead, and dragged the jagged end of it across Harvey's new parka, smearing his coat with blood and slime.

"What—? What the hell are you doing?" Bemis stammered, staggering back, horrified.

"Take a deep breath, counselor. That's what justice smells like in the deep woods. Avery cut Novak a check for his daughter and expected him to take it. I warned you it would blow back, and now it has. I helped make this mess, so I'm going to fix it, but I'm done playing games. I'm going to tell Novak the flat-ass truth about what happened. And he'll give me a name and I'll bring that bastard in. It won't be justice, but I'll have to live with it. This," I said, tossing the bone at his feet, "is the part you have to live with."

As I turned away, Bemis grabbed my arm.

"Just a damn minute, LaCrosse—"

Pure cussedness on my part. As he jerked me around, I used the momentum to slap him across the face. Harder than I meant to. He went down like a sack of cement, staring up at me in stunned disbelief.

"I'll—I'll have your badge for that!"

"No, you won't. I'd love to tell a judge about this mess, Harve, but your boss wouldn't like it. And just so we're clear? If you ever lay hands on me again, I'll break your goddamn jaw. C'mon, get up." I offered him my hand, but he brushed it away angrily and staggered to his feet.

A black carrion beetle the size of my thumb was working its way through the muck on his overcoat.

"You've got a bug," I said, pointing at the beetle.

"What? *Oh!*" he gasped, horrified. He tried to brush it away, but the beetle clung stubbornly to the fabric, scarfing its lunch.

Harvey plucked it off and cast it aside, but his fingertips came up smeared with Derek Patel's remains. It was too much. Stumbling into the brush, he dropped to his knees in the snow, retching up everything but his spleen.

I almost felt sorry for him.

But I couldn't spare the time. I needed to get to Novak fast.

To tell him the truth. And destroy him with it.

I picked up my partner at the shore highway, where patrolmen were taping off the original dump site. Racing back into Valhalla with lights and sirens, we crossed the river to Poletown, to Carl Novak's run-down double-wide.

I carried the femur with me. Technically it was evidence, but the forest den wasn't really a crime scene. The coyotes were only guilty of being coyotes.

When Carl Novak answered my knock, I simply handed him the savaged bone, explained what it was and where I'd found it. And what had actually happened the night his daughter died.

It took a moment for the horror of it to sink in. But when it did, Novak sagged against the doorjamb like he'd been slammed across the knees with a Louisville Slugger.

And then he gave us the hired killer's name.

A familiar one.

Joni Cohen was right. When you do police work in your hometown, you're bound to run into people you know.

"Holy crap," Zina said, scanning the screen of her laptop. We were in my Jeep, idling in Novak's driveway, waiting for a prowl car to show, to take him into custody.

"What have we got?" I asked, keeping an eye on Carl Novak, as he said his goodbyes to his wife and remaining kids on his porch. Dry-eyed now, but he looked decades older. In utter despair.

"Oskar Sorsa, Big Ox," Zina read. "Six foot seven, two-eighty. Two-time loser, both busts tied to the meth trade, three years on the first fall, four more on his second. Ganged up in prison with the Aryan Militia. The LEO lists him as a violent offender. Presume to be armed, approach with caution. Paroled to Valhalla after his latest hitch. Elkhart Road? I don't recognize that address."

"It's in the state forest. His grandfather had a cabin back there."

"You know this guy?"

"I used to see him around logging jobs, back in the day. Never worked with him. He had a rep as a bad-ass then. Sounds like prison made him worse."

"How do we handle him?"

"*We* don't," I said, swiveling in my seat to face her. "He's a woodsmoke boy, a survivalist. If we go out there with an army, he'll rabbit into the backcountry and we'll be chasing him for a year. If I talk to him one-on-one, maybe he'll come in peacefully."

"And if he doesn't?"

"If I'm alone, at least he won't run." I shrugged. "You wait here with Novak for the prowl car. Make sure he doesn't hurt himself."

"So you can go after Sorsa alone? You're making a mistake, Dylan."

"At least I'm consistent. I've botched this thing from the beginning, Zee. I'm going to close it out."

She was right. Going alone is always a mistake. And I knew it.

But I was past caring. I needed this done.

Elkhart Road trails off into the bottomlands east of Valhalla. Low swampy ground, only fit for ducks and muskrats.

And poachers. When I rolled into the overgrown yard at Sorsa's backwoods cabin, he was dressing out a deer.

The swamp buck was hanging from a large pine, spread-eagled and eviscerated, eyes glassy, its tongue lolling. Ox was peeling off its hide like a bloody blanket, rolling it down from a circular incision at the animal's throat. He straightened slowly as I stepped out of the Jeep. Still holding the dripping skinning knife.

I'm six-one in my socks, but the Viking type facing me was nearly a foot taller, dressed in grimy coveralls, his hands and wrists streaked with gore from the gutted buck.

Forty or so, his sandy hair was a wild tangle around the edges of a greasy engineer's cap. Hard gray eyes. His narrow face was permanently reddened by the wind and prison hooch, and marked with a striking set of scars. Three vertical gashes in one cheek, livid as war paint. Gouges from a chainsaw kickback. Savage and ugly. And not uncommon in the backcountry.

He eyed my back trail uneasily a moment, expecting an army to come roaring in behind me. When he realized I'd come alone, he relaxed a bit. Probably figured he could handle me. Maybe he was right.

I checked out the yard as I stepped out of my Jeep. A rust-bucket white pickup was parked beside a cabin so warped and faded it looked like a natural part of the forest. Cords of firewood were stacked neatly along the outer walls. A trio of antlered deer skulls were nailed over the door. Trophy bucks. None smaller than ten points. A Model 94 Winchester lever-action was leaning against the doorframe.

"Who are ya?" Sorsa demanded. I could smell whiskey off him six feet away.

"Detective Dylan LaCrosse," I said, showing him my shield. "Major Crimes."

"I ain't done nothin' major." He gave me a screwball grin, showing broken teeth, stained meth yellow. "Nothin' minor, neither."

"Rifle season closed December first, Ox. That buck's illegal."

"Ain't no season on roadkill. Found this bastard dead in a ditch. Kilt by a truck."

"Then the truck must have shot it in the eye. I can see the bullet hole from here."

Sorsa frowned at the deer, then jammed a thumb into the bloody eye socket, obliterating the wound by gouging out the flesh.

"C'mon, LaCrosse, the DNR don't care if a man takes meat off-season to feed himself. You gonna rat me out?"

"I don't give a rip about the deer, Ox. I'm here about a boy. Derek Patel."

He didn't say anything. But his eye strayed to the Winchester on the porch. Figuring his odds. The gun was only a few yards away. Loaded? Damn straight. He'd only used one round to kill the buck and probably reloaded that one immediately. Out here, weapons stay loaded. Plus, he was still holding the skinning knife. I could practically see the wheels turning in the big guy's meth-fried mind as he mulled over the geometry of murder. It was painful to watch.

I could have pulled on him then, taking control of the situation. But I didn't. I waited instead.

"I got nothin' to say about no boy," he said at last.

"I don't need a confession, Ox. Carl Novak already gave you up, chapter and verse. But you can still do yourself some good. Did you do the killing alone? Or did you have help?"

He thought about saying nothing. Or go screw yourself. Same answer, really. But we were past that now. And we both knew it. He edged sideways a half-step. Casually, like he was relaxing. But it moved him a foot closer to the rifle on the porch.

"I didn't need no help," he spat in contempt. "The kid was mud people."

"Mud people?"

"Brown people, or black. One of them low races. Not like us."

Low races? This snaggle-toothed Neanderthal, butchering a buck like a freaking caveman, actually thought he was superior—I took a breath.

"Okay, you took him alone. How'd you manage it?"

"Easy. I pulled up next to his car, asked him for directions. Clocked him with a sap. Not hard really, but he was already bandaged up. Sap put him down, all the way. Never moved once on the run out to the woods." Ox edged sideways, another step nearer to the gun. Maybe two yards to go. A single stride for a guy his size. I let him do it, more interested in getting the absolute truth now. Keeping him talking.

"Where did you dump the body?"

"On state land, near the highway. Lot of coyotes around there. I zipped him open. Scavengers will shy away from the scent of people, but if you slit the belly open, spill the guts out on the ground?

They don't smell like people no more. Just guts. Coyotes freak out, fight each other to rip it up. They'll eat anything if you open it up first. Even mud people."

He said this last inching over the final half-step, watching my eyes. When I didn't react, he nodded. He knew then that I wasn't going to.

"Last question," I said. "This one's important, Ox. When you zipped that kid open and left him for the coyotes? Was he dead? Or just unconscious?"

Sorsa grinned at that, shaking his head. Almost ready now. Not caring that I knew it.

"To be honest, LaCrosse? I can't really say for sure. What's the difference?"

"It matters. To me."

"Nah, it don't," he said, shaking his shoulders, loosening up. "All that matters now is, I ain't goin' back to prison."

"No," I agreed. "Probably not." But I kept my hands at my sides. Made no move for my weapon.

Making it his call. Either way.

The wind was picking up, swirling snow devils across the yard, twisting the gutted buck slowly at the end of its rope, dark blood oozing down from its body cavity, pooling beneath it. I felt a sudden chill that had nothing to do with the wind. Only the emptiness in Sorsa's eyes—

He glanced toward his truck—but it was a feint. Flipping the bloody knife at my head with more force than I thought possible, he lunged for the rifle.

Instinctively I ducked away from the flashing blade. Too late! It banged off my forehead, slashing it open, stunning me. Dropping to one knee, I clawed for my weapon, pulling it just as Ox rolled to the rifle on the porch.

He threw the Winchester to his shoulder just as my gun came up, both of us cutting loose in the same split second, our shots nearly simultaneous. I couldn't tell who fired first.

His rifle slug burned past my cheek, so close I felt the heat of the muzzle blast. My first round flew high and wide, blowing a chunk out of the doorframe.

He was jacking in a fresh round when my second shot nailed him dead center. So did the next three.

Pete DeNoux wasn't the only one raised on the rules. When you shoot something, you damn well put it down.

I spent three days on suspension while the state police conducted an independent investigation, then I had to face a shooting board, in a conference room at Hauser Center. Three command officers from Lansing and me. I was entitled to have an attorney present. Didn't ask for one. Maybe I should have.

Some officers serve their entire careers without drawing a weapon. I'm guessing the bureau chief who chaired the review was one of them.

He kept rephrasing the same pointed questions. Why had I sought out a violent felon, a suspected murderer, alone? Why had I attempted an arrest without calling for backup?

Had I ever met the decedent? Had any previous dealings with him? Did I bear him a grudge?

"I knew who Ox was," I admitted. "In high school, I spent my summers working in the woods, swinging a chainsaw. You hear about guys who are okay, guys to avoid. I thought Sorsa would be more likely to come in peacefully with someone he could relate to."

"But you couldn't convince him?" the captain pressed. "How hard did you try?"

"Not very," I admitted, tired of the dance. "When I suggested it, he threw a skinning knife at my head and went for his rifle."

He waited for me to expand on that. I didn't.

"I'd say you misjudged the situation pretty badly."

I didn't rise to that either. He was certain I'd gone after Ox alone for reasons of my own.

He was right.

Sorsa had taken blood money to murder a boy he didn't know. There's no redemption for a crime like that, no way back. But there was no grudge involved. If he'd surrendered peacefully, I would have brought him in alive.

He didn't.

So I kept my answers brief, my tone neutral. And in the end, the board decided the case on the facts. Sorsa was an enforcer for the Aryan Militia, a convicted felon in illegal possession of a firearm, and the sole suspect in a homicide. He died with a loaded rifle in his hands and I had a gash in my forehead that took eight stitches to close. The board conferred for twenty minutes. Then ruled the shooting as self-defense.

Justified.

I'd won, I suppose. It didn't feel like it.

After the hearing, I headed back to my office at the House. I needed time alone, to think things through. But Todd Girard was there, waiting for me. It was just as well. It saved me the trouble of tracking him down.

He was in the visitor's chair beside my desk. I dropped into my swivel chair, facing him. Neither of us offered to shake hands.

"You roughed up Harvey Bemis," Todd said.

"Sorry about that," I said. "It should have been you."

"Me?"

"You served in the sandbox, right?"

"Helmand, eight months," he said. "What's that got to do with anything?"

"Ever sit in on a tribal council?"

"No. Look, Dylan—"

"Bear with me. Tribal councils are pretty straightforward. No judges, no lawyers. Just clan chiefs and their bodyguards, an imam for a referee. Everybody comes strapped, nobody pretends to be neutral. They all push for their own interests. Like we did at the Jury's Inn."

"What's your point?"

"Avery was protecting the Champlins," I continued. "The Champlins were protecting their boy, all of us were looking out for the college. Everybody had a voice. Except the one who mattered most. The snow angel. Julie Novak. That was your job, Todd. To speak for the victim. Instead you gallantly stepped aside, to avoid a conflict of interest. And you handed the case off to Bemis. Only he didn't speak for the victim. Didn't even pretend to. He thinks his job is keeping you happy. And he did that, by protecting your friends."

"I never asked him to."

"You didn't have to ask! You knew how he'd play it. So did the rest of us. But we let it pass. Because it gave us the outcome we wanted. A closed case, a four-year school, serious cash for the Novaks. A good outcome, till it went off the rails. I'm not laying the blame on you, Todd, we all own a piece of it. All we can do now is try to set it right."

"What do you want, Dylan?"

"Two things," I said flatly. "First, Bemis is out. Kick him to the curb. He doesn't have the soul for this job."

I expected an argument. Didn't get one. He just nodded. "And the other?"

"Give Novak a break, Todd. Some kind of a deal."

"Not a chance," Girard said, shaking his head. "The man paid for a murder, Dylan. He caused the death of an innocent boy."

"He didn't know he was innocent! If we'd given him the truth instead of buying him off—"

"Maybe he would've murdered the Champlin boy instead!" Girard snapped. "We'll never know, will we? We only know what he did."

"We put him in a lousy situation and he made a lousy choice. I'm not saying he walks, but we owe him something. What can you do?"

"I—hell." Girard looked away, chewing the corner of his lip. "If he serves the minimum with no more trouble, I'll consider a humanitarian release. That's the best I can offer."

"Then I guess it'll have to do."

"Not quite," he said, meeting my eyes dead-on. "I need a straight answer from you. About Sorsa."

"What about him?"

"If you'd brought him in breathing, I could have used his testimony against Novak to put them both away for life. You told the board you went alone, hoping he'd surrender. Was that true?"

I didn't say anything.

"I didn't think so," he said, rising, looking down at me. In every sense. He waited a moment for me to say something in my defense. When I didn't, he turned and stalked out.

He left angry, thinking the worst. Thinking he knows an ugly truth about me.

But he's wrong.

I chewed over his question a good long while after he left.

I've known Todd since high school. I didn't want to lie to him.

But I couldn't tell him the truth.

Because I don't know what it is.

Some night, many years from now, maybe I'll wake in the dark and know to a certainty what really happened in that clearing. I'll know that I gave Ox Sorsa a choice because I hoped he'd surrender. Or because I hoped he wouldn't.

For now, I'll have to live with not knowing.

So will Todd.

I worked at my desk the rest of the afternoon, catching up on paperwork. When I headed out into the fading twilight, a gentle snow was falling. Downy flakes, swirling on the wind. But as I walked to my car, I slowed, then stopped.

Listening.

Up the block, in Memorial Park, a children's choir was on the bandstand singing Christmas carols, their voices carrying clear and pure in the gathering dusk.

Without thinking, I fell in step with a throng of shoppers and families and passersby, all of us drawn by the music, gathering around that small stage. Letting the old songs carry us back to a time when the world was a simpler place. Or we were too young to know the difference.

*Peace on earth, good will to men.*

It's tough to argue with that.

But as I listened to the voices ringing in the icy air, my gaze strayed to the far corner of the park, where a winged figure stands watch over a memorial, a stone tablet that bears the names of the Great Fallen. Local boys who died in the first War to End All Wars. And in all the wars since.

It's a long list.

The mourning angel that guards it was aglow, decorated for the holidays with glittering lights, her hands spread wide in benediction, a marble teardrop frozen on her cheek.

And my throat seized up. And I couldn't breathe.

I wonder if I will *ever* see an angel again without remembering that shining schoolgirl sleeping in the snow.

I hope not.

ANDREW BOURELLE

# Cowboy Justice

FROM *Law and Disorder*

JACK PUT FOUR shells of double-ought buck into the twelve-gauge, chambered a round, then added the fifth shell. His breathing was shallow. He wondered how he was going to get through this. Beside him in the passenger seat, David had already loaded the 30.06 and the .270 and seemed to be waiting patiently. A Kenny Chesney song about a guy leaving his summer fling and heading back to Cleveland was playing on the stereo and Jack turned it off.

"I thought you liked Kenny Chesney," David said.

"He ain't bad. It just ain't the right kinda music for now is all."

David nodded and looked out the window. They were parked in an empty Raley's parking lot. The sun wasn't up yet; the black of night was turning gray. They had guessed this might be the best time to make their move. With meth users, it wouldn't matter if it was three in the morning or three in the afternoon. At least at dawn they'd have some light to shoot by.

"Take this, would you, brother?" Jack said, handing over the shotgun.

David put it next to the rifles, all three leaning against the bench seat between them, butts on the floor, barrels pointed toward the back window of the truck. The two rifles both had black scopes. David would be using them. The shotgun was just backup. On the floor were boxes of ammunition, more than they'd be able to use. Jack picked the Derringer off the seat and checked it. He'd already checked it once. Two shots. That was it. He took a deep breath.

"I still think we should just go in shooting," David said.

"No," Jack said. "This is the best way. Just trust me, okay?"

"I trust you. It's just you could be dead inside before I fire a god-damn shot."

"Ain't gonna be that way. These are druggies. Speed freaks. They're gonna have guns, but they ain't gonna know how to use them."

"You said that already."

"If they ever fired them at all, it was out in the desert at bottles and cans."

"You said that a hundred times already."

"Most of them ain't never shot something real, something moving. Just pretend they're deer and do what you do when you got a buck in your sights."

David shook his head. "That don't change the fact that it'd be better if we just went in together, guns blazing."

"They got cameras. They'd see us coming and be waiting at the front door with who knows what kind of firepower. We're gonna be able to shoot better than them but that's 'cause we're prepared and they ain't. If we give them time to be ready, things might be different. We talked about that a hundred times already too."

David shook his head like he always did when he still disagreed but didn't want to argue.

"This is the way we're doing it. It's the best way."

Truth was Jack wanted to keep his baby brother as far away from the fight as possible. He didn't want both his brothers dead. But he couldn't pull this off by himself. David was a good shot with a rifle—probably better than Jack, even at sixteen—and putting him in the truck would be a relatively safe place.

Jack checked the Derringer again, then promised himself it would be the last time.

"You ready?" he said.

"Yep."

Jack believed his little brother. But he wasn't so sure about himself.

"Better go ahead and get down."

David crouched onto the floor and covered himself with a quilt their grandma had made. He pulled the guns toward him and covered them too. Jack put the Derringer inside his hat, tore off a piece of duct tape from the roll sitting on the seat, and taped the gun inside. He put the hat on. He'd practiced this; the gun fit nicely.

Jack started the truck and pulled out of the parking lot. The five weeks since Jamie's death had led him to this point. He and David had spent three of those weeks camping at Lake Tahoe, driving down into Carson City every night, asking questions, trying to find people. They were surprised by what they found going on in a town that didn't seem all that big or special. Which probably meant this kind of stuff was happening everywhere. But their hunt was over. Now was this thing. And by noon they'd be done. David wanted to stop outside the city and get whores at the brothel before heading back to Montana. To celebrate. But Jack said they ought to see how they felt after it was all over. Truthfully, he didn't know what to expect. He figured he'd never be the same person again after what they were about to do. Never. David neither probably. That is, Jack thought, if we ain't dead.

"All right," Jack said as he pulled onto the street where the house was. "We're here."

They'd driven down the street a few times in the past week, trying to scope out the neighborhood. On their second drive by, David had seen the camera in the tree, so they waited a couple days before coming back. The last time they'd come, they sprung for a rental car so the drug dealers wouldn't recognize his truck. They didn't know how carefully anyone was monitoring the camera (or cameras, if they hadn't spotted all of them), but they wanted to be cautious.

Jack stopped several houses from their target, parking the truck on a slight curve about a hundred yards away to give David a good shooting lane down the street. They'd discussed this. It would be hard on Jack getting back to the truck after the shooting started, but David's rifles would be able to reach out a lot farther than anything the guys inside would have. So the distance was in their favor.

"This is it, brother," Jack said.

"Good luck." David didn't stir; he spoke from beneath the blanket.

Jack's heart beat hard. Sweat slid down his skin inside his button-down shirt.

"I'm leaving the window down," he said. "You probably won't be able to hear the Derringer, but listen anyway. Be ready when I come busting out of that place."

"When you grab a gun," David said, "don't get nothing too complicated."

"I reckon I'll grab what I can grab."

"Grab something you know how to use is all I'm saying. You don't want to be fumbling with the damn safety or figuring out how to get a round in the chamber."

"I ain't gonna have time to be choosy, I don't think."

"Don't miss."

"You neither."

Jack got out of the Chevy and started walking down the street. His boot heels clicked on the pavement, loud in the morning silence. His hat felt heavy on his head, weighed down by the Derringer. They'd talked about him dressing different, trying to fit in better, but they decided once he opened his mouth, the people in the house would figure him for a redneck anyway. He'd had a shaved head and worn the same green clothes as everyone else in boot camp, but it didn't stop them from nicknaming him Hillbilly. Might as well make it part of his story.

Jack thought as he approached the house, If we can't kill the sons of bitches, if it all goes to hell, please just let David get away.

He'd been nervous from the start about bringing David. But just because he was sixteen didn't mean he had any less right to want to avenge Jamie than Jack did. Jack had never been as close to David as he had been to Jamie, and Jamie had probably been closer to his little brother than his older. Jack was eight years older than David; Jamie had been born right in between them. When Jack had gone into the army, David was a kid still; when he came back, his baby brother was a young man, already shaving and dipping snuff, with a pretty girlfriend and a deer mounted on the wall bigger than any he or Jamie had ever shot. And Jamie was gone to college in Reno. Jack had been in such a hurry to get away from Montana, but when he was away he missed the ranch and the mountains and waking up in the morning in the house and having breakfast with his brothers. When he came back, though, it was all different. And then there was this; how had it gotten so bad that he was here now, walking down some Carson City street with a gun under his hat?

The neighborhood wasn't bad, some crappy houses and some nice ones. A white cat hurried across the street in front of him. An automated sprinkler kicked on at one house; one nozzle was busted and sprayed water all over the sidewalk. Jack walked right down the center of the street. He thought of a gunfighter in an old western walking down Main Street and into trouble; he told himself this was going to be different from the movies he'd watched growing up.

The house was nondescript. Beige siding. Roof in need of repair. A couple of brown patches in the lawn. A few trees out front, nothing too big.

He ignored the camera. He stepped over a dead bird. He tried to control the shaking in his hands. The door swung open even before he raised his hand to knock. A white guy in a pair of cutoff jeans and a T-shirt. The guy was thin; he had red hair and an unruly beard. Could have been thirty-five, but probably was twenty-five and just worn the hell out. His shirt said *Misfits* on it in green letters; Jack wondered if that was some kind of rock band. The guy had one hand behind his back. A skinny Mexican kid who couldn't have been eighteen stood behind him, wearing jeans and no shirt. His ribs stood out like slats on a fence.

"What the hell you want, cowboy?" the redheaded guy asked.

Jack tried to keep his voice confident but reverential. "Sorry to just show up like this, man, but I need some crystal."

"I don't know what you're talking about," the man said without hesitating.

"Stu Kicking Bird told me this was the place to come. He's dry, and I can't wait."

Misfit looked at him for a moment.

"Come on. Let's talk inside."

Jack fought the urge to turn and look down the street toward David.

When the door was shut, the one with the *Misfits* shirt pulled his hand out from behind his back. He didn't point the gun at Jack but just showed him that it was there. It was a .357 Magnum with a sandalwood grip, like something a gun collector might have, not a drug dealer. Jack pretended it didn't bother him.

They were in a small foyer, closed in by a second thick oak door that looked a heck of a lot more secure than the one in front. Jack hadn't expected this. He'd wanted to get in, find an opportunity, shoot one or two guys real quick, grab a gun, then head out the door, shooting as he went. A second door was an obstacle. Not a big one, but anything was trouble when he didn't have much room for mistakes anyway.

"Arms up," Misfit said.

Jack raised his arms, and the Mexican came in to pat him down. If they checked his hat, he'd have to make a move for Misfit's gun, but he probably wouldn't be able to get it. The Mexican was thorough, even checking Jack's boots, but he ignored the hat.

"I know y'all are a distributor and you wouldn't normally deal with a guy like me," Jack said. "But Stu was dry and I ain't got time to keep looking."

"Why the hurry?" Misfit said.

"I'm just driving through from L.A.," Jack said, wanting to get the story out quickly. "My sister was down there using and I'm trying to get her back home to Wyoming where I can get her some help. But I'm a realistic man and I know she can't just quit. I'm just trying to get enough to get home so I can get her some help."

Both men stared at him suspiciously.

"I ain't a user but I ain't judging y'all. I just want to get my sister through this. I been out looking all night and all I found was Stu. All I want is to get some stuff an y'all won't never see me no more."

"Where's your sister at?" Misfit asked.

"She's at a motel, sicker'n a dog."

"Well," Misfit said, "you're going to have to talk to Gabe. He makes the decisions."

Gabe—the name he and David had heard over and over again. That's the guy, Jack thought. No matter what happens afterward, I'll get him at least.

The Mexican pounded against the second door; there wasn't a handle on this side.

"Open up!"

A white guy with a nose ring and a shaved head opened it. As Jack stepped inside the house, the smell of the cooking meth hit him. It stank like chemical cleaners. He was instantly light-headed, like he'd stood too fast. He tried to walk straight, to pretend it wasn't bothering him. The others didn't seem to notice.

Misfit led him into the kitchen. A group of people were sitting at a table working. Jack tried to get his bearings, tried to count the people and determine what kind of situation he was in. But his wooziness wasn't going away—it was getting worse. He felt nauseous, dizzy. Not all that different from the time in boot camp when they had to go into the tear-gas chamber. He saw a table full of equipment: burners, pans, boxes of cleaning supplies. He saw bags of powder on the counter, lots of them. An AK-47 was leaning against the wall and an Uzi was sitting by the sink next to a box of Cheez-Its.

Misfit led him through the house and he followed. A couple guys were sitting on the sofa watching an old Clint Eastwood western. Jack couldn't tell which one. Beer bottles and ashtrays were all over the coffee table, and a sawed-off shotgun. A pit bull in the corner stood up and started barking at him, then someone—Jack couldn't figure out who—yelled at it. It sat back down. Jack noticed the dog was lying near a rusty brown stain about the size of a stop sign on the gray carpet. Jack wondered if it was blood.

They went down a hall and Misfit knocked on a door.

"There's a cowboy here to see you."

"A what?" It was a girl's voice.

Misfit cracked the door.

"A cowboy. He's just passing through. Said Stuart Kicking Bird told him where to go."

"Jesus fucking Christ." A male voice this time. "Okay. What the fuck ever."

Misfit opened the door, and Jack looked past him and saw it was a bathroom. A pretty Indian girl sat on a chair facing the tub, where a man was lying in bathwater. Several candles were burning. Incense. A two-by-four lay across the tub, spanning the guy like a bridge. A black rubber strap and an empty syringe sat on the wood. A pistol sat on the linoleum floor by the tub.

"Wow," the girl said. "He really is a cowboy."

Jack reached up and tipped his hat.

"Ma'am," he said.

It wasn't something he would normally do. He felt giddy.

The guy in the tub shifted to get a better look at Jack. He had brown hair, shaggy and almost to his shoulders. The hair on his face was an unruly mess somewhere between a beard and a few days' stubble. His eyes were so bloodshot Jack could see the red from where he was.

"Well, come on in, cowboy," Gabe said, his smile suggesting he found this funny in a way no one else quite would.

The girl stood.

"I'll leave you two alone," she said.

She walked past Jack and stared at him as she passed by, so close that he could smell her over the chemicals. She was so pretty he couldn't believe it. Not pretty in any done-up way. Just cute. Long straight brown hair. Clean almond-colored skin. Eyes dark like rich fertile soil. Why couldn't he meet a girl like this back home?

"Be nice to him," she said to Gabe, not taking her eyes off Jack. "He's a cute cowboy."

Jack smiled at her. He wondered if there was still hope for her. He thought about not going through with it all, then he stepped into the bathroom, telling himself to get his head straight.

"Pedro frisked him," Misfit said. "Motherfucker's clean."

Misfit shut the door behind him, leaving Jack alone with Gabe.

"Sit down," Gabe said, picking up the pistol, a Glock, and laying it on the two-by-four.

Jack sat.

Jack stared, unblinking, at the campfire. He and David had hardly spoken all evening. They built the fire, cooked hot dogs over the flames, and sipped beers in a sort of robotic daze. Now a mound of red and orange coals lay beneath the few logs. The coals were hot, twisting with orange and red and black shapes. Jack could see images in the coals, like flaming clouds. Faces, tortured visages. But he couldn't seem to make himself look away. He felt almost like he was losing his mind. He'd looked at his brother's dead body in the Carson City morgue that afternoon, and now he couldn't quite make sense of anything.

Across the fire, David pulled out his can of Kodiak, hit it against his palm to pack it, and then put a pinch in his lip. He spit into the fire.

"Want some?" he said.

Jack shook his head no.

David took a deep breath. "I tell you what," he said.

Jack knew immediately that his brother had been planning to say what he was about to, had been mulling it over all evening, waiting for the right moment.

"That lawman ain't gonna do a goddamn thing," he said.

"Nope." Jack put another log on the fire without looking at David. The wood caught immediately, and the flames rose. The night was chilly—it was summer, but they were in the mountains—and Jack's back was cold while his knees, close to the fire, were hot.

"He might as well have said, 'He's just some drug dealer; it ain't like he was somebody who mattered.'" David spat onto the log. The tobacco juice sizzled like hot grease. "Like they got better things to do. This is Carson City. How many murders they got here?"

"I don't know," Jack said, taking his hat off, setting it on a log.

He put his elbows on his knees and his head in his hands, running his fingers back and forth through his hair. He closed his eyes but could still see flashes of orange on the inside of his black lids. The fire was dry against his face and hands. All he could think about was what he should have done differently. He'd seen something was wrong with Jamie when he was home for Christmas, and he suspected it was drugs. But he never guessed how far Jamie must have been involved in that world. He'd wanted to say something, take him aside and give him a good talking-to. Instead, though, when he drove him to the airport, they were silent most of the way, and as he shook his hand and said goodbye, all he'd said was, "If you ever need anything, let me know, okay?" Jamie nodded and that was it. The last time he saw his brother alive.

"Well, if the law ain't gonna do nothing," David said, "I think we should."

Jack looked into the fire again and not at David. He'd been thinking the same thing, speculating on how realistic it would be for him to ask around town and track down who Jamie had been hanging around with. Then, if he could figure it out, could he go through with killing those who'd done in his brother? Jack's four years in the army fell between the two Gulf wars; he'd never been in combat but felt confident he'd be able to handle himself.

"I say we go home, get some shit—guns—and come back and start asking questions." David spat. "What do you think?"

"I been thinking the same thing." Jack paused for a long time and then, still looking into the fire, said, "Only just me, not you."

"He was my brother too," David said.

He was right. Even at sixteen, David was old enough to want his brother's murderers brought to justice.

"I know," Jack said. "Still."

"I ain't a kid no more. I can shoot as well as you. I—"

"Just shut up and let me think," Jack said.

Jack thought about going home, telling his ma and pa what happened, and trying to put the whole thing behind him like a bad memory. But he already had memories in his mind that he couldn't push away, things he wished he'd done to help Jamie before it got this far. He hadn't said anything when Jamie failed out of the University of Nevada and moved to Carson City with friends. He just figured it was his brother's life to do what he wanted with. And then at Christmas, with Jamie looking so pale and as thin as a post, Jack hadn't done anything. Jamie had smiled just like always, like nothing bothered him. His grin had always been infectious, but in December all Jack could think about was how yellow his teeth seemed to look. And yet he still didn't say anything.

So, he thought, staring into the fire, *you gonna fail your brother again?*

"Okay," he said. "We'll come back and ask some questions, see what happens."

"And kill them that killed Jamie?"

He looked up from the flames at David. "If we can."

David smiled. His face was stained with shadows cast upward from the fire. His eye sockets were dark holes; his forehead was in darkness. Only his grin was aglow from the orange flames. Jack shuddered, wondering if he'd just made a mistake. David spat into the fire, and the juice sizzled.

The air was clearer in the bathroom and Jack immediately began to feel better.

"What brings you to my home?" Gabe asked, settling back into the water. He didn't seem to care that he was meeting a stranger while naked in a bathtub.

Jack looked around. There was a big window above the tub, stained white with shower scum but not covered by any curtain. The mirror over the sink was cracked. The toilet was open and the water inside was yellow. A double-barrel shotgun leaned against the wall by a pile of *Penthouse* magazines.

"Uh," Jack said, looking into the tub. He saw Gabe's penis, floating in the water, pointing up. He saw the dark hair on the man's stomach and chest swaying in the water like weeds in a pond. He looked Gabe in the face. He was afraid and he didn't want to be.

"Uh," he said again, taking off his hat, careful not to show the gun, and shaking his head. "I'm sorry. My head's spinning a bit from the chemicals in the air. I'm sure y'all don't notice, but I'm a virgin when it comes to this stuff."

"Pure in heart and soul," Gabe said, grinning. "A real fucking cowboy."

"I don't know about pure," Jack said. "Just unfamiliar is all."

He was feeling better and better.

"Where you from, boy?" Gabe said, imitating Jack's accent.

Jack opened his mouth and almost said Montana. He caught himself and said, "Wyoming. I'm coming back from L.A., where my little sister was into some stuff. I'm taking her home, but I just need to get her a quick fix so I can get her back and into a program of some sort."

Gabe just looked at him.

"I'm sorry to show up at your door like this. I just need enough to get her through till Wyoming. She's pretty sick right now."

Holding his hat in his lap, Jack reached in and fingered the Derringer. He wished he'd brought a knife. He'd never guessed he'd get an opportunity to be alone with this guy.

Gabe shifted in the water, getting more comfortable. "You remind me of a friend of mine," he said.

The Glock sat on the board, but both the guy's hands were in the water.

"Yeah," Jack said.

"Had an accent like yours. Probably a lot like your sister. From the middle of nowhere. Got involved in some shit he wasn't ready for. Good kid, though. He was a fucking hoot."

"Yeah."

"I could just listen to him talk all night long, man. Just get high and listen to him."

"What was his name?"

"Jamie," Gabe said. "From Montana."

Jack half thought the guy was messing with him and any second he would grab the Glock and point it at him.

"What happened to him?" Jack asked.

"Jamie. He pissed me off. We're not on speaking terms right now."

Jack remembered his brother: napping on the couch, smiling with pure happiness after taking a big trout out of the river, sneaking in drunk at two in the morning and unable to keep himself from laughing while Pa yelled at him, wiping sweat from his face and complaining while they made hay in the barn. He saw Jamie hooting as the two of them rode through the pasture together, pushing their horses into a lope and heading home for supper. Jack saw his brother's face, expressionless and plastic, on the slab in the morgue, his throat open like a second wide grinning mouth, his windpipe visible like a limp white tongue.

"Say something country, man," Gabe said. "Say something like, *tighter than a bull's ass in fly season.* Or *hotter than a whore on dollar day. As nervous as a fart in a windstorm.* Say something country and I'll sell you what you came for."

"I got one," Jack said. "I got one y'all are gonna love."

"Yeah?"

"Yeah," Jack said.

He pulled out the Derringer and lunged forward, sending his hat flying. He put his left hand over the Glock, holding it down, and thrust the Derringer into Gabe's face. Gabe pulled back against the porcelain wall behind him and Jack jammed the gun into his eye. Jack saw terror on Gabe's face and felt a thrill from it.

"James Fisher was my brother," he said, and squeezed the trigger.

He'd shot enough deer to know that bullet wounds didn't look like they do in the movies. This was no different. He'd shot Gabe in the left eye, but blood was coming out both sockets. And his nose and his ears. Like a grenade had gone off inside the man's brain.

Jack forced himself to stop looking. The sound had been more a pop than a loud blast, but Jack knew it would be enough to get the attention of everyone else in the house. He tried to move as fast as he could. He shoved the Glock into his waistband, then locked the door. It was cheap fiberboard and could be busted apart in seconds, but it might buy him some time. He grabbed the shotgun.

"What the hell's going on in there?" The voice sounded like Misfit. Right on the other side of the door.

Jack glanced at Gabe. Half the water was red now, and Jack's hat was floating at Gabe's crotch.

Something crashed against the door. The lock held, but Jack heard wood splinter. He didn't think it would take many more hits like that. He pointed the shotgun at the window above the tub and squeezed both triggers. There was a double click. He broke the gun and saw both barrels were empty.

"Damn," he said, and tossed the gun into the bathwater.

Misfit crashed against the door again. More splintering.

"Hey, Misfit," Jack yelled, pulling out the Glock.

"Huh?"

Jack pointed the Glock at the door where he thought Misfit would be and started pulling the trigger. He lost count at four rounds and stopped himself a few shots later. The noise was deafening in the little room. His ears rang. Gunsmoke filled the air in a thick cloud. He pointed the Derringer at the window and fired. It only put a small hole in the glass, so he shot it again with the Glock. Glass came down onto Gabe and into the red water.

Jack heard shouting from behind the door. Screaming. The dog was barking. A baby started crying.

What the hell they got a baby in a place like this for? Jack thought.

His heart was pounding hard, even harder than when he jumped out of an airplane for the first time. He put one foot on the tub, kicking the two-by-four and a candle into the water, then stopped. How many bullets do I got left? Two? One? None?

He stepped away from the tub. He unlocked the door and yanked it open. Misfit lay on the floor, bleeding into the carpet like a gutted deer staining the snow. Two men were down at the end of the hall, both with guns. Jack fired at them and they jumped for cover. His gun went *click click click*. He dropped the Glock, grabbed Misfit's .357, and darted back into the bathroom. The AK-47 started up like a buzz saw and ripped into the door. Chunks of wood exploded into the bathroom. Jack jumped out the window headfirst, diving over Gabe and the tub. He heard bullets whine by. He hit the ground hard. He felt pain—in his knees, elbows, chest—and he thought he might not be able to get up in time. He took a deep breath; he tasted fresh air. Then he ignored the hurt and was up and running.

Jack had been the fastest running back in the state in high school, but he'd never run with the football like he ran now. He felt like he was almost flying as he sped around the house, through the yard, and across the street. He jumped and slid across the hood of an LTD. The AK-47 started firing again behind him, and he fell onto the sidewalk, scraping his elbows and forearms on the concrete. He still held the Derringer in one hand, the .357 in the other. He hid behind the wheel, and heard more shots. A shotgun. A pistol. The shooting stopped for a second, and he tried to peek up over the hood. He heard the bullet zip by his head before he heard the blast of the gun. He jerked back down, and more gunfire began. The Ford shook from the bullets slamming into it.

Then Jack heard the familiar crack of David's 30.06. There was screaming, then a second crack, then the screaming stopped.

Jack felt a swelling of pride about David's shooting skill, then he wondered if this was something he should be proud of.

After the third crack of the rifle, all shooting stopped.

Did he get two or three already?

Jack pointed Misfit's revolver at the passenger-side mirror and squeezed the trigger. He jammed the Derringer into his pocket and picked up the biggest chunk of mirror he could find and held it up. It took him a few seconds to orient himself through the glass, but then he spotted two bodies, one slumped over in a bush, the other lying in the yard. Then he glimpsed a figure crouched behind a tree. The person had no shirt on—the Mexican kid who'd frisked him? Others were hiding inside the front doorway. There was another crack, and the guy behind the tree went down. The figures in the doorway backed up into the house. He saw, in the side yard, one of the victims of David's shooting had been the pretty Indian girl. She was lying facedown in the grass, her brown hair spread around her in tendrils.

He realized what they were doing in a way he hadn't before. It punched him in the gut. Jack wanted this to be over. He wanted to go back in time and make a different decision.

Then he heard the crack of David's .270. He'd switched rifles, which had been the plan all along. Don't bother to reload until both were empty. Another crack. Falling glass. David was shooting at the house now.

Don't do that, Jack thought. There's a baby in there.

Jack took off running, hunched low. David kept shooting, but no one returned fire from the house.

Only about twenty-five yards away now. He saw a figure coming round the back of the truck, sneaking up behind David. His brother was hanging out the driver's side window, using the window frame to rest his elbow and steady his gun. Who was the guy? Someone he hadn't seen before. Someone who hadn't been in the house maybe. Just coming home.

"Davey," Jack tried to yell, but his voice was just a hoarse whisper. "Davey," he tried again, but it wasn't much louder.

"Goddamn drug dealers," the man said, and shot.

David jerked into the truck. His rifle fell to the pavement. The barrel made a dinging sound when it hit. Jack ran full speed into the street.

The man, wearing pajama bottoms and a tank top, saw him and raised his pistol. He fired but missed. He was middle-aged, with a mustache and a gut. Jack swung his revolver up. He had the flash of a memory of going out into the field with Jamie and David and seeing how fast they could draw and shoot like cowboys. He'd been the best of the three, even good enough to shoot from his hip and hit a bottle thrown into the air. He pointed the gun at the man and held down the trigger and fanned the hammer with his left hand, shooting the guy five times, all in the chest, and kept on firing until the gun clicked three times. The guy went to his knees first, then fell over in the street. Jack had seen people die just like that in the movies—Hollywood had got it right on that one. Behind the man, Jack could see the sun just coming up over the hills to the east, bright, orange, red.

Jack sprinted to the truck, out of breath, a lump in his throat just like the one he'd had when the Nevada policeman called to tell him Jamie was found in a dumpster, his throat slit.

"Davey," he said, coming around and looking in the window.

"Damn it," David said.

He was slumped against the other door, holding his head with one hand. David's fingers were red, and his hair was wet.

"It hurts," David said.

"Ah hell," Jack said, yanking the door open and getting in. He tossed the .357 on the seat. "Talk to me, Davey."

"Shot me in the head," David muttered.

Please, Jack thought. Please let it be one of those miracle shots where the bullet didn't hurt his brain. Please.

"Did we win?" David asked.

"We sure did," Jack said, starting the truck.

He heard a scream and looked up to see a woman running through a yard, heading his way, her eyes focused on the guy lying in the street. She was wailing. Jack grabbed the shotgun and pointed it out the window. He saw she wasn't armed, but he shot anyway. The woman crumpled into the street. She had graying hair, sweatpants, a Mickey Mouse T-shirt that was turning red. Jack looked at the man lying by her feet. Some regular Joe fed up with a drug war happening on his street, playing vigilante. And the lady was his wife.

For a moment the neighborhood was completely quiet. Jack had never heard such silence in his life. Then he heard the sound of the sprinkler. He heard a dog barking. He heard a screen door slam. He heard screaming. He heard sirens.

"Hellfire and damnation," Jack said, and stomped on the gas.

He yanked the wheel to do a U-turn and almost ran over the bodies of the man and woman lying in the street. The back wheels spun, screeching on the pavement, then tearing up over the curb and spitting dirt and grass. The truck jerked like when he took it off-roading, then all four tires were on pavement and he sped away. The sirens were loud now. Behind him, someone ran into the street and shot once at the truck. But the truck was too far away.

"Keep talking," Jack said, glancing at his brother as he ran a stop sign.

"I'm okay," David muttered, but his hand fell away, and his head rolled down so his chin almost rested on his chest. He looked like a drunk unable to keep from passing out. Blood dripped out of his hair and streaked down his face, bright red against his pale skin.

"You're going to be okay, Davey," Jack said, but he heard the panic in his voice. "Trust me, little brother. Just trust me."

Jack's hands shook. His eyes were blurry with tears. He was having trouble seeing. He didn't know where he was going. He screeched around a corner onto Highway 50 and floored the gas, heading east, not knowing why.

"Talk to me, Davey."

Jack's brother muttered something incomprehensible.

Jack pushed the truck to a hundred miles an hour, zipping around cars on the four-lane highway. The sun was up now, a bright, almost blinding blood-red bullet hole in the blue sky in front of him. He realized no police were following him. No drug dealers. But he didn't slow down.

# Rosalee Carrasco

FROM *Ploughshares*

## I

WHEN CHARLOTTE WAS very small, she played a game called Pretty Pretty Princess with her older sisters, and she never once won. One of them always became the prettiest princess, draped in pink or blue or purple plastic beads and a shiny plastic crown.

At eight, she was accepted into the circle of Ashlee, Tabatha, and Danielle, and even though they said to her, *You're not as pretty as us, but we'll let you play with us anyway,* Charlotte conceded to their haughty governance with fawning displays of appreciation and unmitigated devotion and loyalty.

In sixth grade, Charlotte fell in love with Scotty Marlowe. She sat behind him in geography class and mapped the spattering of copper freckles on the back of his neck instead of the primary-colored countries on the blackboard.

Yesterday, Danielle helped her narrow down her dress choice for the eighth-grade dance to a silver number with a conservative neckline and a sexier, asymmetrical piece in "oasis blue." Charlotte was leaning toward the blue dress.

## II

The four girls are the last to finish getting dressed after second-period phys ed class. They are always the last to get dressed because they take their time reapplying fragranced lotion to their ivory limbs, glinting baubles to their discriminating wrists and ears, and expensive, shimmering makeup to their delicate eyelids and lips. Ms. McCreary knows this, so she leaves them to finish preening while she prepares the gym for the next class. Mr. Pickert, their pervy third-period algebra teacher, knows this, but what Ms. McCreary calls "tardy," the girls call "fashionably late" and Mr. Pickert calls "reasonably delayed," as long as they sit in the front row with their long legs emerging from short skirts. Rosalee Carrasco knows this, which is why she chooses this specific time to step into the girls' locker room at Oak View Middle School and reach into the pink, rhinestoned messenger bag at her side. *What do you want, skank?* Ashlee says, looking up, holding a comb with its teeth paused in her straightened, tawny hair. Rosalee pulls out a semiautomatic Smith & Wesson 40 VE. It is heavier in her hand than when she fingered it this morning in her father's desk drawer. She points the cold black barrel at Ashlee.

## III

Tomorrow, Charlotte will stay home from school, where she will lock herself in her bathroom and scrape under her fingernails with a toothpick, and then a metal nail file, and then a little Swiss Army knife. She will struggle to get the blood out from under her nails until the blood that is there is her own.

She will stay home for the remainder of the school year, and she won't answer calls from her friends. Her older sisters will bring her homework from school, and they'll help her complete it on the floor of her bedroom. One of them will show her how to equalize a basic equation while the other kneels behind her, brushing her hair.

When the new school year begins, Charlotte will attend high school in a new district, where nobody asks her questions.

In fifteen years, she will marry a quiet young professor from UC Berkeley, and they will have two daughters.

When they are old enough, she will tell them that they are both the prettiest princess, even though they never ask, and even though she doesn't believe it.

*I*

At just five years old, Ashlee's parents bought her a Shetland pony.

Her mother went to college with James Dewitt, Danielle's father, and this is how Ashlee and Danielle became inseparable.

Ashlee was always second in command because her parents were not as rich as Danielle's (her father moved around real estate, while Danielle's father moved around stocks) and because her mother was half black, though they never spoke of it.

When other little girls asked to play with them, Ashlee laughed.

She played tennis—but only indoors because she'd learned that too much sun was costly.

It was Ashlee who noticed, last week, that the Mexican girl had begun her period and didn't know it. She had a blossom of dark red on the back of her khaki pants. Ashlee pointed it out to the others. Someone (not her, certainly) took a picture with his or her camera phone and posted the picture on Facebook, tagging everyone in the school.

*II*

Rosalee is nervous and angry and she doesn't know what she's doing. She planned this, and she planned what she wanted to say and how she would say it, but she hasn't thought past that. She just wants them to listen to her, to be scared, to feel what it feels like to be powerless. She wants a lot of things. Tabatha takes a step toward a locker, and there's no exit but the one Rosalee is standing in, but Rosalee says *Sit the fuck down* anyway. Danielle stands up and repeats what Ashlee said, without the epithet, and much more calmly: *What do you want?* She stands in a little rectangle of morning sunlight thrown into the room by the small, high windows above the lockers. It puts her perfect face half in shadow. Her hair is perfect and her clothes are perfect, and she was in the middle of doing her makeup, so only her bottom lip is shiny with gloss. She seems in control, even when she's not. Rosalee hates her for this. Rosalee's hand is trembling, the heavy black-and-silver Smith & Wesson is trembling, and when she speaks, her voice is trembling.

She releases the safety, the way the YouTube video showed her. *I want you to pay,* she says.


## III

Tomorrow, Ashlee will go to school. Reporters will sneak onto campus, and one will pop out of a bush like a gangly bird of prey and surprise her. He'll poke a mic in her face and ask if she knew Rosalee was crazy. She'll say, *I didn't think she was crazy. I didn't think about her at all.*

She will stay friends with what remains of her clique through high school, but there will be something off-kilter, as if the shifting of elements within the group has thrown off their center of gravity. She will feel the subtle prick of exclusion when her father loses his real estate job in yet another recession, and after high school, they'll lose touch completely.

In college, Ashlee will stop lightening her hair, and she will experiment with a new drug called Chastity. Things will unravel rapidly. She will drop out of school, and huge chunks of her life will later appear as empty spheres, or as bleary shapes viewed through a glass of water. It will take twenty years for her to clean herself up, and she will, in therapy, retrace it all back to that day in the locker room at Oak View Middle School. She won't go any further than that.


## I

Tabatha was born in October. She was a Libra.

At two years old, Tabatha would not stop eating her crayons, and her mother had to remove all crayons and crayonlike objects from the house.

Her little brother was born when she was five, and when he was two months old, she pinched his nose closed while he slept to see him open his little pink, translucent lips like a fish. Then she kissed him.

When she was six, she gained an appreciation for the proper use of crayons, and turned out to be a capable artist.

In fourth grade, she and her three new friends helped her dad paint a mural with an ocean theme on the wall in her little brother's room.

When she was twelve, she was her brother's hero.

Tabatha Roth was also in love with Scotty Marlowe.

Yesterday, like every Tuesday for the past fifteen years, Tabatha allowed herself to chew gently on a crayon when nobody was looking, before she went to sleep. She liked the feel of wax between her teeth. This crayon color was called "blush."

## II

*Do you want money?* Danielle asks. *We can give you money.* Rosalee is confused for a moment, knits her brow. *I don't want your fucking charity.* She's never cussed this much, and the word *fuck* feels powerful in her mouth. She says it out loud again, just for good measure: *Fuck.* Charlotte, with her reddish curls bouncing irreverently, moves behind Tabatha. Danielle says, coolly, *Well, then, what do you want?* And she crosses her arms like she's not scared, like nothing in the whole world scares her. She learned this from her father, who has always told her that "people are cowards, but Dewitts show no fear." Rosalee feels that she's losing control of the situation, so she aims at the ceiling. The girls all raise their arms and cover their heads with their hands, instinctually, as Rosalee pulls the trigger, which is harder to squeeze than she'd anticipated. She expects the bullet to strike the plaster tiles and cause a shower of white powder to rain down on them, instilling fear. But instead it makes a sharp *ping* on a pipe, and it's several seconds before anyone notices that Tabatha is no longer standing. She is an awkward heap on the floor.

## III

## I

Ms. Janet McCreary was born on a small farm in Pennsylvania, where she milked goats and reveled in lightning storms from her upstairs bedroom window. She saw lightning strike the lone striped maple in the center of a field beneath her window twelve times.

She was a highly precocious child, and she read hungrily, consuming books under her blankets with a flashlight well after her mother turned the lights off. She and her friends spent their time talking about boys and books, but more often books.

Ms. McCreary studied German lit in college but found afterward that her skills were not very marketable. She began teaching PE until she found a position more suited to her.

She met her fiancé, Matthew Parker, on Match.com. Within a year, they'd determined the location and the guest list for their wedding. It would be in June.

Three weeks ago, Ms. McCreary, with much happiness, told her fiancé that she was pregnant. She rigged a game of Scrabble by hiding tiles under the table, and played words like *baby, father,* and *family* until he caught on. He was elated.

## II

Ms. McCreary hears the shot from out in the gym, but it doesn't register with her what it is. This is only a middle school, and she has never heard a real gunshot before. She moves unhurriedly toward the locker room, annoyed with the four girls she left there: What have they done now? As she turns into the locker room, she sees Rosalee from behind. She can see the girls on the ground beyond Rosalee and wonders what they're playing at. *Strange,* she thinks. *Danielle Dewitt is on her knees.* It is then that she sees the gun. She thinks *Scheisse,* because she always curses in German. Ms. Mc-

Creary doesn't know what to do. Her instinct is to talk to the girl, but she hesitates—maybe she should try to subdue her, or go call for help. Her eyes flicker to Rosalee's right, where she's certain she left a softball bat leaning against the wall. She takes a step closer, and she can hear Charlotte on the ground mumbling something over and over, but she can't make out what it is. She takes another step, but stops, and raises her hand silently to her stomach. Charlotte moves her hand from Tabatha's head to her own and touches her temple, leaving a bright smudge like a child's red finger paint. She is saying, *She's dead, she's dead, she's dead.*

## III

Tomorrow, Ms. McCreary will spend much of the day in the police station, giving statements. She will be tired, but more than that she will be afraid she's going to lose her job because she is never supposed to leave kids in the locker room alone. There was death on her watch.

Despite the fact that there were more students in the gym who required supervision than there were in the locker room, Ms. McCreary will be the scapegoat for Ella County School District, and she will lose her job.

In two weeks, she will have an abortion, and she will tell her fiancé that it was a miscarriage. She will tell herself she finds unbearable the thought of bringing a child into a world where things like this happened, where her children would have to play and learn and live—with children *like this.*

In one year, her fiancé will leave her, and she will let him.

In six years, Ms. McCreary will relocate to Germany, where she will teach English and begin writing. She will publish an article titled "Social Violence and Accountability in American Literature" in a modest academic journal.

## I

When Rosalee Carrasco is born to a French mother and Chilean father, she is crying.

Rosalee is always doing and going and performing. She is always trying, and learning.

When she is six, she is feeding her two younger brothers mashed bananas with a tiny rubber-coated spoon because her parents work overtime to pay for her private school.

When she is eight, she is buying trendy pink bracelets and standing nervously in line next to Ashlee at lunch. She is viciously ignored.

At nine, her mother is scolding, *Enfant ingrat! You have nothing to cry about.*

When she is seven and eight and ten and twelve, she is asking *Can I play?*

At thirteen, she is falling in love with Scotty Marlowe. At thirteen, she is understanding.

At fourteen, she is watching herself become a woman in the mirror, and then she is watching herself become a woman on Facebook, and then she is watching the custodian pull dark, bloody tampons from her locker with gloved hands. She is cowering as boys call her "Rosa-leaky."

## II

*Rosalee, honey.* Ms. McCreary says, her voice hardly above a whisper. Rosalee whips around, the gun pointed at chest level, both hands wrapped around the grip. She's been holding it up for only a minute, maybe two, but it feels as if she's been holding it her whole life, and it is heavy. Her eyes are big and round as quarters, and Ms. McCreary can see the whites all the way around her dark pupils. Behind her, all of the girls are huddled around Tabatha's body, and one of the girls—Charlotte—is sniffling. *Rosalee,* Ms. McCreary says again. She steps toward the slight girl, whose dark hair is pulled severely behind her head, making her look older than she is, and whose fear makes her look younger than she is. The teacher holds out her hand, slowly, slowly, her palm up. It is the universal sign for *Give me the gun.* The barrel begins to drop, slowly, slowly. Danielle stands suddenly and says, *She killed Tabatha* in a voice that is a sob and an accusation and a taunt; it is all of these things. *I didn't,* Rosalee cries out. Her words come out high and hollow; they echo without resonance. She spins around wildly, points the gun at Danielle, and Ms. McCreary shouts, *Rosalee!*

## III

Rosalee will be charged with five counts. She will be convicted of three counts, and she will serve four years at a juvenile correctional facility, where she will read Sylvia Plath and ZZ Packer and keep to herself.

When she is released, she will go to community college, where she will major in women's studies. She will become interested in acting, and join a small troupe at a local theater.

She will be quiet and withdrawn, dark and inscrutable. Men will fall in love with her, or rather, they will try to fall in love with her, but she will not let them. People will try to get close to her, but she will push them away.

In her most acclaimed performance, she will star in the role of Wendy, in *Peter Pan*. She will be most convincing when she plays Old Wendy and her young daughter Jane asks her what it is she sees in the darkness. *Nothing,* Wendy says. *Yes,* counters Jane. *You see when you were a little girl.* And Rosalee says, *That is a long time ago, sweetheart.*

For the rest of her life, she will be always doing and going and performing. She will be always remembering.

## I

Danielle Dewitt was a happy, occasionally colicky baby.

Her older half-sister Sophia dressed her up in cashmere and anointed her with makeup when Danielle was four; she looked like a painted porcelain doll.

When she was five, her older half-brother Colin taught her how to fish. She caught a small salmon and threw it back, horrified.

At Mimi's Finishing School for Children, she learned how to read a French dinner menu. At home, she learned how to read people, how to put herself at the advantage.

When she was nine, she stole her sister's beloved diamond stud earrings and flushed them down the toilet.

She considered herself a good, charitable person; she made her father donate to the whales every Christmas.

Last week she conceived of and forced the girls to carry out the prank on the Mexican girl. Danielle said that each girl had to supply an "item" so that none could be exempted if they got caught, except for Tabatha, because Tabatha was a virgin and so hadn't begun using tampons yet. She, however, acted as lookout.

## II

Danielle, who had stood up and stepped forward a moment ago, made brave by the presence of an adult, steps back again. The barrel of the gun is shaking wildly in Rosalee's hand; if she pulls the trigger, the bullet could fall harmlessly wide, or it could hit Danielle right between her pretty blue eyes, a fatal blemish above her straight, narrow nose. Rosalee says, *I didn't kill her, it was an accident,* and behind her Ms. McCreary is nodding her head, *Yes, yes. Of course it was.* Rosalee says to Danielle, motioning with the silver barrel, *Tell her. Tell her it was an accident.* And Danielle says, *It was* while she's exhaling, so they can hardly hear her. *And tell her,* Rosalee says. *Tell her what you did to me.* Danielle's eyes flit, imperceptibly, to Ms. McCreary and then back to Rosalee. *We didn't do anything to you.* Rosalee moves suddenly toward Danielle, the gun at her side. Ms. McCreary is yelling something in the background, but neither girl hears. Rosalee steps up to Danielle, so close their noses are almost touching. They are breathing each other's heavy breaths. Something passes between them: an expression, a quivering of the pupil, an exchange of molecules? Rosalee drops the gun.

## III

Danielle will go to school tomorrow and she will dazzle before the paparazzi. She will be quoted as saying, "I never even spoke to the poor girl before this. She must have been obsessed with us."

She will go to the eighth-grade dance with Scotty Marlowe, and she will look stunning in a slinky, asymmetrical dress that is "oasis blue."

She will use what she'll refer to as "the Tragedy" to get her father to buy her a Hermès Birkin bag, then a Mercedes C-Class when she turns sixteen, and then a shopping trip to Paris at eighteen.

She will go to Sarah Lawrence University, marry a dermatologist, and have three children by cesarean section before she is thirty-five.

She will read *Charlotte's Web* and *James and the Giant Peach* to her children when they are small, and they will bicker for her affection.

One day, just before her youngest daughter begins high school, Danielle will hire a maid named Rosa. She will pause for a moment as she cuts the stem off the bottom of a tulip, and she will think that maybe she knew someone once by that name.

LEE CHILD

# Wet with Rain

FROM *Belfast Noir*

BIRTHS AND DEATHS are in the public record. Census returns
and rent rolls and old mortgages are searchable. As are citizenship
applications from all the other English-speaking countries. There
are all kinds of ancestry sites on the Web. These were the factors
in our favor.

Against us was a historical truth. The street had been built in
the 1960s. Fifty years ago, more or less. Within living memory.
Most of the original residents had died off, but they had families,
who must have visited, and who might remember. Children and
grandchildren, recipients of lore and legend, and therefore possibly a problem.

But overall we counted ourselves lucky. The first owners of the
house in question were long dead, and had left no children. The
husband had surviving siblings, but they had all gone to either Australia or Canada. The wife had a living sister, still in the neighborhood, but she was over eighty years old, and considered unreliable.

Since the original pair, the house had had five owners, most
of them in the later years. We felt we had enough distance. So
we went with the third variant of the second plan. Hairl Carter
came with me. Hairl Carter the second, technically. His father had
the same name. From southeastern Missouri. His father's mother
had wanted to name her firstborn Harold, but she had no more
than a third-grade education, and couldn't spell except phonetically. So Harold it was, phonetically. The old lady never knew it
was weird. We all called her grandson Harry, which might not have
pleased her.

Harry did the paperwork, which was easy enough, because we made it all Xeroxes of Xeroxes, which hides a lot of sins. I opened an account at a Washington, D.C., bank, in the name of the society, and I put half a million dollars into it, and we got credit cards and a checkbook. Then we rehearsed. We prepped it, like a political debate. The same conversation, over and over again, down all the possible highways and byways. We identified weak spots, though we had no choice but to barrel through. We figured audacity would stop them thinking straight.

We flew first to London, then to Dublin in the south, and then we made the connection to Belfast on tickets that cost less than cups of coffee back home. We took a cab to the Europa Hotel, which is where we figured people like us would stay. We arranged a car with the concierge. Then we laid up and slept. We figured midmorning the next day should be zero hour.

The car was a crisp Mercedes and the driver showed no real re- luctance about the address—which was second from the end of a short line of ticky-tacky row houses, bland and cheaply built, with big areas of peeling white weatherboard, which must have saved money on bricks. The roof tiles were concrete, and had gone mossy. In the distance the hills were like velvet, impossibly green, but all around us the built environment was hard. There was a fine cold drizzle in the air, and the street and the sidewalk were both shiny gray.

The car waited at the curb and we opened a broken gate and walked up a short path through the front yard. Carter rang the bell and the door opened immediately. The Mercedes had not gone unnoticed. A woman looked out at us. She was solidly built, with a pale, meaty face. "Who are you?"

I said, "We're from America."

"America?"

"We came all the way to see you."

"Why?"

"Mrs. Healy, is it?" I asked, even though I knew it was. I knew all about her. I knew where she was born, how old she was, and how much her husband made. Which wasn't much. They were a month behind on practically everything. Which I hoped was going to help.

"Yes, I'm Mrs. Healy," the woman said.

"My name is John Pacino, and my colleague here is Harry Carter."

"Good morning to you both."

"You live in a very interesting house, Mrs. Healy."

She looked blank, and then craned her neck out the door and stared up at her front wall. "Do I?"

"Interesting to us, anyway."

"Why?"

"Can we tell you all about it?"

She said, "Would you like a wee cup of tea?"

"That would be lovely."

So we trooped inside, first Carter, then me, feeling a kind of preliminary satisfaction, as if our lead-off hitter had gotten on base. Nothing guaranteed, but so far, so good. The air inside smelled of daily life and closed windows. A skilled analyst could have listed the ingredients from their last eight meals. All of which had been either boiled or fried, I guessed.

It wasn't the kind of household where guests get deposited in the parlor to wait. We followed the woman to the kitchen, which had drying laundry suspended on a rack. She filled a kettle and lit the stove. She said, "Tell me what's interesting about my house."

Carter said, "There's a writer we admire very much, name of Edmund Wall."

"Here?"

"In America."

"A writer?"

"A novelist. A very fine one."

"I never heard of him. But then, I don't read much."

"Here," Carter said, and he took the copies from his pocket and smoothed them on the counter. They were faked to look like Wikipedia pages. Which is trickier than people think. (Wikipedia prints different than it looks on the computer screen.)

Mrs. Healy asked, "Is he famous?"

"Not exactly," I said. "Writers don't really get famous. But he's very well respected. Among people who like his sort of thing. There's an appreciation society. That's why we're here. I'm the chairman and Mr. Carter is the general secretary."

Mrs. Healy stiffened a little, as if she thought we were trying to sell her something. "I'm sorry, but I don't want to join. I don't know him."

I said, "That's not the proposition we have for you."

"Then what is?"

"Before you, the Robinsons lived here, am I right?"

"Yes," she said.

"And before them, the Donnellys, and before them, the McLaughlins."

The woman nodded. "They all got cancer. One after the other. People started to say this was an unlucky house."

I looked concerned. "That didn't bother you? When you bought it?"

"My faith has no room for superstition."

Which was a circularity fit to make a person's head explode. It struck me mute. Carter said, "And before the McLaughlins were the McCanns, and way back at the beginning were the McKennas."

"Before my time," the woman said, uninterested, and I felt the runner on first steal second. Scoring position.

I said, "Edmund Wall was born in this house."

"Who?"

"Edmund Wall. The novelist. In America."

"No one named Wall ever lived here."

"His mother was a good friend of Mrs. McKenna. Right back at the beginning. She came to visit from America. She thought she had another month, but the baby came early."

"When?"

"The 1960s."

"In this house?"

"Upstairs in the bedroom. No time to get to the hospital."

"A baby?"

"The future Edmund Wall."

"I never heard about it. Mrs. McKenna has a sister. She never talks about it."

Which felt like the runner getting checked back. I said, "You know Mrs. McKenna's sister?"

"We have a wee chat from time to time. Sometimes I see her in the hairdresser's."

"It was fifty years ago. How's her memory?"

"I should think a person would remember that kind of thing."

Carter said, "Maybe it was hushed up. It's possible Edmund's mother wasn't married."

Mrs. Healy went pale. Impropriety. Scandal. In her house. Worse than cancer. "Why are you telling me this?"

I said, "The Edmund Wall Appreciation Society wants to buy your house."

"Buy it?"

"For a museum. Well, like a living museum, really. Certainly people could visit, to see the birthplace, but we could keep his papers here too. It could be a research center."

"Do people do that?"

"Do what? Research?"

"No, visit houses where writers were born."

"All the time. Lots of writers' houses are museums. Or tourist attractions. We could make a very generous offer. Edmund Wall has many passionate supporters in America."

"How generous?"

"Best plan would be to pick out where you'd like to live next, and we'll make sure you can. Within reason, of course. Maybe a new house. They're building them all over." Then I shut up, and let temptation work its magic. Mrs. Healy went quiet. Then she started to look around her kitchen. Chipped cabinets, sagging hinges, damp air.

The kettle started to whistle.

She said, "I'll have to talk to my husband."

Which felt like the runner sliding into third ahead of the throw. Safe. Ninety feet away. Nothing guaranteed, but so far, so good. In fact bloody good, as they say on those damp little islands. We were in high spirits on the way back in the Mercedes.

The problem was waiting for us in the Europa's lobby. An Ulsterman, maybe fifty years old, in a cheap suit, with old nicks and scars on his hands and thickening around his eyes. A former field operative, no doubt, many years in the saddle, now moved to a desk because of his age. I was familiar with the type. It was like looking in a mirror.

He said, "Can I have a word?"

We went to the bar, which was dismal and empty ahead of the lunchtime rush. The guy introduced himself as a copper, from right there in Belfast, from a unit he didn't specify, but which I guessed was Special Branch, which was the brass-knuckle wing of the old Royal Ulster Constabulary, now the Police Service of Northern Ireland. Like the FBI, with the gloves off. He said, "Would you mind telling me who you are and why you're here?"

So Carter gave him the guff about Edmund Wall, and the appreciation society, and the birthplace, but what was good enough earlier in the morning didn't sound so great in the cold light of midday. The guy checked things on his phone in real time as Carter talked, and then he said, "There are four things wrong with that story. There is no Edmund Wall, there is no appreciation society, the bank account you opened is at the branch nearest to Langley, which is CIA headquarters, and most of all, that house you're talking about was once home to Gerald McCann, who was a notorious paramilitary in his day."

Carter said nothing, and neither did I.

The guy continued, "Northern Ireland is part of the United Kingdom, you know. They won't allow unannounced activities on their own turf. So again, would you mind telling me who you are and why you're here?"

I said, "You interested in a deal?"

"What kind?"

"You want to buy a friend in a high place?"

"How high?"

"Very high."

"Where?"

"Somewhere useful to your government."

"Terms?"

"You let us get the job done first."

"Who gets killed?"

"Nobody. The Healys get a new house. That's all."

"What do you get?"

"Paid. But your new friend in the very high place gets peace of mind. For which he'll be suitably grateful, I'm sure."

"Tell me more."

"First I need to check you have your head on straight. This is not the kind of thing where you make a bunch of calls and get other people involved. This is the kind of thing where you let us do our work, and then when we're gone, you announce your new relationship as a personal coup. Or not. Maybe you'll want to keep the guy in your vest pocket."

"How many laws are you going to break?"

"None at all. We're going to buy a house. Happens every day."

"Because there's something in it, right? What did Gerald Mc-Cann leave behind?"

"You got to agree to what I said before. You got to at least nod your head. I have to be able to trust you."

"Okay, I agree," the guy said. "But I'm sticking with you all the way. We're a threesome now. Until you're done. Every minute. Until I wave you off at the airport."

"No, come with us," I said. "You can meet your new friend. At least shake hands with him. Then come back. Vest pocket or not, you'll feel better that way."

He fell for it, like I knew he would. I mean, why not? Security services love a personal coup. They love their vest pockets. They love to run people. They love to be the guy. He said, "Deal. So what's the story?"

"Once upon a time there was a young officer in the U.S. Army. A bit of a hothead, with certain sympathies. With a certain job, at a certain time. He sold some obsolete weapons."

"To Gerald McCann?"

I nodded. "Who as far as we know never used them. Who we believe buried them under his living room floor. Meanwhile, our young officer grew up and got promoted and went into a whole different line of work. Now he wants the trail cleaned up."

"You want to buy the house so you can dig up the floor?"

I nodded again. "Can't break in and do it. Too noisy. The floors are concrete. We're going to need jackhammers. Neighbors need to think we're repairing the drains or something."

"These weapons are still traceable?"

"Weapon, singular, to be honest with you. Which I'm prepared to be, in a spot like this. Still traceable, yes. And extremely embarrassing, if it comes to light."

"Did Mrs. Healy believe you about Edmund Wall?"

"She believed us about the money. We're from America."

The guy from Special Branch said, "It takes a long time to buy a house."

It took three weeks, with all kinds of lawyer stuff, and an inspection, which was a pantomime and a farce, because what did we care? But it would have looked suspicious if we had waived it. We were supposed to be diligent stewards of the appreciation society's assets. So we commissioned it, and pretended to read it afterward. It was pretty bad, actually. For a spell I was worried the jackhammer would bring the whole place down.

We stayed in Belfast the whole three weeks. Normally we might have gone home and come back again, but not with the Special Branch copper on the scene, obviously. We had to watch him every minute. Which was easy enough, because he had to watch us every minute. We all spent three whole weeks gazing at each other, and reading crap about dry rot and rising damp. Whatever that was. It rained every day.

But in the end the lawyers got it done, and I received an undramatic phone call saying the house was ours. So we picked up the key and drove over and walked around with pages from the inspection report in our hands and worried expressions on our faces—which I thought of as setting the stage. The jackhammer had to be explicable. And the neighbors were nosy as hell. They were peering out and coming over and introducing themselves in droves. They brought old Mrs. McKenna's sister, who claimed to remember the baby being born, which set off a whole lot of tutting and clucking among her audience. More people came. As a result we waited two days before we rented the jackhammer. Easier than right away, we thought. I knew how to operate it. I had taken lessons, from a crew repairing Langley's secure staff lot.

The living room floor was indeed concrete, under some kind of asphalt screed, which was under a foam-backed carpet so old it had gone flat and crusty. We tore it up and saw a patch of screed that was different from the rest. It was the right size too. I smiled. Gerald McCann, taking care of business.

I asked, "What actually happened to McCann?"

The Special Branch guy said, "Murdered."

"Who by?"

"Us."

"When?"

"Before he could use this, obviously, whatever it is."

And after that, conversation was impossible, because I got the hammer started. After which the job went fast. The concrete was long on sand and short on cement. Same the world over. Concrete is a dirty business. But even so, the pit was pretty deep. More than just secure temporary storage. It felt kind of permanent. But we got to the bottom eventually, and we pulled the thing out.

It was wrapped in heavy plastic, but it was immediately recognizable. A reinforced canvas cylinder, olive green, like a half-size oil drum, with straps and buckles all over it, to keep it closed up tight, and to make it man-portable, like a backpack. A big backpack. A big, heavy backpack.

The guy from Special Branch went very quiet, and then he said, "Is that what I think it is?"

"Yes, it's what you think it is."

"Jesus Christ on a bike."

"Don't worry. The warhead is a dummy. Because our boy in uniform wasn't."

Carter said, "Warhead? What is it?"

I said nothing.

The guy from Special Branch explained, "It's an SADM. A W54 in an H-912 transport container."

"Which is what?"

"A Strategic Atomic Demolition Munition. A W54 missile warhead, which was the baby of the family, adapted to use as an explosive charge. Strap that thing to a bridge pier, and it's like dropping a thousand tons of TNT on it."

"It's nuclear?"

I said, "It weighs just over fifty pounds. Less than the bag you take on vacation. It's the nearest thing to a suitcase nuke ever built."

The guy from Special Branch said, "It *is* a suitcase nuke, never mind the nearest thing."

Carter said, "I never heard about them."

I said, "Developed in the 1950s. Obsolete by 1970. Paratroops were trained to jump with them, behind the lines, to blow up power stations and dams."

"With nuclear bombs?"

"They had mechanical timers. The paratroops might have gotten away."

"Might have?"

"It was a tough world back then."

"But this warhead is fake?"

"Open it up and take a look."

"I wouldn't know the difference."

"Good point," I said. "Gerald McCann obviously didn't."

The guy from Special Branch said, "I can see why my new friend wants the trail cleaned up. Selling nuclear weapons to foreign paramilitary groups? He couldn't survive that, whoever he is."

We put the thing in the trunk of a rented car and drove to a quiet corner of Belfast International Airport, to a gate marked *General Aviation,* which meant private jets, and we found ours, which was a Gulfstream IV, painted gray and unmarked except for a tail number. The guy from Special Branch looked a little jealous.

"Borrowed," I said. "Mostly it's used for renditions."

Now he looked a little worried.

I said, "I'm sure they hosed the blood out."

We loaded the munition on board ourselves, because there was no spare crew to help us. There was one pilot and no steward. Standard practice, in the rendition business. Better deniability. We figured the munition was about the size of a fat guy, so we strapped it upright in a seat of its own. Then we all three sat down, as far from it as we could get.

Ninety minutes out I went to the bathroom, and after that I steered the conversation back to rendition. I said, "These planes are modified, you know. They have some of the electronic interlocks taken out. You can open the door while you're flying, for instance. Low and slow, over the water. They threaten to throw the prisoner out. All part of softening him up ahead of time."

Then I said, "Actually, sometimes they do throw the prisoner out. On the way home, usually, after he's spilled the beans. Too much trouble to do anything else, really."

Then I said, "Which is what we're going to do with the munition. We have to. We have no way of destroying it before we land, and we can't let it suddenly reappear in the U.S., like it just escaped from the museum. And this is the perfect setup for corroboration. Because there's three of us. Because we're going to get questions. He needs to know for sure. So this way I can swear I saw you two drop it out the door, and you two can swear you saw it hit the water, and you can swear I was watching you do it. We can back each other up three ways."

Which all made sense, so we went low and slow and I opened the door. Salt air howled in, freezing cold, and the plane rocked and juddered. I stepped back, and the guy from Special Branch came first, sidewinding down the aisle, with one of the transport container's straps hefted in his nicked and scarred left hand, and then came the munition itself, heavy, bobbing like a fat man in a hammock, and then came Carter, a strap in his right hand, shuffling sideways.

They got lined up side by side at the open door, their backs to me, each with a forearm up on the bulkhead to steady himself, the munition swinging slackly and bumping the floor between them. I said, "On three," and I started counting the numbers out, and they hoisted the cylinder and began swinging it, and on three they opened their hands and the canvas straps jerked free and the cylinder sailed out in the air and was instantly whipped away by the slipstream. They kept their forearms on the bulkhead, looking out, craning, staring down, waiting for the splash, and I took out the gun I had collected from the bathroom and shot the guy from Special Branch in the lower back, not because of any sadistic tendency, but because of simple ballistics. If the slug went through-and-through, I wanted it to carry on into thin air, not hit the airframe.

I don't think the bullet killed the guy. But the shock changed his day. He went all weak, and his forearm gave way, and he half fell and half got sucked out into the void. No sound. Just a blurred pinwheel as the currents caught him, and then a dot that got smaller, and then a tiny splash in the blue below, indistinguishable from a million white-crested waves.

I stepped up and helped Carter wrestle the door shut. He said, "I guess he knew too much."

I said, "Way too much."

We sat down, knee to knee.

Carter figured it out less than an hour later. He was not a dumb guy. He said, "If the warhead was a dummy, he could spin it like entrapment, like taking a major opponent out of the game. Or like economic warfare. Like a Robin Hood thing. He took a lot of bad money out of circulation, in exchange for a useless piece of junk. He could be the secret hero. The super-modest man."

"But?" I said.

"He's not spinning it that way. And all those people died of cancer. The Robinsons, and the Donnellys, and the McLaughlins."

"So?" I said.

"The warhead was real. That was an atom bomb. He sold nuclear weapons."

"Small ones," I said. "And obsolete."

Carter didn't reply. But that wasn't the important part. The important part came five minutes later. I saw it arrive in his eyes. I said, "Ask the question."

He said, "I'd rather not."

I said, "Ask the question."

"Why was there a gun in the bathroom? The Special Branch guy was with us the whole time. You didn't call ahead for it. You had no opportunity. But it was there for you anyway. Why?"

I didn't answer.

He said, "It was there for me. The Special Branch guy was happenstance. Me, you were planning to shoot all along."

I said, "Kid, our boss sold live nuclear weapons. I'm cleaning up for him. What else do you expect?"

Carter said, "He trusts me."

"No, he doesn't."

"I would never rat him out. He's my hero."

"Gerald McCann should be your hero. He had the sense not to use the damn thing. I'm sure he was sorely tempted."

Carter didn't answer that. Getting rid of him was difficult, all on my own, but the next hours were peaceful, just me and the pilot, flying high and fast toward a spectacular sunset. I dropped my seat way back, and I stretched out. Relaxation is important. Life is short and uncertain, and it pays to make the best of whatever comes your way.

MICHAEL CONNELLY AND DENNIS LEHANE

# Red Eye

FROM *FaceOff*

*2005*

AS A PRACTICE, Harry Bosch did his best to stay out of tunnels, but as he came out of Logan Airport a tunnel was unavoidable—either the Ted Williams or the Sumner, take your pick. The rental car's GPS chose the Williams, so Harry drove down and deep under Boston Harbor. The traffic backed up at the bottom and then completely stopped as Bosch realized that the timing of his red-eye flight from L.A. had landed him in the heart of morning rush hour.

Of course, the tunnel was much bigger and wider and was well lit in comparison to the tunnels of his past and those of his dreams. He was also not alone in his predicament. The passage was wall to wall with cars and trucks—a river of steel under the river of water, only one of them flowing at the moment. But a tunnel is a tunnel and soon the chest-tightening feeling of claustrophobia took hold. Bosch started to sweat and impatiently honked the horn of his rental in impotent protest. This apparently only served to identify him as an outsider. The locals didn't honk, they did not rail against that which they could not change.

Eventually, traffic started moving and he finally emerged, lowering his window to let in the fresh air. He made a mental note to find a map and then chart a way back to the airport that did not include going through a tunnel. Too bad the car's GPS didn't have a No Tunnels setting. He would have to find his way back to the airport on his own.

The LAPD's Open-Unsolved Unit's travel protocol called for Bosch to check in with the local authorities immediately upon arrival in another city. In this case that would be the District E-13 offices of the Boston Police Department in Jamaica Plain. This was the district that included the address Bosch had for Edward Paisley, the man whose DNA Bosch had come to take—surreptitiously or not.

Bosch, however, often trampled on the official cold case protocol. He usually followed his own protocol, which involved getting the lay of the land first and maybe putting an eye on his quarry—then going in to meet and greet the local constabulary.

Bosch planned to check out Paisley's address, maybe get a first look at him, and then check into the room at Courtyard by Marriott he had reserved on Expedia. He might even take a short nap after check-in, to make up for the lost sleep on the flight out. In the early afternoon he would go to District E-13 and tell the captain or major in charge that he was in from L.A. on a fifteen-year-old cold case murder. He would then most likely be paired with a divisional detective who had fallen from favor with command staff. Squiring around a visiting detective following a lead on a 1990 cold case was not a choice assignment.

Two nights before, at a bar on Warren Street in Roxbury, Dontelle Howe had asked Patrick Kenzie, "You got kids?"

Patrick half nodded, a bit confused on how to answer. "One on the way."

"When?"

"Any day now."

Dontelle Howe smiled. He was a trim black man in his early thirties, with close-cropped dreads and clothes so crisp you could smell the starch from two rooms away. "First?"

Patrick nodded.

"Ain't you a little old?" Dontelle took another dainty sip from the one brandy he allowed himself every weeknight. Weekends, he'd assured Patrick, he could drink his weight in Henney, but weeknights and Sundays he kept his limit at one because every morning he drove a bus full of forty-five children from their homes all over the city to Dearborn Middle School in Roxbury, about two blocks from the bar where he'd agreed to meet Patrick after work.

"A little old?" Patrick checked himself in the bar mirror—a

little grayer, okay, a little heavier, fine, a little less on top than he would have hoped, sure, but not bad for forty. Particularly forty years lived as hard as he'd lived his. Either that, or he was bullshitting himself, which was just as likely. "You don't look like you'll be auditioning for any boy bands yourself, Dontelle."

"But I already got two in grade school. Time they're in college and me and the woman are kicking it somewhere in Florida? I'll *be* your age."

Patrick chuckled and drank some beer.

Dontelle Howe's voice grew deeper, more somber. "So no one's looking for her? *Still?*"

Patrick made a mezza-mezza motion with his hand. "Police think it's a custody thing. Father's a real piece of shit, and no one can find him. No one can find her, either, so they think it's a case of one plus one equals she'll turn up."

"But she's twelve, man."

"She" was Chiffon Henderson, a seventh-grader Dontelle Howe picked up every morning from the Bromley-Heath Housing projects in Jamaica Plain and dropped off nine hours later in the same spot. Three nights ago, Chiffon had left her bedroom in the back of the unit she shared with two sisters and her mother. The leaving wasn't in dispute; the question of whether it had been voluntary was. She'd exited through a window. No signs of struggle or forced entry, though her mother had told police that Chiffon often left her window open on a mild night even though she'd been warned a thousand times not to. The police were focusing on Chiffon's father, Lonnie Cullen, a deadbeat dad four times over to four different households, who hadn't checked in with his parole officer this past weekend and couldn't be found at his last known address. There was also some talk that Chiffon may have started seeing a boy who lived in one of the other buildings in the projects, though no one knew his name or much about him.

Chiffon's mother, Ella Henderson, worked two jobs. By day she checked in patients for four ob-gyn partners at Beth Israel; nights she cleaned offices. She was a poster child for the burdens of the working poor—so much time spent trying to feed your kids and keep the lights on that you never spent any time with them until the day they told you it was too late to start trying.

Two days ago, she'd checked in Patrick's wife, Angie, for her final appointment before their child, expected to enter the world a week from today, would be delivered. As Ella Henderson dou-ble-checked the insurance info and verified the parents' dates of birth, she began to weep. It was weeping without drama or noise, just a steady stream even as her polite smile remained in place and her eyes remained fixed on her computer screen.

Half an hour later, Patrick had agreed to ask around about her daughter. The lead cop on the case, Detective Emily Zebrowski, had a current caseload of twelve open investigations. She told Patrick she welcomed his help, but she saw no evidence of an abduction. She admitted if it were an abduction, Chiffon's bedroom was the place to do one, though—a tall elm towered over her window and those above her; her building was at the rear of the Heath Street complex and the city was five months behind replacing bulbs in the lamps back there that had been shot out by drunken persons unknown on New Year's. Emily Zebrowski told Patrick, however, that no one heard a peep that night from Chiffon Henderson's bedroom. People rarely vanished involuntarily, the detective said; that was more something you saw on TV than encountered in the real world.

"So your operating theory?" he'd asked.

"Her father," Detective Zebrowski said. "Guy's got priors the way other guys have nose hair."

"To what end?"

"Excuse me?"

"He's a scumbag," Patrick said, "I get it. But his scumbagged-ness makes sense usually, right? There's motive behind it. He steals one of his kids, he wants to get paid or get the mother off his back for something. But here the mother's got no money, she's never sued him for child support or alimony, and what guy with his psychological makeup wants to bring his twelve-year-old daughter back to his spot, have her ragging on him from dawn to dusk?"

Detective Zebrowski shrugged. "You think d-bags like Lonnie Cullen think things through before they do them? If they did, they wouldn't know the number on their orange jumpsuits better than their own birthdays. He did it because he's a criminal and he's an idiot and he has less impulse control than a flea at a livestock auc-tion."

"And the boyfriend angle?"

"Looking into it."

Two nights ago Dontelle said to Patrick, "But you don't be-lieve it?"

Patrick shrugged. "Deadbeat dads dodge their kids, they don't kidnap 'em, not the ones who've been out of the picture as long as Lonnie has. As for the boyfriend theory, she's, what, shacked up with him for three days, they never go out to grab a bite, call a friend?"

"All I know," Dontelle said, "is she seemed like a sweet kid. Not one of them typical project girls who's always frontin', talkin' shit. She was quiet but . . . considerate, you know?"

Patrick took another drink of beer. "No. Tell me."

"Well, you get a job like mine, you got to do a probation pe-riod—ninety days during which they can shitcan you without cause. After that, you with the city, man, gotta fuck up huge *and* be named Bin Laden for the city be able to get rid of your ass. I hit my ninety a couple weeks ago and not only did Chiffon congratulate me, she gave me a cupcake."

"No shit?" Patrick smiled.

"Store-bought," Dontelle said, "but still. How sweet is that?"

"Pretty sweet." Patrick nodded.

"You'll see in about twelve years with your kid, they ain't too into thinking about others at that age. It's all about what's going on up here"—he tapped his head—"and down there"—he pointed at his groin.

They drank in silence for a minute.

"Nothing else you remember about that day? Nothing out of the ordinary?"

He shook his head. "Just a day like any other—'See you tomor-row, Chiffon,' and she say, 'See you tomorrow, Dontelle.' And off she walk."

Patrick thanked him and paid for the drinks. He was scooping his change off the bar when he said, "You had a probationary pe-riod?"

Dontelle nodded. "Yeah, it's standard."

"No, I know, but I guess I was wondering why you started so late in the school year. I mean, it's May. Means you started in, what, February?"

Another nod. "End of January, yeah."

"What'd you do before that?"

"Drove a tour bus. Drove from here to Florida, here to Montreal, here to P-Town, all depended on the season. Hours were killing me. Shit, the *road* was killing me. This job opened up, I jumped."

"Why'd it open up?"

"Paisley got a duey."

"Paisley?"

"Guy I replaced. Other drivers told me he was a piece of work, man. Show up with forty kids in his charge, eyes all glassy. Even the union wouldn't protect him after the last time. Drove the bus off the side of the Legion Highway, right?" Dontelle was laughing in disbelief. "Damn near tipped it. Gets out to take a piss. This is at six-thirty in the ante meridiem, feel me? He gets back in, tries to pull back off the shoulder, but now the bus *does* tip. That's Lawsuit City there, man. Forty times over."

"Paisley," Patrick said.

"Edward Paisley," Dontelle said, "like the ties."

Paisley lived on Wyman Street in a gray row house with fading white trim. There was a front porch with an old couch on it. Bosch drove by the place and then circled the block and went by again before finding a parking space at the curb a half block away. By adjusting his side-view mirror he had a bead on the front door and porch. He liked doing one-man surveillances this way. If somebody was looking for a watcher they usually checked windshields. Parking with his back to his target made him harder to see. Edward Paisley may have had nothing to do with the murder of Letitia Williams all those years ago. But if he did, he hadn't survived the last fifteen years without checking windshields and being cautious.

All Bosch was hoping for, and that he'd be happy with, was to see some activity at the home to confirm that Paisley was at the address. If he got lucky, Paisley would go out and grab a cup of coffee or a bite to eat at lunch. Bosch would be able to get all the DNA he'd need off a discarded cup or a pizza crust. Maybe Paisley was a smoker. A cigarette butt would do the trick as well.

Harry pulled a file out of the locking briefcase he took on trips and opened it to look at the enlargement of the photo he'd pulled the day before from the Massachusetts RMV. It was taken three years earlier. Paisley was white, balding, and then fifty-three years old. He no longer had the driver's license, thanks to the suspension that followed the DUI arrest six months ago. Paisley tipped a school bus and then blew a point-oh-two on the machine and with it blew his job with the school district and possibly his freedom. The arrest put his fingerprints into the system, where they were waiting for Bosch. Sometimes Harry got lucky that way. If he had pulled the Williams case eleven months earlier and submitted the prints collected at the crime scene for electronic comparison, there would have been no resulting match. But Bosch pulled the case four months ago and here he was in Boston.

Two hours into his surveillance Bosch had seen no sign of Paisley and was growing restless. Perhaps Paisley had left the house for the day before Bosch could set up on the street. Bosch could be wasting his time, watching an empty house. He decided to get out and do a walk-by. He'd seen a convenience store a block past the target address. He could walk by Paisley's address, eyeball the place up close, then go down and pick up a newspaper and a gallon of milk. Back at the car he would pour the milk into the gutter and keep the jug handy if he had to urinate. It could be a long day watching the house.

The paper would come in handy as well. He'd be able to check the late baseball scores. The Dodgers had gone into extra innings the night before against the hated Giants and Bosch had gotten on the plane not knowing the game's outcome.

But at the last moment Bosch decided to stay put. He watched a dinged-up Jeep Cherokee pull into a curbside slot directly across the street from his own position. There was a lone man in the car and what made Bosch curious was that he never got out. He stayed slumped a bit in his seat and appeared to be keeping an eye on the same address as Bosch.

Bosch could see he was on a cell phone when he first arrived, but then for the next hour the man remained behind the wheel of his Jeep, simply watching the goings-on on the street. He was too young to be Paisley. Late thirties or early forties, wearing a baseball cap and a thin gray hoodie over a dark blue graphic T. Something about the cap gave Bosch pause until he realized it was the first one he'd seen in a city filled with them that didn't have a *B* on it. Instead it had what appeared to be a crooked smiley face on it, though Bosch couldn't be positive from the other side of the street. It looked to Bosch like the guy was waiting for somebody, possibly the same somebody Bosch was waiting for.

Eventually, Bosch realized he had become a similar object of curiosity for the man across the street, who was now surreptitiously watching Bosch as Bosch was surreptitiously watching him.

They kept at this careful cross-surveillance until a siren split the air and a fire truck trundled down the road between them. Bosch tracked the truck in the side mirror, and when he looked back across the street he saw that the Jeep was empty. The man had either used the distraction of the passing fire truck to slip out, or he was lying down inside.

Bosch assumed it was the former. He sat up straight and checked the street and the sidewalk across from him. No sign of anyone on foot. He turned to check the sidewalk on his own side and there at the passenger window was the guy in the baseball hat. He'd turned the hat backward, the way gang squad guys often did when they were on the move. Bosch could see a silver chain descending from the sides of his neck into his graphic T, figured there was a badge hanging from it. Definitely a gun riding the back of the guy's right hip, something boxy and bigger than a Glock. The man bent down to put himself at eye level with Bosch. He twirled his finger at Bosch, a request to roll the window down.

The guy with the Hertz NeverLost GPS jutting off his dashboard looked at Patrick for a long moment but then lowered his window. He looked like he was mid-fifties and in good shape. Wiry. Something about him said cop. The wariness in his eyes for one; cop's eyes—you could never believe they truly closed. Then there was the way he kept one hand down in his lap so he could go inside the sport coat for the Glock or the Smith if it turned out Patrick was a bad guy. His left hand.

"Nice move," he said.

"Yeah?" Patrick said.

The guy nodded over his shoulder. "Sending the fire truck down the street. Good distraction. You with District Thirteen?"

A true Bostonian always sounded like he was just getting over a cold. This guy's voice was clean air; not light exactly but smooth. An out-of-towner. Not a trace of Beantown in that voice. Probably a fed. Minted in Kansas or somewhere, trained down in Quantico and then sent up here. Patrick decided to play along as long as he could. He tried to open the door but it was locked. The guy unlocked it, moved his briefcase to the back seat, and Patrick got in.

"You're a bit away from Center Plaza, aren't you?" Patrick said.

"Maybe," he said. "Except I don't know where or what Center Plaza is."

"So you're not with the Bureau. Who are you with?"

The man hesitated again, kept that left hand in his lap, then nodded like he'd decided to take a flier.

"LAPD," he said. "I was going to check in with you guys later today."

"And what brings the LAPD out to JP?"

"JP?"

"Jamaica Plain. Can I see some ID?"

He pulled a badge wallet out and flipped it open so Patrick could study the detective's badge and the ID. His name was Hieronymus Bosch.

"Some name you've got. How do you say that?"

"Harry's good."

"Okay. What are you doing here, Harry?"

"How about you? That chain around your neck isn't attached to a badge."

"No?"

Bosch shook his head. "I'd have seen the outline of it through your shirt. Crucifix?"

Patrick stared at him for a moment and then nodded. "Wife likes me to wear it." He held out his hand. "Patrick Kenzie. I'm not a cop. I'm an independent contractor."

Bosch shook his hand. "You like baseball, Pat?"

"Patrick."

"You like baseball, Patrick?"

"Big-time. Why?"

"You're the first guy I've seen in this town not wearing a Sox hat."

Patrick pulled off his hat and considered the front of it as he ran a hand through his hair. "Imagine that. I didn't even look when I left the house."

"Is that a rule around here? You've all got to represent Red Sox Nation or something?"

"It's not a rule, per se, more like a guideline."

Bosch looked at the hat again. "Who's the crooked smiley-faced guy?"

"Toothface," Patrick said. "He's, like, the logo, I guess, of a record store I like."

"You still buy records?"

"CDs. You?"

"Yeah. Jazz mostly. I hear it's all going to go away. Records, CDs, the whole way we buy music. MP3s and iPods are the future."

"Heard that too." Patrick looked over his shoulder at the street. "We looking at the same guy here, Harry?"

"Don't know," Bosch said. "I'm looking at a guy for a murder back in nineteen-ninety. I need to get some DNA."

"What guy?"

"Tell you what, why don't I go over to District Thirteen and check in with the captain and make this all legit? I'll identify myself, you identify yourself. A cop and a private eye working together to ease the burden of the Boston PD. Because I don't want *my* captain back in L.A. catching a call from—"

"Is it Paisley? Are you watching Edward Paisley?"

He looked at Patrick for a long moment. "Who is Edward Paisley?"

"Bullshit. Tell me about the case from nineteen-ninety."

"Look, you're a private dick with no 'need to know' that I can see and I'm a cop—"

"Who didn't follow protocol and check in with the local PD." He craned his head around the car. "Unless there's a D-13 liaison on this street who's really fucking good at keeping his head down. I got a girl missing right now and Edward Paisley's name popped up in connection to her. Girl's twelve, Bosch, and she's been out there three days. So I'd love to hear what happened back in nineteen-ninety. You tell me, I'll be your best friend and everything."

"Why is no one looking for your missing girl?"

"Who's to say they're not?"

"Because you're looking and you're private."

Patrick got a whiff of something sad coming off the L.A. cop. Not the kind of sad that came from bad news yesterday but from bad news most days. Still, his eyes weren't dead; they pulsed instead with appetite—maybe even addiction—for the hunt. This wasn't a house cat who'd checked out, who kept his head down, took his paycheck, and counted the days till his twenty. This was a cop who kicked in doors if he had to, whether he knew what was on the other side or not, and had stayed on after twenty.

Patrick said, "She's the wrong color, wrong caste, and there's enough plausible anecdotal shit swirling around her situation to make anyone question whether she was abducted or just walked off."

"But you think Paisley could be involved."

Patrick nodded.

"Why?"

"He's got two priors for sexual abuse of minors."

Bosch shook his head. "No. I checked."

"You checked domestic. You didn't know to check Costa Rica and Cuba. Both places where he was arrested, charged, had the shit beat out of him, and ultimately bought his way out. But the arrests are on record over there."

"How'd you find them?"

"I didn't. Principal of Dearborn Middle School was getting a bad feeling about Paisley when he drove a bus for them. One girl said this, one boy said that, another girl said such and such. Nothing you could build a case on, but enough for the principal to call Paisley into her office a couple times to discuss it." Patrick pulled a reporter's notebook from his back pocket, flipped it open. "Principal told me Paisley would have passed both interviews with flying colors but he mentioned milk one time too many."

"Milk?"

"Milk." Patrick looked up from his notes and nodded. "He told the principal during their first meeting—he'd already been working there a year; the principal doesn't have shit to do with hiring bus drivers, that's HR downtown—that she should smile more because it made him think of milk. He told her in the second meeting that the sun in Cuba was whiter than milk, which is why he liked Cuba, the white lording over everything and all. It stuck with her."

"Clearly."

"But so did the Cuba reference. It takes work to get to Cuba. You gotta fly to Canada or the Caribbean, pretend you banged around there when in fact you hopped a flight to Havana. So when her least favorite bus driver got a DUI while driving her students, she eighty-sixed his ass straightaway, but then started wondering about Cuba. She pulled his résumé and found gaps—six-month unexplained absence in eighty-nine, ten-month absence in ninety-six. Our friendly principal—and remember, Bosch, your principal *is* your pal—kept digging. Didn't take long to find out that the six months in eighty-nine were spent in a Costa Rican jail, the ten months in ninety-six were spent in a cell in Havana. Plus, he moved around a lot in general—Phoenix, L.A., Chicago, Philly, and finally Boston. Always drives a bus, and only has one known relative—a sister, Tasha. Both times he was released from foreign jails, he was released into her custody. And I'm willing to bet she walked a bag of cash onto her flight that she didn't have with her on the flight back home. So now, now he's here and Chiffon Henderson is not. And you know everything I know, Detective Bosch, but I bet you can't say the same."

Bosch leaned back against his seat hard enough to make the leather crackle. He looked over at Patrick Kenzie and told the story of Letitia Williams. She was fourteen years old and stolen from her bedroom in the night. No leads, few clues. The abductor had cut out the screen on her bedroom window. Didn't remove the screen, frame and all. Cut the screen out of the frame with a razor and then climbed in.

The cut screen put immediate suspicion on the disappearance. The case was not shunted aside as a presumed runaway situation the way Chiffon Henderson's would be fifteen years later. Detectives from the major crimes unit rolled that morning after the girl was discovered gone. But the abduction scene was clean. No trace evidence of any kind recovered from the girl's bedroom. The presumption was the abductor or abductors had worn gloves, entered and quickly incapacitated the girl, and just as quickly removed her through the window.

However, there was one piece of presumed evidence gathered outside the house on the morning of the initial investigation. In the alley that ran behind the home where Letitia Williams lived investigators found a flashlight. The first guess was that it had belonged to the abductor and it had inadvertently been dropped while the victim was carried to a waiting vehicle. There were no fingerprints on the flashlight, as it was assumed the perpetrator had worn gloves. But an examination of the inside of the flashlight found two viable latent fingerprints on one of the batteries.

It was thought to be the one mistake that would prove the abductor's undoing. But the thumb and forefinger prints were compared to those on file with the city and state and no match was found. The prints were then sent on to the FBI for comparison with prints in the Bureau's vast data banks, but again there was no hit and the lead died on the vine.

In the meantime, the body of Letitia Williams was found exactly one week after her abduction on a hillside in Griffith Park, right below the observatory. It appeared as though the killer had specifically chosen the location because the body would be spotted quickly in daylight hours by someone looking down from the observatory.

The autopsy on the victim determined that she had been repeatedly sexually assaulted and then strangled. The case drew heavy attention from the media and the major crimes unit, but eventually it was shelved. No clues, no evidence, no leads. In 1992 Los Angeles was ripped apart by race riots, and cases like the murder of Letitia Williams dropped off the public radar. The file went to archives until the Open-Unsolved Unit was formed after the start of the new century, and eventually Bosch came to the archived case files and the fingerprints that were matched to Edward Paisley in Boston.

"That's why I'm here," Bosch said.

"Did you come with a warrant?"

Bosch shook his head. "No, no warrant. The prints match is not enough. The flashlight was found in the alley, not in Letitia's bedroom. There is no direct tie to the crime. I came to get DNA. I was going to follow him and collect it. Wait for him to toss a cup of coffee or a pizza crust or something. I'd take it back with me and see if it matches semen collected from the body. Then I'd be in business. Then I'd come back with a warrant and take him down."

They sat in the car and stared out at the street and Bosch could feel Kenzie stewing on something. He wasn't a big man and he had a friendly, boyish face; he dressed in the street clothes of a neighborhood guy, kind of guy would pour your beer or fix your car. On first glance and even on a second, he seemed harmless and sweet, kind of guy you'd be happy for your sister to bring home. But Bosch had spent enough time in his company now to feel a hot wire running in the guy's blood. Most people probably never tripped it. But God help the ones who did.

Kenzie's right knee started to jackhammer up and down in such a way that Bosch doubted he was aware of it. He turned on the seat, looked at Harry. "You said in your case the girl's body was found a week after the abduction."

"That's right."

"But she was dumped there because she would be found almost right away by the people at the observatory."

"Yeah, the body was left at night and noticed the next morning after daylight."

"How long had she been dead?"

Bosch reached to the back seat and opened the briefcase. He brought back a thick blue binder full of records from the case. He spoke as he looked through the pages. He had the answers in his head already. He was just looking at the autopsy report for confirmation.

"She had been dead seventy-two hours when found."

"That's three days. That meant the guy kept her alive for four days."

"Right. The indications were that she was repeatedly—"

"This is the fourth day. If this asshole follows any sort of pattern, well, shit, Chiffon Henderson was taken Monday afternoon." He pointed back down the sidewalk at the gray row house. "We need to get in that house."

Patrick took the front door while Bosch went around back. Patrick had told the L.A. cop he was reasonably proficient picking a lock, but Paisley's front door sported a lock Patrick had never seen before. New, too. And expensive by the looks of it—a $500 lock on a $40 door. Patrick tried a series of picks, but none of them could get to first base with the cylinders. It was like trying to pass a plastic stirrer through a rock.

The second time he dropped a pick, he bent to retrieve it and the door opened in front of him.

He looked up at Harry Bosch standing on the threshold, a Glock dangling from his left hand. "I thought you said you could pick a lock."

"I clearly overestimated my prowess." He straightened. "How'd you get in?"

"He left a window unlocked." Bosch shrugged. "People, right?"

Patrick had expected a dump inside, but the house was quite clean and mostly bare. The furniture was modern Scandinavian—lots of bright white and brighter chrome that clashed with the older wainscoting and dark wallpaper. Paisley was renting; the landlord probably had no idea about the lock.

"Something in here he doesn't want people to see," Patrick said.

"Gotta be in the basement then," Bosch said. He jerked a thumb back at the shotgun layout of the apartment—foyer and living room and then a long corridor that went straight back to the kitchen, all the other rooms branching off it. "I cleared this floor."

"You cleared this floor? How long were you planning to leave me out on the front porch?"

"I figured another half an hour before you snapped and kicked in the door. I didn't have that kinda time."

"L.A. sarcasm," Patrick said as they headed down the hallway. "Who knew?"

Halfway down the hall, on the right, was a door the same dark brown as the wainscoting. Patrick exchanged a look with Bosch and the cop nodded—now would be the time.

Patrick drew the .45 Colt Commander off his hip and flicked the safety off. "You see a bulkhead around back?"

Bosch looked puzzled. "A bulkhead?"

"You know, an entrance to the basement. Double doors, steps down."

Bosch nodded. "Locked from the inside." And then, as though further explanation was needed, he said, "We generally don't have basements in L.A."

"You don't have snow or a wind-chill factor either, so, you know, fuck you." He tossed Bosch a bright, tight smile. "Any basement windows out back?"

Another nod. "Black curtains over them."

"Well, that's bad," Patrick said.

"Why?"

"No one puts curtains over their basement windows around here unless they got a home theater or they're playing Dead Hooker Storage." He looked around the apartment. "Edward does not strike me as the home theater type."

Bosch nodded, his pupils adrenalized to twice their size. "Let's go back out, call it in legit'."

"What if he's down there with her right now?"

That was the dilemma, wasn't it?

Bosch exhaled a long breath. Patrick did the same. Bosch held his hand over the doorknob and said, "On three?"

Patrick nodded. He wiped his right palm on his jeans and read-justed a two-handed grip on his gun.

"One. Two. Three."

Bosch opened the door.

The first thing they noticed was the padding on the inside of the door—at least six inches thick of premium leather soundproofing. The kind one found only in recording studios. The next thing they noticed was the dark. The scant light to find the stairs came from the hall behind them. The rest of the cellar was pitch-black. Patrick pointed at the light switch just past Bosch's ear, raised his eyebrows.

Bosch shrugged.

Patrick shrugged.

Six of one, half a dozen of the other.

Bosch flicked on the lights.

The staircase split the cellar like a spine, straight down the center, and they went down it fast. A black heating oil tank stood at the bottom, quite old, rust fringing the bottom of it.

Without a word, Bosch went left and Patrick went right.

The element of surprise was no longer an option for them.

Only for him.


On the side of the cellar that Patrick chose—the front—the framing was old and mostly unfinished. The first "room" he came upon contained a washer, a dryer, and a sink with a cake of grimy brown soap stuck to the top of it. The next room had once been a workshop. A long wood table abutted the wall, an old vise still fastened to the table. Nothing else in there but dust and mice droppings. The last room along the wall was finished, however. The framing was filled in with drywall on one side and brick on the other, a door in the middle. Heavy door. And thick. The frame around it was solid too. Try and kick in a door like that and you'd finish your day getting fitted for an ankle cast.

Patrick removed his left hand from his .45 and rubbed it on his jeans. He flexed the fingers and reached for the doorknob, holding the .45 cocked awkwardly at about mid-chest level. It didn't look pretty, he was sure, but if he had to pull the trigger, he had a fair chance of hitting center mass on anyone but a dwarf or a giant.

The doorknob squeaked when it turned, proving something a cop had told him years ago—you always made the most noise when you were trying to be quiet. He threw open the door and dropped to his knees at the same time, gun pointing up a bit now, left hand coming back on the grip, sweeping the room from left to right, sweeping back right to left even as he processed what he saw—

Edward Paisley's man cave.

Patrick edged his way through the doorway onto an Arizona Cardinals rug, drew a bead on a BarcaLounger trimmed in Sun Devils colors. A Phoenix Suns pennant shared space with one from the Phoenix Coyotes, and Patrick had to peer at the latter to realize the Coyotes played in the NHL.

If he learned nothing else from this day, he now knew Arizona had a professional hockey team.

He found baseball bats signed by Troy Glaus, Carlos Baerga, and Tony Womack. Baseballs signed by Curt Schilling and Randy Johnson, framed photos of Larry Fitzgerald and Kurt Warner, Shawn Marion and Joe Johnson, Plexiglas-encased footballs, basketballs, and pucks, Patrick again thinking, They have a *hockey* team?

He picked up a bat signed by Shea Hillenbrand, who'd broken into the Bigs with the Sox back in 2001 but got shipped to Arizona before the Sox won the Series last year. He wondered if that stung or if being able to lie out in the Arizona sun in January made up for it.

He'd guess it didn't.

He was putting the bat back against the wall when he heard someone moving through the cellar. Moving fast. Running, actually.

And not away from something, but toward it.

Harry had worked his way along the back of the cellar, finding nothing but wall and rocky, jagged flooring until he reached a tight space where an ancient water heater met a prehistoric oil heater. The space reeked of oil and mold and fossilized vermin. Had Bosch not been searching for an adolescent in possible mortal danger, he might have missed the corridor on the other side of the heaters. But his penlight picked up the hole in the darkness on the other side of a series of pipes and ducts that were half hanging, half falling from the ceiling.

Bosch worked his way past the heaters and entered a long thin space barely wide enough to accommodate any mammal with shoulders, never mind a full-grown adult male.

As soon as you entered a tunnel, the first problem you noticed was that there was no left, no right, and no place to hide. You went into an entrance and you headed toward an exit. And should anyone who wished you ill pop up at either point Alpha or point Zeta, while you were passing between those points, your fate was in their hands.

When Bosch reached the end of the passageway, he was bathed in sweat. He stepped out into a wide unlit room of dark brick and a stone floor with a drain in the center. He swept the room with his penlight and saw nothing but a metal crate. It was the kind used to house large dogs on family trips. A blue painter's tarp covered it, held to the frame by nine bungee cords.

And it was moving.

Bosch got down on his knees and pulled at the tarp, but the bungee cords were wrapped tight—three of them crossing the crate lengthwise and six crossing it widthwise. The cords were clasped down at the base of the crate and stretched taut so that separating the clasps with one hand was not an option. Bosch placed his Glock by his foot as the crate continued to rock and he picked up the sound of someone mewling desperately from under all that tarp.

He pulled apart the clasps on the first of the three lengthwise cords and still couldn't get a clear view inside. He put the penlight in his mouth and went to work on the second and that's when the room turned white.

It was as if someone had hung the sun a foot above his head or lit up a ballpark.

He was blind. He got his hand on his Glock, but all he could see was white. He couldn't tell where the wall was. He couldn't even see the crate anymore and he was kneeling in front of it.

He heard something scrabble to his left and he turned his gun that way and then the scrabbling broke right, coming around his weak side, and he turned with the Glock crossing his body, his eyes adjusting enough to pick up a shadow. Then he heard the thump of something very hard turn something less hard into something soft.

Someone let out a dull yelp and fell to the floor in all that blinding light.

"Bosch," Patrick said, "it's me. Close your eyes a sec'."

Bosch closed his eyes and heard the sound of glass breaking—popping, actually—and the heat left his face in degrees.

"I think we're good," Patrick said.

When Bosch opened his eyes, he blinked several times and saw the lights high on the wall, all the bulbs shattered. Had to be in the 700-watt range, if not higher. Huge black cones behind them.

Eight lights total. Patrick had pulled back the curtain on the small window at the top of the wall, and the soft early-afternoon light entered the room like an answered prayer.

Bosch looked at Paisley lying on the floor to his right, gurgling, the back of his head sporting a fresh dent, pink blood leaking from his nose, red blood streaming from his mouth, a carving knife lying beneath his twitching right hand.

Patrick Kenzie brandished a baseball bat. He raised his eyebrows up and down and twirled it. "Signed by Shea Hillenbrand."

"I don't even know who that is."

"Right," Patrick said. "Dodgers fan."

Bosch went to work on the bungee cords and Patrick joined him and they pulled back the tarp and there she was, Chiffon Henderson. She was curled fetal in the crate because there was no room to stretch into any other position. Patrick struggled with the door until Bosch just took the roof off the crate.

Chiffon Henderson had electrical tape wrapped around her mouth, wrists, and ankles. They could tell it hurt her to stretch her limbs, but Bosch took that as a good sign—Paisley had kept her caged but possibly unmolested. Bosch guessed that was supposed to commence today, an appetizer to the murder.

They bickered as they removed the tape from her mouth, Bosch telling Patrick to be careful of her hair, Patrick telling him to watch he didn't tear at her lips.

When the tape came free and they went to work on her wrists, Bosch asked, "What's your name?"

"Chiffon Henderson. Who're you?"

"I'm Patrick Kenzie. And this other guy? He was never here, okay, Chiffon?"

Bosch cocked his head.

Patrick said, "You're a cop. From out of town. I can barely get away with this shit, but you? They'll take your badge, man. Unless you got a no-knock warrant in your pocket I can't see."

Bosch worked it through in his head.

"He touch you, Chiffon?"

She was weeping, shaking, and she gave that a half nod, half head shake. "A little but not, you know. He said that was coming. He told me all sorts of things were coming."

Patrick looked at Paisley huffing into the cement, eyes rolled back into his head, blood beginning to pool.

"Only thing coming for this shithead is the strokes that follow the coma."

When her hands were free, Patrick knelt to get at the tape on her ankles and Bosch was surprised when the girl hugged him tight, her tears finding his shirt. He surprised himself when he kissed the top of her head.

"No more monster," he said. "Not tonight."

Patrick finished with the tape. He tossed the wad of it behind him and produced his cell. "I gotta call this in. I'd rather be bullshitting my way free of an attempted murder charge than an actual homicide rap, if you know what I mean, and he's turning a funny shade."

Bosch looked at the man lying at his feet. Looked like an aging nerd. Kinda guy did your taxes out of a strip mall storefront. Another little man with soiled desires and furious nightmares. Funny how the monsters always turned out to be little more than men. But Patrick was right—he'd die soon without attention.

Patrick dialed 911 but didn't hit Send. Instead he held out his hand to Bosch. "If I'm ever in L.A."

Bosch shook his hand. "Funny. I can't picture you in L.A."

Patrick said, "And I can't picture you out of it, even though you're standing right here. Take care, Harry."

"You too. And thanks"—Bosch looked down at Paisley, on his way to critical care, minimum—"for, um, that."

"Pleasure."

Bosch headed toward the door, a door only accessible from the front of the cellar, not the back. Beat the hell out of the way he'd entered the room. He was reaching for the doorknob when he turned back.

"One last thing."

Patrick had the phone to his ear and his free arm wrapped tight around Chiffon's shoulders. "What's that?"

"Is there a way to get back to the airport without going through that tunnel?"

JOSEPH D'AGNESE

# Harm and Hammer

FROM *Alfred Hitchcock's Mystery Magazine*

ONCE A MONTH the man parks his car at the top of her cul-de-sac. He sits behind his steering wheel and plays with his phone until she arrives. She takes no obvious note of him as she drives home from the mall. No looking. No waves. She simply parks in the driveway of her crappy townhouse rental and heads inside, leaving her front door unlocked. She kicks off her shoes, runs to the kitchen, and turns the oven to 350 degrees. Then she dashes upstairs to her bedroom and strips off everything but her bra and panties and slips into the little black dress or sometimes the cute red one. She steps into her Mary Janes, puts on her earrings, and checks her hair and makeup in the mirror. By the time she pops the disks of cookie dough into the oven and begins heating the kettle, the man is already making the rounds of her small back-yard. It isn't much of a yard, but he always likes to check the perimeter and that makes her think sweetly of him.

Eventually he raps his knuckles on the door as he enters. He sits at the table while she serves him tea and cookies. Green tea because he once said it's good for his cholesterol and he's trying to cut down. He's not heavy, but he can easily blow his good looks if he doesn't watch out. She knows he and his wife have recently split, that his wife has taken the kids, that her lawyer is riding him hard.

She knows that she and he can never have a future. But that's not the point. Thinking about him is a nice fantasy for her at this point in her life. And she trusts him. She likes the way he treats her. Like she's a good person. Like she was simply caught up in something she didn't know how to get out of.

Which is only half true.

Marshal Fred is good and kind, with somewhat sad eyes. He probably has a million cases like hers, but he behaves as if she is the only one in whom he can confide. She enjoys their time together, even if it comes only once a month.

But today, it's not his voice she hears coming from the open doorway.

"Callie? Callie Rustan?"

A woman's voice.

A *woman* calling her by that name. The name she'll never get used to.

Fear grips her as she stands at the stove. Her eyes flick to the wooden block. She reaches for the chef's knife.

"Drop it," the voice says.

The dead, distorted faces of the women and children flash before her, and she thinks, *Oh, my God — they found me.*

She whirls to face a short, squat woman in a pantsuit who's got her hand on her holstered weapon and is holding aloft the shield of a federal marshal.

"Where's Fred?" is all Callie can think to say.

Callie sips her green tea alone because Federal Marshal Margaret Bryan coldly declines a cup. Already Callie can feel her spirits sinking.

"He's been reassigned? To where?"

"That's none of your concern, is it?"

This woman knows Callie all of two minutes and she's already showing her who's in charge. Fred was never this way.

"So I'm dealing with you now?"

"That's right."

"You read the file?"

The marshal nods.

"So you know I was coerced."

The woman's blouse is a little tight. She must be in her mid-thirties, Callie thinks. She's the kind of slightly older woman Callie and her girlfriends would have mocked when they hit the clubs at night, back when she lived in the city. She regrets that now. Indeed, with each passing day she is beginning to hate the girl, the child, she was only months ago. Especially since the woman in ill-fitting clothes has the power to make Callie's new life miserable.

"Let me ask you a question," Bryan says. As she says this, she points at Callie's teacup. Not so much accusing her as the cup of tea. "Did you know it was wrong?"

Did she know it was wrong to take a briefcase of cash each week from the tieless man in the Armani suit and beautiful chocolate shoes, and run them through the system, and credit each fresh infusion, minus Timball's cut, into one of the client's nine accounts? Sort of, yes. She didn't need an accounting degree to know that. But she had trusted Eddie Timball. He was one of the top men at the brokerage firm, and she'd been rather flattered and awed by the attention he'd paid her when she first came to work for them. He was a slightly older, handsome man, not her direct supervisor. The other girls had said he was divorced but still played the field. The rumors about his wealth, his cars, his apartment, and his homes had seemed so enticing. It was true, of course. The rumor mill just hadn't factored in that Eddie was in debt up to his slightly receding scalp.

He had said he could not trust just anyone with this, and that if she helped him she would be . . . *rolling in commissions.* His words. He also let her know that if she helped him, she could not breathe a word of this task to anyone. She had seen it as an opportunity. A way to advance. A way to shuck herself of her roommate and get a place of her own. A way to buy nice things for herself. By the time she had figured out what was really going on, she was in too deep. Only later did she realize that the mere act of Eddie's asking had doomed her. *She could not refuse.* She was sentenced the second the words left the glib fellow's lips.

"Yes, I knew," she tells Margaret Bryan.

"But you did it anyway. You did it and you hid it for three years."

Fred had never been like this. He had a way of making it all seem like some vast, unfortunate tragedy in which she was merely a bit player. Eight months ago, when he'd first confronted her in his office, he'd laid out those terrible photos on the table and pointed to each of the faces of the dead. "People always say that they're victimless crimes. You slip them some cash. They give you something. You snort it, shoot it, or smoke it. What's the harm, right? The harm is, it's funding people who do this. And this. And this."

One by one, he carefully pronounced the names of the beaten

or bullet-ridden men, women, and children in the photos. Most of them foreigners.

Even when she'd accepted, even when she'd said yes to save her own life, Fred had never treated her like a criminal. He had never once suggested that her actions had led to what happened to the people in those photographs. But *she* had made the leap. It was only logical. He'd tucked those images away almost immediately. But she saw them still. She was sure she always would.

And later, when they had relocated her to someplace in the southeast, Fred had sat her down and spoken to her as if she were just a kid at a new school. He read her the rules. Don't call attention to yourself. Try to fit in. Join groups, but don't become a leader. Stay off the Internet. Avoid social media. Don't make waves. Above all, don't contact friends and family. They're dead to you.

Fred had sat with her at this table only last month, one hand on a cookie, his other just grazing hers.

She had trusted Eddie Timball. She had trusted Fred. And now both of them were gone.

"In all that time," Bryan says now, "you could have called someone. You could have notified the authorities."

"So that's how it's going to be, huh?" Callie says. She wants to sound tough, but she's out of her league.

"Honey, that's the way it *is*," Bryan says. "Nothing's changed. Nothing's . . ."

She pauses now, lifting her nose to the ceiling.

The smoke detector screams. Persistent, angry, accusatory.

The cookies are burning.

Fred used to say it's all about trade-offs.

Back home in New York, she could buy whatever she wanted, once the infusions of Eddie Timball's commissions started rolling in. She'd had the apartment on the Upper East Side. She had grown accustomed to the clothes, the shoes, the parties, and the guys. And all the freedom in the world.

Now she has less freedom. She is staying put for the foreseeable future. She works a desk job in the management office of a department store in a mall in the middle of nowhere. She tries to do as Fred advised: fit in. She has always been a good student. Always. And so she earnestly tries to do this. She studies the sales circulars that the store she's never heard of puts out, and decides on a new look. She can dress like a young mom, in that outdated preppy look. Loafers and chinos and a bland, sensible sweater. She doesn't like any of these clothes, but she can stomach them.

There are no clubs here. At least, nothing like the ones she frequented in the city. Nothing like the tapas and downtown wine bars and the chic lounges lorded over by bouncers who sized you up to see if you merited entrance. There are no restaurants here run by celebrity chefs. No places where the music thumps so hard that you can feel it in your heart and a round of champagne costs you and your girlfriends seventy, easy. No—instead they have brew pubs and Irish-themed hangouts and honky-tonk roadhouses she wouldn't be caught dead in. The main drag in the center of town is populated with women who dress the way she now does, and who prowl the gift shops on weekends in search of ceramic teddy bears and quilted handbags and scented candles.

There are no cute guys. But more and more, she finds she doesn't even think about this. It's as if she has banned pleasure from her heart. She cannot bear to think about having a man close to her. How can she? How could she let a man into her bed and tell him that her name is Callie? She can't.

She cannot bear to think of her family. Her brother out west. Her sister up north. Her two nieces. She cannot bear to think of her mother, who had been growing weaker and weaker, and relying more on her chair to get around. Never again can the girl the feds call Callie escape to Connecticut to regress into childhood for a long weekend, to eat Dad's chili, to play the baby grand Knabe in the sunroom and watch for the smile to return to her mother's face.

The MS had eroded her mother's ability to play. She and her siblings had been close in age, and all three of them had studied business. All three of them had aped their father in this respect. But the other two were already far more accomplished than she, weren't they? They possessed, perhaps, far more rigorous minds and a slavish knack for industry. While she—well, every time she looked into her brother's or sister's eyes, she sensed that they knew exactly what she was: a vapid, unambitious party girl from the suburbs.

But neither her brother nor her sister had ever learned to play. So the piano would one day pass to her. Or it would have, before her name became Callie Rustan.

So: No apartment. No money. No clothes. No clubs. No guys. No family. No music.

It's as if the world she knows has been annihilated.

She feels like a nun.

But it's a trade-off, right, Fred? In exchange for all this, I get to live.

There's a town about forty minutes north of here, high in the mountains, where tourists prowl and locals flee when the heat gets miserable. It's home to a historic farm with formal gardens and a bike path. In her old life, she would have turned her nose up at such a place, but she's now beginning to appreciate that her choices are limited. She wants to be a model witness. She doesn't want to give Bryan grief.

Both marshals have alluded to having counselors available if she ever wants to talk about her situation. She's tempted. She could use a shrink badly. But she dares not take them up on it. The marshals always speak of reassignment, making it seem as if you can *behave* yourself into a better city. She is beginning to suspect that this promise is a ploy to extract compliance, but she can't risk having her mental health issues—her loneliness, her anger, her guilt—on the record. She wants to do this right. She wants to be well thought of. She wants to put the past behind her.

She wants to be good.

So she works out. She runs the paths and rides the bikes and paddles kayaks down frothy rivers. And one afternoon, she leaves the bike off at the rental barn and wanders through the historic farm area, watching ladies churn butter, printers crank presses, and bakers turn loaves. Inside the blacksmith's shop, an emaciated old man is showing tourists how he makes decorative coat hooks. He pumps the bellows and extracts the glowing iron rod and lays it across his anvil.

*Pound pound pound,* the hammer beats red iron.

His audience watches transfixed as the rod yields to the old man's imagination. Here's the curl of iron. Here, the grooves that denote a tiny leaf. Here, pincers pluck a tiny gargoyle's face from the rod.

The old man spins the hammer like a gunslinger twirling a six-gun.

The audience ahhs adoringly.

She feels as if she's seen something like this as a girl, but she cannot remember when or where. She longs to call her mom right now: *Hi, I know you think I'm dead, but—*

But she can never do this.

The smithy tells how his mentor used to play the anvil like a musical instrument. And then, just like that, he raises his hammers to the anvil and begins to tap out a tune.

The audience is rapt.

*Amazing grace . . .*

Something shifts in her, and she remembers how and why she came to study the piano.

*How sweet the sound . . .*

She remembers how she'd played in a bell chorus through two Christmas seasons when she was in elementary school. How she'd loved that sound so much—clear, high, tinkling, beautiful.

But her mother hadn't thought it wise to study the bells. It wasn't a skill one could be proud of. What was a bell, really? A novelty instrument, good for showing off once a year. No, if she wanted to learn music, she would learn the piano. And so she had, and it had contented her until she'd gotten to high school and began to see that her choice meant she'd never be able to play in the marching band. Back then, she would have gladly switched to the steel drum. God, how she'd loved that high, plunking sound. But her enthusiasm had struck her mother as strange. In their home it was always understood that music was something a young woman did as part of her overall education. The piano was not an end, not a calling, unto itself. At least not for someone like her. Not for someone possessed of such coldly practical parents.

*That sav'd a wretch like me . . .*

My God, she thinks: The voice of the anvil is like the voice of a bell.

"Who'd like to give it a try?" the blacksmith says.

Already his eyes are upon her.


The complex where she lives was built in the eighties, and everything here is a little run down. The garage door opener should probably be replaced, but she dreads calling the maintenance office. It takes her forever to get the door open so the deliverymen can back the truck in. When they lift the antique anvil from the back of their truck, she can see the muscles straining under their shirts and overalls. Her empty garage suddenly smells of their sweat, of the Appalachian hills themselves, of the barn where she found and bought the relic, of manure and gasoline. They set the blackened object on top of a tree stump. One of them asks if her husband really is intending to do his blacksmithing in such a small space. There just isn't enough roof clearance, another explains.

"I'm not married," she says. "It's for me."

This shushes them. They accept their tips and shuffle out with smiles on their faces and perhaps their tongues in their cheeks.

It's not as easy as you'd think to buy an anvil. The cheap ones she can afford at the big-box stores are made of cast iron, and every one of the ironworker websites warns against them. But buying a new, unblemished one made of steel can easily consume more than half her monthly income. They are just *that* expensive. But she soon learns that most smithies buy their tools at auctions or barter with other collectors or craftsmen. And this is what she does, follows one local lead after another until she finds a retired farm auctioneer who sells antiquated tools out of his barn.

Everyone she meets—everyone—assumes she is taking up smithing, because that's what so many of the artistic young people of the region seem to be doing these days. They're returning in droves to the old folkways. Part of her thinks that's actually a fine cover. Fred would probably be proud of her for exploiting such a misdirection.

But she only wants to hear that sound again. Her confidence is robust for someone so young, but she knows she has a few things going for her. She knows music, she can sight-read, and she has a good ear. Every instructor she's ever had has told her this, and she has no reason to doubt them. *Of course* she has a good ear. She is a good student. She will work as hard as she can. She will not fail.

But the anvil is tough.

She has no way of knowing if the assortment of hammers she's bought at the big-box store are appropriate. On the subject of playing the anvil as a musical instrument, the Internet is largely silent. She finds countless videos of Verdi's Anvil Chorus from *Il Trovatore,* of leather-aproned men or women pounding out that famous melody as the chorus of gypsies sings along. But she longs to conjure a sound that is wholly different.

More delicate, elegant, and purer.

For a long time, the sound emanating from the steel seems flat and dull. There is none of the distinct loveliness she heard that day in the old smithy's barn.

But she tries. Oh, she tries.

The music store at the mall coughs up some decent sheet music, which she uses as a guide only. And strangely, she discovers that she only wants to play church music. "Amazing Grace," of course. "Ave Maria." "How Great Thou Art." At the tractor store—she cannot believe the day she walks into it—she finds a pair of roomy overalls that sprout loops at her hips and promise to give her thighs the requisite range of movement.

Each night that summer she sucks down her dinner and retires to the garage to squat over the thing and play. The anvil sounds again and again, and each night, after a few hours, her ears ring and her hands hurt and her palms stiffen.

At work, while she files paperwork, she hears it still.

The sound is good. Just not good enough.

Like her.


If the smithy is surprised to see a woman so young dressed in overalls and work boots and so closely quizzing him on this particular sideline of his craft, he doesn't show it. He listens to her story as he sits at the picnic table behind his shop and tears into a pulled pork sandwich doused with smoky orange sauce. His voice is gravelly, his teeth bad, his glasses distinctly unstylish.

He is plainly ugly.

But the second she thinks this, she begs his silent forgiveness. *Am I such a bad person?* she wonders. *Was the old me really that bad?*

"You're lucky buying an old one," he tells her. "Most of the anvils made today are just not going to give you that ringing sound. They really don't make them the way they used to. The rest is just practice." He cocks his head, crowlike, and asks, "How are you holding the hammers?"

Good question. She holds them as if she is about to drive a nail, but he scoffs when she tells him this. He looks at his scuffed Timex.

"You want it to be like a drumstick. Firm, but loose and gentle-like. You want to cultivate muscle memory. You know what that is?"

"Like I know it but don't *know* I know it."

"Yep. Like your hands just know what to do. Look, I don't have much time, but I can show you a few things. If you were looking to apprentice, I got to say no. I just don't do that anymore. I'm just putting on a show for the tourists here."

"I just want to make it sing."

"Well, okay then. I can show you a few things. But you mind my asking something? Why in the heck would a pretty girl like yourself want to do such a thing?"

She is appalled that she doesn't have an answer.

It's only later, when the weather turns and the mall grows ever busier, that she begins to get the first glimmer of an answer. But it is not an answer she can articulate clearly. She can only feel it building within her when she plays. Only then do the faces of the dead recede and seem to bear witness to her concerts.

So much of her life is on autopilot now. In the back of her mind as she works the day job is the thrum of sound, the plink and patter of the hammer. Up, dress, work, lunch, work, back home—and then the steel. On weekends when she can, she prowls the flea markets on Old Highway 6, looking for various types of hammers and chisels she can use to produce different sounds. At night sometimes when she collapses in front of the TV she can feel herself running the notes the way she used to do when she was studying the piano.

*Amazing grace . . .*

Her closed fist taps out the melody on empty air.

*How sweet the sound . . .*

And this is why she doesn't quite know how to respond to the question the smithy asked her a month ago now. If pushed, she will only say that she wants to make music. Beautiful music. She *needs* it to be beautiful. But that alone is not enough. She cannot deny that when she's beating out a melody against that steel, she derives a pleasure she never felt when she played the piano, or even the bells.

You knew, didn't you? You knew all along that it was wrong.

Yes, I knew. But damn you for saying so.

*Tink.*

Damn you, Eddie, for asking me to do it.

*Tink, tink, tink. Smack.*

Damn the feds for making her life so banal and lonely.

Oh, really? Poor *you*. People *died*.

All she wants to do is strike the hammer. To crush and pound it until it reverberates in her soul. Her life this past year has massed itself into a ball of anguish. Each night, as she makes the journey from the flat to the horn, she imagines she is chasing the pain away, nattering it, worrying it to the edge of the steel until it drops away into space.

She hopes too that the steel is changing her. God help her for saying so, but that smithy is an ugly man. She despises herself for thinking such a thing, but it's so. And yet, when he bends to the anvil and plays, he becomes something else. She wants that. But she worries sometimes that she has more anger bound up inside her than the hammers will ever be able to chase away. Anger at herself. Her parents. Eddie Timball. The feds. Margaret Bryan. Maybe even dear, kind Fred.

*No wonder my music isn't beautiful.*

Around Christmas that year the smithy looks up from his work when the next round of tourists leave. There's a light snow falling outside. Framed in the doorway is the young woman dressed in a Carhartt jacket. Two hammers hang from the loops at her hips like sidearms.

"So you're a cowboy now, is that it?" he says.

She smiles, draws, and flawlessly executes the blacksmith's own gesture: twirls the hammers like six-guns before catching them. She loves doing this now. Loves feeling the heft of the handles as they swing back home to her grasp.

"Can I show you something?" she says.

He nods his assent. As she comes behind the railing, stripping off her jacket, his eyes take in the muscles along her arms. He sips from his flask.

He is taller than she is, so she has to bend lower to reach his anvil. The second her hammers bite steel, she thinks, My God, his is so much clearer, so much purer. Must be the construction.

But she pushes these thoughts from her mind and plays "And Did Those Feet in Ancient Time."

The old man stops sipping at his flask.

She plays a good long while. She remembers Blake's song from childhood, but back then she never thought about the words. In the last month that's all she has done.

*Bring me my Bow of burning gold . . .*

*Bring me my Arrows of desire . . .*

Today she tortures herself for not paying better attention when she was younger. How could I have been so thoughtless? The dead poet's words touch her now.

*I will not cease from Mental Fight . . .*

The words speak to every striving instinct she has for something better. She wants to be good. She craves it.

Her eyes are moist when she looks up. But the old man has a smile on his face.

"That's a churchly hymn now, isn't it? Well, I'd say you done the good Lord proud today," he says.

She hears applause and is stunned to see that another round of tourists have come in from out of the cold. A bunch of them in the barn, clapping. Moms, dads, grandmas, kids.

She smiles and twirls the hammer in her right hand. Then the left. And slings them both in the loops of her overalls.

It's nice. She feels good. Real good. Maybe not beautiful, but close.

Then she notices that three of the dads have video cameras. All of them pointed at her.

She doesn't notice the truck until the Friday after Christmas, when it seems as if the whole world has descended on the mall to lob returns or cash in gift cards. The black Chevrolet truck following her as she pulls out of the mall looks a lot like the one she saw on the cul-de-sac this morning. She peels out ahead of it at the turn signal and tries to put the vehicle out of her mind. She figures she's imagining things.

The truth is, the videos have spooked her. For weeks now, ever since she showed off at the farm, she's been surfing all the amateur video websites in search of them, without any luck. That's a good thing. Maybe the tourists who filmed her didn't feel moved to post their videos. Maybe it's not what they do. Maybe the footage didn't turn out that well. Or maybe they've been distracted by Christmas.

She needs the steel badly tonight. And as soon as she gets into the garage—the space heater throwing out some BTUs, the hammers and chisels arrayed on the concrete to her right—she is able to finally tap out the notes that will bring her to the "Ave Maria."

She doesn't know the original words, and that's part of the problem. If you don't know how to pronounce the words, you don't know how the syllables break. She's translating from some sheet music for drums that sits on a music stand to the left.

*Gratia plena.* Full of grace.

She never had the chance to study Latin, but now the pings against steel bring her to tears.

*Ora . . . ora pro nobis . . . peccatoribus.*

Pray for us sinners . . .

She pauses. Drops the hammers. Braces her hands against the anvil and lets the tears come. Behind the garage door she can hear the insistent ringing of her phone. *Let it ring.* But then it beeps. Message left.

She dries her eyes and goes to check it in the kitchen. *MB* has called a half-dozen times. Margaret Bryan. Dammit. When she last saw Maggie, Callie hadn't mentioned the videos to her. No way was she going to give the fed any reason to play the bad cop. The videos were gone. Bullets dodged. End of story.

She listens to the first message.

Anxiety in the woman's voice: "You have to call me, okay?"

Callie begins to dial, but as she does, Bryan calls again.

"Are you there?" Margaret says. "Where are you?"

*Where would I be on a Friday night, Maggie?*

"At home, why?"

"I need you to listen to me, okay? You need to get out of there. Get out of the house and get to the police station. Just go inside. Don't say a *word* to them. You just sit there. I don't care who comes in asking for you. You just refuse to leave, you hear me?"

"What is this? Am I in trouble?"

"I'm driving up with another agent, okay? But the roads are bad. We're hitting some snow outside Atlanta. *But I will be there, Callie.* You just need to listen to me."

"Just level with me, okay? Is this because of the videos?"

"What?"

*Dammit—she didn't know. And you just went ahead and told her.*

Callie steps to the window of the townhouse and nudges the curtains. At the top of the cul-de-sac, a large shape. The truck?

"I'm going," she says into the phone. "I'm going right now."

She hangs up. She turns to get her car keys when the knock comes at the door. She pads back to the living room to look out the window. The large shape is now parked in her driveway.

The knock now more insistent. The knob turning. "Dammit, Callie," a voice says. "Open the damn door. I know you're there."

Relief floods her. She knows that voice. She opens the door to find Marshal Fred standing there. Fred the fed, dressed in street clothes, not the suit. Sneakers on his feet. Dark sweatshirt. As his eyes slide down her overalls, she senses his confusion. She is not the witless child she was months ago. She is not even a girl anymore. And he has changed too. He looks heavier, stressed, exhausted.

"Why didn't she tell me you were coming?" Callie says.

"Who?" he says, stepping into the room.

"Margaret."

"Bryan called you?"

She nods. He swears under his breath. Hangs his head. Then he starts to close the door by feel and produces the weapon. Not his service weapon. Another one. Smaller, stubbier, older.

"What's this all about?"

"I'm sorry, Callie," he says, and for a moment she buys the hurt in his eyes and voice. "She's bleeding me dry. I had to do something. I'm sorry," he says again. "It was the only thing I could think of. It's just . . . it's just a transaction."

And then it hits her. She knows the truth.

*Oh God. This isn't—*

She backs away.

The ball-peen hammer hanging at her left hip comes to her hand almost without thinking. She flings it. The steel catches him in the chest. Knocks him back against the door and halfway out of the house. She's not around to see it. She's already down the hall, heading for the garage.

If she can get to the steel-clad security door.

But when she gets to the garage she realizes that the security door locks from *inside* the house. And when she hits the switch to raise the garage door, all she hears is a futile groan from the automatic door opener. Dammit. She has never gotten it fixed.

No time.

She hears him calling her. Trying to reassure her. Trying to reason with her.

She kills the lights.

When he enters the garage, his hair disheveled, his eyes wild, she hits him hard across the wrist with the music stand. He half drops. The gun clatters. She tries to leap over him to run inside. But he catches her and throws her to the concrete. Mounts her. Grabs her by the neck.

All light, all air, seems to shrink to pinpricks.

Her hands scrabble frantically to scratch his face, scratch his eyes. But he ably dodges her.

She tries to claw his arm with one hand.

Her other hand is over her head.

Reaching.

Her hand touches wood. It comes to her hand like an old friend.

*Bring me my Spear: O clouds unfold!*

She's forgotten that the other tool is still in the loop at her hip. Her right hand reaches for it now. Her eyes are nearly blind, her ability to think is seconds from being squeezed away, but somehow she doesn't have to think. Her hands do it all.

The hammers rise together in unison.

They drum their way down the man's skull, chasing away sin, chasing away evil. The sound is nothing like a bell. It is terrible, awful, fatal. Not at all beautiful but immensely satisfying.

Sirens make terrible music. She lets that sound and the flashing lights wash over her when the authorities come to take the body. Later that night she is bundled in a blanket as the car rockets south toward Atlanta. Margaret Bryan sits close to her in the back seat, another marshal driving. Maggie is remarkably kind; keeps trying to explain to her what will happen next. A safe house for a few days. A debriefing. A reassignment, for sure.

Maggie's voice is soft, tinged with anger. "I'm so sorry it took us so long to figure it out. We didn't believe what we were see-ing—hearing. He cut a deal with the guy who was looking for you and Timball. You probably didn't know, but Fred had some . . . money problems. He and his wife, they're going through some is-sues."

*The divorce. I know.*

Callie thinks she has said these words but she has not. She has merely nodded. The words are echoing inside her.

*He sold me out. For money.*

The marshal is talking about making plans. About seeing the counselor in Atlanta. About needing to make new arrangements.

About how it's going to be fine. Like starting over again in a new school.

"I know you probably aren't up for this right now," Bryan says. "But I want to make this clear. We're pulling you out. A new city. A new home. A new identity. Everything."

Callie forces herself to speak. "I need my things. My tools."

"We'll get what we can. But make no mistake: you're starting over, you understand? You can't take anything from your old life."

*My new old life, you mean.*

Once, she was a foolish young girl. Then she became a woman named Callie. But now she is not even that.

*I'm starting over all over.*

*Again.*

Beside her, Maggie relaxes. Looks at her quizzically. "Yeah. What was that back there? Did you take up woodworking or something?"

She wants to explain but can't find the words. Maggie pats her blanket. She means it to be reassuring. Comforting. It's a big gesture for her.

But the woman they once called Callie takes no comfort in any of it. She has lowered the volume on Maggie's voice, the car engine, the road, the shush of the falling snow. She has hied herself over to an inviolable place. A cocoon of steel, where only the patient fall of the hammer can keep her safe.

JEFFERY DEAVER

# The Adventure of the Laughing Fisherman

FROM *In the Company of Sherlock Holmes*

SOMETIMES IT'S OVERWHELMING: the burden of knowing that the man you most admire isn't real.

Then the depression that you've fought all your life creeps in, the anxiety. The borders of your life contract, stifling, suffocating.

And so slim Paul Winslow, twenty-eight, was presently walking into the neat, unadorned office of his on-again, off-again therapist, Dr. Levine, on the Upper West Side of Manhattan.

"Hello, Paul, come on in. Sit down."

Dr. Levine was one of those shrinks who offered basic armchairs, not couches, for his patients. He spoke frequently during the sessions, wasn't afraid to offer advice, and asked, "How do you feel about that?" only when it was important to know how his patients felt. Which was pretty rare.

He never used the verb *explore.*

Paul had read Freud's *Psychopathology of Everyday Life* (not bad, though a bit repetitive) and the works of Jung and Horney and some of the other biggies. He knew that a lot of what brain docs told you was a crock. But Dr. Levine was a good man.

"I did the best I could," Paul now explained to him. "Everything was going along okay, pretty much okay, but over the past couple of months it got worse and I couldn't shake it, you know, the sadness. I guess I need a tune-up," Paul added, smiling ruefully. Even at the worst times, his humor never wholly deserted him.

A laugh came from the mouth of the clean-shaven, trim physician, who wore slacks and a shirt during the appointments. His glasses were unstylish wire-rims, but that seemed to fit his casual style and friendly demeanor.

Paul had not been here for nearly eight months, and the doctor now glanced through his patient's file to refresh his memory. The folder was thick. Paul had seen Dr. Levine off and on for the past five years and had been to other shrinks before that. Diagnosed from a young age with bipolar and anxiety disorders, Paul had worked hard to control his malady. He didn't self-medicate with illegal drugs or liquor. He'd seen therapists, attended workshops, taken medicine—though not regularly and only those run-of-the-mill antidepressants ingested by the ton in the New York metro area. He'd never been institutionalized, never had any breaks with reality.

Still, the condition—which his mother also suffered from—had sidelined him. Never one to get along well with others, Paul was impatient, had little respect for authority, could be acerbic, and never hesitated to verbally eviscerate the prejudiced and the stupid.

Oh, he was brilliant, with an IQ residing well up in the stratosphere. He'd zipped through university in three years, grad school in one. But then came the brick wall: the real world. Teaching at community colleges hadn't worked out (you don't necessarily have to get along with fellow professors, but a modicum of tolerance for your students' foibles is a requirement). Editing for scientific publishers was equally disastrous (the same problem with his bosses and authors). Recently he'd taken up freelance copyediting for one of his former employers, and this solitary job more or less suited, at least for the time being.

Not that money was important; his parents, both bankers, were well off and, sympathetic to their son's condition, established a trust fund for him, which supported him nicely. Given these resources, he was free to live a simple, stress-free life, working part-time, playing chess at a club in the Village, dating occasionally (though without much enthusiasm), and doing plenty of what he loved most: reading.

Paul Winslow didn't care much for real people, but he loved the characters in fiction. He always had.

Lou Ford and Anna Wulf and Sam Spade and Clyde Griffiths and Frank Chambers and Mike Hammer and Pierre Bezukhov and Huck Finn . . . a hundred others made up Paul's circle of intimates. Harry Potter was a good friend, Frodo Baggins a better one.

As for vampires and zombies . . . well, better not to get Paul started.

Yet no fiction, high-brow or low-, captivated him like the short stories and novels of one author in particular: Arthur Conan Doyle, the creator of Sherlock Holmes.

Upon his first reading, some years ago, he knew instantly that he'd found his hero — a man who reflected his personality, his outlook, his soul.

His passion extended beyond the printed page. He collected Victorian memorabilia and artwork. Sitting prominently on the wall in his living room was a very fine reproduction of Sidney Paget's pen-and-ink drawing of archenemies Holmes and Professor Moriarty grappling on a narrow ledge above Reichenbach Falls, a scene from the short story "The Final Problem," in which Moriarty dies and Holmes appears to. Paul owned all of the various filmed versions of the Holmes adventures, though he believed the old Grenada version with Jeremy Brett was the only one that got it right.

Yet in recent months Paul had found that spending time in the world of the printed page was growing less and less comforting. And as the allure of the books wore off, the depression and anxiety seeped in to fill its place.

Now, sitting back in Dr. Levine's bright office — shrink contempo, Paul had once described it — he ran a hand through his unruly black curly hair, which he often forgot to comb. He explained that the high he got from reading the books and stories had faded dramatically.

"It hit me today that, well, it's lame, totally lame, having a hero who's fictional. I was so, I don't know, *confined* within the covers of the books, I'm missing out on . . . everything." He exhaled slowly through puffed cheeks. "And I thought maybe it's too late. The best part of my life is over."

Paul didn't mind the doctor's smile. "Paul, you're a young man. You've made huge strides. You have your whole life ahead of you."

Paul's eyes, in his gaunt, narrow face, closed momentarily. Then sprang open. "But how stupid is that, having this hero who's made up? I mean, they're only books."

"Don't dismiss the legitimate emotional attraction between readers and literature, Paul. Did you know tens of thousands of Victorians were inconsolable when one character in a Dickens book died?"

"Which one?"

"Little Nell."

"Oh, *The Old Curiosity Shop*. I didn't know about the reaction."

"All over the world. People were sobbing, milling around in the streets, talking about it."

Paul nodded. "And when it looked like Sherlock Holmes died in 'The Final Problem,' Doyle was so hounded, one might say, that he had to write a sequel that brought him back."

"Exactly. People love their characters. But apart from the valid role that fiction plays in our lives, in your case I think your diminished response to Sherlock Holmes stories is a huge step forward." The doctor seemed unusually enthusiastic.

"It is?"

"It's a sign that you're willing—and *prepared*—to step from a fictional existence to a real one."

This was intriguing. Paul found his heart beating a bit faster.

"Your goal in coming to see me and the other therapists in the past has always been to lead a less solitary, more social existence. Find a job, a partner, possibly have a family. And this is a perfect opportunity."

"How?"

"The Sherlock Holmes stories resonated with you for several reasons. I think primarily because of your talents: your intelligence, your natural skills at analysis, your powers of deduction—just like his."

"My mind does kind of work that way."

Dr. Levine said, "I remember the first time you came to see me. You asked about my wife and son—how was he doing in kindergarten? But I didn't wear a wedding ring and had no pictures of family here. I never mentioned my family and I don't put any personal information on the Internet. I assumed at the time you were just guessing—you were right, by the way—but now I suspect you deduced those facts about me, right?"

Paul cocked his head. "That's right."

"How?"

"Well, as for the fact you had a child and his age, there was a tiny jelly or jam fingerprint on the side of your slacks—about the height of a four- or five-year-old hugging Daddy at breakfast. And you never have appointments before eleven A.M., which told me that you probably were the spouse who took your child to school; if he'd been in first grade or older you would have gotten him to school much earlier and could see patients at nine or ten. You did the school run, I was assuming, because you have more flexible hours than your wife, working for yourself. I was sure she had a full-time job. This *is* Manhattan, of course—two incomes are the rule.

"Now, why a son? I thought the odds were that a girl of that age would be more careful about wiping her fingers before hugging you. Why an only child? Your office and this building are pretty modest, you know. I guessed you weren't a millionaire. That and your age told me it was more likely than not you had only one child. As to the wife, I suspected that even if you had had marital problems, as a therapist you'd work hard to keep the marriage together, so divorce was very unlikely. There was the widower factor, but the odds seemed against that."

Dr. Levine shook his head, laughing. "Sherlock Holmes would be proud of you, Paul. Tell me, that comes naturally to you?"

"Totally natural. It's kind of a game I play. A hobby. When I'm out, I deduce things about people."

"I think you should consider using these skills of yours in the real world."

"How do you mean?"

"I've always thought you were misplaced in academia and publishing. I think you should find a job where you can put those skills to work."

"Like what?"

"Maybe the law. Or . . . Well, how's this: you studied math and science."

"That's right."

"Maybe forensics would be a good choice."

"I've thought about that," Paul said uncertainly. "But do you think I'm ready? I mean, ready to get out in the real world?"

The doctor didn't hesitate. "I absolutely do."

Several days later Paul was doing what he often did at 10 A.M. on a weekday: having a coffee at Starbucks near his apartment on the

Upper West Side and reading. Today, however, it was not fiction he was engrossed in, but the local newspapers.

He was considering what Dr. Levine had told him and was trying to find some way to use his skills in a practical way. He wasn't having much luck.

Occasionally he would look around and make deductions about people sitting near him—a woman had broken up with a boyfriend, one man was an artistic painter, another was very likely a petty criminal.

Yes, this was a talent.

Just how to put it to use.

It was as he was pondering this that he happened to overhear one patron, looking down at her Mac screen, turn to her friend and say, "Oh, my God. They found another one!"

"What?" the companion asked.

"Another, you know, stabbing victim. In the park. It happened last night. They just found the body." She waved at the screen. "It's in the *Times*."

"Jesus. Who was it?"

"Doesn't say, doesn't give her name, I mean." The blonde, hair pulled back, ponytail, read. "Twenty-nine, financial adviser. They shouldn't say what she does without giving her name. Now everybody who knows a woman like that's going to worry."

Paul realized this would be the man—*surely* a man, according to typical criminal profile—who was dubbed the "East Side Slasher." Over the course of several months he'd killed two, now three, women. The killer took trophies. From the first two victims, at least, he cut off the left index finger. Postmortem, after he'd slashed their jugulars. There'd been no obvious sexual overtones to the crimes. Police could find no motives.

"Where?" Paul asked the Starbucks blonde.

"What?" She turned, frowning.

"Where did they find the body?" he repeated impatiently.

She looked put out, nearly offended.

Paul lifted his eyebrows. "It's not eavesdropping when you make a statement loud enough for the whole place to hear. Now. *Where* is the body?"

"Near Turtle Pond."

"How near?" Paul persisted.

"It doesn't say." She turned away in a huff.

Paul rose quickly, feeling his pulse start to pound.

He tossed out his half-finished coffee and headed for the door. He gave a faint laugh, thinking to himself, The game's afoot.

"Sir, what're you doing?"

Crouching on the ground, Paul glanced up at a heavyset man, white, pale white, with slicked-back, thinning hair. Paul rose slowly. "I'm sorry?"

"Could I see some identification?"

"I guess, sure. Could I?" Paul held the man's eyes evenly.

The man coolly displayed his NYPD detective's shield. The detective said his name was Carrera.

Paul handed over his driver's license.

"You live in the area?"

"It's on my license."

"Doesn't mean it's current," the detective responded, handing it back.

He'd renewed two months ago. He said, "It is. West Eighty-Second. Near Broadway."

They were just north of the traverse road in Central Park, near the pond where the Starbucks woman had told him the body had been found. The area was filled with trees and bushes and rock formations. Grass fields, trisected by paths bordered with mini-shoulders of dirt—which is what Paul had been examining. Yellow police tape fluttered, but the body and crime scene people were gone.

A few spectators milled nearby, taking mobile phone pictures or just staring, waiting to glimpse some fancy *CSI* gadgets perhaps. Though not everyone was playing voyeur. Two nannies pushed perambulators and chatted. One worker in dungarees was taking a break, sipping coffee and reading the sports section. Two college-age girls roller-bladed past. All were oblivious to the carnage that had occurred only fifty feet away.

The detective asked, "How long have you been here, Mr. Winslow?"

"I heard about the murder about a half hour ago and I came over. I've never seen a crime scene before. I was curious."

"Did you happen to be in the park at around midnight?"

"Was that the time of death?"

The detective persisted. "Sir? Midnight?"

"No."

"Have you seen anyone in the park recently wearing a Yankees jacket and red shoes?"

"Is that what the killer was wearing last night? . . . Sorry, no, I haven't. But is that what the killer was wearing?"

The detective seemed to debate. He said, "A witness from a street-sweeping crew reported seeing somebody walk out of bushes there about twelve-thirty this morning in a Yankees jacket and red shoes."

Paul squinted. "There?"

The detective sighed. "Yeah, there."

"And he was in his street-sweeping truck?"

"That's right."

"Then he's wrong," Paul said dismissively.

"I'm sorry?"

"Look." Paul nodded, walking to the traverse. "His truck was over there, right?"

The detective joined him. "Yeah. So?"

"That streetlight would've been right in his face, and I'd be very surprised if he'd been able to see writing on the jacket. As for the shoes, I'd guess they were blue, not red."

"What?"

"He would only have seen them for a second or two as he drove past. An instant later his mind would have registered them as red—because of the afterimage. That means they were really blue. And, by the way, they weren't shoes at all. He was wearing coverings of some kind. Booties, like surgeons wear. Those are usually blue or green."

"Covering? What're you talking about?" Carrera was rocking between interested and irritated.

"Look at this." Paul returned to dirt he'd been crouching over. "See these footprints? Somebody walked from the body through the grass, then onto the dirt here. He stopped—you can see that here—and stood in a pattern that suggests he pulled something off his shoes. The same size prints start up again here, but they're much more distinct. So your suspect wore booties to keep you from finding out the brand of shoe he was wearing. But he made a mistake. He figured it was safe to take them off once he was away from the body."

Carrera was staring down. Then he jotted notes.

Paul added, "And as for the brand? I guess your crime scene people have databases."

"Yessir. Thanks for that. We'll check it out." He was gruff but seemed genuinely appreciative. He pulled out his mobile and made a call.

"Oh, detective," Paul interrupted, "remember that just because the shoe's big—it looks like a twelve—doesn't mean his *foot* is that size. It's a lot less painful to wear two sizes large than two sizes smaller, if you want to fool somebody about your stature."

Paul's impression was that the cop had just been about to say that the suspect had to be huge.

After Carrera had ordered the crime scene back and disconnected, Paul said, "Oh, one other thing, detective?"

"Yessir?"

"See that bud there?"

"That flower?"

"Right. It's from a knapweed. The only place it grows in the park is in the Shakespeare Garden."

"How do you know that?"

"I observe things," Paul said dismissively. "Now. There's a small rock formation there. It'd be a good place to hide, and I'll bet that's where he waited for the victim."

"Why?"

"It's not unreasonable to speculate that his cuff scooped up the bud while he was crouched down, waiting for his victim. When he lifted his foot to pull off the booties here, the bud fell out."

"But that's two hundred yards away, the garden."

"Which means you haven't searched it."

Carrera stiffened, but then admitted, "No."

"Just like he thought. I'd have your people search the garden for trace evidence—or whatever your forensic people look for nowadays. You see so much on TV. You never know what's real or not."

After he'd finished jotting notes, Carrera asked, "Are you in law enforcement?"

"No, I just read a lot of murder mysteries."

"Uh-huh. You have a card?"

"No. But I'll give you my number." Paul wrote it down on the back of one of the detective's cards and handed it back. He looked up into the man's eyes; the cop was about six inches taller. "You think this is suspicious, I'm sure. I also wrote down the name of the chess club where I play, down in Greenwich Village. I was there last night until midnight. And I'd guess the CCTV cameras in the subway—I took the number 1 train to Seventy-Second—would show me getting off around one-thirty. And then I went to Alonzo's deli. I know the counterman. He can identify me."

"Yessir." Carrera tried to sound like he hadn't suspected Paul, but in fact even Lestrade in the Sherlock Holmes books would have had him checked out.

Still, at the moment, the detective actually offered what seemed to be a warm handshake. "Thanks for your help, Mr. Winslow. We don't always find such cooperative citizens. And helpful ones too."

"My pleasure."

Carrera pulled on gloves and put the bud in a plastic bag. He then walked toward the garden.

As Paul turned back to examine the scene, a voice behind him asked, "Excuse me?"

He turned to see a balding man, stocky and tall, in tan slacks and a Polo jacket. Topsiders. He looked like a Connecticut businessman on the weekend. He was holding a digital recorder.

"I'm Franklyn Moss. I'm a reporter for the *Daily Feed*."

"Is that an agricultural newspaper?" Paul asked.

Moss blinked. "Blog. Feed. Like RSS. Oh, that was a joke."

Paul gave no response.

Moss asked, "Can I ask your name?"

"I don't know. What do you want?" He looked at the recorder. Something about the man's eager eyes, too eager, made him uneasy.

"I saw you talking to the cop, Carrera. He's not real cooperative. Kind of a prick. Between you and I."

You and me, Paul silently corrected the journalist. "Well, he was just asking me if I saw anything—about the murder, you know. They call that canvassing, I think."

"So, did you?"

"No. I just live near here. I came by forty-five minutes ago."

Moss looked around in frustration. "Not much good stuff, this one. Everything was gone before we heard about it."

"Good stuff? You mean the body?"

"Yeah. I wanted to get some pix. But no luck this time." Moss

stared at the shadowy ring of bushes where the woman had died.
"He rape this one? Cut off anything other than the finger?"

"I don't know. The detective—"

"Didn't say."

"Right."

"They always play it so close to the damn chest. Prick, I was saying. You mind if I interview you?"

"I don't really have anything to say."

"Most people don't. Who cares? Gotta fill the stories with something. If you want your fifteen minutes of fame, gimme a call.
Here's my card." He handed one over. Paul glanced at it and then
pocketed it. "I'm writing a sidebar on what people think about
somebody getting killed like this."

Paul cocked his head. "I'll bet the general consensus is they're
against it."

All the next day, Paul had been in and out of the apartment constantly, visiting the crime scenes of the Upper East Side Slasher,
getting as close as he could, observing, taking notes. Then returning and, as he was now, sitting at his computer, continuing his research and thinking hard about how to put into practical use everything he'd learned from his immersion in the Sherlock Holmes
books.

His doorbell rang.

"Yes?" he asked into the intercom.

"Yeah, hi. Paul Winslow?"

"Yes."

"It's Detective Carrera. We met the other day. In Central Park?"

Hm.

"Sure. Come on up." He hit the button to unlock the door.

A moment later there came a knock on the door. Paul admitted
the detective. Breathing heavily from the two-story walkup—he apparently hadn't waited for the elevator—the man looked around
the apartment. Maybe his cop training precluded him from saying,
"Nice digs," or whatever he would say, but Paul could tell he was
impressed by the small but elegant place.

His trust fund was really quite substantial.

"So," Paul said. "Did you check me out? I'm guessing you did,
'cause you don't have your handcuffs out."

Carrera, who was carrying a thick dark-brown folder, started to deny it but then laughed. "Yeah. You weren't much of a suspect."

"Perps *do* come back to the scene of the crime, though."

"Yeah, but only the stupid ones give the cops advice . . . and good advice, in your case. The shoe was a Ferragamo, size twelve—you got a good eye. So our perp's pretty well-off."

"And you checked the indentation?"

"It was pretty deep. He's a big man, so the shoe's probably the right fit."

"How old was the shoe?"

"They couldn't tell wear patterns."

"Too bad."

"And you were right about the jacket. The street cleaner didn't really see the logo. He was speculating—because it was black and had the cut of a Yankees jacket his kid owns. Trying to be helpful. Happens with witnesses a lot."

"Remember the back lighting. It might not have been black at all. It could have been any dark color. Can I get you anything?"

"Water, yeah. Thanks."

"I'm having milk. I love milk. I drink a glass a day, sometimes two. You want some milk?"

"Water's fine."

Paul got a glass of milk for himself and a bottle of Dannon for the detective.

He returned to find the man studying the shelves. "Man, you got a lot of books. And that whole wall there—true crime, forensics."

"I'm thinking maybe someday I'll study it. Go to school, I mean. I've got degrees in math and science."

"That's a good start. All the good crime scene cops I know have science backgrounds. Hey, let me know if you need advice on where to go, what courses to take."

"Yeah? Thanks."

Carrera turned away and said, "Mr. Winslow?"

"Paul."

"Okay, and I'm Al. Paul, have you heard that sometimes police departments use civilians when there's a tough investigation going? Like psychics."

"I've heard that. I don't believe in psychics. I'm a rationalist."

"Is that somebody who doesn't believe in the supernatural?"

"That's right."

"Well, that's me too. But one thing I *have* done in the past is use consultants. Specialists. Like in computer work. Or if there's been an art theft, we'll bring in somebody from a museum to help us."

"And you want me to be a consultant?" Paul asked, feeling his heart pounding hard.

"I was impressed, what you told me in the park. I've brought some files from the UNSUB two-eight-seven homicides—that's what we call the perp."

"Police don't really use the word *slasher* much, I'd guess."

"Not too, you know, professional. So, Paul. I was wondering if you could take a look at them and tell us what you thought."

"You bet I would."


George Lassiter was upset.

The forty-year-old Manhattanite, whose nickname in the press was the sensationalist but admittedly accurate "Upper East Side Slasher," had a problem.

No one was more meticulous than he was when it came to planning out and committing his crimes. In fact, part of the relaxation he experienced from murder derived from the planning. (The actual killing—the *execution,* he sometimes joked—could be a letdown, compared with the meticulous planning, if, say, the victim didn't scream or fight as much as he'd hoped.)

Taking scrupulous care to select the right kill zone, to leave minimal or confusing evidence, to learn all he could about the victim so there'd be no surprises when he attacked . . . this was the way he approached all his crimes.

But apparently he'd screwed up in the latest Central Park murder near Shakespeare Garden and Turtle Pond a few nights ago.

The solidly built man, dressed in slacks and a black sweater, was now outside an apartment on Eighty-Second Street, on the Upper West Side of Manhattan. Lassiter had returned to the crime scene the next morning, to see how far the police were getting in the investigation, when he'd noted a skinny young man talking to Albert Carrera, whom Lassiter had identified as the lead detective on the case. The man seemed to be giving advice, which Carrera was obviously impressed with.

That wasn't good.

After the young man had left the crime scene, Lassiter had followed him to his apartment. He'd waited a half hour for someone to exit the building, and when an elderly woman walked down the stairs, Lassiter had approached her with a big smile. He'd described the man and had asked his name, saying he looked like somebody Lassiter had been in the army with. The neighbor had said he was Paul Winslow. Lassiter had shaken his head and said that no, it wasn't him. He thanked her and headed off.

Once home, he'd researched Paul Winslow at the address he tracked him to. Very little came up. No Facebook page, Instagram, Twitter, Flickr, LinkedIn . . . no social media. A criminal background check came back negative too. At the least, it was pretty clear the young man wasn't a professional law enforcer, just a private meddler.

Which didn't mean he wasn't dangerous.

He might even have seen Lassiter step out of the hiding place in the Shakespeare Garden and grab Ms. Rachel Garner around the neck, throttling her to unconsciousness and then carrying her into the park. For the knife work.

Or seen him slip away from the scene around midnight after he was through. That was more likely; after all, Lassiter had seen Paul staring at the very spot where he'd slipped away from the bloody murder site.

Why hadn't he called the police then? Well, possibly he'd spent the night debating the pros and cons of getting involved.

It was Paul's apartment that he was surreptitiously checking out at the moment. His intention had been to follow the young man again and find out where he worked, perhaps learning more about him.

But then, lo and behold, who came knocking at the front door, carrying a big fat file folder?

Detective Carrera, in need of a tan and a workout regimen.

What to do, what to do?

Several thoughts came to mind. But, as always, he didn't leap to any conclusions right away.

Think, plan. And think some more.

Only then could you act safely and your crimes be successful.


"We did find something," Al Carrera was telling Paul as he spread the contents of the case file out before them on the coffee table.

"In the rocks, where you said the UNSUB waited—Shakespeare Garden."

"What was it?"

"Indentations that match the bootie prints. And a tiny bit of wrapper, food wrapper. Forensics found it was from one of those energy bars that campers and hikers eat. From the paper and ink analysis we found it was a Sports Plus bar—their four-ounce peanut-butter-and-raisin one. Probably the perp's, because of the dew content analysis. That told us it'd been dropped on the ground about midnight."

"Your people are good," Paul said. He was impressed. He recalled that Sherlock Holmes had his own laboratory. Conan Doyle, a man of science himself, had been quite prescient when it came to forensics.

The detective lifted an envelope, eight and a half by eleven. "These're the pictures of the crime scenes—and the victims. But I have to warn you. They're a little disturbing."

"I don't know that I've even seen a picture of a real body. I mean, on the news I have, but not up close." He stared at the envelope, hesitated. Finally he nodded. "Okay, go ahead."

Carrera spread them out.

Paul was surprised to find they were in color—vivid color. He supposed he shouldn't have been. Why would police photographers use black-and-white when nobody else did nowadays?

As he stared at the unfiltered, bloody images, Paul felt squeamish. But he thought back to the Sherlock Holmes stories and reminded himself to be as detached and professional as his hero.

He bent forward and concentrated.

Finally he offered, "Some observations. He's really strong. You can see the bruises on their necks. He didn't have to reposition his hands. He just gripped and squeezed and they went unconscious—not dead, mind you. The amount of blood loss tells us they were stabbed while still alive. Let's see, let's see . . . All right, he's right-handed. A lefty pretending to be right wouldn't have gotten the cuts so even in the soft tissue."

"Good."

"Also he's cautious, very aware and observant. Look at his footprints in the dirt at all three scenes. He's constantly standing up and walking to the perimeter and looking for threats. Smart."

Carrera wrote.

Paul tapped the picture that showed the perp's bloody hand-print on the ground, perhaps as he pushed himself up to a standing position. "Look at the thumb. Interesting."

"What?"

"It's not spread out very far—which you'd think it would be if he was using the hand for leverage to rise."

"I see it."

"That might mean that he spends a lot of time on a computer."

"Why?"

"People who regularly type tend to keep their thumbs close in, to hit the spacebar."

Carrera's eyebrow rose and he jotted this down too.

Paul gave a faint smile. "He's a fisherman."

"What?"

"I'm fairly certain. See those marks on the victims' wrists?"

"Ligature marks."

Paul squinted as he shuffled through the pictures. "They're about the thickness of fishing line. And see how he made those incisions *before* he removed the victims' fingers. That's how you skin fish. And, yes, the energy bar—just the sort of food a fisherman would take with him for lunch or a midmorning snack."

Paul sat back and glanced at Carrera, who was writing feverishly. The young man said, "If he *is* a fisherman, which I'm pretty sure he is, he probably has a lake house somewhere in the tri-state area. We know he's got money. He's not fishing with the locals in the East River. He'll go out to the country in his BMW. Wait," Paul said quickly with a smile, noting Carrera had started to write. "The Beemer's just a guess. But I'm sure his car's a nice one. We know he's upper-income. And the arrogance of the crimes suggests that he'd have an ostentatious car. Mercedes, BMW, Porsche."

After he finished writing, Carrera asked, "Is there any reason he'd take the index finger?"

Paul said, "Oh, I think it's an insult."

"Insult. To who?"

"Well, to you. The police. He's contemptuous of authority. He's saying someone could point directly to the killer and you'd still miss it. He's laughing at you."

Carrera shook his head at this. "Sonofabitch."

Paul looked over the pictures once more. "The laughing fisherman," he mused, thinking that would make a good title for a Sherlock Holmes story: "The Adventure of the Laughing Fisherman."

Carrera snapped, "Laughing at us, the prick."

Then Paul cocked his head. "Fish . . ."

"What?" Carrera was looking at Paul's focused eyes as the young man strode to his computer and began typing. After a moment of browsing he said, "There's fishing in Central Park—the Lake, the Pond, and Harlem Meer. Yes! I'll bet that's where your perp goes fishing . . . for his victims." He glanced at Carrera eagerly. "Let's go take a look, maybe see if we can find another wrapper or some other evidence. We could set up surveillance."

"It's not authorized for a civilian to go on field operations."

"I'll just tag along. To observe. Offer suggestions."

Carrera debated. "Okay. But if you see anyone or anything that looks suspicious, I take over."

"Fine with me."

Paul collected his jacket from the den and returned to the living room. Pulling it on, he frowned. "There's something else that just occurred to me. I'll bet he knows about you."

"Me? Personally?"

"You and the other investigators."

"How?"

"I'm thinking he's been to the crime scenes, checking out the investigation. That means you could be in danger. All of you. You should let everyone on your team know." He added gravely, "Sooner rather than later."

Carrera sent a text. "My partner. He'll tell everybody to keep an eye out. You should be careful too, Paul."

"Me? I'm just a civilian. I'm sure I don't have anything to worry about."

Paul Winslow's apartment was pitifully easy to break into.

After James Lassiter had seen Paul and Carrera leave the place—it was about two hours ago—he'd had slipped around back and jimmied the basement door. Then up a few flights of stairs to the apartment itself. The lock-pick gun had done the job in five seconds, and he'd slipped inside, pleased to note that the place didn't have an alarm.

Piece of cake.

He now stood in the bay window of the dim living room, scanning the street. He was wearing latex gloves and a stocking cap. Lassiter had been impressed with the fancy apartment; the opulence worked to his advantage. Having so many nice things in an unalarmed house? Just the place for a robbery. He'd decided that Paul couldn't be a victim of the Upper East Side Slasher, because then Carrera and the other investigators would know immediately that Paul's advice—which might lead to Lassiter—was accurate. No, the crime would be your basic break-in, the burglar surprised when Paul stepped into his apartment.

His plan was that if Carrera returned with Paul, he'd slip out the back and wait another day. But if the young man returned alone, Lassiter would throw him to the floor and pistol-whip him. Blind him, shatter his jaw. Put him in the hospital for months and render him useless as a witness. Murder ups the ante exponentially in a crime. Police frankly don't care so much about a beating, however serious.

*Jesus, look at all the books . . .* Lassiter almost felt bad thinking that blinding him would pretty much finish his days as a reader.

*But it's your own fault, Mr. Meddling Winslow.*

A half hour later, Lassiter tensed. Yes, there was Paul returning from the direction of Central Park. Alone. The cop wasn't with him. When the young man stepped into a quick mart, Lassiter drew his gun and hid behind the front door, which opened onto the hallway of Paul's building.

Three minutes passed, then four. He was awaiting the key in the latch, but instead heard the sound of the buzzer.

Lassiter cautiously peered through the eyehole. He was looking at a fisheye image of a pizza delivery man, holding a box.

He nearly laughed. But then wondered, *Wait, how had the guy gotten through the front security door without hitting the intercom from outside?*

*Oh, shit. Because Paul had given him the key and told him to ring the buzzer, to draw Lassiter's attention to the front door. Which meant—*

The gun muzzle touched the back of Lassiter's neck, the metal cold. Painfully cold.

"Settle down there, Lassiter," Paul said in a calm voice. "Drop the gun, put your hands behind your back."

Lassiter sighed. The pistol bounced noisily on the wood floor.

In an instant, expertly, Paul had cuffed his hands and picked up the gun. Lassiter turned and grimaced. The young man did not, it turned out, have a weapon of his own. He'd bluffed, using a piece of pipe. Paul nodded to the door and said, "I gave him the key outside and told him to let himself in the front door. If you were wondering. But you probably figured."

The buzzer rang again and Paul eased Lassiter onto the floor.

"Don't move. All right?" The young man checked the gun to see that it was loaded and ready to fire, which it was. He aimed at Lassiter's head.

"Yes. Right. I won't."

Paul pocketed the gun and turned the apartment lights on. He stepped to the door, opened it.

He took the pizza box and paid. He must've left a real nice tip; the young man said an effusive, "Well, thank you, sir! You have a good night! Wow, thanks!"

Paul didn't care much for pizza. Or for any food really. He'd only placed the order to distract Lassiter and give him the chance to sneak in the back door. He did, however, have a thirst. "I could use a glass of milk. You?"

"Milk?"

"Or water? That's about all I can offer you. I don't have any liquor or soda."

Lassiter didn't respond. Paul walked into the kitchen and poured a glass of milk. He returned and helped Lassiter onto a chair. He sipped from the tall glass, reflecting on how different he felt, how confident. The depression was gone completely, the anxiety too.

Thank you, Dr. Levine.

Paul regarded the glass. "Did you know milk has a terroir too, just like wine? You can tell, by analysis of the milk, what the cows were eating during the lactation period: the substances in the soil, chemical residues, even insect activity. Why do you wrap your trophies in silk? The fingers? That's one thing I couldn't deduce."

Lassiter gasped and his eyes, wide, cut into Paul's like a torch.

"I know it wasn't on the news. The police don't even know that." He explained, "There was a single bloody thread at one of the scenes. It couldn't have come from a silk garment you were wearing. That would be too ostentatious and obvious for a man on a killing mission. Silk is used for cold-weather undergarments, yes, but you wouldn't have worn anything like that in these temperatures; very bad idea to sweat at a crime scene. Weren't the days better for people like you when there was no DNA analysis?"

Did a moan issue from Lassiter's throat? Paul couldn't be sure. He smiled. "Well, I'm not too concerned about the silk. Merely curious. Not relevant to our purposes here. The more vital question you have surely is how I found *you*. Understandable. The short answer is that I learned from the newspaper accounts of the murders that you're an organized offender. I deduced you plan everything out ahead of time. And you plan the sites of the killings and the escape routes meticulously.

"Someone like that would also want to know about the people tracking him down. I decided you'd be at the scene the morning after the killing. I observed everyone who was there. I was suspicious of the man sipping coffee and reading the sports section of the *Post*. I was pretty sure it was you. I'd known that the clue about the Ferragamo shoe was fake—why take off the booties in the dirt, when you could have walked three feet farther onto the asphalt and pulled them off there, not leaving any impressions for the police? That meant you weren't rich at all but middle-class—the shoes were to misdirect the cops. I knew you were strong and solidly built. All of those described the *Post* reader pretty well.

"When I left the scene I was aware that you followed me back here. As soon as I got inside I grabbed a hat and new jacket and sunglasses and went out the back door. I started following *you*—right back to your apartment in Queens. A few Internet searches and I got your identity."

Paul enjoyed a long sip of milk. "An average cow in the U.S. produces nearly twenty thousand pounds of milk a year. I find that amazing." He regarded the unfortunate man for a moment. "I'm a great fan of the Sherlock Holmes stories." He nodded around the room at his shelves. "As you can probably see."

"So that's why the police aren't here," his prisoner muttered. "You're going play the big hero, like Sherlock Holmes, showing up the police with your brilliance. Who're you going to turn me over to? The mayor? The police commissioner?"

"Not at all." Paul added, "What I want is to *employ* you. As my assistant."

"*Assistant?*"

"I want you to work for me. Be my sidekick. Though that's a word I've never cared for, I must say."

Lassiter gave a sour laugh. "This's all pretty messed up. You think you're some kind of Sherlock Holmes and you want me to be your Watson?"

Paul grimaced. "No, no, no. My hero in the books"—he waved at his shelves—"isn't *Holmes*. It's *Moriarty*. Professor James Moriarty."

"But wasn't he, what do they say? Holmes's nemesis."

Paul quoted Holmes's words from memory: "In calling Moriarty a criminal you are uttering libel in the eyes of the law—and there lie the glory and the wonder of it! The greatest schemer of all time, the organizer of every deviltry, the controlling brain of the underworld, a brain which might have made or marred the destiny of nations—that's the man!"

He continued, "Holmes was brilliant, yes, but he had no grand design, no drive. He was passive. Moriarty, on the other hand, was ambition personified. Always making plans for plots and conspiracies. He's been my hero ever since I first read about him." Paul's eyes gazed affectionately at the books on his shelves that contained the stories involving Moriarty. "I studied math and science because of him. I became a professor, just like my hero."

Paul thought back to his session with Dr. Levine not long ago.

*The Sherlock Holmes stories resonated with you for several reasons. I think primarily because of your talents: your intelligence, your natural skills at analysis, your powers of deduction—just like his . . .*

Dr. Levine had assumed Paul worshipped Holmes, and the patient didn't think it wise to correct him; therapists presumably take role modeling of perpetrators like Moriarty, even if fictional, rather seriously.

"Moriarty only appeared in two stories as a character, was mentioned in just five others. But the shadow of his evil runs throughout the entire series, and you get the impression that Holmes was always aware that a villain even smarter and more resourceful than he was always hovering nearby. *He* was my idol." Paul smiled, his expression filled with reverent admiration. "So. I've decided to become a modern-day Moriarty. And that means having an assistant just like my hero did."

"Like Watson?"

"No. Moriarty's sidekick was Colonel Sebastian Moran, a retired military man who specialized in murder. Exactly what I need. I wondered whom to pick. I don't exactly hang out in criminal circles. So I began studying recent crimes in the city and read about the Upper East Side Slasher. You had the most promise. Oh, you made some mistakes, but I thought I could help you overcome your flaws—like returning to visit the scene of the crime, not planting enough fake evidence to shift the blame, attacking victims who were very similar, which establishes patterns and makes profiling easier. And for heaven's sake, eating a power bar while you waited for your victim? Please. You are capable of better, Lassiter."

The man was silent. His expression said he acknowledged that Paul was correct.

"But first I needed to save you from the police. I helped Detective Carrera come up with a profile of the perp that was very specific, very credible . . . and described someone completely different from you."

"Maybe, but they're out there looking for me."

"Oh, they are?" Paul asked wryly.

"What do you mean?"

He found the cable box remote. He fiddled for a moment. "You know, in the past we'd have to wait until the top of the hour to see the news. Now they've got that twenty-four/seven cycle. Tedious usually but helpful occasionally."

The TV came to life.

Actually it was a Geico commercial.

"Can't do much about those," Paul said with a grimacing nod at the screen. "Though they can be funny. The squirrels're the best."

A moment later an anchorwoman appeared. "If you're just joining us—"

"Which we are," Paul chimed in.

"NYPD officials have reported that the so-called Upper East Side Slasher, allegedly responsible for the murders of three women in Manhattan and, earlier tonight, of Detective Albert Carrera of the NYPD, has been arrested. He's been identified as Franklyn Moss, a journalist and blogger."

"Jesus! What?"

Paul shushed Lassiter.

"Detective Carrera was found stabbed to death about 5 P.M. near the Harlem Meer fishing area in Central Park. An anonymous tip—"

"*Moi,*" Paul said.

"—led authorities to Moss's apartment in Brooklyn, where police found evidence implicating him in the murder of Detective Carrera and the other victims. He is being held without bond in the Manhattan Detention Center."

Paul shut the set off.

He turned and was amused to see Lassiter's expression was one of pure bewilderment. "I think we don't need these anymore." He rose and unhooked the handcuffs. "Just to let you know, though, my lawyer has plenty of evidence implicating you in the crimes, so don't do anything foolish."

"No, I'm cool."

"Good. Now when I decided I wanted you as an assistant, I had to make sure somebody else took the fall for the killings. Whom to pick? I've never liked reporters very much, and I found Franklyn Moss particularly irritating. So I datamined him. I learned he was quite the fisherman, so I fed Carrera this mumbo-jumbo that that was the killer's hobby.

"Earlier today I convinced Carrera we should go to Central Park, one of the fishing preserves there, to look for clues. When we were alone at the Meer I slit his throat and sawed off his index finger. That's a lot of work, by the way. Couldn't you have picked the pinkie? Never mind. Then I went to Moss's apartment and hid the knife and finger in his garage and car, along with some physical evidence from the other scenes, a pair of Ferragamos I bought yesterday, and a packet of those energy bars you like. I left some of Carrera's blood on the doorstep so the police would have probable cause to get a warrant."

Paul enjoyed another long sip of milk.

"The evidence's circumstantial, but compelling: he drives a BMW, which I told Carrera was his vehicle—because I'd seen it earlier. Public records show he has a lake house in Westchester—which I also told Carrera. And I suggested that the ligature marks were from fishing line, which Moss had plenty of in his garage and basement . . . You used bell wire, right?"

"Um, yes."

Paul continued, "I also fed the detective this nonsense that the killer probably spent a lot of time keyboarding at a computer, like a blogger would do. So our friend Moss is going away forever. You're clean."

Lassiter frowned. "But wouldn't Carrera have told other officers *you* gave him the profile? That'd make you a suspect."

"Good point, Lassiter. But I knew he wouldn't. Why bring the file to me here in my house to review, rather than invite me downtown to examine it? And why did he come alone, not with his partners? No, he asked my advice *privately*—so he could steal my ideas and take credit for them himself." Paul ran his hand through his hair and regarded the killer with a coy smile. "Now, tell me about the assignment—about the person who hired you. I'm really curious about that."

"Assignment?"

But the feigned surprise didn't work.

"Please, Lassiter. You're not a serial killer. I wouldn't want you if you were—they're far too capricious. Too driven by emotion." Paul said the last word as if it were tainted food. "No, you came up with the plan for the multiple murders to cover up your real crime. You'd been hired to murder a particular individual—one of the three victims."

Lassiter's mouth was actually gaping open. He slowly pressed his lips back together.

Paul continued, "It was so obvious. There was no sexual component to the killings, which there always is in serial murders. And there's no psychopathological archetype for taking an index finger trophy—you improvised because you thought it would look suitably spooky. Now, which of the three was the woman you'd been hired to kill?"

The man gave a why-bother shrug. "Rachel Garner. The last one. She was going to blow the whistle on her boss. He runs a hedge fund that's waist-deep in money laundering."

"Or—alternative spelling—'waste-deep,' if it needs *laundering*." Paul couldn't help the play on words. "I thought it was something like that."

Lassiter said, "I'd met the guy in the army. He knew I did a few dirty tricks, and he called me up."

"So it was a one-time job?"

"Right."

"Good. So you can come to work for me."

Lassiter debated.

Paul leaned forward. "Ah, there's a lot of carnage out there to perpetrate. Lots of foolish men and women on Wall Street who need to be relieved of some of their gains, ill- or well-gotten. There're illegal arms sales waiting to be made, and cheating politicians to extort and humans to traffic and terrorists who may hold intellectually indefensible views but have very large bank accounts and are willing to write checks to people like us, who can provide what they need."

Paul's eyes narrowed. "And, you know, Lassiter, sometimes you just need to slice a throat or two for the fun of it."

Lassiter's eyes fixed on the carpet. After a long moment he whispered, "The silk?"

"Yes?"

"My mother would stuff a silk handkerchief in my mouth when she beat me. To mute the screams, you know."

"Ah, I see," Paul replied softly. "I'm sorry. But I can guarantee you plenty of opportunities to get even for that tragedy, Lassiter. So. Do you want the job?"

The killer debated for merely a few seconds. He smiled broadly. "I do, professor. I sure do." The men shook hands.

BRENDAN DuBOIS

# Crush Depth

FROM *Ice Cold*

IN THE NEW HAMPSHIRE island community of New Castle, Michael Smith spent nearly a month conducting a surveillance op at an oceanfront park called the Great Island Common. It was small, with a tennis court, gazebo, and picnic tables and benches scattered on a scraggly green lawn. There was a stone jetty sticking out into the near channel, from which ships entered and left nearby Portsmouth Harbor to the Atlantic, and across the narrow channel was the state of Maine.

Near the stone jetty was a good downstream view of the Portsmouth Naval Shipyard, which had been building warships for the U.S. Navy since 1800.

It was now one year after the hammer-and-sickle flag had been lowered for the last time over the Kremlin, and sitting in a rented blue Toyota Camry, Michael thought it ironic that his work and the work of so many others was still going on, despite peace supposedly breaking out everywhere.

Cold war or hot war, there was always plenty of work to be done.

He stepped out of the Camry, started walking to the jetty. It was a warm day in late May. As with every previous Wednesday, his target was sitting on a park bench adjacent to the jetty, an old man with a metal cane balanced between his legs, looking down the channel, at the buildings, cranes, and docks of the shipyard.

Michael walked around the park bench, sat down, and gave a quick glance to the man about three feet away. He seemed to be in his late sixties, wearing a white cloth jacket, partially zippered up, a blue baseball cap with the U.S. Navy emblem in the center, dungarees, and black sneakers that had Velcro snaps. He looked over at Michael, then turned his gaze back to the shipyard. His nose was large with big pores, his face leathery and worn, white eyebrows about the size of butterfly wings.

"Nice day, huh?" Michael asked.

There was a pause, and the man said, "Yeah, it sure is."

"But I bet fog can come up pretty quick, thicken everything up."

"You know it."

He sat still for a bit longer, not wanting to spook the man. All those months and weeks, poring over the dusty files, then making last-minute travel arrangements, and then ending up here. He had finally made it, and he didn't want to screw it up.

"Think the shipyard will close now that the Cold War is over?"

A shrug. "Beats the hell out of me. But somethin' that's been there for nearly two hundred years, it'd be a shame if it did."

"I agree," Michael said, putting warmth into his voice. "I mean, there are good-paying jobs over there, with a lot of skilled guys and gals, am I right? Working with their hands, having special knowledge, knowing how to build subs."

"Nobody over there builds subs," the man declared.

"Excuse me? It's a shipyard, isn't it?"

"Yeah, but all they do now is overhaul work or the occasional repair. Last time they built a sub over there was the USS *Sand Lance*. Launched in 1969."

"What kind of submarine was that?"

"An attack sub. Sturgeon class. Used to hunt Russian missile subs."

"Oh. I see."

Michael kept quiet, folded his hands in his lap. Looked back at the older man, said, "Excuse me for asking this, I get the feeling you worked there. True?"

A long pause. The old man rubbed his hands along the top of the cane. "Yeah. I did. A pipefitter."

Michael felt a small sense of triumph, tried to keep it out of his voice and expression. "You miss it much?"

"The people," he said quickly. "You miss the guys you worked with. A real smart bunch of fellas, could pretty much figure out how to solve any kind of problem, no matter what it was, no matter if it was welding or electronics or anything else. Most of the times, we finished the boat under budget and on schedule. A great, great group of guys."

"Sounds like it," Michael said. "Makes it good to know that the place might still stay open."

The old man kept quiet, and Michael stayed with him a few minutes longer, and said, "Lots of birds out there today."

"Mostly seagulls," the old man said. "More like rats with wings, not sure if they count as birds."

Michael spoke softly. "Ever see a kingfisher?"

"No," he said sharply. "Never have."

He let it be, and after a couple of minutes got up and said, "So long," and walked back to his rental car.

Good ops were like going fishing. Getting that initial nibble was always encouraging.


Exactly a week later, Michael came back to the Great Island Common and once again found the old man sitting at the same park bench, like he had never left. He sat down, and when the guy glanced over, he put his hand out and said, "Michael."

The man took his hand. It was wrinkled and rough. "Gus."

"Glad to meet you, Gus."

They sat there for a while, and Gus said, "What brings you here?"

Michael sighed. "You know, Gus, sometimes I just need to sit outside and get some fresh air. I work in an office, and after a while, you realize, man, is this it? Is this your life? Moving papers from one pile to another. Going to lots of meetings. Moving some more papers around. Kissing the right ass. Go home, go to bed, get up and do it again. Blah."

Gus stayed quiet, and Michael said, "I know this sounds crazy, but sometimes, you know, sometimes I envy guys like you. Worked with your hands. Building things. Fixing things. Could point to something at the end of the day. Could say, hey, that submarine that just got launched, I had a part of it."

"Well . . . it wasn't easy work."

"Oh, man, yeah, I know that. I know it was hard, dirty, and maybe dangerous. But I'm sure you felt like you were helping out the country, you know? Helping defend it by making the navy strong. Me? End of the day, end of the month, what do I get? I moved some papers around and made some middle managers happy. So what?"

Gus cackled. "Yeah, managers. Always tend to get in the way, don't they. Paperwork, procedures, forms, checklists. If it wasn't for completed and filled-out forms, made you think whether they could breathe or not."

"They sure do. Man, so how many submarines did you work on?

Gus shrugged. "Lose track. Eighteen, maybe nineteen."

"So you were there when they went from diesel subs to nuclear?"

"That I was."

"Bet security was really something, back then."

Gus didn't say anything, and Michael wondered if he had gone too far. He waited, wondering what to say next.

The old man finally said, "Yeah, it was something. Had to be. We were in the middle of the Cold War, weren't we?"

Michael nodded. "People tend to forget that, don't they?"

"Well, I don't."

"Neither do I." Michael got up. "Tell me, you ever see a kingfisher fly by here?"

A firm shake of the head. "Nope, can't say I ever have."

The third time, the third Wednesday, it was overcast, with a steady breeze coming off the Atlantic, whitecaps making the channel choppy. But Gus was still sitting there, watching the gray buildings and cranes of the shipyard.

Michael sat down, having brought two cups of coffee with him. He passed one over to Gus, who took it and murmured, "Thanks, appreciate it."

"Not a problem."

A cargo ship was making its way slowly out of the harbor, being escorted by two tugboats. Michael watched it slide by and said, "Your dad work at the shipyard?"

"No, he was navy."

"Oh. During World War II?"

"Kinda. He joined up just as it was wrapping up. Went to Japan as part of the occupation forces, right after the war ended."

"I see."

"Me, I got into the shipyard in the late 1940s, just as a kid."

"Bet your dad was proud of you."

"Yeah, you'd think," he said, speaking slowly. "But my dad . . . something in the navy really changed him. Didn't talk about his duty for a long, long while. But he hated the fact I had anything to do with the military."

"Really? That sounds strange. I mean, you read all those books and see those television shows about 'the Greatest Generation.' It seems most guys were proud of their service. My grandfather, he fought the Nazis during the war. Said it was the best four years of his life. Nothing ever came close to giving him that close bond, of being part of something larger than him, fighting against fascism."

Gus took a noisy slurp from his coffee. "Yeah, but the war was pretty much over when my dad joined up. No more fighting. Just occupation duty."

"Something must have happened to him, back then."

Michael sensed he had gone too far. It seemed Gus was staring at something very, very far away. His orders told him to do something, but he couldn't do it. Not yet.

He didn't know enough.

Finally Gus said, "This coffee is good. Thanks."

Michael sat with him for a little while and then got up.

"Later, Gus."

The old man didn't say anything else.

In nearby Portsmouth, the Federal Building in the center of the city contained offices from the post office to the Armed Forces Recruiting Centers to the local office of the FBI. Michael parked nearby and walked for a bit, arriving at a room where he made a phone call to give an update.

His supervisor was brusque with him. "You should be wrapped up by now."

"I'm close. I don't want to spook him."

"This whole thing can blow up in our faces unless it gets handled right. So handle it."

"I will."

"You better."

And then his supervisor hung up.

*

The Wednesday next, Michael came to the park bench where Gus sat. In addition to bringing two coffees, he had brought a bag of doughnuts. Gus grunted when he saw the doughnuts. "My doc says I shouldn't eat this stuff."

"What do you say?"

"My doc should mind his own goddamn business."

The doughnuts came from a local bakery—not a chain shop—and they were tasty and filling as both men ate. Michael took in the channel, the bridges, the brick buildings of Portsmouth, and the cranes and gray buildings of the shipyard.

"You said you worked on a lot of subs over the years," Michael said. "Any one of them stand out in your mind?"

Gus took a good mouthful of coffee. "No, not really."

"You sure? I think there'd be at least one that stuck out in your mind."

"Nope."

"Not even the USS *Thresher?* You sure?"

Gus paused, one hand holding the coffee cup, the other holding a half-eaten cruller. He coughed. "What do you know about the *Thresher?*"

"It was built over there, at the shipyard. Came back for some overhaul work in 1963. Went out one morning for a test dive off Cape Cod. Something went wrong. It sank, all hands lost. One hundred twenty-nine crew members and civilians. Hell of a thing."

Gus lowered his shaking hands, let the coffee and the cruller fall to the ground. Michael said, "Went out on April 10, 1963. A Wednesday. Funny thing, huh? Every time I come by here and you're sitting here, looking at the shipyard, it's a Wednesday. What a coincidence, eh?"

"Sure," Gus said. "A coincidence."

"Never a Tuesday. Or Friday. Or Saturday. Only Wednesday. Why's that?"

No answer.

Michael pressed on. "Tell me. You ever see an osprey out there?"

Gus turned to him, tears in his eyes. "Who the hell are you, anyway?"

Michael took out a leather wallet with a badge and identification and held it up for Gus to look at. Gus looked at it, sighed, and sat back against the park bench. He seemed to age ten years from one heartbeat to another.

"How did you do it, Gus?" Michael asked. "How did you sink the *Thresher?*"

Michael waited, thinking he now knew this guy pretty well, and Gus didn't disappoint. He didn't argue, he didn't deny, he didn't try to get up and run away.

Gus just seemed to hold on to his cane tighter. "Wasn't meant to sink the damn thing. That wasn't the plan."

"What was the plan, then?"

Gus said, "You told me the code words, in the right sequence. You should have figured it out, you and the rest of the FBI."

Michael put his identification away. "You'd be surprised at what we don't know."

"You seem to know enough."

"No, not really," Michael said. "Biggest thing for me is, why didn't you bail out once I said 'kingfisher' that first day?"

Gus turned to him. "What? Where would I go? Shuffle off to my assisted living facility? Empty out my savings account and take a Greyhound to Florida? I didn't know who the hell you were . . . so I waited you out. Maybe you were a birdwatcher. Maybe not. I'm old enough now I don't really give a shit."

Michael knew his supervisor wanted him to wrap this up as quickly as possible, but he was patient. Maybe too patient, but he wanted to make sure he had this one settled before proceeding.

"So what can you tell me, Gus?" he said. "How did it start?"

"You go first," he said. "How the hell did you find out about me, after all these years?"

Michael laughed. "What, you haven't been watching the news last year? In case you didn't get the memo, the goddamn Evil Empire has collapsed. The Communist Party's practically outlawed, peace is breaking out, and the Soviet Union is no more."

"So?"

"So when you got a country that's collapsing, the army's being called out to harvest potatoes and their navy is sinking dockside, then everything's for sale. Everything! So we've had guys going over to Moscow and other places, passing out the Benjamins, getting files and dossiers. You wouldn't believe the old secrets that are being given up. We had special squads lined up to get answers to old puzzles . . . I put in for the JFK squad but I was assigned to naval matters. And we found your dossier . . . or parts of it. Got your real name, your job at the shipyard, and your assignment for the *Thresher.*"

Gus sighed. "I never got contacted after she sank. I thought I was in the clear. Thought they had forgotten me."

Michael said, "Then you don't know how they operated. The KGB had a seal they'd put on some of their more sensitive documents. *Dolzhny khranit'sya vechno.* Know what that means? It means 'to be kept forever.' That's how their minds worked. They thought they'd be victorious against us evil capitalists, so nothing would ever be burned or shredded. Their proud files would be kept forever."

Gus looked out at the channel, and Michael said, "But something was missing in your dossier, Gus. It's why you did it. Was it money? Were you that hard-pressed for money back in the 1960s? Was it gambling? Medical bills for a family member? Did the KGB promise you a ton of cash?"

"No, nothing like that. It wasn't for the money. Didn't get paid a dime."

"So why did you do it, Gus? Why did you betray your country? Sabotage a nuclear-powered submarine, the first in its class, a sabotage that would sink it and kill everyone on board?"

The old man sighed. "You wouldn't believe me."

"Try me. C'mon, let me in on it."

"Why?" he shot back. "To make it look good on your arrest report?"

Michael laughed. "Who said anything about arresting you?"

Gus turned, shocked. "Then why the hell are you here? What's going on?"

"Didn't you hear what I said earlier? We're getting old questions answered, puzzles figured out. I didn't say anything about arrests, now, did I?"

The old man slowly turned his head back. Michael said, "Look, the JFK squad. They're compartmentalized, so I don't know what they're learning. But suppose they did find something out. Like somebody in the KGB ordered the hit on JFK. Or if Oswald really was sent over as a patsy to cover up for whoever really did it. What, you think the president will hold a news conference and say nearly thirty years of official history and explanations were wrong? And by the way, let's start a new Cold War to get revenge for what the Reds did back in '63?"

There was a siren sounding out by the shipyard, which eventually drifted silent. "Same thing with you, Gus. We just want to know how it happened, why it happened, and fill in those gaps in the secret histories. And once those gaps are filled, I'll leave you here and I promise, you'll never be disturbed, ever again."

Gus seemed to ponder that for a few moments, and, his voice quiet, he said, "My dad."

"What about him?"

"It was his fault."

Michael was so glad he hadn't rushed things, because this was certainly a new bit of information. Gus sighed. "My dad. A gentle guy. Never once hit me. Was a deacon at our local Congregational church. Didn't really belong in the military at all. But they were calling everybody up back then, teenagers, fathers, guys with glasses or some medical conditions. A cousin of his, he said to my dad, Curt, 'Curt, join the navy. You'll sleep at night in a bunk, you won't be in a muddy trench, you'll have food three times a day, no cold rations, and no marching.' So he joined the navy."

Gus rotated his cane twice. "Since he was so smart and quiet, he was assigned to some military evaluation team. He and a bunch of others were sent to Hiroshima and Nagasaki, to check on what the places were like after the atomic bombs had been dropped a month earlier. It was horrifying, he told me later, all these blasted buildings, the trees burnt stumps, and wounded and burnt people still stumbling around."

"That's war," Mike said.

Gus shook his head. "No, Dad thought differently. It may have ended the war, but it also opened the door to something much more terrifying, something that could go beyond destroying cities to destroying whole peoples, whole countries, even the damn planet itself. He said every day and night there just sickened him. He said going across the Pacific, not once did he get seasick, but he was nauseous and threw up a lot when he was in Japan."

"That's why he didn't want you to join the military, do anything that had to do with defense."

"You got it. He only talked about it as he got older, and then, in 1962, he got lung cancer. Pretty funny, since he never smoked a cigarette or a cigar in his life. His doc told me privately that he probably kicked up a lot of radioactive dust when he was going through Nagasaki and Hiroshima, kept on breathing it in. By then I was married, to a nice girl called Sylvia, had two young boys, and I was working at the shipyard, making good money. My dad died that October. I was his only son, so I went through some of his things. That's when I found the movies."

"What kind of movies?"

"My dad, he told me that he and the others, they were forbidden to take photos at Hiroshima and Nagasaki unless it was part of their official work. But somehow Dad got a hold of an eight-millimeter movie camera, even used color film. I think he went out on his own and took these short little movies. No sound, of course, but you didn't need sound to figure out what was going on."

Michael let him sit quiet for a few moments, wind coming off the water flapping the loose ends of Gus's white zippered jacket. "What were the movies like?"

A heavy, drawn-out sigh, like the man next to him had just finished climbing an impossibly high peak. "I still dream about them, even though it's been thirty years. I found a projector and one night hung up a white bed sheet in the basement and played them. The city . . . you see those TV reports, about a tornado hitting some city out in the Midwest? Just piles of rubble and debris. That's what it was like. Except the rubble had burned . . . there were places along the sides of bridges or cement walls where the flash from the bomb had burned in shadows . . . and the last bit of the third film, it was the people. Still walking around in shock at what had happened to them. One plane, one bomb . . . there were these two little boys . . . about the age of my own little fellas . . . looking at the camera, looking at my dad . . . they were barefoot . . . the clothes they was wearing was filthy . . . and each was holding a little ball of rice. And you could tell they was brothers, they looked the same . . . even were hurt the same . . ."

The old man's voice dribbled off. Michael cleared his throat. "How were they injured?"

"The right side of their faces. Scabbed and crisscrossed with burns. Like they were walking down a street, going in the same direction, when the bomb hit and burned them. Oh, I know they were the Japs, the enemy, and lots said they deserved it for what they did at Pearl Harbor and Bataan. But when I saw it, in 1962, the war had been over a long time. All I saw was two kids, all I saw was my two boys, burned and barefoot in the wreckage of their city."

Michael saw the emotion in the man's face, the tears coming up in his eyes, and it came to him. "You said your father died in October 1962. That's when the Cuban missile crisis was, when we almost got into World War III with the Russians. You put the two together, didn't you?"

"Yeah," he said, his voice hoarse. "Had Sylvia take the two boys up to a hunting camp of ours, over in Maine, with food and supplies. She said it wasn't right to take 'em out of school, but I also said it wouldn't be right to have 'em vaporized or burned in Portsmouth, because, by God, we were a goddamn target for the Russians. That and the SAC base over in Newington. And a couple of times I went out drinking in some of the bars in Portsmouth, and got drunk and pissed off, and said that damn fool Kennedy was going to kill us all, burn us and flatten our cities, because he got kicked in the nuts at the Bay of Pigs fiasco in Cuba, and had to prove he was a real man to his bootlegger daddy."

"Somebody heard you, then."

Gus said, "Oh yeah. Somebody heard something, who passed it on to somebody else, and one day a guy came by and bought me some drinks. Said he was in the government, trying to work for peace, but he and the others were fighting against the hawks that were controlling JFK. He spun a good yarn, the bastard, and said if I was truly for peace, I could help things out. And I said, how? And he said, well, the *Thresher*'s being overhauled. If the overhaul took longer and longer, if problems cropped up, if things were delayed, that would help him and the others. Put things over budget. He and the others could help JFK rein in the Defense Department, help him work for peace with the Russians."

"And what did you say?"

"I told 'im to go to hell . . . but he was sly, he was wicked sly. Wouldn't take no for an answer. Showed me his ID, said he worked for the Department of Defense. Even took me to his office, just outside of the SAC base."

"All faked, wasn't it?"

"'Course it was," Gus said. "But I was too young, too dumb. He kept on going back to Hiroshima and Nagasaki. He said, Look, back then, the Japs were our mortal enemies. Now we're best buds. We're buying their radios and soon we'll be buying their televisions. That's what happens in wartime. Your enemies become your friends. Look at Germany and us. So who can say what we and the Russians will be like ten or twenty years down the line? But the big difference was the bomb. The next war would be fought with the bomb, and this guy — Chandler was his supposed name — said, You know what Einstein said about World War IV?"

Michael said, "Beats the hell out of me."

"Einstein said the fourth world war would be fought with sticks and stones. That's what he said." Another long sigh. "I watched those movies again, and I made up my mind. I told Chandler I'd help, but only to delay things. Not to hurt anybody. He gave me a tiny black box to smuggle in during my next work shift, which is what I did. A week later the *Thresher* went out on a shakedown cruise, never came back . . ."

Gus coughed. Tears were rolling down his cheeks. "What was worse . . . I mean, the whole thing was bad. All those poor sailors, all those poor families. But what made it worse was knowing there were seventeen civilians on board, guys from my own shipyard, guys from companies like Raytheon. You think, hey, the military, they sign up to put their lives on the line, that's the risk. But these civilian techs . . . I'm sure they thought it was a thrill, to go along on this test dive, to make sure things worked . . . and then they sure didn't. Can you imagine that, you're a civilian, having a blast on this top-secret sub, thinking about bragging to your coworkers when you got back, figuring out what you could tell your wife and kids . . . and then alarms. Navy crewmen running around. Shouting. The sub tilting its nose up, sinking by the stern . . . knowing in your bones that the water wasn't shallow enough to hit bottom . . . only knowing you were going to be dead within seconds . . ."

Michael said, "The naval inquiry said it appeared a pipe broke, releasing water that shorted out instrument panels, that led to the reactor shutdown . . . and they couldn't keep her up, until she went to crush depth . . ."

Gus said, "Sure it said that. What else would they say? Sabotage, at one of the most secure shipyards in the country? I went to that office building where Chandler was supposedly hanging out. Empty. It was all a front. I thought about killing myself, about giving myself up . . . and I thought about Sylvia and the boys. And I tried to forget it . . . tried really hard."

"But here you are, Gus. Every Wednesday."

Gus leaned forward on his cane. "I lost Sylvia two years ago. Both boys are married, doing fine. One in Oregon, the other in California. I'm here by myself, and every Wednesday I come here. Pray for them. Pay tribute to them. And ask forgiveness."

"For how much longer?"

Gus shrugged his shoulders. "Until the very end, I guess."

"Does anybody else know about you and . . . what happened?"

"God, not at all."

"Do you have any evidence from what happened back then?"

"Like what?" Gus shot back. "Pictures of me with that damn Russian? Written instructions on how to sabotage a submarine?"

Michael slowly nodded, and then Gus turned to him, eyes still watery, face flushed. "But what about me now, eh? You and the FBI, you know it all. What now?"

"What I promised," Michael said, taking out a little notepad and a ballpoint pen, which he clicked open. "That you'll never be bothered, ever again."

And with one practiced motion, he took the pen and jabbed it into the base of Gus's neck.

Gus looked stunned. He coughed, gurgled. A few words were whispered, the last one much quieter than the first.

Michael checked the old man's neck for a pulse.

Nothing.

He put the pen and notebook away and walked back to his rental car.

Two days later, after his supervisor held a debriefing, his boss shook his head and said, "Misha, you need to know your history better."

"How's that?"

"Two things," the stern man said. "First, you told the American that your grandfather had fought the Germans for four years. Maybe your grandfather did, but the first time Americans fought Germans was in North Africa in 1942. That would be three years, not four. And you said your grandfather was proud to fight fascism. That's crap. Americans fought the Krauts, the Germans, the Nazis. They weren't fighting fascism."

He just shrugged. "Got the job done, though, didn't I?"

"But you didn't have to be sloppy. We can't afford to be sloppy. The damn Americans are in a loving and forgiving mood. Ready to lend us billions so long as we play nice. If they find out some of our old secrets—like that damn attack submarine and how we sank it—they won't be in a loving and forgiving mood. Got it?"

He sighed. "Heard you twice the first time."

The supervisor walked past the office window, which offered a good view of the Kremlin's buildings and where the white-blue-red flag of the new Russian Federation flew.

"Misha, you're a romantic at heart. You probably write poetry in your spare time . . . but stay focused. Now. What did you leave out of your official report?"

"What makes you think I left anything out?"

"Previous experience from that Swedish schoolteacher who helped Olof Palme's assassin escape."

He crossed his legs, shook his head, still in disbelief. "The ship-yard worker, he managed to say something as he was dying."

"What did he say—'Go to hell, you bastard'?"

Another shake of the head. "No. He said thank you. That's what he said. Thank you. Like he was thanking me for ending his life, ending the guilt. Can you believe that?"

His supervisor sat down heavily in his chair. "When it comes to Americans, I can believe almost anything. They spend fifty years threatening to burn us off the map, and now they offer us loan credits and McDonald's. What can you say about a foe like that?"

"Makes you wonder who really won the Cold War."

His supervisor, a sharp-eyed man named Vladimir, said, "Who says it's over?"

JOHN M. FLOYD

# Molly's Plan

FROM *The Strand Magazine*

THE BANK STOOD at the west end of Palmetto Street, an old gray lady of a building in an old gray part of town. Only two things made it remarkable. First, it had a long porch with incongruous white columns, as if someone had started to build a plantation home, then, during the process, had forgotten how one looked. Second, it was located on a semicircle of buildings where a mile of featureless pavement with no side alleys and only one cross street came to a dead end.

This strange setting, a fireman's nightmare, had an unplanned but definite advantage: the bank had never been robbed. The street was narrow and often clogged with delivery trucks and double-parked cars. Its west end was a sort of commercial cul-de-sac containing the bank and two other buildings with iron fences between them, and its east end was home to one of the city's largest police stations. There was simply no good escape path for would-be bank thieves, and as a result they practiced their trade elsewhere. Smart rustlers tend to avoid box canyons.

Branch manager Donald Ramsey was fond of saying that no one on earth was brave enough or foolish enough to attempt to rob his bank.

He was mistaken.

At 12:57 P.M. on the first Thursday of December, Owen McKay pushed open the front door of the Palmetto branch and stepped into the lobby.

Owen was a short man, and thin as a hobo's wallet. His outfit consisted of a cheap overcoat, faded blue jeans, gloves, sneakers, a baseball cap, and sunglasses. If you passed him on the street, the word *odd* might come to mind; *threatening* would not.

He stopped just inside the entrance, took a checkbook from his pocket, and pretended to look at it as he studied his surroundings. It was just as Molly had said. Four tellers side by side behind a twenty-foot-long counter to his left, a glass-enclosed office, empty and silent in the back corner, and two platform officers—customer service reps, Molly had called them—at desks along the left wall. Only three things looked unusual. There were no customers (this was the slowest day of the week, and only a few minutes before midday closing time), no drive-up teller windows (there was no driveway to drive up), and no branch manager (he was attending his weekly Rotary Club luncheon). All these made Owen's task easier.

The door to the vault was closed. Molly had told him it was usually standing open. A minor glitch—it meant he would require the help of the assistant manager, who was acting as a teller today and was easy to identify since he was the only male in the room besides Owen. Cecil Woodthorpe looked like everyone's image of a low-level banker: balding, pudgy, and middle-aged, with round eyeglasses and round ears that stood straight out from his head like rearview mirrors.

Owen also located the closed-circuit surveillance camera, mounted near the top of the side wall. Perfect. It was aimed not at him but at the teller area and the center of the lobby. According to Molly, he'd be safe as long as he stayed near the front door.

*Ah, Molly.*

Owen had loved Molly Fremont from the moment he first saw her in his high school gym class. They'd dated throughout their senior year, and when he joined the army and she enrolled at a community college that fall, the separation seemed only to increase their feelings for each other. A year later, they married, and seven years after that—ten months ago—he took an assignment at an army recruiting center on Oakwood while she left her job modeling sports outfits to take a teller position at the Palmetto Street branch of a regional bank. It was a bad move on both their parts. Their combined salaries barely paid the rent. Three months ago, she had quit her teller job to try to get back into modeling. At twenty-six, she was blond and trim and still looked stunning in just about anything, but she didn't have an agent anymore, and that industry was struggling like all the others.

One night last month, as they sat in their apartment on the other side of town, picking at their TV dinners and watching CNN's coverage of a rash of bank robberies a thousand miles away, Molly had an idea.

For weeks afterward, she fiddled with schedules and escape routes and contingency plans, and the final result was Owen standing here now, inside the front door of the bank, with Molly's checkbook in his hand, surveying the lobby from the corner of his eye and feeling a slight but irritating urge to use the bathroom.

He drew in a long breath, exhaled slowly, removed the glove from his right hand, took a .22 pistol from his overcoat pocket, pointed and aimed, and shot the eye out of the surveillance camera.

The effect was almost comical. Six heads snapped up, every mouth hanging open in stunned disbelief.

"Back up," Owen shouted. "Back up two steps from your desks. NOW!"

They obeyed immediately. So far, so good, he thought. Molly had told him there was a silent-alarm button at each desk and teller station, but he felt sure no one had yet had time to press one. That was the reason he'd chosen not to use a silencer. A gunshot at close range creates a handy shock effect.

Well, that wasn't quite true. *He* hadn't chosen not to use a silencer. *Molly* had. Owen, truth be told, wasn't much of a planner. What he was good at was shooting things and hitting what he aimed at . . . and taking orders. In the military, he'd had a lot of experience at both. On this occasion, Molly's orders were clear. All he had to do was follow them.

He threw a quick glance out the door. Nobody in sight. He doubted anyone outside had heard anything — one of the advantages of a small-caliber weapon. Besides, Molly had assured him that the walls themselves were almost soundproof, especially with the thick glass in the door and the absence of windows.

Quickly, Owen threw the deadbolt, yanked down the door shade, and turned again to face the lobby. Behind the teller stations and the CSR desks, Cecil Woodthorpe and the five women were standing rock-still, their backs flat against the walls. One of the ladies had her hands up.

Owen moved to the middle of the lobby, concentrating on the tellers, remembering his wife's instructions. *Don't waste time having them empty their cash drawers — the big money's in the vault. And don't make them file out into the lobby and lie down on the floor.* Since robbers often order them to do that, Molly had said, there'd been some talk at the bank about installing an additional button near the gate leading out of the teller area. She wasn't sure if that had yet been done, but she didn't want to take any chances.

"You," Owen said to Woodthorpe. "Go to the end of the counter, climb over it, and come out here with me. And make it quick."

Woodthorpe didn't move. He seemed to be smirking.

"Now!" Owen said.

The bald man calmly shook his head. "No."

The second gunshot was as sudden and unexpected as the first. All the women let out little yelps. One of the CSRs folded to the floor in a faint. Cecil Woodthorpe hadn't moved at all, except for his eyes. They seemed to have grown so wide they might've popped from his head.

A neat hole about the size of a collar button had appeared in Woodthorpe's oversized right ear. Just behind him, a similar hole was visible in the sheetrock of the side wall. Bright blood trickled from his ear onto his white shirt.

"Let's go," Owen said, beckoning with the smoking gun barrel.

He didn't have to ask again. Within five seconds, a dazed Woodthorpe was over the counter and standing at rigid attention. One hand was clapped over his ear. All signs of arrogance had vanished.

"Take this," Owen said, pulling a folded black nylon duffel bag from its clasp inside his overcoat. "Unlock the vault and fill the bag to the top. Understand?"

The new, attitude-adjusted Cecil Woodthorpe snatched the bag, hurried over to the vault door, and started twirling dials. Even the women seemed to have undergone a change, Owen noticed. They were all visibly trembling and scarcely breathing, eyes pointed straight ahead. All of them now had their hands raised. A little blood is a fantastic incentive, Owen decided. His drill team at the base would probably have won top honors every week if his commander had taken the trouble to shoot a hole in someone's ear now and then.

The vault door swung open. With barely a pause, Woodthorpe dashed inside and started cramming cash into the duffel. Owen moved to a spot just outside the vault and watched him work. The clock on the wall said 1:02. Right on schedule.

"Big bills only," Owen called. Woodthorpe, working with great intensity, just nodded. His ear seemed to be bleeding less, a fact that didn't seem to lessen his newfound eagerness to please.

Owen wiped a sheen of sweat from his forehead and reviewed the steps of his plan, ticking them off in his mind.

His biggest worry was Donald Ramsey, the branch manager. Ramsey didn't usually return from his Rotary lunch until one-thirty or so, but nothing was certain. If he happened to be early, the locked and shaded door wouldn't surprise him, but if he used his key and encountered the deadbolt, he'd know what was up and would call in the cavalry. Besides, Molly hadn't wanted him here at all. "Ramsey could hurt us," she'd said to Owen one night. "He's tough, and he's smart too. While I worked there, he did a good job." Owen had replied, half seriously, "He had good help."

She had laughed at that, he remembered. God, how he loved hearing her laugh.

He wished she were here with him now.

Owen checked his watch. He'd been inside the bank almost eight minutes. Pretty much what they'd planned on. But he had to be careful not to let down his guard. The next few minutes might well determine whether he would spend his future on a tropical beach making love or in a federal prison making license plates.

"Hurry it up in there," Owen shouted, although he couldn't imagine anyone working any harder or faster than Woodthorpe was. The man was a bag-filling maniac.

At that moment something—Owen never knew what—made him turn and look at the platform area on the far side of the room, and what he saw made his heart leap into his throat. The CSR who had fainted hadn't fainted at all, or if she had, she'd regained consciousness; at this instant, she was propped on one trembling elbow and was stretching her other hand up toward her desktop.

"Get away from there," Owen roared.

Too late. Her right forefinger was pressed flat against a little red button on the side of her desktop. Owen fired without thinking, putting two bullets into the walnut edge of the desk and neatly cutting the wire that ran from there to the floor. But that was also too late. The alarm, he knew, had already sounded—not here in the bank lobby but in the police station down the street.

Mistake, he thought. Big mistake.

But not critical. Molly had anticipated something like this, the way she anticipated most everything. *Stick to the plan.*

He glanced around wildly, making sure nothing else was amiss. It wasn't. Cecil Woodthorpe, still emptying shelves like a madman, appeared to have ignored the whole incident. The black duffel looked almost full now, bulging at the sides. No one else had moved. The lady who had pressed the button sat on the floor beside her desk, hugging her elbows and staring at Owen with wide brown eyes. She looked amazed to still be alive.

Owen's mind was whirling.

He tried not to think about the alarm. From what Molly had remembered about the bank's emergency drills—and from a couple of false alarms she'd seen last summer—it would take the cops at least six minutes to get here. Plenty of time.

"Okay," he called to Woodthorpe. "That's enough. Get out here." The assistant manager hurried through the vault door, breathing hard, and handed over the bag. He couldn't seem to take his eyes off the pistol. He probably figured the only thing worse than getting shot would be getting shot twice. Owen opened the bag and examined the contents, burrowing his free hand several layers deep. The duffel was literally stuffed with packets of hundred-dollar bills.

Without another word, Owen zipped the bag shut and backed carefully across the lobby to the door. The room was as quiet as a tomb. He reached the door, raised one edge of the shade with his gun barrel, and peeked out.

The coast was relatively clear. Across the way, an elderly man with a straw hat and a cane was walking a ratty-looking poodle; just down the street to the left, a bread truck was parked underneath a sign that said LEO'S BAKERY; on the sidewalk near the truck, a little girl was skipping rope, her breath making white clouds in the chilly air; to the right, near the end of the cul-de-sac, an old gray-haired woman in a purple flowered dress and a ragged coat was pushing a shopping cart full of trash bags. She stopped occasionally to inspect the contents of the garbage cans at the curb and stuff anything interesting into one of her bags.

Owen turned and flicked his gaze over the lobby one last time, then put his ear to the door and listened a moment. No sirens. At least not yet.

*Now or never.* He released the deadbolt, heaved a deep breath, and opened the door.

Three minutes earlier, two city policemen had received the call, swerved onto Palmetto Street, and aimed their cruiser west toward the bank. Officer Scott was almost as short as Owen McKay, and considerably wider. The other—Mullen—was so tall and long-faced he'd acquired the nickname Muldoon, from a TV police comedy that had aired long before he was born.

"Don't forget," Mullen said, "to mention me to your sister."

Scott, who had no intention of letting Mullen get within a mile of his sister, gave him a dark look. "You're not her type."

"Why not let me be the judge of that?"

"Because I've seen your judgment in action," his partner said, watching the traffic. They were almost there. "Like right now. How about keeping your mind on the job?"

"This call, you mean?" Mullen snorted. "It's another false alarm, Scotty. You know nobody would rob that bank."

The words were barely out of his mouth when they both saw, fifty yards away, a short dude in a ball cap and tan overcoat running down the steps of the bank building. The guy was holding a black duffel bag in his gloved left hand and a pistol in his ungloved right. "That must be Nobody," Scott said, screeching to a stop in the middle of the street.

The suspect saw them and dodged left, putting the parked bread truck between him and the police cruiser. By the time the officers were out of their car and peeking past the truck with guns drawn, the guy was dashing across the cul-de-sac toward a wrought-iron fence between two buildings. *We've got him,* Scott thought. *There's no way out of here.*

At that point, three things happened at about the same time: the little girl wisely dropped her jump rope and ducked into the bakery, the old bag lady in the purple dress pushed her grocery cart into the cul-de-sac from across the street, and the dog walker with the straw hat—spotting the fleeing robber—abandoned his poodle, raised his cane, and marched toward the running man as if ready to do battle.

Both the cops and the gunman shouted to the old man to get the hell out of the way. He kept coming. The suspect, without slowing, fired a single shot; the old guy's hat was snatched off his head as if the wind had taken it, landed ten feet behind him, and rolled into the gutter.

Crouching beside the truck, Officers Scott and Mullen paused and looked at each other. The old man stopped too. He felt around on top of his head for a second or two and, apparently realizing what had happened and that he was unhurt, lost all interest in engaging the enemy. Simply put, he got the hell out of the way.

The bag lady, unfortunately, did not.

At the sound of the gunshot, the gray-haired woman stopped dead, looked around in confusion, and then started running, pushing her cart blindly along in front of her.

The fleeing robber almost missed her—and would have, if she hadn't run straight into his path. As things turned out, he slammed into the side of her shopping cart at top speed, tumbling it and her and himself onto the ground and spilling old shoes and magazines and clocks and black plastic garbage bags all over the pavement. Still holding the gun, the robber scrambled to his feet, glanced once at the cops, picked up the fallen duffel bag, and sprinted again toward the barred fence in the wall bordering the cul-de-sac.

"Freeze!" Officer Scott shouted, and fired into the air. The two cops couldn't fire at the suspect; the woman in the coat and dress was waddling around gathering her belongings and jamming them into bags, directly between them and the escaping robber. As they watched helplessly, the suspect reached a gate in the fence and stopped there, tugging in vain at the vertical wrought-iron bars. Behind him Scott shouted again, and fired another warning shot.

That seemed to make up the robber's mind. He shrugged out of his overcoat, dropped it, and—with stomach sucked in and head turned sideways—put his right leg between and through the bars, followed by his right arm, shoulder, head, and torso. The space between the bars couldn't have been more than eight inches, and it seemed impossible that he could make it. But he did. Within seconds he eased the rest of his body through to the other side.

Except for his left hand.

The hand holding the black duffel bag.

The bag, packed full, was far too big to fit. Even from a distance, the cops could see his face. First it registered surprise, then
frustration, then anger, then defeat. After another moment's hesitation, the suspect released his grip and let the bag fall to the sidewalk beside his overcoat. He stared sadly through the bars at it for
a second more, then turned and fled. Those in the street behind
him saw him dash down a gloomy alleyway, jog left, and disappear.

Scott and Mullen broke cover and ran past the old lady to the
gate. Mullen peered through it, then reached out to touch its bars,
gauging the distance between them. "That was one skinny dude,"
he said.

Scott picked up the dropped duffel bag, hefted it a couple of
times, and unzipped the top. He stared for a moment at the bills
stacked inside. "And almost a rich one."

"Be careful," Mullen said. "We need prints off of that."

"No need—he was wearing gloves. On the hand holding this, at
least." Scott looked up at the ten-foot gate in the fence and added,
"Wonder why he didn't throw the bag over first."

"Probably never thought of it. Things happened too fast. Besides, it looks heavy."

"It is."

A crowd was gathering. The old lady in the purple dress was
still scooping up her treasures, packing them into her trash bags
and the pockets of her coat and reloading her rickety cart. She
was limping a bit and mumbling a lot, but looked more angry
than hurt. Down the street, the mangy-looking poodle was walking
around trailing its leash and finally sat down in the gutter beside
the straw hat. Its owner, Scott thought, was probably still running.

Thunder rumbled somewhere in the distance. A misty rain began to fall.

Officer Scott tucked the duffel bag under his arm, picked up
the robber's discarded overcoat, and studied the faces in the
crowd. He knew the branch manager, Ramsey, but didn't see him
among the onlookers. It occurred to him that the bank folks might
still be holed up inside. Or locked up. "We better check out the
crime scene," he said.

Mullen grinned. "I'm ready. One of the tellers—Debbie something?—she's a knockout."

Scott sighed, rolled his eyes, and headed across the cul-de-sac toward the bank.

"Nothing against your sister," Mullen called.

The Palmetto branch probably hadn't seen this much activity since its grand opening, Debbie Martingale thought. Twenty minutes after the incident, detectives and reporters and bank executives from downtown were all over the place, although none of them seemed to be accomplishing much. What did seem to be happening was a lot of back-slapping and congratulating. After all, the bag containing the money had been recovered, nobody had been killed, and the only person injured—the arrogant Cecil Woodthorpe—had turned his battle wound into an opportunity to be more obnoxious than ever. Secretly, Debbie Martingale wished the robber had aimed about four inches to the right.

The most surprising thing was, no one seemed overly concerned that the robber had gotten away. And, though no one had asked her opinion, Debbie had a theory about that.

The first two policemen at the scene—one, she thought, resembled Francis Muldoon on the old *Car 54, Where Are You?* reruns—were saying that the suspect would probably be easy to locate because he'd been forced to flee on foot, and thus his getaway car was probably still parked somewhere up the street. When they found it, DMV records could produce a name, address, etc.

Debbie thought they were wrong. She had watched, through the glass of the front door, as the robber jogged down the bank's tall steps. She'd seen him shoot the hat off the old man's head, crash into the bag lady, and run straight toward that gate in the fence. And she was fairly convinced that any hesitation he'd shown before squeezing his body past those iron bars was play-acting, plain and simple. She thought he'd known very well beforehand that he could fit between those bars if he had to. No getaway car would be found, because he hadn't planned that kind of getaway. He had planned to walk out—either down the street or through the fence.

But her scenario, like the fence, had holes in it. What about the money? Had he forgotten to throw the bag over the gate first, or—in all the excitement—not had time to? And where exactly had he planned to walk, if he'd not been forced to exit through those bars? Those were big questions, big enough to keep her from voicing her theory. Besides, she had other things to think about at the moment. Cecil Woodthorpe, who was standing in a knot of reporters, had turned and was pointing at her. As she watched, he left the group and marched in her direction.

Great, she thought. *Now what?*

In a third-floor hotel room a quarter mile from the bank, a woman in a bathrobe and slippers stood at the room's only window, watching the drizzle and smoking a cigarette, rubbing the bruise on her hip. Her hair was still damp from the rain; she'd wrapped a white towel around it.

She idly studied the traffic in the street below. People walking and people driving, here and there and everywhere. How did the song go? *Like a circle in a spiral.* To her, all those people mattered not one whit. It didn't even matter that the room she was in, like most in this part of town, was old and seedy.

She heard a knock at the door. She tensed, cinched the bathrobe's belt a bit tighter, and crossed the room. The door had neither peephole nor chain, so she put one hand on the knob and one ear against the wood, listening. "Who's there?" she called.

Immediately she heard the quiet clicks of doors opening up and down the hallway. They wouldn't be opening far, she knew—just enough for a quick look. She'd checked into the room two days ago, knowing that most of the other guests in this hotel were either pushers or users, and thus generally uninterested in anyone who was not.

"Department of Human Services," a voice answered. "May I come in?"

Still listening, she heard those same doors clicking closed again. She could sense the sighs of relief, and the thoughts: *Welfare Department. Not the cops.*

The woman took a last draw on her cigarette, unlocked and opened the door, and limped back across the room to drop the butt into an empty Coke can. Behind her, Owen McKay stepped through the open door into the room. His baseball cap was gone, his sweatshirt was soaked, and one knee of his blue jeans was ripped from the same collision that had bruised her hip.

She turned to face him, and when she did, he raised his shirttail and drew a pistol from his belt. Then he took a roll of yellow masking tape from the pocket of his jeans.

"I assume you're not really from the DHS," she said.

"You assume correctly," he replied, smiling. "Come here."

Cecil Woodthorpe leaned forward and said, with solemn intensity, "We need a count."

He and Debbie Martingale were standing together in the back room. He had one hand cupped gingerly over his now-bandaged war injury; the other was holding the still-zippered black duffel bag that he had so energetically packed full of vault cash thirty minutes earlier.

"Why?" Debbie asked.

He hefted the bag onto the table between them. "The reporters need to know exactly how much money was involved in the robbery attempt. When you're done counting, report the total to Ramsey." Branch manager Donald Ramsey, who was currently being interviewed by one of the less-known reporters, had arrived at the bank moments ago looking like a kid who'd received a birthday balloon after the party was over.

*"Ramsey,"* Debbie said to herself. This morning it would've been "Mr. Ramsey." *New career plans, Cecil?*

When Woodthorpe turned to leave her to her task, she unzipped the heavy bag, looked inside, and, despite herself, murmured, "Whoa."

Woodthorpe stopped and turned. "What is it?"

"There must be a fortune here." She reached in to touch a bound packet of bills. "Packs and packs of tens, all the way to the top."

He frowned. "Good God, Martingale. No wonder your cash drawer doesn't always balance. You can't tell a ten from a hundred."

"What?"

"Hundreds," he said patiently. "The idiot told me he wanted big bills only. I filled the bag with hundreds."

Now Debbie was the one frowning. Carefully, she fanned one of the packets with her thumb, examining each bill. She *had* been wrong, she noticed. It wasn't a packet of tens. But it wasn't hundreds either. It was a packet of blank paper with one ten on top.

Barely breathing, she took out more bundles. They were all the same: one ten-dollar bill on top, ninety-nine rectangles of plain paper beneath it. Digging underneath the top packets, she made another discovery. The rest of the bag was filled with stacks of old newspapers.

She looked up into Woodthorpe's suddenly pale face.

"Which idiot are you referring to?" she said.

Owen McKay kept his eyes on the woman as he tore off a strip of masking tape and cut it with his teeth. His eyes flicked away only once, to sweep the room. The suitcases packed and ready in the corner, the shirt and trousers laid out neatly on the bed, the black duffel bag sitting open and empty on the table, along with dozens of bundles of bills, stacked in groups of ten bundles each. On the floor beside the table stood a shopping cart full of trash bags. One of the bags was outside the cart now and in the woman's hands; she was holding it open in front of him. He focused again on her face.

"The garbage collection business seems to be doing well," he said.

She shrugged. "I can't complain."

"How much?" he asked as he worked with the tape.

"Nine hundred sixty thousand. If I counted right." She was still looking at him, still holding the mouth of the trash bag open for him. The only sound in the room was the patter of cold rain on the window.

Finally Owen finished wrapping his pistol with masking tape. It was, he had read, the only way to be sure that metal detectors would never locate it. Then he dropped the gun and the roll of tape into the open bag, followed by his sunglasses and the false mustache he'd peeled from his upper lip. He could see that the bag already contained a gray wig, a purple flowered dress, a ragged black coat, and some kind of makeup kit.

She closed the trash bag, secured its top with a twist-tie, and set it aside. "What took you so long?"

"Cops were just down the street. I walked back down to Jefferson and came in from the other way." He nodded toward the window. "How about the van?"

"Loaded and ready."

Owen smiled as a thought occurred to him. "How many pillows did you have to use to fill out that dress?"

"Not as many as I'd thought I would," she said, and laughed. "Too many pizzas lately." She uncoiled the towel from around her hair and handed it to him. He used it to dry his rain-wet face, then turned his gaze again to the money on the table and the clothes she'd laid out for him on the bed.

"Old woman," he said, "you do good work."

Molly Fremont McKay laughed and ran her fingers through her blond hair. "I have good help," she said. And stepped forward, into his arms.

As they embraced, two thoughts were foremost in his mind. The first was that it was finally over. The plan had worked.

The other was how much he loved hearing her laugh.

# A Bottle of Scotch and a Sharp Buck Knife

FROM *Thuglit*

EVERYONE KNOWS THIS KID. He is dirty and dumb and sits in a corner, lonely, but not alone. His face has an involuntary twitch, and when he makes eye contact, his lids and cheeks squeeze his eyes shut. We call him Blinky. Blinky rolls with it, though, smiles big and toothy when kids shout his name across the schoolyard.

It is late fall and coat season in the eastern part of northern California. Our mothers stuff us into puffy jackets, force homespun beanies all the way over our eyes, both to be ditched as soon as we break onto the playground. We throw them over the scalloped tips of a chain-link fence; fill the yard with sounds of tetherball leather-slapping hammerfists, the creaking of chain links on the swing set, and children hollering.

Blinky is there too, his goofy smile breaking out occasionally, his frayed denim jacket always on, tugged down to his wrists.

I am king of the tetherball. I am strong and I know how to use the momentum to keep the ball turning my way. I ignore the pain when the tide turns and I have to use my palms to stop the ball.

"Come on, Blinky. Step up. Ready to challenge the king?"

But Blinky just shoves his hands in his coat. "Nah, Emmett. Um good. I'll get you next time."

"Okay."

Mr. Glass steps onto the blacktop, crosses the first hopscotch square, extends his arm.

"Who the fuck's he waving at?" Flynn says, safely away from any adult ears.

"Dare you to flip 'im the bird?"

"Yeah. Fuck you, Emmett. You just don't want no one to dethrone you."

"What'd be the difference if you were in detention?"

"Again. Fuck you."

But Blinky leaves our group, heads toward Mr. Glass, kicking orange and brown leaves. His hands never leaving his coat and his elbows crooked out like broken bird wings.

Our lives are run by the sound of school bells and our mothers' voices. A week takes forever to pass and a year is an eternity. Our walk home is an unknown distance, but we talk like it spans the galaxy.

We trudge home, backpacks full of books and nothing but swear words in our mouths. Our journey broken by a barbershop, a gas station, and endless fields of wheat-colored scrub grass. The gravel crunches under our feet and Flynn spins the pedals of his bike backward, making a metallic ratcheting noise.

Me, Maxine, Flynn, Brady, and Blinky. Blinky's headphones are on, the ones with the turquoise earpieces. I can hear New Kids on the Block blaring, Blinky's head bob missing "You Got It" by half a beat.

Brady pulls the headband and the turquoise foam tilts off his ear. "What's wrong with you? You trying to burn a hole in your ear?"

"Just thinking," he says, kind of dreamily. I hear the click of the Stop button and the headphones rest on his shoulders. Blinky stares off at something somewhere.

"It's okay. I like loud music too," Maxine says, pats his arm. To Brady, "Where'd you come up with 'burn a hole in your ear'?"

Brady shrugs. "It's what my mom says to my brother every time he puts his Walkman on. Is it not true?"

"Do you believe everything your mother tells you?" Flynn says. He's on his bike and pedals around us.

"Is it not true then? The ear-burning thing? What? Don't laugh."

But it just encourages us.

Blinky salutes us, turns off into Heaven's Acres trailer park.

After we're past, Flynn says, "Where do you think he got the Walkman? It's brand-new. And a Sony."

"Maybe his dad? His birthday's in a couple months," Maxine offers.

Over my shoulder I see Blinky's place. The rust on the window screen, the piece of aluminum that was bent in a storm two winters back, still flapping unchallenged in the breeze. "Yeah. Sure," I say, 'cause I like that she sees the best in folk, and 'cause I like her.

Flynn and Brady live on one of the newer residential streets. Built up just in time for the paper mill's new addition. Flynn offers to give Maxine a goodbye hug. He stops his bike, opens his arms wide.

"No. I know it's hard, but try not to be a weirdo."

Undeterred as ever. "All right. Your loss. It would have been rockin'."

Two more blocks, and Maxine's place is right on the corner. Her house is pristine—green cut lawn, edged, and the house crisply painted in blues and grays. Her dad steps onto the porch, raises his hand.

I wave back. The badge on his chest winks in the afternoon light. "Why does he come out like that? See you tomorrow."

"To greet me. 'Cause he wants to see me. Don't your parents do that?" She touches the cuff of my sleeve. Squeezes. "Bye, Emmett."

The pressure on my arm is all I can think about for the rest of the day.

My home is an old farmhouse an acre down a dirt driveway. It sits in the shade of a big oak caught in the grip of wisteria vine, slowly being strangled to death by lilac blossoms.

The house is empty, quiet in a sleepy kind of way. I microwave mac 'n' cheese, add a handful of Fritos as a topping from an opened bag on top the fridge. I adjust the rabbit ears slightly to NBC and watch an episode of *Highway to Heaven*. Michael Landon saves the day, his prose poignant and potent, wrapping the episode in a lesson learned.

I find Roxy—my mutt of unknown origin—lounging on the back porch. I touch her coarse black fur and she is immediately drawn to life and at my side, ready for adventure. We walk through waist-high flaxen grass, slip over a barbed-wire fence. The grazing cows pay us no heed, other than to follow us with their eyes, their mouths always moving, chewing.

Old Spooky is a charred oak tree at the edge of the property, blackened branches reaching for the sky. I wonder if it was struck with lightning or was caught in the path of a wildfire. The bark is black ash and feels like coal in my hand.

I hear the truck, my dad's Toyota, and stay in the field a while longer. Later there's the high buzz of my mom's hatchback and Roxy and I head in.

Dinner is baked chicken and mashed potatoes and store-bought biscuits. My father nurses a beer, only taking his eyes from the paper long enough to take another forkful of food. My mother tells us about the diner and the interesting customers passing through. She asks about my day and I shrug it off. "It's okay."

The paper crinkles in my father's grip. "That's good. I'd have bad news about life if sixth grade is kicking your ass."

"What about your day?" Mom asks him.

"You want me to talk about how hot it is in the mill?" His patented answer for anything concerning his work. The black-inked four-leaf clover on his forearm wrinkles as he shifts his grip. Then his eyes go back to the paper.

Silence follows us after that, and I do the dishes, stack it all to dry in the rack, watch the clouds slink over the sky for the night.

It's almost winter when Blinky pulls a Rubik's Cube out of his pocket. I see the side, the little squares a random assortment of colors. It makes me laugh. "Blink. Where'd you get that? Was that a recess game?"

"Nope. It's mine." He blinks both eyes at me in quick succession. He twists the little cube this way and then that. Then he raises the cube up, each side a solid color.

"No way."

"Holy shit," Flynn says. "You're a genius. But like . . . a retarded genius." Maxine smacks the back of Flynn's head and the sharp noise makes me laugh. "Ouch. Come on, man. You know exactly what I mean."

"Where'd you get that, Blinky?" Max asks.

Blinky does the thing with his eyes, but in a shy way. He shoves the perfect cube deep into his denim. It causes his cuff to ride up, reveals the blue and black just above his wrist. Blinky immediate pulls it back into place.

"You okay?"

"See ya tomorrow, Emmett," he says, and then tucks his chin to his chest, shuffles into Heaven's Acres.

"That was pretty amazing," Brady says. "I've had one since Christmas, and I can only ever get two sides to match."

"My dog got three sides done on mine," Flynn says.

"Oh . . . uh-huh, sure. Why don't you help him out?" Brady laughs at his own joke.

Flynn doesn't miss a beat. "Well, I don't want to ruin the challenge for him, Brady."

"Where's Blinky even getting this stuff? Last week he had a set of Micro Machines, a couple days ago he had a brand-new deck of Garbage Pail cards. He even had the new Acne Amy, didn't even know it was out yet."

"Think Blinky's stealing stuff?" I ask.

I get a round of laughs for the line.

"From where?"

"Closest Toys-R-Us is in Red Bluff."

Flynn gets a smile. "So Blinky gets up in the dead of night, sneaks out of the creaky-ass trailer, walks to Red Bluff, breaks into the mall, then Toys, then he picks a single item, then he resets all of the alarms and hitches a ride back here in time for breakfast."

"So how's he getting the stuff?" But only the wind answers.


After Sunday church, Flynn and I steal away, borrow his dad's tackle box and two of his poles. It's cold, but we pedal hard and our speed and youth keep us warm as we ride our ten-speeds to Battle Creek. A mile down Carter Street and we see a familiar faded and frayed denim jacket walking along.

We stopped beside him. "Blinky. What are you doing out here?"

"Oh. You know," he kind of sing-songs and stares at the tops of his shoes.

Flynn just gives me a shrug.

"We're going fishing, you wanna come?"

"What're you fishing for?"

"Fish," Flynn says.

Blinky laughs—to himself, I think. "Okay."

So I take both the poles and the tackle, and Blinky rides on Flynn's foot pegs. It takes a while, but we park the bikes on a dead log and trek down the pebble bank. We bait hooks with grubby worms and cast into the middle of a tired but clear stream.

We talk shit and our lines bob, fish swimming right past our lines. Flynn breaks out a single stolen cigarette and a paper book of matches. We pass the Camel back and forth, cough with every gasp of nicotine, and feel cool and adult as the creek burbles at our feet.

"Okay," Flynn says as he coughs out a cloud. "If you had to do it with a teacher. Which one?"

"Gross," I say.

"Come on. You know you've thought about it."

"They're too old."

"Not too old for boning. Bet their skin's all soft and papery."

"Fine. If you'll stop talking about this, Mrs. Fletcher."

"That is gross," he says. "You're disgusting."

"You started this."

"Emmett. No one made you say Mrs. Fletcher. You did that yourself." After a moment, "You gross bastard."

"Okay, ass. Who'd you do it with?"

Flynn just shakes his head. "I would never do that. It's gross. You know in Mrs. Fletcher's house, they're not granny panties, they're just panties."

I'm still fuming when Blinky chimes in. "Mr. Glass isn't too old. He doesn't even have gray hairs."

I look at Flynn and we laugh so hard the cigarette falls out and dies at the water's edge. "You're a fucking gem, Blinky," he says through the tears. "A fucking gem."

We bike back at dusk, the world turned soft and smooth by gray shadowed light.

Blinky hops off in front of Heaven's Acres. "That was a nice place. Thanks. Nicest place I ever been." He says it so earnestly, not even Flynn laughs.

I start walking Max to her classes. I don't know why. We just get to talking and I like that our steps match so easily. I like a lot of things about her. The late bell sounds for fourth period; the halls empty.

We stand alone and still outside her class. "You're gonna be late," she says, but with a smile.

"Totally worth it," I say, smiling with all my teeth.

A door opens behind us. Mr. Glass and Blinky come around the corner, whispering harshly to each other. Mr. Glass is stooped down, hand on Blinky's shoulder, his mouth close to Blinky's ear.

Mr. Glass straightens, pulls his hand away and squeezes it into a fist, then puts it behind his back. It's wrong somehow, intimate almost. I can't help but stare.

Then he's back on. "Emmett. Maxine. You're late for class."

Max ducks into her class.

Mr. Glass looks me right in the eye. "Something else, Emmett? Something else I can help you with?"

"Nope." To Blinky I say, "See you after school, Blink," but he doesn't even look up. My mind is weirdly full and my stomach hurts and my footsteps sound loud on the tile.

The feeling follows me as we walk home, and I spend the whole time looking at Blinky. He looks different or is different. Something. Maybe I've seen him wrong this whole time.

The others talk about class and Mrs. Charles's receding hairline and winter break. I make all the right noises in the right places but don't participate.

The others trail off and Max stops in front of her house, pushes loose strands of blond hair behind her ears. "Thanks for walking me to class. It's nice."

"Did you see Glass and Blinky today?"

"Yeah. I thought we were going to get detention."

"Did they seem weird to you?"

"I don't know. I guess." She bites her bottom lip. "Weird how?" The front door opens and her father steps out. She turns. "See you Monday."

Home is familiar and normal and I find a dead bantam chicken on the back porch, its black-and-white feathers mottled with drops of red now. "Shit."

I find Roxy shamed under the porch, feathers still sticking to her bloody maw. It takes a while, but I coax her out and clean her mouth with a garage rag. Then I bury the chicken in the back field, tap the fresh earth down with the shovel blade. I put everything back, clean the dirt and red from under my nails. And pretend like it didn't happen.

I'm on the floor watching TV when Mr. Speakman's car pulls into the drive. My dad greets him on the porch. After a few moments, my dad comes in. "Emmett. You seen any bantam chickens on the property?"

I try to make my face blank. "Nope."

"'Cause something got into Gary Speakman's coop, killed six of his hens. He's still missing three."

I just shrug, turn my head back to *Cheers*, but my hearing strains for the muffled sounds on the porch.

It is the dead of night when something yanks me by the hair and throws me to the floor. *"Oof,"* and the wind goes out of me. The bedroom light is snapped on and it seems bright and stark and pierces my bleary vision.

My father's imposing frame lords over me. "You're a dipshit." My father's voice is even and calm and his black clover tattoo is so dark it must drink the light.

"Yessir," I wheeze.

"Good. I'm glad we're starting off on the right tone. Get your boots and coat."

I dress as instructed and find him in the kitchen. There's a pot of coffee going and the earthy aroma permeates the air. The dead chicken sits on the kitchen table. A ring of dirt and feathers forms a brown halo. The back door is open and Roxy sits on the other side of the screen, tongue out, tail thumping. Her muzzle is brown with dirt and feathers.

My father pours himself a cup, takes a long sip. "So Roxy musta killed the Speakman chickens, felt bad about it, got my shovel, dug a perfectly round hole, buried said chicken, then put my shovel back with freshly turned soil on it. But later she decided she didn't feel that bad and wanted to eat the chicken anyway, so she dug it up and fought a coon for it on the back porch. You tracking, Emmett?"

"Yessir."

"I understand you don't want your dog to be in trouble. I don't know why you would lie to me. And you are horrible at it. I knew soon as I asked, saw your whole face go white."

"Yessir."

"Hey. Look at me. Whatever else you think of me, I'm not gonna punish your dog for being a dog. And I can't help you with any problems if I don't know about them. Okay?"

"Yeah. Okay."

"Good. Get a box of matches and some lighter fluid. We're gonna fix this one together."

So we put the dead bird, some paper, and two logs of oak into our burn barrel, then I squeeze a half-bottle of lighter fluid into the can. It all goes up in a *whoosh* of flame. The flames flicker, play light across my father's face. "See. Fire cleanses all. Should take care of it. If there's a skeleton left, you can break it up with my framing hammer. Not the finish hammer, though. The framing one."

"Okay."

"Emmett . . . what are the two things that can solve any problem?"

I say my dad's mantra. "A bottle of Scotch and a sharp Buck knife."

"Who's the Scotch for?"

"Me."

"Good. And the knife?"

"Whoever is the problem."

"That's right. Sometimes you need both." He messes my hair. "Got an early overtime shift at the mill. Enjoy your Saturday. Stay with the fire till it dies down." He tromps through the grass, never spilling a drop of coffee.

The fire is plenty hot, turns everything to ash.

After some sleep I wake and shower and feel hunger stirring me. Mom's in the kitchen, sipping steamy coffee, reading a romance novel at the table. "Long night?" she says.

"Yup."

"You okay?"

"Yeah."

"Want some waffles?"

"Please."

So I eat waffles smothered in butter and thick maple syrup, and watch Garfield and Bugs and later on the Ninja Turtles. And I feel better, normal.

Mom cleans the house around me and I mow the front lawn, around the oak and under the wisteria. I almost hit the paper but stop and overhand it onto the porch. When I'm done my shirt sticks to the sweat on my back, and I wipe my forehead across my sleeve.

Inside I hear soft crying in the kitchen. Mom's got the paper out, flat on the table. "You okay?" I say.

"Oh Emmett, I'm so sorry." She blinks puffy red eyes, motions to the paper, and I read the headline:

Body Discovered at Battle Creek
Alfie Johnson, 12, Presumed Suicide

"Who's Alfie Johnson?"

My mother looks at me, and then cries more. Eventually the tears subside and she says, "Your friend. Blinky. That's his real name."

"No. No way." My mind is too small and I can't make this idea fit. "I just saw him yesterday."

"I'm sorry, honey, but he's gone. It looks like he loaded all his pockets down with rocks and then walked to the middle of the creek and laid down." She starts crying again.

I could see Blinky in my mind's eye, lying at the bottom of the creek. For some reason, his eyes were open in my imaginings. "I need to talk to my friends. Can I go out?"

"I don't know."

"Come on, Mom. Brady and Flynn and Max were his friends too." She takes a deep breath. "Okay. But be careful."

The ten-speed can't go fast enough, but I just keep pushing the pedals harder. I ditch the bike in Max's driveway. The door opens after my rapid-fire frantic knocks. Max's dad answers, and whatever's on my face is enough. "She's in her room," he says softly.

Max is sobbing into her pillow, and it's the saddest thing I've ever heard. I knock on her doorframe and she sits up, her face puffy and red.

"Hey," I say, to say something.

Then she's up and her arms are around my neck. We sit on her bed and talk for a long time, about Blinky and the awfulness of the world and how he shouldn't have left us. Max cries and I squeeze her—like if I do it right, I can make it better. I must have been doing it wrong, though, cause I ended up crying too.

Monday comes and there's a school assembly. A guy in a tie shows up, tells us through a microphone that it's okay to feel how we're feeling, and that time will slowly make things normal again. He talks about tragedy and sense of loss, and strategies for dealing with them, but whatever empathy he's trying to convey is lost in the electronic sound system.

Off in the corner, by the basketball banners, I see Mr. Glass leaning on the wall, arms crossed and nodding sincerely to the speaker's words. My stomach does a somersault.

I find Flynn at his locker. "You bring it?"

"Yup." He hands me the Rubik's Cube and I tuck it in my bag. "Even got some B-nocs. You really think this is gonna work?"

"I think he's gonna be sheet-white when he sees it."

"What does that prove? You think Maxine's dad can put him in jail on a reaction?"

"I just wanna prove it to myself."

"Then what?"

"Then nothing. I just wanna know I'm right."

Flynn looks at me for a long moment. "Uh-huh. Sure."

Maxine plays distracter for us. "Just be charming," I tell her.

"What does that mean?"

Flynn laughs. "Just be yourself. Trust me."

We go to the teachers' lounge, and from the hall Maxine asks two teachers a question with an upward inflection. She smiles as they both step out. She walks down the hall and they just follow. Flynn and I walk in right behind them. Flynn pulls the blinds up all the way and cuts the cord so they can't be lowered. I find Glass's locker, put the cube right on top.

We walk right past the two teachers and I hear Max. "Thank you so much. You guys are great, really. I gotta get my books, but thanks for the explanation."

Smoker's Hill sits across the parking lot and right in front of the teachers' lounge window. Max catches up. "That was easy."

"What'd you ask them?"

"Just how the class schedule worked. Which classes were for which periods. They were really nice about it."

"It's October," Flynn says and we both laugh. We laugh even harder at Max's frown.

We wait on the hill, Flynn with his binoculars and me with the scope off my dad's Marlin. One of the high school smokers wanders over. "Girls' locker room is on the other side, fellas," he tells us, blowing smoke out the side of his mouth.

"Gross. Get out of here," Max says, and chases him away with a glare.

There's mass movement after the second-period bell sounds. We wait, eyes glued to the teachers' lounge. They file in, drinking coffee and carrying folders. Glass opens the locker and backs away. He shuts the door quickly and turns, looking at everyone in the room.

And he is sheet-white.

"Holy shit," Flynn says.

"What?" Max asks. "What'd he do?"

I think about what I'm going to do. I think about Max's smile, and how I never want to be out of its brightness. "Nothing," I say. "I thought he'd react to the cube, but he didn't. I musta been wrong about him." Then I drop the scope in my bag, ignore Flynn's frown, and go to class.

I wake early, meet my dad in the kitchen. It's still coal-dark outside and he's only on his first cup of coffee. "Morning," he says.

"You were something, right? Before you were a millwright?"

He frowns, folds the paper neatly, puts it aside. "I surely was."

"I have questions."

"I may have answers," he says. And he does, answering them all in his calm manner. It's strange, meeting him for the first time.

Armed with knowledge, I prep my stuff, and the following day we go to Blinky's funeral. It's the only time I've ever seen him in a suit. The boy in the box looks like a poor wax caricature of my friend. Max hugs me fiercely and Flynn tries to be tough. Brady cries more than Max.

People stand, say nice things, say all the right things, but none of it unties the knot in my stomach.

Glass even speaks, tears rolling down his cheeks. "Alfie was a beautiful boy. He had charms the world will never know, and it is a little darker here without him."

I don't cry, I just look at Glass and let the heat of my rage turn the tears to steam.

After, in the parking lot, Glass comes over. "I know he was your friend, but I feel like he was mine too." He hugs us each and I want to crush his spine. I feel slimy and poisonous as I pull away. His eyes are shiny and wet and full of sorrow and I want to put them out with my thumbs.

That night I lie in bed, unable to sleep, staring at my ceiling, waiting. At midnight I grab my special bag, pull on sweats, and walk my ten-speed to the end of the drive before I get on. Then I ride, a river of adrenaline carrying me along. I lean into the pedals, stomp my feet. There's the pressure of the bag on my back and the cool night air on my face and a sense of peace.

I'm sweating when I reach my destination. There is only stillness and starlight with me on the street. When I knock, I see the lights come on one by one as he moves through the house. Something moves behind the peephole. I grip the ax handle hard and the door opens for me.

"Emmett?" Glass says sleepily. "What . . ."

But I drive the ax handle into his stomach and he grunts in surprise, steps back, stoops to a knee. I bring the ax down on his back and side and shoulders and I go on until my arms are tired and Glass is a curled ball on the floor. I close the door, bind his hands and ankles with fishing line.

He cries the whole time. "Why?"

I move through the house, snapping on lights. There's three bedrooms—a master, an office, and one full of brand-new, in-the-box toys. Simon Says and He-Man action figures, and yo-yos. I almost vomit. There's a Polaroid on his nightstand.

Blinky. Smiling, holding a toy.

I toss the picture on the floor in front of Glass's withered form. "This is why."

"What? I didn't do anything to Alfie. I would never. I only wanted him to be happy." Glass clears his throat, puts some beef behind it. "If you let me go now, I won't say anything to the police, Emmett. You could go to jail . . . prison even."

I pick up the picture. "Hey, Mr. Glass, I have a question. Why do you have a picture of Blinky?"

He laughs. "Don't be jealous, Emmett. Alfie needed extra attention. He was a special boy."

"Why was this photo taken in this house?" I look around. "Right there on that wall."

Only silence answers me, and in the quiet it strikes me that I sound just like my father.

So I gag him, drag him out to his car, put my bike and bag in the trunk. His car is weird, but I've had plenty of practice driving on the farm. The strangest thing is driving on smooth roads. No one passes and nothing moves.

When we get to my home, I drive the last leg with the lights off and kind of coast in. The dome light comes on when I open his door and he screams behind the duct tape. I drag him out despite his struggle and drop him on the tarp, right next to the burn barrel. I think of Blinky, beneath the water, staring up. I hope there was blue sky for him to see. I don't know why.

"This can't be settled with Scotch," I tell him. The snick of the Buck knife opening is loud in the cloudless night.

Soon I have the burn barrel going nice and hot, a few logs of oak and a whole container of lighter fluid. When my dad comes out, coffee mug in hand, gray light has painted the horizon starless. He leans over the barrel. "Jesus." And after a moment, "You're definitely going to need the hammer. Remember—"

"I know. The framing hammer."

"Well, a finish hammer with dings on the face is no good," he says reasonably. "Now about that car out front . . ."

And he tells me that lesson.

STEVEN HEIGHTON

# Shared Room on Union

FROM *New England Review*

THEY WERE PARKED on Union, in front of her place, their knees locked in conference around the stick shift, Janna and Justin talking, necking a little, the windows just beginning to steam. We'd better stop, she said. I should go now. It was 1 A.M., a Thursday night turned Friday morning. Squads of drunken students were on the town. So far nobody had passed the car. *Hey, take it to a Travelodge, man!* Nights like this, that sort of thing could happen—one time a rigid hand had rammed the hood, another time someone had smacked the passenger window a foot from her ear, Justin's fingers in her hair stopping dead.

I won't miss this part, he told her.

I really should go, Jus.

Friday was her "nightmare day," a double shift at the upscale café/bistro where she was now manager. Thursday nights she insisted on sleeping at her own place, alone. Sleep wasn't really the issue, he sensed. This seemed to be a ritual of independence, and he knew she would maintain it strictly, having declared she would, until they moved in together in the new year. Other nights of the week they slept at his place or hers. They would be moving into a storm-worn but solid Victorian red-brick bungalow, three bedrooms, hardwood floors, in a druggy neighborhood now being colonized by bohemians and young professionals. Justin and Janna were somewhere on the chart between those categories. In March they planned to fly, tongues somewhat in cheeks, to Las Vegas to get married.

These separate Thursday nights, this symbolic vestige (as he saw

it), tore him up in a small way. He could never take in too much
of her. He had never been in this position before—the one who
loves harder and lives the risk of it. It hadn't been this way at first.
Then it was this way, then it wasn't, and now it was again, but more
so. This must be a good thing, he felt—this swaying of the balance of desire—and he would try to work out in his mind why it
was a good thing, and the words *reciprocal* and *mutuality* would pop
up from somewhere, and the idea of a "marital dance," which he
thought he had probably read somewhere, yes, definitely . . . and
his mind would start to drift, unable to concentrate on the matter
for so long, and he would simply want her body next to his again.
For now, no excess seemed possible.

Okay, he said. I know.

I'll see you tomorrow, Jus.

Great.

From somewhere the remote, tuneless roar of frat-boy singing.
Possibly the sound was approaching. One of the ironies of existence in this city of life-term welfare and psychiatric cases was that
the student "ghetto," on a weekend night, could be as dangerous
as any slum north of the Hub or in the wartime projects further
up. She tightened her eyes and peered through the misty windshield. She had a vertical crease between her brows and it would
deepen when she was tired. That one hard crease; otherwise her
face was unlined.

What's that?

The boys seemed to be receding, maybe turning south toward
the lake. Then another sound—the flat tooting ring of a cell
phone, as if right behind the car. Still in a loose embrace they
looked back over their shoulders. Someone was there, a shadow,
as if seen through frosted glass, standing by the right fender.

*What? Yeah, but I can't talk right now. Right, I'm just about to. What's
that? Yeah, I believe so.*

I'd better go, she said.

I'll walk you in.

It's okay, she said. She didn't move.

*Call you in five minutes,* the voice said in a clumsy, loud whisper.
*Me you, not you me, okay?* The shadow wasn't there by the fender.
There was a rapping on the driver's side window, a shape hulking.
Justin let in the clutch and pinched the ignition key but didn't
twist. With his free hand he buffed a sort of porthole in the steam

of the window. That middle-class aversion to being discourteous, even to a lurking silhouette at one in the morning.

*Open it,* the voice said roughly. No face visible in the porthole. Justin twisted the key.

*Don't!*

Jus, he's got something, stop!

*It's not a fake—open the fucking door.* The man clapped the muzzle to the glass. Behind the pistol a face appeared: pocked and moon-colored under the sodium streetlights, eyes wide and vacated. A too-small baseball cap, hair long behind the ears, dark handlebar mustache.

Justin got out slowly, numbly, and stood beside the car, his eyes at the level of that mustache. The man put the pistol to Justin's chest. An elongated, concave man. Some detached quarter of Justin's mind thought of an extra in a spaghetti western—one of the dirty, stubbly, expendable ones. A hoarfrost of dried spittle on the chin.

Janna was getting out on her side, he could hear her.

Just give him the keys, Justin.

There.

And your wallet, the man said. Nice key chain. And your bag, ma'am. Come on.

*Ma'am,* he'd said. Justin dug for his wallet. His fingers and body trembled as though hypothermic. The night wasn't cold—mild air was lofting up from Lake Ontario and Justin smelled the vast lake in the air, a stored summer's worth of heat. The pupils in the man's pale eyes were dilated with crystal meth, or coke, Justin guessed, aware again of that aloof internal observer—that scientist—though actually in his life he was impulsive to a fault, and in his work he progressed by instinctive leaps instead of careful, calibrated steps. He lacked focus but he had energy, good hunches. Two years past his PhD he was in medical research at the university, assisting in a five-year study of fetal alcohol syndrome. No shortage of study subjects in this city.

The pistol looked small to him, maybe a fake, but his knowledge of weapons was vague. He gave his wallet and then, with a sudden instinct to politeness, reached across the roof of the car and received from Janna her olive suede handbag—to pass it to the man. Janna's crease was sharply incised, her green eyes tight and stony. No plea for heroics there. She looked dazed and indignant, he didn't know at whom.

The man got into the car. Justin, as if waiting to be dismissed, stood by the door as it was pulled shut. Your door too, the man told Janna — the voice gone thinner, higher. She shoved it to, the door bouncing back open — the seatbelt buckle. Don't slam it that way! he yelled, a man now sustaining an affront to his property. She got the door closed. Frozen, Justin and Janna meshed glances over the roof. The man was trying to start the car. Something wrong there. On stiff, stiltlike legs, Justin edged around the back of the car toward Janna — Janna retreating, as if from him, though more likely toward the door of her building.

The man swung open the car door and shouted, What kind of vehicle *is* this, man?

It's a Volvo. Volvo 240.

I mean what's its *problem?* The man sprang out of the car and stood teetering by the door, across from them now, eyeing them with ice-clear but unfocused eyes. Possibly drunk as well. He flapped the pistol in the air as he talked in his breathy, squashed tenor. Justin glanced around. The streets were empty.

I don't know, Justin said. It's a standard. You don't drive standard?

His assumption that a townbilly would know how. Pickup trucks and so on. The man's brow clenched, as if at some inward struggle. Drunk too, yes.

Why didn't you *tell* me?

Well, Justin started. The word soaked up whatever breath he had.

I can't drive fucking stick!

Oh, Justin said, eyes on the wagging pistol. I'm sorry.

I hardly ever drive, the man said, quieter.

It's all right, Justin said.

Just leave the car, Janna said, monotone, a digital voice on a recording. You've got our stuff.

The man's cell phone went off like a siren.

Stay there, both of yous.

The pistol aimed vaguely at the space between Justin and Janna. Justin wanted to bridge that space and at the same time move as little as possible. The man had the cell phone to his ear. Janna was rigid. She was a quick, fidgety type—frozen that way she was not herself, a wax replica.

Right, but I said I'd call back. How's that? I don't know why the fuck the thing hasn't come, you call them back yourself! I know, I know, that's why I said don't use them anymore, didn't I? Yeah. That's right. And pineapple on just half this time, right? And don't call back. I might be longer, there's no car now. No, I don't want to now. I'll deal with it.

He jabbed the cell phone into his jacket. He looked to either side.

Into the trunk, both of yous.

What? Justin said.

The man flicked the key over the roof of the car. It slid off the near side and plinked down among the leaves and rotting oak mast along the curb.

Hurry up!

Just take our stuff, you don't need to—

Panicking, the man trained the gun on them over the roof of the car, straight-armed, both hands on the grip, a cop at a police car barricade. They might be dead in a second and the afterimage Justin would take with him into oblivion would be from prime-time television.

Open the trunk!

Okay.

I've got to fucking *walk* now.

Still thinking and seeing with weird clarity, Justin bent down for the key, and as he stood up he studied the key chain in his hand. A tiny plastic bust of Elvis. A gift from her, last Valentine's Day. He walked to the trunk and opened it. This was all right, though. There would be people passing, and the trunk was spacious, as trunks go. The guy wasn't taking them into an alley and shooting them. And though Justin had forgotten his cell phone tonight, he knew that she had hers, she always did, and maybe it wasn't in her handbag now, sometimes she kept it in her jacket.

I'm not getting in there, Janna said.

Get in, the man whispered.

No, I can't, please.

Janna, please.

Stop! she hissed in a private way, straight at Justin, her eyes round with rage.

The man's skinny arm pushed her toward the trunk and she gasped. Justin, flat-palmed, shoved at the caved chest under the denim jacket—did it without thinking. The man swung the gun and the butt cracked Justin in the side of the head. He saw a screen of blue light, heard a fizzing sound like static or a can of beer being opened, as he sat back into the trunk. A sick, cold feeling, nausea in the bones, plummeted down his spinal column to his toes. Beaten, he tucked up his dead legs and curled obediently into the trunk. She was making a faint blubbering sound as she climbed in after him. No, I won't, she said as she climbed in. I can't. Please.

Get in, Justin and the man said at the same time. Now just move your foot, the man told her, his voice still quiet but in a different way, maybe appeased, maybe appealing for a sort of understanding. The trunk was deep. It snapped closed, and after a second there was a sound of steps running off. The sound-space between the strides was long, and Justin had an image, projected on the sealed darkness around him, of the man loping away up Union, long arms dangling, almost simian, mouth slack and panting under the droopy mustache. In their politically civilized circle, people didn't use words like *trash* or *skag* about the distressed elements—addicts, parolees, the generationally poor—who made the city's north side seem more like a slum in Jackson, Mississippi, than part of the old limestone capital of Canada. But now in his anger the words occurred to him. And what he should have done. What he would be doing mentally for weeks to come, rewinding the scene, recutting it.

Fucking yokel. Cops will have him by tomorrow. Are you all right?

No. She expelled the word on a faint puff of breath. He was groping in the dark for her shoulder. He found her breast instead and she seemed to recoil, though there was no room for that. In the deeps of the trunk, furled on their sides in mirror image, they lay with knees pressed together, faces close. Her breaths, coming fast, were hot, coppery, sour.

Janna? He found her shoulder and she didn't move.

She said, Could air be running out already? I feel like it is.

No, no way. And the car's ten years old. We'll get some air in here.

I don't feel it.

Breathe slower, he said. Do you have your cell?

In my bag. It's gone. I didn't want to get in. Why did you just get in?

I didn't. You saw, he smacked me. I was out for a second. He would have shot us. My head is—

I can't be *in* here, Justin. I can't! You knew that too. That I'm claustrophobic.

He'd never seen her this way. Even in private she was always capable, composed, professional, as though feeling herself under constant scrutiny by some ethical mentor. Too much so, he sometimes felt. How she would never miss a day's workout in the spring and summer while training for her annual triathlon, whatever the weather or her, their, schedule. How she would talk of getting "more serious" about the sport next year, maybe doing more events. Even her recreation—nights out, parties, vacations—she undertook in this same carefully gauged manner, pacing herself. Only so much fun. Only this much frivolity and no more. As if she was afraid of some tipping point.

Till now he had not let on to himself how her discipline—what he had so long lacked and craved—was coming to irk him.

I've told you I'm claustrophobic. Why didn't you tell him?

He probably wouldn't have known the word. Christ, my head.

Of course he would know it.

And I didn't *know*. I mean, I thought you were just saying that before. Everyone says they're claustrophobic.

I don't even like when you pull the quilt over us!

To make love, he thought, in an exclusive cocoon, cut off from the world.

I'm sorry, Jan, he said. The throb in his head was worsening and something was gouging into his hip. Maybe a tool? Something useful here? Of course there were no tools in his trunk. He felt the thing, an old ballpoint pen. His mouth was parched.

And I really have to pee, she said.

That's just nerves, he said. His own guts were wheeling. But it calmed him somewhat, being the one in control like this, consoler and protector.

What's that?

A car revved past, humping out a heavy rap number, the octave dropping as it receded, as if in sadness or fatigue. Justin realized that he'd shouted—both of them had shouted for help, though at the last moment somehow he had tightened the syllable to *Hey*.

You forgot your cell, didn't you? she whispered.

There'll be more cars.

They can't *hear* us, Justin. You always forget your cell! I knew it.

People'll be going by.

Not till the morning. I feel like there isn't, there won't be enough air.

Don't worry, there will.

And I *really* have to go.

She'd never sounded so much like a small girl. Or girly woman. And sometimes he'd longed for that, for a small, unshielded part of her to give itself over to his chivalry and guardianship. But this went too far. Her stomach (invisible now, though as he jabbed the LED on his watch, 1:22 A.M., he got a subaquatic glimpse of her nestled form)—her stomach had a washboard look, tanned, much harder and stronger than his own. She was crying, whimpers mixed with convulsive little intakes of breath, like a child post-tantrum. Finding her hands, he held them close between their chests. The trunk seemed to be rocking slightly as if from the adrenaline thump of his pulse, their hearts together. Spending the night together after all. He'd studied murky ultrasound images of curled fetuses, and one time twins—soon to be FAS siblings—the victims of ignorant, careless, or despairing parents. Entombed in their toxic primordial sea, the two had seemed to be holding each other in a consoling embrace.

Help, help, she was calling weakly.

Another car passed, slower. Again he yelled involuntarily, aware of a swelling node of panic he was compressing under his heart.

Might have let us go if you said I was claustrophobic.

Okay, Janna. He tried to speak normally. A laryngeal whisper came out. Let me think.

I mean, he won't want us to die in here! He doesn't want to go to jail for that!

You're going to be fine, Jan.

How the fuck do *you* know if I'm going to be fine! You didn't even remember I'm claustrophobic!

Janna.

You're supposed to be a doctor!

I'm not a doctor, you know that. Jesus.

You're crushing my *hands*, Justin!

Her whine seemed to split his head. This felt like the most savage hangover—worse than the worst he had undergone in university and grad school, before he met Janna and set his life on a stabler footing. A student of booze, he had been. *My years of research,* he would quip.

Jesus, Janna, calm down.

Why is no one walking past? Most nights I lie there and it's, it's, it's like an endless parade of people walking past. Yahoos shouting.

Someone will. Don't worry. We'll call. I—

I just *knew* you wouldn't have your cell. How can we call if—

Shut up! I mean *call.*

This just fueled her. She wrung her hands free, panting in the tight space. No, no, you're *not* a doctor and it's lucky. You've got no—no—you can never just be *together,* can you, Justin? Why can't you just *arrange* yourself for once? It makes me crazy! You're always—

I'm telling you, enough.

Oh, your bedside manner.

Her breaths were shallow, the sour smell filling the trunk.

You're going to hyperventilate, Janna. That's the only way you won't get enough air, if you hyperventilate.

I can't help it! Get me out of here, Justin!

What are you doing?

Okay. Okay—I'm on my back, I'm pushing up with my feet. You do it too.

Janna—

Like a leg press. I'm strong. It's an old car.

Ten years isn't old for a Volvo. This came to him from somewhere—a line from some ad? His father, years ago? She was grunting, doing her press. At the fitness center she used a personal trainer and was toying with the idea of becoming one herself. After a few seconds he rolled onto his back and tried it. It was tight, the angle too acute.

Come on, she breathed out, please please please please. Come on, come on.

The only motion, a slight flexing of the metal. Then more of that suspensioned rocking, below. A passerby might think lovers were in the back seat of the car.

I hear something, he said. He wanted to cover her panting mouth with his hand. Listen.

Oh god, it's someone. Help! she said, but with no breath in it.

Hello! he yelled, amazed at how the enclosure, and somehow the darkness too, seemed to stifle the shout. He squirmed out of his leg-press crouch as steps approached. This move involved shoving contortions, Janna crying out weakly, cursing him as his knee met her shoulder, he guessed. He didn't care now. This was the point in the old film where the hero slaps the hysterical woman and she gets a hold of herself, grateful, admiring, won over.

He got his mouth up against the crack of the trunk, near where it latched. Hello! Help!

The footsteps stopped.

In here, please! We're in the car!

The trunk, Janna whispered.

We're in the trunk!

Footsteps approached. They sounded heavy, solid. A good thing.

Someone in there?

Yes.

Yes! Janna called with a sob. Her breathing was slower, though still shallow.

What, there's two of you?

Yes.

What are you doing in there? A faint slur yoked the words together. The voice was low and throaty—older. Actually, the voice sounded a bit tickled.

We got locked in. A guy robbed us.

No way! What a fucking drag! I never seen anything like this.

Please, Janna said.

Can you just open the trunk? Justin said. The key might be in the lock there. Or maybe on the ground somewhere.

Hmm. Not in the lock.

Or just call the police. My fiancée is claustrophobic.

Yeah? The wife, she's got that too, as a matter of—

Have you got a phone?

What's that? Oh yeah, at home. Let me see if I can see a key around here.

The key chain is of, uh . . . it's Elvis, his head.

Not having much luck here. The man started to whistle softly, in tune. *It's now or never.*

I think I'm going to pee, Janna whispered.

Hold on, Justin said. Would you please hurry up, mister?

186 STEVEN HEIGHTON

Hey, I'm doing my best for you, chief!

Maybe you should just go call the cops.

No! Janna said. The key has to be around here!

He might've just stole it, the man said. It's not on the road here.

I don't see why he would have, Justin said stubbornly, hoping the words into truth.

Why didn't he take the car? Nice car. I like these European cars.

He tried, Justin said, reaching to hold Janna's quivering shoulder. He couldn't drive standard.

A momentary silence, then the man burst out in snorty guffaws. Oh, now that's too good! he said finally. Guy couldn't drive standard!

I can't hold it, Janna said. Oh god.

It's all right, Justin whispered.

Oh *god,* get me *out* of here, *please!*

Go call the cops now, please! Justin yelled.

All right, yeah, I will so. I will now. But I was just wondering something first . . .

What?

Got nothing but shit for luck these days. Never the luck, the wife says. If you know what I'm saying. Could you give me a little retainer?

A what?

You know, a retainer. It's legal talk, like on TV. A fee. He paused and then said, firmly, Slip me out some money, whatever you got. I need it. Then I'll call the cops for you. There's a pay phone up the street.

I told you, we were just robbed!

Justin, wait.

We don't have a cent. How the fuck can you ask—

Justin!

Now hang on a minute, chief—I told you, I'm broke, and I'm going to be doing you a favor. I mean, I prefer not to have anything to *do* with cops if it's up to myself. This is going out on a limb for me. It's not like you can't afford it. Look at this car. This fucking *Volvo.*

But we—

It's okay, Janna said, I have something. Some money.

What? Justin said.

Just slip whatever you got through the crack, here by the latch. I can pry, maybe. I got some keys here.

My keys, Justin said. Janna, what are you —

I always keep a twenty separate, she said, in case.

Of course, Justin whispered.

What?

Of course you do, he told her, and now in his mind he saw, not with doting amusement but a stressed rage, Janna opening doors with her hooked pinkie, or with the same fey digit keying in her PIN at the automatic teller. This although, as he'd told her, on any given day a person encountered a dozen infectious agents which, if you were weakened enough, could make you ill or worse. But she was strong — probably all the more so for her years of working with the public at the bistro, where she also did the pinkie thing. Where it must be seen as a stylish or campy affectation, not another symptom of her leery, meticulous nature.

A twenty is good, the man said. Try to slip it through here.

No! Justin said. Put the money away, Janna. He was groping in the dark, flashing the LED, trying to find her hand.

Justin, for God's sake, I'm going to get us out of here. Someone has to.

Let her give me the money, asshole. The voice was closer now, the man kneeling, it seemed. I think you can slip it out here.

How do we know you'll even help us, Justin said, if we give you the money?

It's like you got a choice here? The voice was sneering. Justin inhaled sharply. Then the man added, *Duh!* — and this, for Justin, was the end. This soft little *duh*.

Fuck you! You can take our keys and your phone call and your — shove them up your ass, if you know how to find it. And I'm going to find you tomorrow! The cops are going to —

A horrific slamming beat down on them from above, then it seemed to emanate from all directions, a pummeling they felt inside, slower and steadier than their bolting hearts, as the man hammered the trunk with a fist or the flat of his hand. It could have been a street gang smashing the car with tire irons, bats. Justin rushed his hands to his ears and then to Janna's ears, to protect what was left of her nerves. Stop! he cried. The slamming went on, Janna making a steady high whine of pain or terror. He

tried pushing up on the trunk with his fist to absorb the vibra-
tions. He rammed his palm upward once, a feeble counterblow
the man nevertheless must have felt, because now he whacked the
metal harder and faster. Justin curled on the floor of the trunk,
clamping his palms over Janna's ears, then over his own, back and
forth. Though their bodies were jammed together at many points,
in this extremity he was fully alone. She must feel the same. He
guessed she must feel the same. The beating ended. Heavy footsteps stalked away. The night was quiet again. She was breathing
slower—small, sobby catches of breath coming at longer intervals.
There was a smell like ammonia and he thought he felt dampness
through the right knee of his jeans. He rested a hand on her hip.
She seemed to be drifting into a kind of sleep, or a gradual faint,
her nervous system, he guessed, no longer able to take the stress.

Now that he didn't have a conscious Janna to coax along, the
full weight of his own fear and anger returned. He sobbed for a
moment, no tears, eyelids clamped on dryness. Not for the first
time he wondered if they actually could suffocate in here. Maybe
that was why she'd lost consciousness. His breathing felt tight, but
that could just be fear. The trauma of his head blow. A car passed,
then another, and he made no effort to cry out.

After a time, soft footsteps approached.

Hello! Please help us! He tried to shout gently, afraid of ripping
Janna from her stupor.

Is someone in there? A soft tone, a sort of eunuch voice—the
vocal equivalent of the footsteps. Justin explained things, trying
to sound calm, murmuring through the crack through which he
felt, just once, a cool breath of air. The man listened with a few
faint sounds of encouragement. He seemed to be kneeling close
to Justin's mouth. The man was an orderly, he said, on his way to
the hospital to start his shift on the maternity ward. It was almost
5 A.M. He would flag down the first car he saw, he said, and get
somebody to phone the police, or he would find a pay phone, or
call from the hospital if all else failed. That would be ten minutes
from now. He would run. The odd, adenoidal voice trailed off,
and soft steps—rubber-soled, Justin guessed—jogged away into
the night.

Justin left his head against the cool of the metal, his mouth as
near as possible to the crack from which that one clean breath of
air had seemed to seep. As another draft reached him, tears surged

into his eyes with a wide-angle shot of great vaporless skies and fenceless emerald meadows . . . like a tourist still of the prairies, although he could *smell* the fields. There would be air enough, at least. The police would come soon.

Surely, whatever happened, they would live differently now.

A car was nearing slowly. It cruised past—perhaps the police, searching for the Volvo they had been told to look for. But the car didn't double back. Another passed, then another. The sparse traffic of early dawn. It was 5:12. In the eerie light of his watch, her sleeping face was peaceful except for the abiding crease between her eyes. Now she was nestled hard against him in the cold, his arm tight around her, his hand splayed wide on her back to cover as much of her as he could. Were old married couples ever buried in the same coffin? he wondered. He had never heard of it, but surely it happened. Or was there some law against it? Another half hour passed and the little predawn rush hour seemed to end. Why was he not mystified, or at least puzzled, by this latest lack of help, or by its slowness? He felt just numb. There was never any telling. Now and then other cars came from the west or from the east, but none slowed or stopped. Real help would come eventually, of course—the sidewalks would soon be thronged. Another hour or two. Three at most. What was another hour or two in a lifetime together?

· · ·

A curious thing he noticed in the years after: in company, he and Janna would often discuss that night, either collaborating to broach the story on some apt conversational cue (which they would both recognize without having to exchange a glance), or readily indulging a request from guests, or hosts, to hear it for the first time, or yet again. And even when passing through a troubled spell in their marriage, they would speak of each other's actions that night only in proud, approving ways. Janna with her granite will, he would say, had faced a claustrophobic's worst nightmare and remained the more rational of them throughout. *She'd probably have got us out of there hours earlier if I'd just listened.* Justin, she would insist, had been competent and forceful the way she had always wanted him to be and had kept her from totally "losing it." Justin would then profess chagrin at how he himself had lost it, screaming at their potential savior, though in fact he was partial to the memory of that recklessly manly tantrum—and on Janna's face, as she watched him replay the scene, a suspended half-smile would appear, a look of fond exasperation. But when the story was done and they left to drive home, or their guests did, a silence would slip between them—not a cold or embarrassed silence, but a pensive, accepting one—and they would say nothing more of that night or its latest rendition. When they were alone together, in fact, they never spoke a word of it.

JANETTE TURNER HOSPITAL

# Afterlife of a Stolen Child

FROM *The Georgia Review*

## *1. Darien*

CHANCE OF THUNDERSTORMS was the forecast and so naturally Simon offered to drive Melanie and the children into town. All the mothers in Bayside made a social thing out of daily shopping, nothing more than a status notch in my humble opinion — my viewpoint being that of observant neighbor — and the Goldbergs certainly cared about status in a conspicuously nonchalant way. The daily trip to the butcher, the baker, the greengrocer, and the beeswax-candle-maker signified leisure and summer and Long Island and the right sort of environmental angst. The mothers shopped for locally grown vegetables and free-range chickens and fresh-baked artisanal bread. The town market was a half mile inland from the Goldbergs' house, the dunes and the beach 200 yards the other way.

People walked or rode bikes. Bayside was so tranquil, the summer regulars said, that you could hear the cedar shakes swell when it rained, yet Simon could always imagine 101 forms of harm. He was a city boy, used to knowing what to watch for, what to listen for. Serenity made him nervous. I can vouch for this. I visited them once (before the event) in their unnecessarily large apartment on the Upper West Side. There I saw Simon almost at ease.

I visited their Manhattan place afterward too, just once, to offer condolence.

There was an edgy quality to that meeting, although it was before the police declared me a "person of interest."

It is perhaps relevant to explain that I was not the owner of the house next door in the Hamptons. For that momentous year I was subletting. I am a nomad by instinct, I come and go, and for that very reason I adapt quickly to each new address. I am a listener and I am a watcher and I'd wager that within a few weeks I know as much of everyone's business as the long-term residents know.

"You could get drenched," Simon said to Melanie on that day in Bayside, the day that would make headlines in the *News* and the *Post*.

"So?" she said.

Simon sighed and rolled his eyes at me. We were on opposite sides of the hedge between the summer houses, both spraying for powdery mildew and black sooty mold. "The long walk in wet clothes," he explained as to a child. "Pneumonia."

"Nonsense." Melanie was clipping the rain cover to the double stroller, each fastener snapping shut with a *thock*, a very satisfying and reassuring sound. "If it rains, I'll roll this down and they won't get a drop on them. See?" She demonstrated and Simon set down the sprayer and walked over to the shell-grit path. "And as for me," Melanie said, "I've always adored walking in the rain." She began humming that old Johnny Ray song and they both peered through the plastic windshield at their children. I couldn't see very well from beyond the hedge, so I'm guessing here. Six-month-old Jessica was fast asleep, her little soft-boned form slumped low in the canvas seat. Joshua, whose second birthday they had so recently celebrated, pawed at the plastic from inside.

"He doesn't like it," Simon said. "He feels trapped."

"Don't be silly." Melanie made a funny face at Joshua through the plastic and Josh laughed and perhaps he made a funny face back. "Anyway," she said, rolling the plastic back up and securing it in two canvas loops, "we probably won't even need it. You know how incredibly local these thunderstorms are. It can be raining on one side of the street and not on the other."

That, Simon thought—and I always knew what he was thinking; I zeroed in on him as a confider of secrets within twenty-four hours; I have a talent for picking victims—that was precisely what was so alarming: the sheer arbitrariness of harm, the way it could touch down like the flick of a whip, random, focused, and deadly. "I wish you'd let me drive you," he said. "If there's lightning, you're not to shelter under a tree."

Melanie laughed. "You want to keep us all in cotton wool." She stood on tiptoe to kiss him. "Poor Simon. Here we are giving you a whole morning to work on your book and you're going to waste it on worry."

"I'm spraying for mold," he said. "And then I'm mowing. You'll be back before I get to my book."

"We'll go to Joan's for lunch. We'll spend the afternoon there. You can have the whole day."

I watched Simon bend over to kiss the sleeping Jessica on her forehead. When he leaned toward Joshua, his son squirmed and giggled and pulled his T-shirt up over his face.

"You haven't shaved," Melanie said. "You're scratching him."

Simon tugged at the soft cotton shirt, pulled it back from over his son's eyes. "I see you," he said, and his son squealed with hyperexcited glee.

"Say bye to Daddy," Melanie said.

Simon waved. He watched till they turned the corner before he came back to the hedge.

"I know you think I'm neurotic," he said, "but they seem intolerably fragile to me."

I went on spraying. It wasn't the kind of statement that required a response.

Simon steamrollered on in his melancholy academic way, as he usually did and does. "Harm seems so arbitrary. So . . . malevolent. It terrifies me."

"I've got a dental appointment in town," I said, as much to shut off the spigot of his pathetic and privileged anxiety as anything else. "Later this morning. I'll keep an eye on them for you."


## 2. Melanie

"I don't like that man," she tells the children. "He watches us. We're going to have to get shades on our windows." She wipes a thin film of salt from her cheek. The sea breeze, deceptively cool on the beach, turns sticky on the landward side of the dunes. Her sweat is dripping into her eyes. It stings. "Maybe we should have taken your daddy's offer, Joshua," she says. "It's so *hot*. I hope it *does* pour. Wouldn't that be lovely, punkin? I just adore walking in the rain."

The walk seems twice as long on sultry days.

"We'll go to Joan's house after the shopping," she says. "We can all cool off in her pool."

Melanie has an easy elegance about her. She wears white linen pants and a racer-back navy top. Her sandals are Birkenstocks. She swims and jogs and plays tennis. She has worked on getting her waistline back since Jessica's birth, but the truth is, already she is toying with the idea of getting pregnant again. There is something so gorgeously languid about that fecund state. It must be the earth-mother syndrome.

She brakes the stroller and leans into the front to fan the children. "Poor babies," she says. "I thought there'd be more of a breeze. As soon as we've got the vegetables and the bread, we'll get ice creams, Josh, okay?" She bends low and covers their silky little cheeks with kisses. "You're so delicious, I could eat you," she tells them. "Even your sweat smells good."

Jessica sleeps on, oblivious. Joshua is drowsy but smiles at the kiss and the thought of ice cream.

"Chocolate," he murmurs.

"Okay. Chocolate. It'll be cooler when we get into town."

There are spreading trees that make a green tunnel of Main Street. Outside Ryan's Bakery, two strollers are parked in the shade. Melanie maneuvers to the head of the line so that Josh will have a clear view of the dogs. They are tethered by their leashes to the bike rack and they rub noses and sniff behind each other's tails. She sets the stroller hard up against the plate-glass window, directly under the oversized decal of the *R,* and pushes the brake lever with her foot.

Of course she has never stopped replaying that moment. She has never stopped wishing, she has never stopped asking *What if?*

What if she had nestled her little ones behind the Nelson toddler, at the back of the line, beneath the final gold-leafed *Y* of Ryan's Bakery, would the world have tilted a different way on its axis? Would the climate have changed? Would a different child have been taken?

"Mommy will just be inside a few minutes, Josh. If Jessica wakes, you can sing her the lollipop song, okay?"

"Okay."

"Then chocolate ice cream," Melanie promises. "After we get the baguettes."

## 3. Joshua

There are three dogs and one of them is lifting its leg. Joshua watches the little river of sunlight spurt out and twist like string, then fall into a black puddle beside the curb. He tries to see exactly where the yellow turns dark. The puddle smells like Jessica when her diaper is wet.

Right now, Jessica has the sleep smell and the baby-powder smell. There is a little bubble of drool on her chin. Joshua leans over to wipe it but his leather harness won't let him go. He fiddles with the buckle but it ignores him. He tugs. He manages almost to kiss Jessica on her cheek.

There is always plenty of kissing, Daddy kissing him, Mommy kissing him, everyone kissing everyone all over.

And then something arrives, a swooping thing like a black crow coming at him, the jab of its vicious beak. Abrupt change of weather, end of kissing time, but Josh can't understand. There is a van that pulls up, dogs yapping, a knife, he knows knife, he sees a knife and his harness lets go. It's like a fast fierce wind that flattens, that blows everything flat (the bakery smell, Jessica, the dogs), *rush, crash, his body seizing up, he can't breathe* . . . He can't even figure out who it is, but it's someone he seems to know and there's another smell he seems to recognize, not Jessica, not the dogs. Is it the man who watches?

*Your mommy said* . . .

This isn't right. It doesn't feel right. But he seems to know that face, he knows that smell.

*You have to come with me, your mommy said* . . .

"*Mommy!*" he screams in sudden terror, but a hand is clamped over his mouth.

And then the thunderstorm? The black sky? Black clouds over his head?

Joshua is always trying to remember what he remembers. There are opaque things that swirl around and around in fog like clothes in a washing machine. They are there, he knows they are there, but he can never quite see them clear. He catches glimpses of what he once knew, fragments that tantalize. He remembers Jessica. He remembers baby smell and sleep smell. He remembers car-seat smell and that other smell. He remembers Mama and chocolate. He remembers the dogs.


## 4. Melanie

The smell of a bakery is like the smell of babies, it's like pregnancy, that yeasty rising. Tonight she is going to talk Simon into letting Joshua sleep in their bed, all four of them curled up together like fresh croissants. Simon thinks Joshua is too old for this, that it isn't healthy for him, that it will turn him into something squishy and damageable. And yet when Joshua is in his own room, in his own bed with side rails, it is Simon who wakes every hour and gets up to check. Just in case.

"You're the one who's babying him," Melanie accuses. "You're drip-feeding him a steady diet of anxiety. You're conditioning him to be a nervous wreck."

"No I'm not."

"Yes you are. It's in your genes, I guess."

"Maybe it *is* in my genes, it probably is, which is exactly why I want to toughen him up. That doesn't mean that *I* can stop worrying, but he doesn't have to know I keep watching. He's learning independence when he sleeps in his own room."

"When we're all cuddled up together in the same bed, he's learning safety and happiness. What's wrong with that?"

"It's tempting fate. It's creating an illusion. It makes me nervous."

"You know," Melanie says, "most of the time things turn out well."

"You're wrong. Most of the time things do *not* turn out well, and when they do, it's dangerous to expect that to last."

Of course it is precisely Simon's obsessive and protective anxiety that Melanie finds so attractive, so much more appealing than the thuggish frat boys she dated in college. She loves his gentleness, his passion for music (classical and jazz), his scholarly mind, the sheer and vast volume of his knowledge about everything. She loves his city-boy's awed attention to their pocket-handkerchief garden on Long Island and to the plants on their balcony in Manhattan. Simon is the grandson of immigrants, blue-collar urban.

His grandfather was a cellist in the old country, a deliveryman on the Lower East Side.

Melanie comes from rural midwestern stock and has the small-town top-of-the-heap gift of self-confidence, possibly a little misplaced, but boundless. She won a scholarship to an Ivy League college and that is where she and Simon met. They despised the preppies, of course, but picked up the bohemian variation, which is why they have a summer place on Long Island and why Melanie is buying baguettes.

The bakery is such a small and intimate place that the five customers constitute a crowd.

"Doesn't this place smell heavenly?" someone asks, and the general response is a murmuring so low and contented and prolonged that it sounds like a Bach chorale.

"Ryan, what do you call these little flaky-pastry things that look like butterfly wings?"

"Those are palmiers," Ryan says, offering a sample. "Take, take," he urges. "Irresistible, don't you agree?"

The women love to ask questions and Ryan loves to expound: on whole grains, on sunflower seeds, on the requisite buttery nothingness of French croissants, on madeleines, on baguettes. Melanie browses the racks of loaves. She and Jenny Nelson exchange chitchat while they wait, and then it is Jenny's turn. Jenny watches as Ryan wraps her fragrant loaves in a tissue scarf, then places them in brown paper bags. "Got to run," she says. "Listen! That's Jason's mommy-siren. It'll get louder by the second and we'll see the stroller rocking like a ship in a storm if I'm not quick."

Both Melanie and Jenny look out through Ryan's streak-free plate-glass window. In the spaces between the large gold-leaf letters of his decal, the strollers — or, more accurately, the canvas hoods — are dark blocky shapes that look like garbage bins or thunderstorm clouds. There are now only two toddler conveyances. The wide gap in the middle corresponds to the gap between the *Ryan's* and the *Bakery* peel-off words.

"I'm parked in front of you," Melanie says. "Under the *R*."

"Yours are enviably quiet. How do you manage that?"

"Pure luck of the draw, and liable to change any second."

"Patience is definitely not a Jason thing," Jenny says. "Oh jeez, will you listen to that wail?"

"Believe me, mine can outdo him. They're capable of sounds that would leave police sirens for dead."

"You're just saying that to make me feel better. I've never once heard Josh throw a tantrum."

"Oh believe me, he can and he does. In fact, the quiet's unnatural. But Jessica's asleep and Joshua's watching the dogs. He loves puppies."

"Bye," Jenny pushes open the door with one shoulder.

"Bye. See you later at Joan's?"

"Not sure. I've got my in-laws visiting this week."

"All the more reason."

They both laugh.

Melanie buys a baguette, half-a-dozen croissants, four palmiers, and two little strawberry tarts. She pays. Someone is coming in as she leaves, there's a delivery van pulling out from the curb, and Jenny is already halfway down the block. "Hey, Josh!" Melanie calls as she stuffs her purchases into the shopping-bag pocket behind Joshua's back, "I'm all done. Aren't those puppies cute?"

"Josh, are you asleep . . . ?

"Joshua . . . ?

"Josh . . . ?"

Very suddenly, the earth lurches out of orbit, the sidewalk tilts, and Melanie is sliding at a sickening heart-stopping speed toward a free-fall into the void.


## 5. Darien

I was the one who had to break the news to Simon. It wasn't planned. I happened to drive by the bakery very shortly after the event (in my car, not in the delivery van), when the police were everywhere, sending out radio alerts. I couldn't see Melanie.

"What happened?" I asked a policeman.

"A child has been stolen," he said. "A two-year-old."

"*Stolen?* That's a strong word. Not just gone missing, the way kids do?"

"A two-year-old can't unbuckle himself from a safety harness. It's been cut."

"Oh my God! And the baby girl?"

I knew instantly that that was a mistake but not a fatal one. The policeman narrowed his eyes and paid the kind of attention that has the effect of making me unnaturally calm and alert. I guess the challenge of getting out of dead ends (so to speak) turns me on.

"What baby girl?" he asked.

"I don't know," I said. "I thought I heard someone say something about a double stroller and a baby girl."

"She wasn't taken," the policeman said.

Later, I don't doubt he was the one who had me declared "a person of interest" after the abandoned van was found, but before that I drove back to the house to tell Simon. I was as gentle and compassionate and consoling as only a kind neighbor can be. "I'm afraid I've got some bad news," I said when he opened the door.

## 6. Simon

The second Simon opens the door he knows. All his life he has been bracing himself for this, looking back over his shoulder, waiting for when the moment would arrive.

And he has always known it would. He grew up with grandparents who turned pale and held still whenever they heard a knock on the door, with parents who passed the anxiety on.

"What?" he asks, or tries to ask, though his breath makes no sound at all. "What? Tell me." He grabs a handful of Darien's shirt as though grasping the nettle. He is spooked by Darien's eyes.

Nothing, Simon thinks, will ever be more terrible than this moment.

As things turns out, he is wrong.

He does not yet know how wrong he is.

## 7. Ryan the Baker

The police want to know what Ryan saw, but Ryan saw nothing that could help. His morning passed, as all mornings pass, inside the cozy cocoon of ovens and bread and pastries and the pleasing *ding* of the till.

"You didn't pay attention to the strollers?" the police want to know.

"There are always strollers," Ryan says. "They are always parked outside. The store is too small for them, and the mothers can't push them over—"

"So you were not aware of how many strollers were parked outside at the time? You didn't see—?"

"I see them, I suppose. I don't pay attention. They come and go, but in the season there are always strollers. One, two, three. I can't recall."

"You didn't see anyone remove a child?"

"I'm too busy. The only time I see outside my window is when no customers come."

"What time of day would that be?"

"In the season, almost never. In winter, most of the day."

"And why exactly did you call 911?"

"Because Mrs. Goldberg, who'd just bought a baguette and croissants and four palmiers and two strawberry tarts, came running back into my store holding her baby girl so close that my first thought was, That baby will suffocate. She's killing it."

"What did she say?"

"She was sobbing and incoherent and then she fainted. My floors are heart pine and clean, but she fell on the baby."

"Was anyone else in the store?"

"Yes, another client had just come in. Mrs. Goldberg's baby was wailing, high-decibel, the way babies do, and the woman—the new customer—reached for the baby but changed her mind. So I put a loaf of whole-grain under Mrs. Goldberg's head—it was the only pillow I had to hand—and I got the baby out from under and cuddled it—I'm a grandfather, you know—and then I called 911."

"Why do you think your other customer changed her mind?"

"What?"

"Why do you think one of your customers changed her mind about taking the baby?"

"Oh. That's not something . . . You know, reasoning was not at the forefront of my mind. It's just something I happened to notice, the way she reached and then pulled away; or maybe it was something I didn't notice till afterward, playing it back. Felt out of her depth, that customer, I would say. And so did I, to tell you the truth. But the reason could have been—if anyone was acting on reason, which isn't something I'd swear to—it could have been Mrs. Goldberg's face."

"Meaning?"

"She looked deranged."

"Yet when the ambulance came," the police say, "you were still holding the baby. Why?"

Ryan puckers his brow, pondering this. "The baby was crying. What else could I do? And Mrs. Goldberg was . . . I think she was in a state of shock."

"She was unconscious?"

"She seemed to be. I think she was."

"For how long?"

"I really don't know. Probably minutes, just minutes. I was pretty strung out myself. I really wasn't conscious of time. And then the ambulance came and took them both."

"Do you have any other information that might help us?"

"She always called the children her 'punkins.' She doted on them. She was a lovely gracious lady, one of my regulars. She came in every day in the season and always bought fresh-baked, which tells you a lot."

"Any further comments?"

"I can't get my mind around how fast . . . I mean, ten minutes at most, she wasn't in the store more than that. She came in with that kind of glow she has—you couldn't help noticing it, she was so *alive,* such a happy and courteous . . ."

"And then?"

"And then deranged. It gives me bad dreams, the way she looked. I haven't slept well since it happened."

"We have to ask you this," the police say. "Is there any chance Mrs. Goldberg might have planned this? Faked this?"

Ryan stares at them. Perhaps a whole minute passes before he can speak. "I think," he says, "that if you weren't cops, I'd land a punch on your jaws that you wouldn't forget in a hurry. But I know you're just doing your job. And I suppose you must see a lot of slime."

"We understand how you feel," one cop says. "But can you answer the question for the record?"

"There is no way in a million years," Ryan tells them, "that Mrs. Goldberg could have or would have faked this."

## 8. Melanie

This is like the worst hangover ever. This is like wishing you were dead. This is like having your lungs full of nettles or prickles or barbed wire. No. Worse than that. It is as though your lungs are crammed with broken glass. Breathing hurts.

Then again, it is like being smashed in the surf by a humongous wave, a rogue wave, knowing you are going under but desperately fighting the rip, the tearing, the gaping hole where your babies have been swept from your arms.

Please, please, please, you beseech the ocean, I will willingly drown if that will save them.

Where is she . . . ? And where is . . . ?

What is this bleeding gaping hole?

Melanie's heart is yammering in vibrato, her eyes flicker from the ceiling to the tube taped to her forearm to the nurse.

Then she remembers but hopes she is just waking, that she is recalling fragments of a horrible dream.

She is afraid to ask anything at all.

"Your baby is here," the nurse says gently. She lays Jessica on Melanie's chest, but this agitates Melanie.

"Take her, you take her, she's not safe with me. Where's Simon?"

The nurse places Jessica in a crib and attends to the drip, professional, calm, increasing the amount of sedation. "Your husband is on his way," she says.

"And my son?" She makes herself say it. "My son, Joshua?"

"Everyone is looking for Joshua. They will find him."


## 9. I, Joshua

Sometimes I configure the script this way, sometimes another, but I am ever more certain that I have the right cast, the right play. I call my script "Afterlife of a Stolen Child" and I am the expert on this case, though I have no interest whatsoever in publication, in HBO, in Oprah, or in anything but a missing segment of myself. All my research was done online via websites for missing children. I combed thousands of search engines and these were my constant keywords: male child, blond, blue eyes, same birth month and birth year as mine, case never resolved.

This is the one.

I've read everything. I know everything that has ever been put on the record (in police files, in interviews, in print) about the father, the mother, the baby sister, the baker, the baker's regulars, the creepy neighbor who was "a person of interest."

I have photographs. I've had them blown up and framed and hung on the walls of my room. This is Simon, this is Melanie, this is Jessica. The resemblance, I think you will agree, is striking. I've tracked the players through cyber detective and paid by credit card online.

Now I know in advance what you are thinking. What's the payoff here? Who is the con man? What exactly does he get out of this? And I'll be the first to confess that I myself have aliases, several in fact, and yes, there's a certain kind of payoff for me.

I cover my tracks.

And so you suspect I'm impervious, without empathy or pain, but it isn't so. Believe me, it isn't so. I ask you this, and I ask you to think seriously before you formulate your answer: Why do con men do what they do?

And I leave you this clue: I have been this certain before but have been wrong, and yet I desperately need to be right.

This time, I believe I am right.

This time, no stone has been left unturned. I know who has died and who's still living, I know their addresses, their phone numbers, where they work, and where they have ever worked. I know that Simon and Melanie split up within a year of the event, that both have remarried, that Simon has had other children and Melanie has not, that both drink more than is wise, and both are on antidepressants.

I know that Jessica, the little sister, is married and has young children and that she is rostered for duty at a child-care center one day a week. The other mothers find her neurotically anxious about the little ones in her care. *She hovers too much,* they whisper. *She almost smothers.*

What I don't know—what no one knows, what even Google and Yahoo and Wikipedia don't seem to know and can't make up—is what happened to Joshua and how Joshua came to be me.

I have a need—a compulsion, perhaps—to write all the possible scripts, but the three protagonists are constant and essential, though ever-changing within their chameleon selves:

Simon, Melanie, Darien.

I move them around like chess pieces on a board, especially Darien, because somebody did this, but how was it done so quickly? And what did he do with the child?

Joshua cannot remember.

Hard as I try to insert him, Joshua is always absent from the text.

You think, therefore, that the claimants—all of them, and I know I am not the first—are opportunists or sociopaths. You will point to the recent breakdown of Simon, to his interview with the *New York Times* following my phone call, an interview first desperately hopeful, then angry, then incoherent.

And you think I was not similarly distraught?

Consider this: I, Joshua (aka Joshua X), can recall nothing before my sixth birthday, in spite of another set of parents (good parents in a standard middle-class way; I hold nothing against them), in spite of siblings, in spite of family albums that record third birthday, fourth birthday, fifth birthday, and so on, but nothing earlier. *We didn't have a camera before that,* the older siblings say, and it does indeed seem to be true, because there are no photographs of the earliest years of the brothers and sisters of my other family, the family of record.

*You weren't expected,* they say. *You came late. You were something of an accident but everyone adored you, you were such a beautiful child.*

Perhaps everyone adored me, probably they did, but I always knew I was the cuckoo in the nest. I wasn't expected and I didn't belong.

It is essential, therefore, that I create Simon and Melanie as doting parents, because that is what was stolen from me. I was the center of the world of that beautiful mythical pair. Neither could recover from my loss, I insist on that. My absence destroyed them.

And here is Melanie, enlarged and framed on my wall, glowing mother of toddler and baby, both in her arms. Night after night, I dream myself into that cradle of her arm.

I admit it: I'm in love with my mother. I press my lips, every night, against hers.

In other circumstances, that might be disturbing, but not—given my history—in mine.

When I was an innocent infant, two years old, a wrong so massive was done to me that only Greek tragedy can contain it. I point to Aeschylus, Sophocles, Euripides: they alone are equal to my tale.

And Darien?

Perhaps I need him even more than I need my mother. I need to know what he did and I need to understand why. He is the one player I have not been able to trace. This much I have established: that there was a summer neighbor who was briefly—as far as the local police were concerned—"a person of interest." He was brought in for questioning, but there was not enough evidence to hold him. He vanished. He has left no aliases, no cyber tracks, though there has been speculation, over time, that he could be a serial killer and pedophile.

One more thing: my family, my *other* family, the ones who have me pinned like a butterfly within the frame of the family album, that family (officially mine) claims to recall my unanticipated (though joyfully greeted) birth. Lately, as they have become more bewildered and then more frosty and then more anxious (and sometimes angry) about what they call "my obsession," they have begun to urge a certain kind of test. DNA, they cajole, would settle this thing.

Why do I resist? they want to know.

"Why did you name me Joshua?" I parry.

We didn't, they lie. They profess to show my birth certificate which indicates a different name, my name of record; they profess to offer swabs of their own DNA. So why do I continue to resist?

Why do I resist? I ask myself.

It's like this.

I've read accounts of anguished boys who were born into female bodies; of tortured girls who emerged, slime-wet, in the obstetrician's hands and were recorded as male.

A birth certificate is one thing, but it is not conclusive.

I may not know who I am, but I know who I'm not.


## 10. *Simon*

He knows Melanie believes that he blames her, but in fact it is himself that he blames. On some level, he *knew*. Why didn't he drive them into town? Why didn't he trust his gut?

Perhaps he blames her a little for mocking his fears.

If she had not been so emphatically self-confident, if she had not given him the sense that she privately found him neurotic, too coddling, overanxious . . . Of course, she always denies that. She always claims that she found his fearfulness endearing.

He does not entirely trust her with Jessica anymore because she seems to withhold herself from their baby, almost—for a second—to recoil when contact is made. The body language is subtle, a micro-detail perhaps, but Simon takes note. Unseen, he watches his wife studying Jessica in her crib: the way Melanie stands there, blank and quizzical, as though she does not recognize her own child. Simon cannot help noticing and he is profoundly disturbed.

Sometimes Melanie sees him watching and she lets her huge and mournful dark-ringed eyes rest on his face. "You don't trust me with Jessica," she accuses, her tone a dull sludge of desolation.

"That's nonsense," he lies.

"You're right not to trust me," she says. Her voice is flat. "What kind of a mother loses her child?"

When Jessica wakes in the night, which she does much more often now, it is Simon who picks her up and cuddles her and walks up and down the hallway patting her little diapered butt, singing to her the Yiddish lullabies his own grandmother used to sing.

He cannot talk to Melanie about this.

It is true that he begins to ask himself, Is Jessica safe with her mother?

Simon has put a mattress and a sleeping bag on the floor in Jessica's room. That way he can hear micro-changes in her breathing at night.

## 11. Melanie

Grief is a great sucking whirlpool, more ferocious than a hurricane's eye.

Guilt is wildfire, indifferent, implacable, inexorable, foul, and all-consuming.

The battle strategy of the Grief & Guilt Forces is *scorched earth*. They take no prisoners. They have no mercy. They destroy.

Even in deepest sleep, Melanie's dreams know the truth. She will never be eligible for parole. How could she have been looking at bread loaves, swapping chitchat with Jenny Nelson, when some pervert was ravaging the stroller outside the window and she never even looked?

By random mischance, channel surfing, weeks later she hears a sliver of debate: "Many species," a naturalist—a media expert—says, "are known to kill their own young." He mentions lions, hippos, bears, wolves, domestic cats. "So why should we be surprised," he asks, "in regard to the recent episode of the stolen child, if we should eventually learn—"

Melanie cuts off the TV. She barely reaches the bathroom before she throws up.

She is afraid for Jessica, afraid to touch her.

She is afraid to sleep because of the dreams that come.

She tries not to remember these dreams, but they swarm her: the dream of the beach that turns to quicksand and swallows her children; the dream of shallows that swirl into a deadly funnel and suck her little ones down; the dream of the neighbor who stalks, and kidnaps, and kills, but only after unspeakable acts.

She knows that Simon blames her, and he is right.

She blames herself.

She has trouble attending to what Simon says. Between the beginning and the end of any sentence, she loses her way. His voice is like announcements at an airport: full of sound and fury, signifying something essential, but not something she is able to understand.

## 12. I, Joshua

Of course I need her to be distraught. I need her, fifty years later, to yearn for me, to reach for me in her sleep, never to stop mourning, never to stop dreaming of me.

I need her to yearn for me as I yearn for her.

But I do hold her accountable, after all.

She has to suffer.

## 13. Simon

He has begun to remember small things: her sexual eagerness when they first met, the way it excited him.

Where did she learn that?

Was she already pregnant?

Was Josh his son?

He begins to torment himself with these questions. She had admitted to relationships, several, engaged in as a clueless under-graduate wanting to please.

And had he likewise engaged . . . ? Yes, of course he had, he confessed, though the encounters had meant nothing at all.

Exactly, she had said. Same thing. Those fleeting connections meant nothing at all, although once, with a married man, a friend of her father's, a breath of rural midwestern air blown into New England, the connection had been not entirely nothing, at least not from her point of view. Indeed, it had been full of nostalgia and a warm sense of going back home.

Until the next morning.

The next morning she was embarrassed and appalled, or so she told Simon.

Now he wonders: was this enticement and entrapment?

How seductively devious she had been.

How hungry and how virtuous and how protective and ravenous he had felt.


## *14. Melanie*

She thinks she possibly knows who did it.

She found out she was pregnant the same day her father's friend called to say he'd be making another business trip back east. I'm desperate to see you again, he said.

No, she said. We made a terrible mistake. This can't go on.

It was a dreadful mistake, he agreed, but it happened. We didn't plan it, but now it's fate. It's our destiny. I have to see you.

Of course she should have said *I'm pregnant,* but she never did.

We're guilty of every kind of betrayal, she said instead. I can't live with this. You're my dad's best friend.

And he said, I can't leave my wife and my children, but I won't let you go.

You have to, she said. Or I'll tell my dad.

Something happened then. Something turned ugly. She could instantly tell from his voice.

If you do, he said, I'll tell him it was you who seduced me. I'll show him the photographs that you don't even realize I took. I'll let him know what a slut you are.

You'll never see me again, she said.

It was like sinking into deep still water with chains on her feet. She did not want to come up for air. She hibernated. She moved. She got an unlisted number.

An old friend, bumping into her on the street, was shocked by the smudges beneath her eyes. "My God, what's happened to you? You look like a refugee."

"I'm depressed," Melanie confessed. "And I'm in hiding. Bad judgment, bad love affair."

The friend dragged her out to a party and Simon was there. Simon and Melanie danced and he took her home. A change in the weather set in.

Yet always Melanie has had the sense that somebody's watching. She looks over her shoulder a lot. She fears that her father's best friend is a stalker and that he took back his son.


## 15. I, Joshua

I toy with this as a possible scene, a tentative reason for why the marriage of Simon and Melanie went down the drain. Advantages: it would neatly explain certain details, the awkward details, for instance the detail that my official father, the midwestern farmer, is my biological progenitor (as I fear that the tests would insist). It would explain the age gap between my older siblings and myself. And it offers this additional appealing fact: I would be the son of Melanie and her father's best friend, which would amount to a double connection. My heart flutters. It warms to this idea.

Beyond that, there is the huge and purely *narrative* temptation of Melanie as Mary Magdalene.

But the theory does not compute—there are too many holes—and it runs counter to my profound and instinctual knowledge that my mother—Melanie—was pure and was struck down by my disappearance, by grief, and by consuming but irrational guilt.

## *16. Darien*

I could see when I visited their place on the Upper West Side that things were unraveling. The marriage was falling apart. I confess it gave me an indecent frisson, to be the unknown cause of so much havoc.

Melanie could have been drugged (though I don't think she was). It excited me to think I had the power to drain her vivacity so rapidly and so utterly. If women attracted me, I think I would have found her irresistible (the fragility, the vulnerability, that sense of asking to be destroyed). But of course it was the replication in her son that seduced me.

I remember picking up a framed photograph from the mantel in their Manhattan apartment. "What a beautiful child," I said.

Simon was without affect of any kind.

They were polite and offered Scotch, a single Highland malt, very fine.

I thought of saying—just to throw an ax into their oh-so-immaculate lives—*After I fucked his little ass, I buried him in the backyard next door, not fifty feet from your sandbox and swings and from the powdery mildew on your hedge.*

## *17. I, Joshua*

Of course the most terrible thing for all of us—for Simon, Melanie, Jessica, myself—is the not knowing, the never being able to know.

Yet the need for hope is so desperate and so bottomless and so ravenous that the siren song of substitution is ever audible, its haunting melody calling, calling, luring us toward a tolerable end.

Blessings come where we least expect them, and shared loss has brought Jessica to me.

## *18. Jessica*

Except from photographs, she has no memory of Joshua, but what her body remembers is another thing altogether.

After the divorce, after her mother's lengthy and numerous so-journs in a series of clinics, Jessica remained with her father, who filed for custody—a suit that was uncontested. Simon, both before and after his remarriage, before and after his brand-new children, was devoted to Jessica's well-being. He consulted pediatricians and family therapists and orthopedic specialists, one after the other. No cause could be found for the constant pain in Jessica's right shoulder and along her right hip.

*It feels,* she told multiple specialists, *as though my arm and my leg have been ripped off, as though one side of my body has no skin.*

"Amputation fantasies," one therapist wrote in her file. "Not an uncommon disorder. For the patient, the pain is real."

‘ For years she got by on cortisone shots, but when the first e-mail came she was magically cured. *I've tracked you down,* the e-mail said. *I think I might be Joshua. Could we meet?*

She waited all of ten seconds before responding: *Yes, yes, yes. When and where?*

And when he rang the doorbell, her body knew.

She had been waiting for him for fifty years.

## *19. Darien*

I keep cyber tabs on the names of all the children, and I admit I get a certain kind of thrill at the frequency with which those names crop up in the news. (I get e-mail alerts whenever my tracking engine picks up a name on the list.) It excites me and mystifies me that twenty years, thirty years, fifty years later, there are people who still claim to be suffering pain. I ask myself, Could this be true?

I confess to a certain kind of envy.

I myself would not even remember the names, and certainly not the faces that went with them, if I did not keep a digital and photographic record, but the buzz from browsing the album grows ever more faint. On the other hand, the images that do still grab me are the burial spots, on each of which I have kept a pictorial and topographical notation, and sometimes I think—in the interests of posthumous fame and immortality—that I should arrange to have the archive mailed to the police or to the press in the wake of my death as evidence—like framed degrees on a wall—of superior intelligence and skill.

So many graves? Yet never caught? Destination Guinness.

For the record, I got no particular pleasure from the killing. It was simply necessary to shut them up.

Here is a tip for mothers, offered free: it has been scientifically shown that the decibel level of a toddler crying is equal to the decibel level of a chainsaw and only slightly lower than the cacophony of a jet plane taking off. I leave it to the mothers to do the math. Silence is golden. It could save your child's life.


## 20. *I, Joshua*

According to DNA, my official father is indeed my biological father, though we are strangers. Jessica, who has a cordial though distant relationship with her father, visits her mother regularly and often has her mother stay with her. Melanie as grandmother is both doting and nervous. When she is reading *Where the Wild Things Are* to the children, she will sometimes fall silent for one minute or ten.

She is waiting for Joshua, Jessica says.

There is, according to DNA tests, no genetic link between Jessica and myself. Nevertheless, we are inseparable now. We speak on the phone every week. At Thanksgiving and Christmas, her children climb all over me and call me Uncle Josh.

The heart finds what it needs to find.


## 21. *Thanksgiving*

When Melanie arrives each November for Thanksgiving dinner, she brings a sweet potato and caramelized pecan casserole and a bottle of wine.

"You were too young to remember, Jess," she says each time, "but that's what I did for the last Thanksgiving on Long Island, before, you know . . ."

"I know, Mom."

"Your father's parents always came, and your grandmother had extremely strict rituals that had to be obeyed. The only nonkosher element was my casserole. It was the last time . . ."

"I know, Mom," Jessica says, embracing her. "Mom, I want you to meet a friend of mine from Iowa."

The name means nothing to Melanie, though the guest vaguely reminds her of someone she might once have known. "Have we met before?"

"Possibly," he says.

She watches the way he cavorts on the carpet with the children, the way he plays cowboys and Indians from behind the sofa-fort and the circled wagons of cushions.

"You are very good with children," she tells him.

Halfway through dinner, she asks, "Why do you keep staring at me?"

"I'm sorry," he says, blushing and looking away. "I didn't realize."

"I think I missed your name."

"That wasn't my real name," he says. "My real name is Joshua."

Melanie goes very white and still. Her hands tremble. After some minutes she says quietly, "You are a very nice man, but you are not my son. Jessica, I think I'll go upstairs and lie down for a while."

Melanie drifts into sleep and uneasy dreaming. She is in a vast and confusing railway station, bigger than Grand Central, and it is essential that she not miss her train, yet every platform is blocked with NO ENTRY signs. Somehow she has wandered from the concourse into the lobby of a huge hotel—the Hyatt Regency, perhaps?—and there is a room she must find. Yet every elevator she takes will not stop at the floor she needs. She tries the floor above, the floor below, and frantically hunts for stairs, but they don't exist. She walks miles of corridor, then begins running because time is almost up. She climbs out a window onto a fire escape which is moving the way an escalator moves, except that it moves very slowly and only goes down. It tips her into a back alley near the Midtown Tunnel and she descends into dark.

Vehicle headlights blind her.

She makes her way along a treacherous catwalk meant only for emergency workers.

She runs and runs and runs.

I will be lost forever, she thinks, but I will keep on going until I find my way home.

And then, suddenly, there is sunlight ahead and the tree tunnel of Main Street and puppies tethered to bike racks and she is inhaling the most glorious smell of fresh-baked bread. Without any effort on her part, she is inside Ryan's, and through the window she can see the stroller.

She sees the van pulling up.

There is still time.

She rushes outside and scoops her babies into her arms.

"Thank God," she tells Ryan, bursting back in through his doorway. "I've found my way home."

Ryan cannot tell if she is sobbing or laughing, but he wraps all three of them in tissue and perfumes them with cinnamon and yeast.

Melanie covers Joshua and Jessica with kisses and whispers in Joshua's ear, "We've found our way home and we'll never leave again. I promise that this is where we'll stay."

RICHARD LANGE

# Apocrypha

FROM *Bull Men's Fiction*

IF I HAD money, I'd go to Mexico. Not Tijuana or Ensenada, but farther down, real Mexico. Get my ass out of L.A. There was this guy in the army, Marcos, who was from a little town on the coast called Mazunte. He said you could live pretty good there for practically nothing. Tacos were fifty cents, beers a buck.

"How do they feel about black folks?" I asked him.

"They don't care about anything but the color of your money," he said.

I already know how to speak enough Spanish to get by, how to ask for things and order food. *Por favor* and *muchas gracias*. The numbers to a hundred.

The Chinese family across the hall is always cooking in their room. I told Papa-san to cut it out, but he just stood there nodding and smiling with his little boy and little girl wrapped around his legs. The next day I saw Mama-san coming up the stairs with another bag of groceries, and this morning the whole floor smells like deep-fried fish heads again. I'm not an unreasonable man. I ignore that there are four of them living in a room meant for two, and I put up with the kids playing in the hall when I'm trying to sleep, but I'm not going to let them torch the building.

I pull on some pants and head downstairs. The elevator is broken, so it's four flights on foot. The elevator's always broken, or the toilet, or the sink. Roaches like you wouldn't believe too. The hotel was built in 1928, and nobody's done anything to it since. Why should they? There's just a bunch of poor niggers living here,

Chinamen and wetbacks, dope fiends and drunks. Hell, I'm sure the men with the money are on their knees every night praying this heap falls down so they can collect on the insurance and put up something new.

The first person I see when I hit the lobby—the first person who sees me—is Alan. I call him Youngblood. He's the boy who sweeps the floors and hoses off the sidewalk.

"Hey, D, morning, D," he says, bouncing off the couch and coming at me. "Gimme a dollar, man. I'm hungry as a motherfucker."

I raise my hand to shut him up, walk right past him. I don't have time for his hustle today.

"They're cooking up there again," I say to the man at the desk, yell at him through the bulletproof glass. He's Chinese too, and every month so are more of the tenants. I know what's going on, don't think I don't.

"Okay, I talk to them," the man says, barely looking up from his phone.

"It's a safety hazard," I say.

"Yeah, yeah, okay," he says.

"Yeah, yeah, okay to you," I say. "Next time I'm calling the fire department."

Youngblood is waiting for me when I finish. He's so skinny he uses one hand to hold up his jeans when he walks. Got fuzz in his hair, boogers in the corners of his eyes, and smells like he hasn't bathed in a week. That's what dope'll do to you.

"Come on, D, slide me a dollar, and I'll give you this," he says.

He holds out his hand. There's a little silver disk in his palm, smaller than a dime.

"What is it?" I say.

"It's a battery, for a watch," he says.

"And what am I supposed to do with it?"

"Come on, D, be cool."

Right then the front door opens, and three dudes come gliding in, the light so bright behind them they look like they're stepping out of the sun. I know two of them: J Bone, who stays down the hall from me, and his homeboy Dallas. A couple of grown-up crack babies, crazy as hell. The third one, the tall, good-looking kid in the suit and shiny shoes, is a stranger. He has an air about him like he doesn't belong down here, like he ought to be pulling that suitcase through an airport in Vegas or Miami. He moves and laughs like a high roller, a player, the kind of brother you feel good just standing next to.

He and his boys walk across the lobby, goofing on each other. When they get to the stairs, the player stops and says, "You mean I got to carry my shit up four floors?"

"I'll get it for you," J Bone says. "No problem."

The Chinaman at the desk buzzes them through the gate, and up they go, their boisterousness lingering for a minute like a pretty girl's perfume.

"Who was that?" I say, mostly to myself.

"That's J Bone's cousin," Youngblood says. "Fresh outta County."

Trouble. Come looking for me again.

The old man asks if I know anything about computers. He's sitting in his office in back, jabbing at the keys of the laptop his son bought him to use for inventory but that the old man mainly plays solitaire on. He picks the thing up and sets it down hard on his desk as if trying to smack some sense into it.

"Everything's stuck," he says.

"Can't help you there, boss," I say. "I was out of school before they started teaching that stuff."

I'm up front in the showroom. I've been the security guard here for six years now, ten to six, Tuesday through Saturday. It's just me and the old man, day after day, killing time in the smallest jewelry store in the district, where he's lucky to buzz in ten customers a week. If I was eighty-two years old and had his money, I wouldn't be running out my string here, but his wife's dead, and his friends have moved away, and the world keeps changing so fast that I guess this is all he has left to anchor him, his trade, the last thing he knows by heart.

I get up out of my chair — he doesn't care if I sit when nobody's in the store — and tuck in my uniform. Every so often I like to stretch my legs with a stroll around the showroom. The old man keeps the display cases looking nice, dusts the rings and bracelets and watches every day, wipes down the glass. I test him now and then by leaving a thumbprint somewhere, and it's always gone the next morning.

Another game I play to pass the time, I'll watch the people walking past outside and bet myself whether the next one'll be black or Mexican, a man or a woman, wearing a hat or not, things like that. Or I'll lean my chair back as far as it'll go, see how long I can balance on the rear legs. The old man doesn't like that one, always yells, "Stop fidgeting. You make me nervous." And I've also learned to kind of sleep with my eyes open and my head up, half in this world, half in the other.

I walk over to the door and look outside. It's a hot day, and folks are keeping to the shade where they can. Some are waiting for a bus across the street, in front of the music store that blasts that *oom pah pah oom pah pah* all day long. Next to that's a McDonald's, then a bridal shop, then a big jewelry store with signs in the windows saying COMPRAMOS ORO, WE BUY GOLD.

A kid ducks into our doorway to get out of the sun. He's yelling into his phone in Spanish and doesn't see me standing on the other side of the glass, close enough I can count the pimples on his chin.

*"Por que?"* he says. That's "Why?" or sometimes "Because." *"Por que? Por que?"*

When he feels my eyes on him, he flinches, startled. I chuckle as he moves out to the curb. He glances over his shoulder a couple times like I'm something he's still not sure of.

"Is it too cold in here?" the old man shouts.

He's short already, but hunched over like he is these days, he's practically a midget. Got about ten white hairs left on his head, ears as big as a goddamn monkey's, and those kind of thick glasses that make your eyes look like they belong to someone else.

"You want me to dial it down?" I say.

"What about you? Are you cold?" he says.

"Don't worry about me," I say.

Irving Mandelbaum. I call him Mr. M or Boss. He's taken to using a cane lately, if he's going any distance, and I had to call 911 a while back when I found him facedown on the office floor. It was just a fainting spell, but I still worry.

"Five degrees then," he says. "If you don't mind."

I adjust the thermostat and return to my chair. When I'm sure Mr. M is in the office, I rock back and get myself balanced. My world record is three minutes and twenty-seven seconds.

*

I've been living in the hotel a while now. Before that it was someplace worse, over on Fifth. Someplace where you had crackheads and hypes puking in the hallways and OD-ing in the bathrooms we shared. Someplace where you had women knocking on your door at all hours, asking could they suck your dick for five dollars. It was barely better than being on the street, which is where I ended up after my release from Lancaster. Hell, it was barely better than Lancaster.

A Mexican died in the room next to mine while I was living there. I was the one who found him, and how I figured it out was the smell. I was doing janitorial work in those days, getting home at dawn and sleeping all morning, or trying to anyway. At first the odor was just a tickle in my nostrils, but then I started to taste something in the air that made me gag if I breathed too deeply. I didn't think anything of it because it was the middle of summer and there was no air conditioning and half the time the showers were broken. To put it plainly, everybody stunk in that place. I went out and bought a couple of rose-scented deodorizers and set them next to my bed.

A couple of days later I was walking to my room when something strange on the floor in front of 316 caught my eye. I bent down for a closer look and one second later almost fell over trying to get up again. What it was was three fat maggots, all swole up like overcooked rice. I got down on my hands and knees and pressed my cheek to the floor to see under the door, and more maggots wriggled on the carpet inside the room, dancing around the dead man they'd sprung from.

Nobody would tell me how the guy died, but they said it was so hot in the room during the time he lay in there that he exploded. It took a special crew in white coveralls and rebreathers two days to clean up the mess, and even then the smell never quite went away. It was one of the happiest days of my life when I moved from there.

J Bone's cousin, the player from the lobby, is laughing at me. His name is Leon. I'm not trying to be funny, but the man is high, so everything makes him laugh.

It's 6:30 in the afternoon outside. In here, with the tinfoil covering the windows, it might as well be midnight. I suspect time isn't the main thing on the minds of Leon and Bone and the two girls passing a blunt on the bed. They've been at it for hours already and seem to be planning on keeping the party going way past what's wise.

The door to Bone's room was wide open when I walked by after work, still wearing my uniform. I heard music playing, saw people sitting around.

"Who's that, McGruff the Crime Dog?" Leon called out.

Some places it's okay to keep going when you hear something like that. Not here. Here, if you give a man an inch on you, he'll most definitely take a mile. So I went back.

"What was that?" I said, serious but smiling, not weighting it one way or the other.

"Naw, man, naw," Leon said. "I was just fucking with you. Come on in and have a beer."

All I wanted was to get home and watch *Jeopardy,* but I couldn't say no now, now that Leon had backed down. I had to have at least one drink. One of the girls handed me a Natural Light, and Leon joked that I better not let anybody see me with it while I was in uniform.

"That's cops, man, not guards," I said, and that's what got him laughing.

"You know what, though," he says. "Most cops be getting high as motherfuckers."

Everybody nods and murmurs, "That's right, that's right."

"I mean, who got the best dope?" he continues. "Cops' girlfriends, right?"

He's wearing the same suit he had on the other day, the shirt unbuttoned and the jacket hanging on the back of his chair. He's got the gift of always looking more relaxed than any man has a right to, and that relaxes other people. And then he strikes.

"So what you guarding?" he asks me.

"A little jewelry store on Hill," I say.

"You got a gun?" he says.

"Don't need one," I say. "It's pretty quiet."

I don't tell him I'm not allowed to carry because of my record. We aren't friends yet. Some of these youngsters, first thing out of their mouths is their crimes and their times. They've got no shame at all.

"What you gonna do if some motherfucker comes in waving a gat, wanting to take the place down?" Leon says.

I sip my beer and shrug. "Ain't my store," I say. "I'll be ducking and covering."

"Listen at him," Leon hoots. "Ducking and covering. My man be ducking and covering."

The smoke hanging in the air is starting to get to me. The music pulses in my fingertips, and my grin turns goofy. I'm looking right at the girls now, not even trying to be sly about it. The little one's titty is about to fall out of her blouse.

Leon's voice comes to me from a long way off. "I like you, man," he says. "You all right."

Satan's a sweet talker. I shake the fog from my head and down the rest of my beer. If you're a weak man, you better at least be smart enough to know when to walk away. I thank them for the drink, then hurry to my room. With the TV up loud, I can't hear the music, and pretty soon it gets back to being just like any other night.

Except that I dream about those girls. Dreams like I haven't dreamed in years. Wild dreams. Teenage dreams. And when I wake up humping nothing but the sheets, the disappointment almost does me in.

The darkness is a dead weight on my chest, and the hot air is like trying to breathe tar. My mind spins itself stupid, names ringing out, faces flying past. The little girl who'd lift her dress for us when we were eight or nine and show us what she got. My junior high and high school finger bangs and fumble fucks. Monique Carter and Shawnita Weber and that one that didn't wear panties because she didn't like how they looked under her skirt. Sharon, the mother of one of my kids, and Queenie, the mother of the other. All the whores I was with when I was stationed in Germany and all the whores I've been with since.

The right woman can work miracles. I've seen beasts tamed and crooked made straight. But in order for that to happen, you have to be the right man, and I've never been anybody's idea of right.

We close from one to two for lunch, and I walk over and eat a cheeseburger at the same joint every afternoon. Then I go back to the store, the old man buzzes me in, and I flip the sign on the door to OPEN. Today the showroom smells like Windex when I return. Mr. M's been cleaning. I sit in my chair and close my eyes. It was a slow morning—one Mexican couple, a bucktoothed kid and a pregnant girl looking at wedding rings—and it's going to be a slow afternoon. The days fly by, but the hours drag on forever.

Around 3:30 someone hits the "Press for Entry" button outside. The chime goes off loud as hell, goosing me to my feet. Peering through the window, I see a couple of girls. I don't recognize them until the old man has already buzzed them in. It's the two from the other night, from the party in J Bone's room. They walk right past me, and if they see who I am, they don't show it.

Mr. M asks can he help them. "Let me look at this," they say, "Let me look at that," and while the old man is busy inside the case, their eyes roam the store. I realize they aren't interested in any watches or gold chains. They're making maps, scoping out the cameras and trying to peek into the back room.

I look out the window again, and there's Leon standing on the curb with J Bone and Dallas. They've got their backs to me, but I know Leon's suit and Bone's restless shuffle. Leon throws a glance over his shoulder at the store, can't resist. There's no way he can see me through the reflections on the glass, but I duck just the same.

I go back and stand next to my chair. I cross my arms over my chest and stare up at the clock on the wall. There's a way of being in prison, of making yourself invisible while still holding down your place. I feel like I'm on the yard again or in line for chow. You walk out that gate, but you're never free. What your time has taught you is a chain that hobbles you for the rest of your days.

The girls put on a show, something about being late to meet somebody. They're easing their way out.

"I could go three seventy-five on this," the old man says, holding up a bracelet.

"We're gonna keep looking," they say.

"Three fifty."

"Not today."

The old man sighs as they head for the door, puts the bracelet back in the case. Every lost sale stings him like his first. The girls walk past me, again without a glance or nod, anything that a cop studying a tape might spot. The heat rushes in when the door opens but is quickly gobbled up by the air conditioning, and the store is even quieter than it was before the girls came in.

I don't look at Mr. M because I'm afraid he'll see how worried I am. I sit in my chair like I normally do, stare at the floor like always. The girls are right now telling Leon what they saw, how easy it would be, and J Bone is saying, "We should do it today, nigga, nobody but the old man and McGruff in there, and him with no gun."

But Leon is smarter than that. "That ain't how we planned it," he says. "We're gonna take our time and do it right."

Him sending those girls in to case the store doesn't bode well for me. There's no way he didn't think I wouldn't remember them, which means he didn't care if I did. He either figures I won't talk afterward or, more likely, that I won't be able to.

There are lots of Leons out there. The first one I ever met was named Malcolm, after Malcolm X. He was twelve, a year younger than me, but acted fifteen or sixteen. He was already into girls, into clothes, into making sure his hair was just right. I'd see him shooting craps with the older boys. I'd see him smoking Kools. The first time he spoke to me, I was like, "What's this slick motherfucker want with a broke-ass fool like me?" I was living in a foster home then, wearing hand-me-down hand-me-downs, and the growling of my empty stomach kept me awake at night.

Malcolm's thing was shoplifting, and he taught me how. We started out taking candy from the Korean store, the two of us together, but after a while he had me in supermarkets, boosting laundry detergent and disposable razors and batteries while he waited outside. Then this junkie named Maria would return the stuff to another store, saying she'd lost the receipt. We'd hit a few different places a day and split the money three ways. I never questioned why Maria and I were doing Malcolm's dirty work, I was just happy to have him as a friend. Old men called this kid sir, and the police let him be. It was like I'd lived in the dark before I met him.

The problem was, every few years after that a new Malcolm came along, and pretty soon I'd find myself in the middle of some shit I shouldn't have been in the middle of, trying to impress him. "You know what's wrong with you?" Queenie, the mother of my son, once said. She always claimed to have me figured out. "You think you can follow someone to get somewhere, but don't nobody you know know where the hell they're going either."

She was right about that. In fact, the last flashy bastard who got past my good sense talked me right into prison, two years in Lancaster. I was a thirty-three-year-old man about to get fired from Popeye's Chicken for mouthing off to my twenty-year-old boss. "That's ridiculous," Kay Jay said. "You're better than that." He had a friend who ran a chop shop, he said. Dude had a shopping list of cars he'd pay for.

"Yeah, but I'm trying to stay out of trouble," I said.

"This ain't trouble," Kay Jay said. "This is easy money."

I ended up going down for the second car I stole. The police lit me up before I'd driven half a block, and I never heard from Kay Jay again, not a "Tough luck, bro," nothing. It took that to teach me my lesson. I can joke about it now and say I was a slow learner, but it still hurts to think I was so stupid for so long.

When the heat breaks late in the day, folks crawl out of their sweat-boxes and drag themselves down to the street to get some fresh air and let the breeze cool their skin. They sit on the sidewalk with their backs to a wall or stand on busy corners and tell each other jokes while passing a bottle. The dope dealers work the crowd, signaling with winks and whistles, along with the Mexican woman who peddles T-shirts and tube socks out of a shopping cart and a kid trying to sell a phone that he swears up and down is legit.

I usually enjoy walking through the bustle, a man who's done a day of work and earned a night of rest. I like seeing the easy light of the setting sun on people's faces and hearing them laugh. Folks call out to me and shake my hand as I pass by, and there's an old man who plays the trumpet like you've never heard anyone play the trumpet for pocket change.

I barrel past it all today, not even pausing to drop a quarter in the old man's case. My mind is knotted around one worry: what I'm gonna say to Leon. I haven't settled on anything by the time I see him and his boys standing in front of the hotel, so it won't be a pretty speech, just the truth.

The three of them are puffing on cigars, squinting against the smoke as I roll up.

"Evening, fellas," I say.

"What up, officer," J Bone drawls.

Dallas giggles at his foolishness, but Leon doesn't crack a smile. The boy's already got a stain on his suit, on the lapel of the coat. He blows a smoke ring and looks down his nose at me.

"I saw them girls in the store today," I say to him.

"They was doing some shopping," he says.

"I saw you all too."

"We was waiting on them."

He's been drinking. His eyes are red and yellow, and his breath stinks. I get right to my point.

"Ain't nothing in there worth losing your freedom for," I say.

"What are you talking about?" Leon says.

"Come on, man, I been around," I say.

"He been around," Bone says, giggling again.

"You've got an imagination, I'll give you that," Leon says.

"I hope that's all it is," I say.

Leon steps up so he's right in my face. We're not two inches apart, and the electricity coming off him makes the hair on my arms stand up.

"Are you fucking crazy?" he says.

"Maybe so," I mumble, and turn to go. When I'm about to pull open the lobby door, he calls after me.

"How much that old man pay you?"

"He pays me what he pays me," I say.

"I was wondering, 'cause you act like you the owner."

"I'm just looking out for my own ass."

Leon smiles, trying to get back to being charming. With his kind, though, once you've seen them without their masks, it's never the same.

"And you know the best way to do that, right?" he says.

"Huh?" I say.

"Duck and cover," he says.

He's going to shoot me dead. I hear it in his voice. He's already got his mind made up.

Youngblood says he knows someone who can get me a gun, a white boy named Paul, a gambler, a loser, one of them who's always selling something. I tell Youngblood I'll give him twenty to set something up. Youngblood calls the guy, and the guy says he has a little .25 auto he wants a hundred bucks for. That's fine, I say. I have three hundred hidden in my room. It's supposed to be Mexico money, but there isn't going to be any Mexico if Leon puts a bullet in me.

Paul wants to meet on Sixth and San Pedro at 9 P.M. It's a long walk over, and Youngblood talks the whole way there about his usual nothing. He has to stop three times. Once to piss and twice to ask some shaky-looking brothers where's a dude named Cisco. I'm glad I have my money in my sock. I don't like to dawdle after dark. They'll cut you for a quarter down here, for half a can of beer.

We're a few minutes late to the corner, but this Paul acts like it was an hour. "What the fuck?" he keeps saying, "What the fuck?" looking up and down the street like he expects the police to pop out any second. He has a bandage over one eye and is wearing a T-shirt with cartoon racehorses on it, the kind they give away at the track sometimes.

"Show me what you got," I say, interrupting his complaining.

"Show you what I got?" he says. "Show me what you got."

I reach into my sock and bring out the roll of five twenties. I hand it to him, and he thumbs quickly through the bills.

"Wait here," he says.

"Hold on now," I say.

"It's in my car," he says. "You motherfuckers may walk around with guns on you, but I don't."

He hurries off toward a beat-up Nissan parked in a loading zone.

"It's cool," Youngblood says. "Relax."

Paul opens the door of the car and gets in. He starts the engine, revs it, then drives away. I stand there with my mouth open, wondering if I misunderstood him, that he meant he was going somewhere else to get the gun and then bring it back. But that isn't what he said. Thirty years on the street, and I haven't learned a goddamn thing. I hit Youngblood so hard, his eyes roll up in his head. Then I kick him when he falls, leave him whining like a whipped puppy.

I don't sleep that night or the next, and at work I can't sit still, waiting for what's coming. Two days pass, three, four. At the hotel, I see Leon hanging around the lobby and partying in J Bone's room. We don't say anything to each other as I pass by, I don't even look at him, but our souls scrape like ships' hulls, and I shudder from stem to stern.

When Friday rolls around and still nothing has happened, I start to think I'm wrong. Maybe what I said to Leon was enough to back him off. Maybe he was never serious about robbing the store. My load feels a little lighter. For the first time in a week I can twist my head without the bones in my neck popping.

To celebrate, I take myself to Denny's for dinner. Chicken-fried steak and mashed potatoes. A big Mexican family is there celebrating something. Looks like Mom and Dad and Grandma and a bunch of kids, everyone all dressed up. I'm forty-two years old, not young anymore, but I'd still like to have something like that someday. Cancer took my daughter when she was ten, and my son's stuck in prison. If I ever make it to Mexico, maybe I'll get a second chance, and this time it would mean something.

They show up at 2:15 on Saturday. We've just reopened after lunch, and I haven't even settled into my chair yet when the three of them crowd into the doorway. Dallas is in front, a hoodie pulled low over his face. He's the one who pushes the buzzer, the one Leon's got doing the dirty work.

"Don't let 'em in," I shout to Mr. M.

The old man toddles in from the back room, confused.

"What?"

"Don't touch the buzzer."

Dallas rings again, then raps on the glass with his knuckles. I've been afraid for my life before—on the street, in prison, in rooms crowded with men not much more than animals—but it's not something you get used to. My legs shake like they have every other time I've been sure death is near, and my heart tries to tear itself loose and run away. I crouch, get up, then crouch again, a chicken with its head cut off.

J Bone tugs a ski mask down over his face and pushes Dallas out of the way. He charges the door, slamming into it shoulder-first, which makes a hell of a noise, but that's about it. He backs up, tries again, then lifts his foot and drives his heel into the thick, bulletproof glass a couple of times. The door doesn't budge.

"I'm calling the police," the old man shouts at him. "I've already pressed the alarm."

Leon yells at Bone, and Bone yells at Leon, but I can't hear what they're saying. Leon has his mask pulled down now too. He draws a gun from his pocket, and I scramble for cover behind a display case as he fires two rounds into the lock. He doesn't understand the mechanics, the bolts that shoot into steel and concrete above and below when you turn the key.

People on the street are stopping to see what's going on. Dallas runs off, followed by Bone. Leon grabs the door handle and yanks on it, then gives up too. He peels off his mask and starts to walk one way before turning quickly and jogging in the other.

I get up and go to the door to make sure they're gone for real. I should be relieved, but I'm not. I'm already worried about what's going to happen next.

"Those black bastards," Mr. M says. "Those fucking black bastards."

Once they find out about my record, the police get in their head that we were all in it together and it's just that I lost my nerve at the last minute.

"How did you know not to let them in?" they ask me twenty different times in twenty different ways.

"I saw the gun," I say, simple as that.

Mr. M ends up going to the hospital with chest pains, and his son shows up to square everything away. He keeps thanking me for protecting his father.

"You may have saved his life," he says, and I wish I could say that's who I was thinking about.

The police don't finish investigating until after six. I hang around the store until then because I'm not ready to go back to the hotel. When the cops finally pack up, I walk home slowly, all the way there expecting Leon to come out of nowhere like a lightning bolt. There'll be a gun in his hand, or a knife. He knows how it goes: if you're worried about a snitch, take him out before he talks.

I make it back safely, though. Leon's not waiting out front or in the lobby or on the stairs. The door to J Bone's room is open, but no music is playing, and nobody's laughing. I glance in, and see that the room is empty except for a bunch of greasy burger bags and half-finished 40s with cigarettes sunk in them.

I lock my door when I get inside my room, open the window,

turn on the fan. My legs stop working, and I collapse on the bed, exhausted. I dig out a bottle of Ten High that I keep for when the demons come dancing and decide that if I make it through tonight, I'll treat every hour I have left as a gift.

I talk to the Chinaman at the desk the next morning, and he tells me J Bone checked out yesterday, ran off in a hurry. Youngblood is listening in, pretending to watch the lobby TV. We haven't spoken since I lost my temper.

"What do you know about it?" I call to him, not sure if he'll answer.

"Cost you five dollars to find out," he says.

I hand over the money, and he jumps up off the couch, eager to share. He says Leon and Bone had words yesterday afternoon, talking about the police being after them and "You stupid," "No, you stupid." Next thing they went upstairs, came down with their shit, and split.

"What do you think they did?" Youngblood asks me.

"Fuck if I know," I say. "Ask your friend Paul."

"He ain't my friend," Youngblood says. "I put the word out on him. I'm gonna get you your money back."

I'm so happy to have Leon gone that I don't even care about the money. I ask Youngblood if he wants to go for breakfast. He's a good kid. A couple of hours from now, after he takes his first shot, he'll be useless, but right now I can see the little boy he once was in his crooked smile.

He talks about Kobe—Kobe this, Kobe that—as we walk to Mc-Donald's. We go back and forth from shady patches still cool as night to blocks that even this early are being scorched by the sun. Nobody's getting crazy yet, and it doesn't smell too bad except in the alleys. Almost like morning anywhere. I keep looking over my shoulder, but I can feel myself relaxing already. A couple more days, and I'll be back to normal.

Mr. M's son told me before I left the store that it'd be closed for at least a week, but not to worry because they'd pay me like I was still working. The next Thursday he calls and asks me to come down. The old man is still in the hospital, and it doesn't look like he'll be getting out anytime soon, so the son has decided to shut the store up for good. He hands me an envelope with $2,500 inside, calls it severance.

"Thank you again for taking care of my father," he says.

"Tell him I said hello and get well soon," I reply.

The next minute I'm out on the street, unemployed for the first time in years. I have to laugh. I barely gave Leon the time of day, didn't fall for his mess, didn't jump when he said to, and he still managed to fuck up the good thing I had going. That's the way it is. Every time you manage to stack a few bricks, a wave's bound to come along and knock them down.

They run girls out of vans over on Towne. You pay a little more than you would for a street whore, but they're generally younger and cleaner, and doing it in the van is better than doing it behind a dumpster or in an Andy Gump. I shower and shave before I head out, get a hundred bucks from my stash behind the light switch, and stick it in my sock.

Mama-san is carrying more groceries up the stairs, both kids hanging on her as I'm going down.

"No cooking," I say. "No cooking."

She doesn't reply, but the kids look scared. I didn't mean for that to happen.

The freaks come out at night, and the farther east you go, the worse it gets. Sidewalk shitters living in cardboard boxes, ghosts who eat out of garbage cans, a blind man showing his dick on the corner. I keep my gaze forward, my hands balled into fists. Walking hard, we used to call it.

Three vans are parked at the curb tonight. I make a first pass to scope out the setup. The pimps stand together, a trio of cocky little vatos with gold chains and shiny shirts. My second time by, they start in hissing through their teeth and whispering, "Big tits, tight pussy."

"You looking for a party?" one of them asks me.

"What if I am?" I say.

He walks me to his van and slides open the side door. I smell weed and something coconut. A chubby Mexican girl wearing a red bra and panties is lying on a mattress back there. She's pretty enough, for a whore, but I'd still like to check out what's in the other vans. I don't want to raise a ruckus, though.

"How much?" I say to nobody in particular.

The pimp says forty for head, a hundred for half and half. I get him down to eighty. I crawl inside the van, and he closes the door behind me. There's cardboard taped to the windshield and windows. The only light is what seeps in around the edges. I'm sweating already, big drops racing down my chest inside my shirt.

"How you doing tonight?" I say to the girl.

"Okay," she says.

She uses her hand to get me hard, then slips the rubber on with her mouth. I make her stop after just a few seconds and have her lay back on the mattress. I come as soon as I stick it in. It's been a long time.

"Can I lay here a minute?" I say.

The girl shrugs and cleans herself with a baby wipe. She has nice hair, long and black, and big brown eyes. I ask her where she's from. She says Mexico.

"I'm moving down there someday," I say.

My mouth gets away from me. I tell her I was in Germany once, when I was in the army, and that I came back and had two kids. I tell her about leaving them just like my mom and dad left me, and how you say you're never going to do certain things, but then you do. I tell her that's why God's turned away from us and Jesus is a joke. When I run out of words, I'm crying. The tears get mixed up with the sweat on my face.

"It's okay," the girl says. "It's okay."

Her pimp bangs on the side of the van and opens the door.

Time's up.

I've seen enough that I could write my own Bible. For example, here's the parable of the brother who hung on and the one who fell: Two months later I'm walking home from my new job guarding a Mexican dollar store on Los Angeles. A bum steps out in front of me, shoves his dirty hand in my face, and asks for a buck. I don't like when they're pushy, and I'm about to tell him to step off, but then I realize it's Leon.

He's still wearing his suit, only now it's filthy rags. His eyes are dull and overcast, his lips burnt black from the pipe. All his charm is gone, all his kiss-my-ass cockiness. Nobody is following this boy anymore but the Reaper.

"Leon?" I say. I'm not scared of him. One punch now would turn him back to dust.

"Who you?" he asks warily.

"You don't remember?"

He opens his eyes wide, then squints. A quiet laugh rattles his bones.

"Old McGruff," he says. "Gimme a dollar, crime dog."

I give him two.

"Be good to yourself," I say as I walk away.

"You're a lucky man," he calls after me.

No, I'm not, but I am careful. Got a couple bricks stacked, a couple bucks put away, and one eye watching for the next wave. Forever and ever, amen.

THERESA E. LEHR

# Staircase to the Moon

FROM *Alfred Hitchcock's Mystery Magazine*

I WORE LEATHERS to her funeral, along with the pearls. The newspaper said the necklace was worth $70,000 Australian. That's big bikkies in Broome. A small fortune. At least to me. I thought my sister had hocked the necklace. She'd sold her BMW and lost her apartment overlooking Sydney Harbour last year. Just goes to prove what I always told her: you can't be addicted to heaven dust and the material world at the same time.

Our mum had eyed that string of South Sea pearls longer than I care to remember, so I was caught off guard when my twin sister left them to me. I figured her motive was to twist the knife in Mum one last time. It had nothing to do with me. Making amends was not Shinju's style.

The day after the funeral, photos of me wearing her famous pearls and straddling my Ducati at the front of the motorcade plastered the *Herald* and later the Australian gossip magazines. I didn't wear my helmet and Mum said I had an ax to grind. I denied it, but we both knew I'd never forgiven Shinju for the ink-vine scar that runs down the right side of my face. Did I want everyone to know that? Maybe so.

But murder has a way of either bringing families together or driving them apart. In our case, Shinju's homicide squashed us into a world we'd never shared. Mum, Pop, and I leaned on each other, licked one another's wounds. Unfamiliar, sticky emotions drove us to hound the Broome police until they stopped returning our calls and refused to see us at the station.

You may wonder why a screwed-up family with very little ten-

derness for one another would join together. Was it out of love
for Shinju? Or guilt over getting whatever was left in her bank accounts? Was there even enough love left between us to miss her?
I'm not sure. But I have a feeling the way she died had a lot to do
with it.

Shinju and I began our lives sharing the same primordial sea.
Mum said we wrestled in her belly like Jacob and Esau, and we
would've been named after the brotherly-love-gone-awry twins if
we'd been boys. Instead, Pop had his way, naming us with the family business in mind. Even though I was born first, and in my opinion should've been named Shinju, meaning "pearl," I was dubbed
Kashiko—child of the seashore. Turns out Pop was prophetic. I
became the pearl hunter. Shinju wore them.

Unfortunately, as the years went by, Pop's heavy drinking
wrecked our small pearl-diving business. Fewer trips out to sea
meant fewer opportunities to search for oysters, resulting in
smaller profits. By the time we were fifteen, he had to sell our lugger. Without the boat, the business went belly-up.

Fate smiled on my sister, though. When she was sixteen, Shinju
was hired by world-renowned Broome South Sea Pearls as a jewelry model for their Aphrodite's Tears Collection. Strands of dia-
monds and pearls, sapphires and pearls, platinum and pearls hung
across Shinju's back, thighs, small breasts, and even bare bum in
glossy advertisements in international magazines and Australian
TV commercials. Sales at Broome South Sea Pearls doubled. Two
years later, you couldn't take the bullet train in Tokyo, the subway
in New York, or even sip a cup of java in a Broome coffee shop
without her long black lashes and glowing white skin beckoning
you like a seductive sea nymph. Men ogled her, but women idol-
ized her, imagining if they just bought perfectly matched Broome
South Sea pearls the diameter of lychee fruit, her alabaster skin
and black lacquered hair would become their own.

But the fantasy didn't last. My sister died here in Broome two
months ago, the middle of January. I'd just come off a twenty-one-
day stint on a pearling ship. Because I had nothing in the fridge
at the one-bedroom bungalow I rent two blocks from the beach, I
stopped at the Moon market at Town Beach. Bought a couple of
overpriced star fruits, a package of soy nuts, and a liter of alfalfa
juice. Walking home I heard sirens, but didn't think much of it.

Tourists can get crazy as a cut snake on our famous Staircase to the Moon nights.

When there's a full moon the tides recede far from shore, exposing the mudflats in Roebuck Bay. As the moon rises, light reflects off the wet ripples in the sand, creating the illusion of glowing amber steps shimmering straight up to the moon. Tourists overrun Broome every month to see the Staircase to the Moon. Turns out an American couple on their honeymoon found my sister's body on the beach. I don't care for tourists much, but still, I wouldn't want a death haunting my anniversary.

Pop rang me at 1 A.M. When he whimpered the news about Shinju, I couldn't breathe. Then I remembered I woke up gasping two nights before in my bunk on the *Adelaide*. The clock had glowed 10:42 P.M.

Some say identical twins have a special connection. Like telepathy, or ESP. Shinju and I had such ties: unknowingly buying the same outfits, the same bikinis; carrying on conversations without speaking a word; making the same grades on exams in school. Falling for the same boy in Year 9.

Others say it's bunk—there's no science to prove twins can sense each other's feelings and thoughts. But then how would they explain last October, when a horrifying dream woke me? My hands were cold and clammy and my heart flopped around in my chest like a dying fish. I saw Shinju's face, bloodless and still, floating across my bungalow ceiling. I knew it wasn't my face—hers was perfect. Mine has a scar stretching from the temple to the corner of my lip.

I forced myself to sit up, grab the phone, and ring my parents.

"Call Shinju in Sydney," I said. "If there's no answer, ring the police. And make damn sure they send for an ambulance."

Mum didn't ask questions. She knew the bond Shinju and I shared. Her call saved Shinju's life. She'd snorted enough cocaine to kill a bloody roo, then chased it down with six cold ones—Victoria Bitter, her favorite from the old days in Broome. Blamed me for news of her addiction becoming social gossip, and her employer, BSSP, warning her not to let it happen again.

Was it that same connection that woke me on the *Adelaide*? Was 10:42 the time of her death? I decided not to share my morbid thoughts with Pop when he called that night. Instead I told him not to worry, I'd take care of everything at the coroner's office in the morning. Pop hadn't been back on the wagon long enough to be able to say to the coroner, "Yes, this sea-battered body belongs to my little pearl." But after ringing off, I was restless. I pulled on jeans and a T-shirt, slid into a jacket, and grabbed the keys. But once I straddled the bike, my hands started to shake. I couldn't slip the key into the ignition.

A taxi dropped me at the county morgue. The main entrance was unlit. I peered through the window but couldn't make out much — an empty reception desk, some green molded-plastic chairs. I rapped on the door and waited. Nothing. I knocked harder. I was about to ring for another taxi when a young bloke unlocked the door and stuck out his head.

"What the bloody hell?" he said.

"I'm here to identify my sister's body."

He stared at my scar, like everyone does when they first see the hideous thing, then his gaze darted erratically. "Oh, sorry, lady. But, yeah, like we open at eight o'clock. You'll have to come back." He lifted his shoulders in a halfhearted shrug.

A sweet, lemony cloud drifted over me. It wasn't that the dude was smoking weed that ticked me off. It was his bloodshot and dilated eyes. I'd seen Shinju high enough times to guess he'd snorted heaven dust too.

I glanced at his name tag. "Look, Jeff, I don't think I can build up the nerve again to do this." It was a lie. I can face just about anything, but I had my reasons for being there.

He narrowed his eyes and peered at me. "Do I know you?"

"You do now." I stuck out my hand, gave him a hurried shake, and stepped inside. "Kashiko Nakagawa. My sister drowned. Her body was found on the beach at the Mangrove Resort."

He shook his head. "I shouldn't be doing this. I could get in a lot of trouble."

"World's full of trouble, Jeff. And I'd feel just terrible if you lost your job because someone found out what you were really doing on your break. That would bring down a shitload of problems."

He seemed to think about my words, then nodded slowly. "Right-o. Do you have a photo of the deceased?"

I opened my jacket and pulled out a shot Pop had taken of Shinju on an old lugger a few years back. She held a rice-paper parasol to protect her face from the relentless Australian sun. Jeff studied the photo as we walked down the corridor to the holding room. I gave him my sister's name and he checked the labels on a couple of large metal drawers that lined the walls. When he got to the last drawer on the left side, he yanked it open.

Immediately the stench hit me. I clamped my hand over my nose.

"How'd you say your sister died?"

"Drowned," I mumbled.

He tilted his head to one side. "No, I remember this one, heard the coroner talking about her. She was that famous model, right? She didn't drown."

He pulled back the sheet and my mind went blank. Shinju's face, bloated and bluish, was pockmarked where the sea life I loved so much had taken nibbles from her flesh. Her dull hair was matted with sand and salt, and her usually powdered and perfumed skin smelled of rotting meat. A wave of nausea rolled over me.

"That's her," I whispered. "Pop's little pearl." I reached out and smoothed down her eyebrow. Her skin was cold and stiff, and fine sand rolled under my fingertips.

The reek wafted up again. I grabbed an aluminum basin just in time.

Jeff handed me a brown paper towel. "You know," he said as he stared at Shinju's picture, "I've been studying bone structure, and skulls and whatnot. You two could have been twins."

"Yeah, we could have been." I spat out all that was left of my overpriced star fruit. The paper towel was scratchy, but I wiped my mouth again anyway. Spotting a chair, I sat down, bringing the basin with me. Jeff brought me a cup of water.

"How'd the cops know to call my parents?" I asked.

"The cops at the scene thought they recognized her. Went to school with her, they said."

Considering the state of Shinju's body, it was a miracle anyone could have recognized her. Bile stung my airways and I was ready to get out of there. "Don't I need to sign some papers or something?"

"You know, you could have waited until I fixed her up some before identifying the body. You didn't have to come and see her like this."

Yeah, I did. But I didn't tell him that.

Jeff replaced the sheet, slid the steel slab back into the locker, and twisted the handle. He slipped papers from a folder onto a clipboard and told me to sign at all the *X*'s.

There was no place to sign on the first page, so I flipped to the next. *Cause of Death* stopped me. I sped back to the first page and glanced at the document title. Jeff had accidentally handed me the Initial Autopsy Report. I stole a look at him. He was busy texting. Quickly I scanned the report. The last page was an eight-by-ten glossy. At first I thought the photo had to be a mistake. I stared at the object, amazed at what I saw.

After signing the proper paperwork, I handed Jeff some cash for his trouble and left. The taxi dropped me off just after six. My bike was still in the carport where I'd left it, but the front door of my tiny bungalow wasn't. Smashed and splintered, it hung wide open.

I peered in. A tightness cinched my rib cage, constricting my heart. Overturned chairs, strewn cushions, and the contents of my travel duffel littered the room. I threaded my way through, stumbling over a potted orchid. A rattan chair broke my fall, and I lowered myself to the floor, fighting for air. My underwater training kicked in—slower, deeper breaths, relaxed muscles, a cleared mind. I scanned my tiny room. Whoever had broken in was gone, but fear returned and my heart raced again.

I called the cops. Then I crawled onto the slashed sofa and curled up at one end. I had just taken a breath when my hands started to shake. Weeks of physical labor aboard the *Adelaide,* the sight of Shinju's body, and the break-in had taken their toll. I yanked a blanket from the floor and wrapped myself up tight to keep from shattering into a million pieces.

Closing my eyes, I recalled Shinju's disfigured face. "Be careful what you wish for," Pop liked to say. Well, my deep-seated hope had come true: my sister's famous face was finally more hideous than mine. To see her spoiled looks had been my reason for going to the morgue. But nothing could have prepared me for what I'd seen. The long-awaited satisfaction didn't come. Instead I felt my heart rend in two.

I must have fallen asleep, because shouts startled me awake. I pivoted my head backward on the arm of the sofa and viewed my ruined doorway upside down. Even distorted, I'd know Tom Lafroy anywhere. After all, I'd seen him from all angles, even half naked enough times. He carried a piece of door frame, picking his way through the room, calling my name. I leapt from the sofa and grabbed the knife on the coffee table I'd used to slice up my star fruit.

"You've got a lot of nerve," I said.

He looked up, wariness on his sunburned face. "Kashiko, put down the knife." His voice was soft, measured, and touched with just enough of his father's Irish lilt to make my heart skip. "I just heard about Shinju." He fumbled his words then, not sure what to say next. Let him squirm, I thought.

"Are you okay? Your da's been trying to reach you." Righting the wicker chair, he came closer. And I wondered for the millionth time if he'd ever really loved my sister.

"I'll ring him," I said.

"What happened here?" He swung his head around, quickly taking it all in. Reminded me of the way we pearlers search for oysters on the seabed.

"Maid forgot to show up. Now get out of my house."

He shook his head. "You still hate me."

"Shinju's dead. No one else will ever have her. Happy now?" I picked up the dishes from the coffee table.

"That's not fair. She left *me*, remember?"

I tossed the knife into the sink with a clang and turned to face him. "Was that after she found you in bed with a hooker or after you hooked her on cocaine? I forget which came first."

He picked up an extra-large pillow and leaned it against the wall. A painted Aboriginal design covered the pillow's fabric. Shinju had bought it for me with her first paycheck from BSSP a lifetime ago. Back when she was still trying to buy my forgiveness.

"Keep your hands off my stuff," I said.

In two strides he was close to me. Too close. I pushed him, even though in the past I would never have done that. "Get away," I said, and waved my hands. "Out, out!"

"Listen. Shinju was into something way over her head."

I checked at that remark, reviewing the facts I'd gathered from the autopsy report, but I shook it off. "How do I know you aren't just trying to destroy her all over again?"

He lowered his head and leaned toward me in that way I always found unnerving. "We've been friends long enough for you to know I'd never do that." He placed a hand on my shoulder.

I twisted out of his grasp. "Why should I trust you? You falsify your oyster counts more than anyone in the business."

"We need to talk. About Shinju. Let's go for a coffee."

"I don't drink coffee. Remember?" I turned my back and walked toward the bathroom. "You can let yourself out."

"Won't be hard to do. There's no door." He waited a beat, then spoke. "Call me when you're ready."

Once locked in the bath, I pulled out the eight-by-ten I'd snatched from the report and hidden in my jeans. A pearl of extraordinary size sat above a measuring tape. Eighteen millimeters in diameter. Size of a mothball, harshly glinting light. A coroner's photographer can't capture a pearl's radiant luster. Not like the talent at BSSP's advertising agency can. Those blokes could almost convince me *I* needed to buy a strand worth tens of thousands.

I undressed, turned on the shower as hot as I could stand it, and stepped in. Rising steam warmed my face, except along the deadened scar line. I dropped my head back, letting the water stream down my hair and onto my shoulders. I took a deep breath and tried to relax. But my mind wouldn't stop. What did Tom know? And what the bloody hell had Shinju gotten herself into?

When the cops arrived, I took a quick inventory. The only thing missing was an old photo of Shinju and me I'd stuck beneath a Down Under magnet on the fridge. Mum had snapped a fuzzy shot of us on Eighty Mile Beach. At thirteen, we wore our new bikinis with an excitement that only slightly covered our insecurity. Mum told us of young girls who revealed too much and ended up being taken advantage of. Girls right in our neighborhood. But with Shinju's arms locked tightly around my neck, I felt safe.

Turns out the cops, Liam Walker and Cooper Riley, had gone to school with Shinju and me, and were the same ones who'd been first on the scene at the Mangrove. In those days they'd been Shinju and Tom's friends, not mine.

"Damn shame about your sister," Walker said. It had to be the tenth time he'd said it, and I wondered if he'd slept with her in school.

Riley nodded. "She was a beauty, all right." They exchanged a look, and I was sure they were remembering fonder days.

"Yeah," I said. "She made sure she was the beauty of the family."

They became flustered after that. Everyone knew the story, or at least thought they did. How Shinju "accidentally" sliced my face open with an oyster knife. Trying to protect me and Mum during one of Pop's drunken rages was the story Shinju gave.

Walker coughed. "You have any idea who would break in and steal the photo off your fridge?"

"Maybe one of the blokes Shinju slept with in secondary school?"

Riley stole another look at Walker. "Miss Nakagawa, you don't seem too broken up over your sister's death. Any reason for that?"

I had to laugh. "How much time do you have? But if you think I had anything to do with my sister's murder, I've got twenty BSSP divers who'll swear I've been harvesting oysters on the *Adelaide* for the past three weeks."

Riley raised an eyebrow. "I don't recall saying your sister was murdered."

"I've been to the morgue," I said. "I know about the pearl. The bruises on her neck. Just because Shinju and I fought like the devil doesn't mean I don't want justice."

Walker handed me his card. "Call me if you think of anything else."

I would have slammed the door after them if it'd been possible. I called Mum and Pop and told them I'd be over after I cleaned up the mess. Mum said she'd come and help me, but she never showed up. No surprise there.

I remembered my neighbors had renovated their bungalow a few months before, so I asked to have their old front door. I nailed the jamb in place and hung the door as best I could. When I finished, I grabbed my keys and stepped out the back. Locking up, I stared through the kitchenette window. What kind of person would steal a photo of a couple of thirteen-year-old girls? Possibilities raced through my mind, and despite my bravado with the cops, fear seeped deeper into my spine.

Two detectives were sipping tea at the kitchen table when I got to Mum and Pop's. Both were middle-aged, pudgy above the beltline. Gray Suit Number One spoke first.

"The autopsy revealed your daughter didn't drown. She suffocated." He held up a copy of the eight-by-ten glossy like the one I'd snitched. "This pearl was lodged in her throat, Mr. Nakagawa. Ever seen it before?"

My father is a second-generation Australian pearler. His father emigrated from Japan in the thirties, eventually buying a used but seaworthy lugger. He hired Aborigine women as pearl divers instead of immigrant Japanese women because they had larger lung capacities for free diving. My grandfather made steady money, and wasn't a drinker. Can't say the same for Pop. He lost everything—the shop, the equipment, the lugger—by the time I was fifteen. The same year Shinju sliced my face open.

Taking the photo, Pop clicked his tongue in appreciation. Everyone in my family knew a prize when we saw it. "Back in 'eighty-seven, I held a cultured pearl harvested out of Kuri Bay," he said. "It measured sixteen point five millimeters, was light gray in color, and had a nacre depth of point eight millimeters. I thought I was holding a ray of moonbeam."

I leaned against the kitchen counter, nursing a glass of lemon squash. Pop could be poetic when he felt like it. I smelled the faint tang of whiskey spiraling up from the sink drain. Mum or Pop? I wondered. Probably both off the wagon now.

"But no," Pop continued. "I've never seen this pearl before."

Gray Suit Number Two leaned back in our kitchen chair. "Material recovered from under your daughter's fingernails is not from the mudflats in Roebuck Bay. The sand grains are more coarse. Perhaps from one of the islands along the coast. Do you have any idea why she would have been there? Maybe on a photo shoot for BSSP?"

Mum spoke up, her voice shaky. "I don't think so. She spent an hour here, after her business in town. She said she had a flight back to Sydney later that evening."

As always, this was news to me. Shinju would sometimes visit Mum and Pop after a meeting with BSSP. Drop off an ambrosia dessert from the pastry shop, along with a bit of cash. I'd usually find out about it after she'd gone. My parents had given up trying to piece the family back together.

Mum didn't look so good. Worse than usual. She hadn't dyed her hair pitch-black to cover the gray. Her housecoat was rumpled with what looked like gooseberry jam dried on the breast, and her face was puffy. I walked over and sat down next to her. I can't tell you why, but I put my arm around her.

I turned to the first detective. "Any idea of the time of death?"

"Hard to say for certain, but the medical examiner estimates the time to be approximately forty-eight hours ago, give or take eight hours."

I realized two nights ago at 10:42 in the evening would fall in that range.

A familiar but more gentle than usual rap sounded on the back door, and Thomas Lafroy, Sr., stepped in. The Lafroys had lived across the street from us for ten years. When Mrs. Lafroy died from colon cancer last year, Captain Lafroy sold the house. Everything reminded him of her, he said. Her cornflower-blue hydrangea bushes the size of Volkswagen Beetles had definitely suffered at the hands of the new neighbors. The captain hadn't maintained his rugged good looks since his wife died, but it was still easy to see why Shinju had wrapped herself around Tom Jr. from the start. Father and son both had a crooked smile and a confidence that drew women like bottlenose flies to crocs on the barbie.

"Fierce hard time for ye," he said. "So sorry." Unlike his son's slight Irish lilt, Captain Lafroy's brogue was heavy and thick.

Pop got up and fell into Lafroy's arms, wailing like a baby. When Mum joined the group hug, I began to fidget. We were not huggers.

"We're the detectives on the case," said Gray Suit Number Two. "Did you know the deceased, Mister—?"

Captain Lafroy introduced himself and sat down. "I know Kashiko better than I knew Shinju." His thick accent caused *I* to be *oi* and *than* to be *dan*. "I captain BSSP pearling ships, and Kashiko here is one of our best divers. One of only two female divers in the fleet." He tugged on a lock of my hair, something that had always annoyed me but I'd never complained about.

"The captain was the only one who'd give me a chance," I said, and pulled my head away.

"And the other captains are kicking themselves over it." He clasped his hands together and leaned forward. "But about Shinju, detective. She and my son Tom were sweethearts. They talked about getting married, but things didn't work out. Broke up several years back. Upset both the Nakagawas and my wife and me. It was a hard time."

"Whose decision was it to break up, your son's or the deceased's?" the detective asked.

Lafroy stared at his hands, then stole a look at Pop. "Shinju called off the engagement."

"How did your son take the news, Captain Lafroy?"

Tom's father looked at me, and I shook my head, trying to warn him.

"Not well, I'm afraid," he said.

"Captain, did he ever threaten her, harm her in any way?"

Lafroy rubbed his forehead. "Just remember that Shinju dropped the charges."

"And what charges were those, Captain Lafroy?"

"Assault," I said. "Shinju said Tom threatened to strangle her."

The morning of the funeral I woke before sunrise, slid onto the Ducati, and headed for the Japanese Pearl Divers Cemetery on Port Drive. The tombstones, hewn of beach stone and inscribed with various Japanese dialects, are surrounded by a sea of packed dirt and scattered gray pebbles. In better times, Grandfather drove Shinju and me to the cemetery to sweep and weed the graves. Although he hadn't known any of the ancient residents, he said it was a matter of honor to keep their graves presentable. My sister and I couldn't wait for those peaceful Saturday afternoons when we escaped Mum and Pop's clashes and the stench of cigarette butts drowned in whiskey.

I squatted under a gum tree and fingered Shinju's pearls. That peace I longed for didn't come. Instead anxiety spread like a rising tide. I hadn't seen Tom since the morning my bungalow was broken into, but I needed to talk to him. For several days I'd shown up at the police station and asked the suits if they had any information on Shinju or the pearl. I couldn't decide if they were lying to me or just plain inept. Either way, I got nothing from them and called Tom. There was no answer, so I left a message for him to meet me in the morning at the Japanese cemetery at seven-thirty.

When he didn't show by eight, I stood and brushed the dirt from my leathers. Mum had asked me for breakfast. Probably just tea and toast, but I knew she needed me that day. I took a step in the direction of my bike and Tom Lafroy slithered out from behind a six-foot tombstone.

"I got your message." He lifted his face to the breeze and his shoulders visibly relaxed.

I faltered, but only for a moment. "You said Shinju was in over her head. What did you mean?"

He raised an eyebrow. "And g'day to you too." He was unshaven, dressed in jeans and a sweatshirt. I knew he was planning on being at the funeral, but it wasn't scheduled until ten o'clock. He'd be dressed to the nines by then.

"Sorry." I attempted a smile. We both knew it wasn't genuine.

He plucked a pack of Dunhills from his pocket, tapped it against his forefinger twice, then gripped the cigarette with his lips. He was about to pull it from the pack when he saw my face. He spit the ciggy back into the pack and pushed it out of sight with a fingertip. "Sorry. Forgot you can't handle the smoke. Trying to quit anyway."

I pulled the eight-by-ten from my jacket pocket and handed it to him. "The pearl's one in a million, Tom. Something like that can't be kept a secret — unless it came from a stray."

Occasionally currents caused oysters to cut loose from their basket moorings. When BSSP divers found a stray, they were awarded a finder's fee. Any diver caught not returning a stray was fired on the spot. But that wasn't always a deterrent.

Breath from his low whistle grazed my ear as he marveled at the pearl. "Maybe it was a stray. Maybe BSSP produced it. Who knows?"

I frowned. "You're just like those detectives. Holding out on me."

He grabbed my shoulders with both hands, startling me. Then he put a bead on me that caused me to take in a sharp breath of cold air. "What I'm about to say, you have to promise to keep it quiet. At least until we know more."

I wanted to shrug his hands loose and step back to safety, but I needed the information. "Right-o," I said.

He searched my eyes, uncertain, I suppose, whether he could trust me. "The *Indian Princess*," he said finally. "Part of the BSSP fleet. I was having a pint at Jack's about six months ago and heard a rumor about a stray that produced a pearl like that. But it was never returned to BSSP. The diver kept it. I didn't believe it, figured someone was just blowing smoke . . . until I saw the photo of the pearl in the paper. Word was, the diver was working on the *Indian Princess* at the time."

"Who was he, Tom? Between you and me, we know almost every

diver in the fleet. Twenty boats, twenty divers per boat. We can find him."

His hands were still on my shoulders. I felt them tremble, which I found strange. Tom's hands had always felt so strong, so sure. Then his touch disappeared and he straightened my jacket collar.

"Right-o," he said with a forced smile. "I'll get the ship's log from the *Indian Princess* for the last two years. We'll find him."

I returned his smile. Mine, at least, was heartfelt. "Working together again," I said. "Just like old times."

Pain wrinkled his brow, and his smile faded.

That little show of disappointment sent my spirits spiraling downward. "See you at the funeral," I said quickly and backed away.

But his face turned brooding as he pulled out his Dunhills. The ciggy lit, he inhaled deeply. He turned his head sideways to blow the smoke over his shoulder. When he turned back, I thought he was going to say something. Instead he swung his lanky body in the direction of the tombstone and disappeared.

For the next six weeks I spent my time badgering the suits for updates on Shinju's murder investigation and upending bottles of Famous Grouse Scotch into Mum's kitchen sink. But nothing I said or did seemed to make much difference at the police station, or at home. I finally wised up and remembered I couldn't solve Mum and Pop's problems. But maybe I could do something to help find my sister's killer. The pearl was unique. Only a few companies could have produced it. I figured a BSSP pearling ship was a good place to start. I was headed back out to sea and it couldn't have come at a better time. Broome was closing in on me.

Tom and I hadn't crewed together for several seasons, so I was surprised to find him stowing his gear onto the *Adelaide* three cabins down from mine late one afternoon at the end of February.

"Hey, stranger," I said.

He gave me his crooked smile and a quick nod, but that was all I got. After checking my wetsuit, mask, and regulator for signs of wear and damage, I stowed the gear in my locker and headed for the galley. I kept an eye out for Tom, but he never showed. I guessed he ate in the captain's cabin with his father. The cook served grilled saltwater barramundi and fresh veggies. My favorite. Afterward I turned in early. Being the only female diver on the

*Adelaide,* I never had to share a cabin. Not unless I wanted to, of course. But one-nighters in sandy sheets were not my thing. To the blokes on the ship, I was just another mate.

The ship arrived at our destination sometime during the night. Oyster bed locations are guarded secrets, so except for Captain Lafroy and his first mate, the rest of us hadn't a clue about the *Adelaide*'s exact coordinates.

*Pinctada maxima*—the oysters that produce South Sea pearls —are found only in Australian and Tahitian waters. Because *P. maxima* have a short lifespan, just six years, pearl manufacturers have to maintain a steady supply harvested from the ocean. As a diver, my job is to scour the sea floor and snatch as many of the giants as I can during my shift. Oyster season is from January to March. Unfortunately, it's also the high season for the deadliest creature in the world, the box jellyfish. One sting can kill a person in thirty seconds.

My diver's watch buzzed at 5 A.M. I pulled on a one-piece bather, a well-worn kimono, and boat shoes, then padded down to the galley for a cup of green tea. Sounds of the morning routine drifted through the open portholes: shots of compressed air hissing as the ship's air tanks were tested, the flapping and submerging of the sail anchor, and the creaking of the two metal harvesting arms, each dangling six air hoses and tethers, as they swung into place over the water. The ocean lapped lazily against the ship, and I had just closed my eyes to enjoy the familiar sounds when the blaring of Johnny Cash's "Ring of Fire" shattered my peace. Damn that Yank, *and* Tom Lafroy. Besides annoying me with his favorite music too early in the morning, he hadn't come through with what he promised.

"Da says he can't get the *Indian Princess* records from BSSP," he'd told me a few weeks earlier when we met at the Honeyeater Café for an update. He'd sat picking the grilled fennel root and bean sprouts from his soy burger, then smothered the patty with Keen's mustard. "The company's worried the pearl was stolen. Sounds like it might have been a stray, like you suggested. Da says he's tried contacting a couple of his captain buddies, but everyone's clamming up. So I went back to Jack's."

"Find out anything?" I asked as I scraped his discards onto my soy burger.

He shifted his eyes away from me. "The boys said the diver was a new bloke from Sydney. His body was found at Coulomb Point last October."

I noticed for the first time how his fingers tapped a nervous staccato on the table. I wasn't sure he was telling me everything.

But now, as I sat in the galley on the *Adelaide,* Johnny Cash was singing "I went down, down, down, and the flames went higher" through the porthole, and I wondered if I'd been a fool to believe him. I gulped the tea and returned to my cabin to get ready for my shift.

Exposure of just one square inch of skin is deadly during box jellyfish season. An ounce of venom can kill sixty men. Cody, my dive buddy, a mate I'd partnered with numerous times, checked the hood that covered my head and neck, the tightness of my mask, the juncture where my gloves overlapped the nine-millimeter neoprene suit at my wrists. I did the same for him. Once we completed our check, we gave a thumbs-up to the dive master and climbed onto the dive platform. Each of the ship's two metal arms, one port and one starboard, serviced six divers. Fitted with air hoses and tethers, the device allowed us to be pulled along for extended periods with an ample supply of air. All I had to do was scan the uneven seabed and pluck oysters. Easy. Like riding a finely tuned bike.

I was assigned the far tether on the starboard side, my buddy the second from the end. Once underwater and then again on the sea floor, we exchanged a thumbs-up to indicate that our ears had equalized, our air was flowing, and we were good to go. Every five minutes throughout the dive, we were to signal our status. Adjusting the air in our buoyancy compensators, we hovered an arm's reach from the ocean floor.

At a depth of thirty feet, weightlessness as well as the current teased the strain from my muscles. Pulled along by the tether, I spotted speckled cowries and spiral-shaped wentletrap shells tumbling along the seabed. Under a brain coral, a sea slug rippled its purple-trimmed mantle. It was good to be back.

I refocused on my work, straining my eyes to distinguish the oyster shells from the drab underwater terrain. We were paid per oyster, and shifts could amount to big bikkies in your pocket. At the fifteen-minute mark I returned my buddy's signal. My netted bag was half full of oysters, despite the poor visibility. I was certain to return to the surface with a full haul.

Captain Lafroy gradually turned the boat north. The currents were stronger in this section and had churned up the water, making it difficult to see the oysters even though they were as big as supper platters.

I spied a huge oyster shell peeking out from a clump of dead man's fingers when my lungs felt the tug of decreased air flowing through the hose. I calmed myself, slowed my breathing, and looked up, following the heavy black hose that was keeping me alive. The slack in the hose didn't concern me at first, but when I inhaled a small mouthful of saltwater, panic prickled my sense of calm. And when I saw the black tubing descending in lazy loops before me, I knew my lifeline was severed.

I searched for my buddy. We could share his air. The water darkened as an overhead cloud hid the sun. Visibility was now only a few feet. Where was he? My body screamed for air. Instinct to inhale invaded my brain. But if I did, I'd fill my lungs with water. Training kicked in. I flipped onto my back, released my weight belt, and fumbled for the $CO_2$ cartridge attached to my buoyancy compensator. I yanked hard on the cord. The BC expanded like a balloon. Exhaling what little air I had left in a constant flow of little bubbles, I shot toward the surface. With all my strength, I forced myself not to suck in the blackness around me. It seemed thirty feet had turned into a thousand. My lungs ached, but to survive I had to exhale every bit of breath in my lungs. A free ascent would protect me from getting the bends. In theory, anyway.

I popped to the surface like a harbor buoy. Riding the four-foot waves was rough, but I quickly realized a new danger approached. The huge underwater sail anchor—dragged behind the ship to decrease the ship's speed so divers could work—was almost on me. If I got tangled in its cables, I'd be strangled before I could drown.

I heard a shout from the boat. Captain Lafroy threw out an orange ring as the crew fought with my sixty-foot tether line. His aim was off, and the sea roiled, throwing me down into the trough of the wave and the ring onto the crest. Johnny Cash's lyrics rang in my head. *Down, down, down,* he sang. *Down, down, down.* I swallowed a blast of wind-tossed wave and saltwater scathed my windpipe. I watched as a gust lifted the ring into the air, spinning it on its edge like a coin. Finally it fell within five feet of me. Hope ignited the lactic acid in my muscles, boiling it away. I swam hard against the current. When I reached the ring, I shot my arms through and clamped down with everything I had. I floated on my back and was hauled away from the sail anchor cables and toward the boat. Like a giant tuna.

Once on the dive platform, I was stripped of my gear and rolled in a wool blanket. My heart skittered inside my chest like a pinball. I shook like hell. A couple of deckhands lifted me onto a stretcher and carried me below.

"Thanks, mates," I said, once lying in my bunk. The adrenaline rush had drained me. I just wanted to be left alone. They each gave my hand a squeeze and disappeared. I inhaled the salty air mixed with diesel, thankful to the sea gods I was alive. Someone rapped on the door. Tom's head appeared.

He sat next to me on the narrow bunk and tucked the blanket around my legs. "Da called off the harvesting for the day."

I pulled an arm from under the blanket and angled it across my eyes. "The guys won't be happy about that."

"Sea's getting rough anyway. Storm's coming. I checked your air hose. Looks like sun damage. Cracks weakened the rubber. The hose snapped off just below the surface—that's why no one noticed. Your buddy didn't see a thing. Feels like an ass. Da wants all twelve hoses checked. Replaced if necessary. He's just sick about it."

He took my cold hand in his. At once my exhaustion disappeared and my mind was on alert. His hip pressed against mine, and even though I felt an uncomfortable stabbing pain due to the pressure, I didn't want him to move.

"One time I had to do a free ascent like you did today," he said. "Spent twelve hours in a hyperbaric chamber." He frowned. "Diving's risky business. You should take a break from it for the rest of the trip."

I lifted my head, bristling at his words. "Is that a threat?"

"Just a penny's worth of free advice."

"Piss off, Lafroy. And take your pennies with you."

He got up from the bed and pulled up a stool. "Da said to keep an eye on you for the next couple of hours. If you start having symptoms, we'll have to get you a chamber in Broome. Now lie flat. We're headed to one of the islands to ride out the storm."

I lay back down. It was stupid to raise my head and risk nitrogen rising to my brain. I had to admit that Captain Lafroy was right about that. He was also right about the storm. We'd all be safer on one of the nature reserve islands in the Timor Sea where BSSP maintains a pearling operation site.

Tom looked at me through lowered lids. "So what should we talk about?"

I thought back to my time being tossed around in the sea like a Styrofoam cup. Tom had not been part of the first shift of divers, but I didn't remember seeing him on deck during my rescue. Where had he been?

"I dunno," I said finally. "How about the night in Sydney when you tried to strangle my sister?"

He clicked his tongue. "About time someone wanted to hear my side."

The air in the cabin was getting cooler with the storm and I slipped my arms back under the blanket. I wasn't so sure I wanted to hear his explanation. I liked keeping my resentment toward him alive and healthy. But I owed it to Shinju to find out more.

"Shinju wasn't only addicted to cocaine," he began. "She was addicted to the party scene. But I was sick of that life."

I folded my arms under the covers. Tom offered Shinju and me our first joint in Grade 10, our first snort of cocaine a couple of years later. Shinju got pulled in. I bolted in the other direction.

"That night a movie director was giving a party, but I wanted her to stay home. Shinju just laughed, told me I was bonkers. Why should she be with a bloke from Broome when she could party with Sydney's beautiful people? I got angry, told her I wouldn't let her go."

Imprisoned in my bunk, I couldn't see Tom's face too well. But I did hear his heavy exhale.

"I loved her, but I was losing her. A few weeks before, she told me she'd slept with a fashion designer, some famous guy who'd given her some of his stuff to wear. She was cheating on me. It made me crazy."

His voice cracked a bit with the last sentence, but I didn't care. A cantilevered lamp swayed with the rock of the ship, sending Tom's distorted profile skittling across the wall. The storm was on us now.

"So what did you do?"

"I left. Went to a pub around the corner. Got wasted, then came back to the apartment to wait for her. When she got home at four in the morning, we argued again. She threw her shoes at me. Broke off our engagement. The whole thing was ugly as hell."

"She told me you'd strangle her if she left."

He punched the wall with his fist. "I can't remember everything I said that night. All I know is she stormed off to the bedroom and locked the door. I crashed on the sofa. Don't know how long I was out. The door chime woke me. Three Blue Healers from Central Metro stood there, badges all shiny, saying Shinju reported me for assault—that I'd threatened her."

I heard the crinkling of cellophane, a familiar *tap-tap,* then smelled a whiff of fresh tobacco. I was about to protest, but before the words were out of my mouth he said "Sorry" and put his Dunhills away.

"It was nothing but lies," he continued. "I'd never hurt her."

I didn't know what to believe. Shinju had a knack for twisting the knife in your soft underside. But Tom wasn't trustworthy either.

I heard him rise and then felt him sitting on the edge of my bunk again. He flicked back my hair and found where my scar began at my temple. He traced it across my cheek to the corner of my mouth.

"How did this happen?" He spoke slowly, as if he had to think about each word. The walls of the small cabin collapsed and I felt my throat constricting. I was under the sea again, fighting for air.

"Shinju was trying to protect me from Pop."

He gave his head a little shake, then shifted his gaze to the porthole. His breath, warm and moist, fell softly on my face. It smelled of coffee and cigarettes, but for some reason it didn't bother me. Then, as if something other than the steady storm raged outside, he cocked his head. With a raised eyebrow, he turned to look at me again, hand still on my face. "You sticking with that story?"

I didn't answer. Instead I pulled my head away from his touch. "I always check my air hose before diving," I said. "It looked fine to me this morning."

"Huh?" he said.

"What were you doing while I was diving, Tom?"

He stood and walked to the door. "Maybe you should sleep with one eye open. You don't know who you can trust."

\*

To tend the company's offshore oyster farms, BSSP maintains small camps on several island nature reserves. Australia's restrictions for using the sites are simple: take out what you take in. Every crew I'd ever been part of kept the campsites as pristine as possible.

We arrived at the island around 7 P.M. Box jellyfish season was still going strong, so the sixteen-foot Zodiac made several trips until the crew was landed. I made the trip by Zodiac and stretcher. I was getting tired of the constraints, but Captain Lafroy insisted I lie flat for the full twenty-four hours.

There weren't enough cabins for the entire crew, so Tom put me in a cramped storage room next to The Implantation/Extraction Room, TIER for short. In TIER, experts inserted perfectly round plastic balls into each new batch of oysters. The balls served as cores for cultured South Sea pearls. The oysters were then taken to the undersea farms, placed in netted baskets attached to lines, and dropped into the aquamarine waters. The oyster excretes a flow of pearly nacre to cover the plastic seed irritating its body. And the result? The largest and most exquisite pearls cocreated by man and nature. BSSP's claim, anyway.

The plan was for the crew to work at the camp—scrubbing algae off harvested shells, repairing equipment—for a day or two while waiting for the storm to pass. I kept to my room, sleeping on and off the whole day, listening to the wind and rain, going stir-crazy.

Overrested, I was still wide awake after midnight when I heard muffled voices filtering through the wall my room shared with TIER. Was it normal to work around the clock when a new batch of oysters was brought in? I wasn't sure.

As quietly as I could, I slid headfirst onto the floor and belly-crawled closer. I felt silly, pressing my ear against the wall, but I was determined to find out more about BSSP's operations. The water-tank filters next door gurgled loudly and distorted the voices. I readjusted my head as much as I dared and listened.

"I'm out," a male voice said.

Another male voice answered, but his words were muffled. The aquarium tanks splashed and babbled, and I guessed he was standing farther away from the wall between us.

"That bloody pearl was worth a million. Now we've lost it. The coppers have it," the first man continued. "Then you couldn't even make sure her body didn't wash up on shore. 'Take out what you take in,' you insisted. Bloody hell, now there's a murder investigation. And the sister? You promised she wouldn't make it up from that dive alive. I told you, I'm out of it."

Again I couldn't make out the reply. I heard the door open, then slam shut. I returned to the makeshift cot. I always told myself I could handle anything. Now I wasn't so sure. The rupture of my air hose had been no accident. The break-in at my bungalow, I realized, wasn't just some random act. My heart took off running, and the room started to pitch.

I'd recognized the one voice I heard. It belonged to Crowe, a marine biologist responsible for overseeing TIER. Originally from Sydney, he'd transplanted himself to Broome thirty years ago. A pioneer in the cultured pearl industry. And now, at the very least, an accessory to murder.

I pulled the covers over my head and wanted to hide like I did the night I came home after getting a hundred stitches. Back then, I understood that Shinju had slashed my face to destroy my looks. I'd shivered under the sheets and wondered how my life would change. But this was different. This time I'd be dead if Crowe and his accomplice had their way.

The cheap mattress drilled a wayward spring into my kidney, but I was afraid to move, to make a sound. Too weak to stomp down the memories, my mind raced back to the day Shinju cut me.

On that Saturday morning, Tom and I planned to trek out to the flying boat wrecks in Roebuck Bay. We'd figured out we fancied one another, as much as fifteen-year-olds can know such things, and planned to spend the day sloshing the two kilometers to the wrecks and back. Two or three days a month low tide exposes the remains of three WWII Royal Dutch Air Force flying boats buried in the mud. Not very romantic, but I think we both realized it would give us a reason to hold on to each other as we hiked through the mudflats, and we were both keen on that idea.

But as Tom was backing out his dad's truck from the driveway, Shinju popped open the passenger door and squeezed in next to me. I remember the expression on Tom's face. Surprise at first, then obvious irritation. I gave Shinju a fierce look that spelled "Push off!" She ignored it, reached across me, and fiddled with the radio, chattering about the wrecks. Did we know that in 1942

Japanese Zeros raided Broome and destroyed fifteen flying boats in Roebuck Bay?

"Everyone knows that, Shinju." Tom yanked the shifter into reverse and squealed out of the driveway.

How many times since the Lafroys moved in across the street had Shinju and I talked late into the night, wondering what it would be like to kiss Tom? But after two years of playful flirting, Shinju didn't win him. I did. Tom and I had more in common, I suppose. We both loved to dive, trek the nature reserves, walk along Eighty Mile Beach. Shinju and I didn't realize it then, but the day he chose me, Tom Lafroy made the first slice into the one heart my sister and I seemed to share.

Determined to salvage our outing to the wrecks, we ignored Shinju. As we stumbled through the mangrove swamps, Tom held my hand. To keep me from injuring my feet on buried mussels, he lifted me over suspicious pitted mudflats. He wrapped his arms around my waist whenever possible, even though doing so sometimes made it even more difficult to walk. He slipped his fingers through the bikini ties at my hips, and I clung to him whether I needed to or not.

At the wreckage site, an aircraft engine covered with soft coral had settled into the flats. A lonesome jetty post left for posterity angled up from the exposed sea floor. Locals milled about, along with tourists who'd arrived in hovercrafts.

During the war, Dutch refugees from Java, mainly women and children, were evacuated to Broome. Since no accommodations were available in town, flying-boat pilots were instructed to keep their passengers onboard. Aircraft were to be refueled, then continue on their way. But at 8 A.M. on March third, Japanese pilots strafed the moored planes, believing them to be war targets, unaware that innocent civilians were onboard.

The morning Tom, Shinju, and I were there, an elderly Dutch tourist started to retell the story of the strike. Tom and I weren't interested. We'd heard it enough times in school. We moved on and investigated a different plane some distance away. Shinju, I found out later, gave the man her full attention.

"The Nips are a cruel race," he told her. "My grandfather was a pilot for the Dutch Royal Air Force. He was burned alive here in Roebuck Bay when his fuel tank caught fire. His charred body was one of the few recovered." He pointed a finger at Shinju. "You people deserved Hiroshima and Nagasaki."

Although I was nowhere near my sister, I sensed something was wrong. I ran back and found her collapsed in the mud, surrounded by tourists. Tom was right behind me. He picked her up. Her eyes fluttered once and then she nuzzled her head into his neck. A woman told us what had happened, apologizing for the man, who'd returned to the hovercraft.

How Tom carried her the entire way back, I have no idea. By the time we reached the shore, she was able to walk. In the truck cab, she lay down with her head on Tom's lap, her body between us and her sandy feet on my sunburned thighs. Once or twice on the way home I thought I saw her hand snake up Tom's leg, but I couldn't be sure.

Tom carried her to the bedroom Shinju and I shared, laid her on her bed, then backed out without a word. Mum and Pop weren't home, so I stayed with her. She explained what had happened at the wreck site. A slight smile crept across her face when she apologized for ruining my date with Tom. Then she fell asleep. But I wasn't so sure she was sorry.

I showered, towel-dried my hair, and pulled on a thin camisole top and shorts. A hint of lipstick and I was out the door and on Tom's doorstep. I didn't know what Shinju was up to, but I wanted to make sure I didn't lose him.

Captain Lafroy was sitting on the sofa, reading the newspaper. He asked if Shinju was feeling any better. I assured him she was. Tom was in his room, he added, indicating the direction with a tilt of his head.

I was a virgin and Tom said he was too, but I didn't believe it. I was right. He knew exactly what to do. He locked the door, turned on the radio, and lit a candle. What happened that incredible night I've never experienced again.

Sometime in the night, a knock on the door and his mother's voice woke us. I hid in the closet while she asked him questions — did he have a nice time, would he ask me out again, did he remember to take the rubbish to the curb. After she left, he kissed me one last time and I crawled out his bedroom window.

I floated across the street until I heard Pop's angry words through our front door. I slipped inside and saw Mum lift her arms to protect herself. Pop swung his fist, but Mum ducked. Not making the expected connection, he spun with the momentum and lost his balance. When he crashed to the floor, I grabbed Mum. We raced down the hallway, Pop's threats not far behind. I had just pushed Mum through her bedroom door and heard the lock click when Pop spun me around. I was focused on that crazed look in his eye. I didn't notice Shinju holding our grandfather's oyster knife, sharp as broken glass.

Over ten years have passed since that night, and that knife's long gone. But every once in a while, when I look in the mirror, I still feel its razor sting.

The next morning anxious thoughts woke me. Tom believed Shinju was into something over her head. The previous night's partially garbled conversation coiled itself around my stomach and pulled tight. A nutcase was loose on the island, and now his sights were set on me. But then I reminded myself that the reason I left Broome was to find Shinju's killer. Hiding in a storage closet wasn't going to solve this mystery.

Rummaging through my shore bag, I found my dive knife and strapped it above my knee. Then I stuck my head into the hallway. Lab techs scurried in and out of TIER, but I didn't see Crowe. I re-checked the sheath buckle, then quietly shut the door behind me.

I snuck out of the building and ran to the makeshift showers. While fresh water rinsed the scaly salt from my body, I wondered what to do next. I hated acting like a hunted animal, but I wasn't sure who I could trust. Crowe wanted me dead. Who else was my enemy?

I toweled off using the sarong I wore, then rewrapped myself in it. Sticking around a crowd seemed a good idea, so I walked to the small, open-air dining hall, where some of the crew sat on benches taking a coffee break. I saw Cody, my longtime diving buddy, and squeezed in next to him. He apologized several times for not watching me more carefully during the dive, but I couldn't tell him I now knew my broken hose had been no accident. I sipped my tea, wondering who I could confide in.

Freshly shaven, Captain Lafroy entered, ordered a cup of coffee, and was about to have a seat next to the first mate when he saw me. I waved him over.

He gave me a big smile. "How you feeling?" He tugged my hair.

I swatted his hand away playfully. "Did Tom tell you I almost got my oyster quota? Didn't drop a one on the way up."

Captain Lafroy laughed, his crooked smile turned upward in delight. "What's really important is you're alive."

I looked at him carefully. The paunchy middle, the sun-damaged skin, the graying at the temples. This is what his son would look like in another thirty years. But there was one big difference: Captain Lafroy was a man I could trust.

The hall had cleared out some; even my dive buddy had taken off. I wondered if Captain Lafroy would believe me. Crowe wasn't a favorite among the ships' crews. He tossed out what he claimed to be questionable, sickly oysters, which decreased divers' counts. And more importantly, paychecks.

"I need to talk to you. Right away," I said.

Just then Crowe sauntered into the room. He saluted the captain with a tweak of his hair, but when he saw me, he stopped short. His eyes narrowed and his mouth tightened into a thin line. He walked to the counter, ordered, then turned back to stare at me while he waited for his food.

Captain Lafroy looked at his watch. "Sorry, no time. The *Adelaide* suffered some damage from the storm."

I leaned in closer. "It's about Crowe."

The captain laughed again, but this time more heartily. "Do you think he's fudging your oyster count numbers? Look, he's a stickler for keeping the harvest healthy. Cut him some slack." He glanced at Crowe, who was still glowering, then back to me. "Wait a second. What's going on here?"

"I need your help," I whispered. "Can we talk? Somewhere private?"

He sighed. "All right, I'll give you a wee bit of time. How about Sunset Point in thirty minutes?"

I thanked him and left. As I walked back to my room, Crowe and the oyster counts preyed on my mind. If Crowe was stealing pearls, how was he doing it? I needed evidence to convince the captain. The only way to find out was to sneak into TIER.

Once in the building, I tried the lab door. It was locked. I heard no voices inside, only the gurgling of the water tanks. A blast of cold air hit me and I looked up at the overhead vent. I hurried to my little storage room and turned the bolt. I climbed the shelves, unscrewed the vent cover, and hoisted myself up. The ventilation shaft was a tight fit. Luckily my destination was close by.

After checking to make sure I had no company, I dropped through the vent opening and onto a lab table. A photo of Crowe with the BSSP president sat on the largest desk in the room. On Crowe's computer screen, the *Adelaide*'s latest haul was entered on a spreadsheet. I minimized the document, watching it shrink to the bottom of the screen. I found the file from the *Indian Princess*, the ship connected with the pearl found in Shinju's throat, and couldn't make sense of it. I needed more time, but knew my luck was ticking away. A jpeg file entitled *Simms* saved on the desktop caught my eye. I'd worked with a diver named Simms once. I clicked on the file and felt my jaw drop as soon as the photo popped open on the screen. I knew that hand as well as I knew my own. In her palm, Shinju held the pearl that had killed her.

My mind was in a fog as I clambered my way through the vent back to my room. Tom was right about one thing. Shinju was in way over her head. Even so, she didn't deserve to die. I needed Captain Lafroy's help.

The sandy path to Sunset Point ended at a rock outcropping that rose high above the crystalline blue water. The tide was in, covering the craggy formations below. I leaned over, judging the height to be about twenty feet. Shadowy box jellyfish dotted the surface. I sat on a wet rock and turned my face to the sun clambering to get out from behind a cloud. I had just closed my eyes when I heard the rustling of scrub brush. I turned and shaded my eyes from the glare. Because his lip was hiked up in its familiar crooked grin, my first thought was that I was looking at Tom Lafroy, Jr. What was he doing at Sunset Point?

"Your sister loved this spot too. Pity to stain its natural beauty a second time."

I readjusted my brain. The captain was speaking, not Tom, but his words made no sense.

"A free ascent," he said, nodding his head. "Quick thinking. Thought you'd panic, lass. Well, I can still make this work." He tugged on a pair of heavy rubber gloves, the kind oyster scrubbers use to scrape off algae and bacteria.

I tried to speak but couldn't.

"You didn't wait long enough after the scuba accident, Kashiko. You passed out from nitrogen poisoning. You fell, hitting your head against the rocks. A tragedy."

"Wait," I croaked. "First tell me what happened to Shinju."

He shook his head. "She was a pretty little thing when she was young. The first time I saw you and your sister was the day I decided to buy the house across the street from your family. I made up my mind then and there I'd have you both. Just once was all I wanted. There were a few other young girls in the neighborhood as well. That was a lucky chance. I got Shinju, but I guess she figured she'd save you by ruining your looks. She was right about that. Those stitches, that hideous scar turned my stomach."

"You raped her!"

"Let's not bring up the past. Shinju tried that, and look what happened to her."

"You killed Shinju, didn't you?" I said, scraping up every smidgen of courage to keep the terror from my voice. "I have a right to know why."

"Shinju was blackmailing me. Needed big bikkies for her habit. But I couldn't keep up the payments. She threatened to ruin me. A rape charge by BSSP's favorite model? I'd lose everything—my pension, my reputation . . ."

"Your freedom. You belong in jail."

"You don't understand. My wife's cancer bills wiped out our savings. I sold the house, but it wasn't enough."

My mind battled to make sense of things. "That poor diver, Simms, offered Crowe the stray, didn't he? Whose idea was it, yours or Crowe's, to get rid of him?"

The whites of the captain's eyes glistened in the sunlight. "We both fancied the idea of a two-way split instead of a three. Later I brought Shinju to the island and showed her the pearl. She fell in love with it. Agreed to be the hand model for the pearls we stole. But later that day the pearl was missing from Crowe's office."

"You found her here at Sunset Point."

"High on cocaine. She opened her fist and flashed the pearl at me. I demanded it back. She just laughed. Said she'd left a note at your bungalow about the rape so there was nothing I could do. The next moment I thought I saw her throw the pearl over the cliff." He snorted under his breath. "But she tricked me. She must have thrown a shell.

"I lost control. That pearl was worth a mint. I wrestled her to the ground. Pressed her head into the sand. I had to kill her, don't you see? But I didn't figure it out until I read the newspaper. She'd put the pearl in her mouth and choked on it!"

He took a step closer. I shuffled back, teetering on the edge of the rock. The waves crashed on the ancient formations below, sending a fine mist high into the air and onto my bare legs. I bent slightly and pulled my knife from its sheath.

"Now, Kashiko, don't be difficult."

I waved my weapon back and forth, hoping he wouldn't come any nearer. Instead Captain Lafroy lunged at me. I yanked the knife arm high, above his head. He grabbed my other arm, but I twisted, coming around the back of him, slicing off his ear. Howling, he stumbled backward off the edge of the rock. But he still had me in his grasp. In the next moment we were both falling through the air.

In his panic, Lafroy released me. I grabbled for the rock face sliding past me. My thigh bounced off a protruding rock and momentarily slowed my fall. My hands, scraped and bleeding, found purchase and my body slammed into the cliff. Every nerve in my body lit up in pain. A second later I heard the captain's body hit the limestone below with a gruesome crack.

I refused to look down, but the view above did little to console me. I was a full body length down from the ledge. There were no roots or niches to help me climb back up, and my arms were on fire. *Down, down, down,* sang Johnny Cash. Down to the blue below, swarmed by box jellyfish. My body mottled with stings. My death a diver's nightmare.

I noticed a narrow fissure in the rock face above me. My knife angled out from it. I reached for it, shoving the blade deeper into the slit, the metal grinding against the rock. My broken ribs screamed in protest. Placing both hands on the handle, I pulled myself two feet higher.

A shadow fell over me. Tom Jr.'s face twisted as he stared beyond me to where his father's body surely tossed in the surf, surrounded by jellyfish. The anguish I saw stopped my heart.

His eyes shifted to me, then he fell to his knees and gripped my wrists. "Let go of the knife, Kashiko."

"No!" I screamed.

He grasped my wrists harder. "Trust me."

I hated to place my faith in Tom, but my grip was weakening. I took a deep breath and released the knife. He dragged me up and over the ledge, my ribs wailing.

Tom rocked me in his arms. "Oh, God, oh, God. I'm so sorry, Kashiko." He said it over and over. I wished he'd shut up. I couldn't handle the pain in his voice. But he kept rambling. "I knew Shinju was getting money under the table from somebody in Broome. It had to be Crowe, all Crowe, I told myself. But Da acted strange when I asked him about it. Nervous, suspicious. Still, I had no idea about . . . about what he'd done to Shinju."

"You stopped calling me after my face was cut." It was all I could think to say.

"I was fifteen. I was an ass. I'm sorry."

He started to cry, but I wondered if sorry would ever be enough. For any of us.

"Miss Nakagawa?"

I awoke from my drug-induced nap. The two detectives were sipping coffee at the foot of my hospital bed. But my lids were heavy and shut without any help from me. When I inhaled, a jolt of pain reminded me I had three broken ribs.

"Miss?" Suit Number One repeated.

I kept my eyes shut. But I talked. About Shinju, Crowe, and the captain. About the pearl. The unfortunate diver, Simms. But I didn't tell them everything—that the night I slept with Tom, the captain raped my sister. That she cut my face to save me from the same fate. The suits didn't need to know. At least not right now.

My parents drove me home and Mum offered to stay. I think she was a little surprised when I told her she could. She helped me get into an old nightgown and we sat on the small patio behind the bungalow. A full moon glowed overhead.

A few blocks away, the Staircase to the Moon shimmered on the mudflats. When we were little, Shinju and I imagined skipping up those steps to escape the rows at home. Sadly, she found heaven dust a better way to escape her nightmares.

Mum's lids drooped and she slumped sideways in her patio chair, palms lying limply on her lap. Her shoulders seemed narrower than I remembered. When had her skin become so thin across her cheeks?

Slipping one hand into my nightgown pocket, I drew out Shinju's necklace. Each pearl looked unearthly, as if an angel's halo had been captured in a glass ball. I grasped Mum's fingers and gently wrapped Shinju's pearls around our clasped hands. I've never believed in anything as ethereal as a soul. But if there are such things, I hoped my sister's was now free, skipping those amber stairs to the moon.

LEE MARTIN

# A Man Looking for Trouble

FROM *Glimmer Train Stories*

MY UNCLE WAS a man named Bill Jordan, and in 1972, when I was sixteen, he came home from Vietnam, rented a small box house on the corner of South and Christy, and went to work on a section gang with the B & O Railroad. If not for my mother and her romance with our neighbor, Harold Timms, perhaps my uncle would have lived a quiet and unremarkable life, but of course that's something we'll never know.

"He'll do all right," my father said one night at supper. He looked out the window and nodded his head. It was the first warm day of spring, and the window was open. I smelled the damp ground, heard the robins singing. "I'm glad he's back," my father said, and I believe now, for just an instant, my mother and I let ourselves get caught up in his optimism, a gift we desperately needed, although we were the sort of family that never would have admitted as much.

"How's your pork chop?" my mother asked.

"Bill's going to be aces," my father said.

Then we all sat there, chewing, not saying much of anything else at all. Bill was home, safe, and for the time that's the only thing that mattered.

By summer, though, he was fed up with Harold Timms, who happened to be his foreman on the section gang. It was generally known throughout Goldengate that Mr. Timms was keeping time with my mother, a fact that rankled Bill day in and day out, because on the job he was tired of acting like he didn't know better.

My father, a withdrawn man who kept his troubles to himself, had apparently decided to ignore my mother's adultery.

"I have to do what Harold Timms tells me every day," Bill said to my father one Sunday afternoon when they were in the shade of the big maple alongside our house, changing the points and plugs on our Ford Galaxie. "And all the while everyone in town knows he's getting it steady from your Annie."

I lay on my bed, listening. Out my window, I could see Bill leaning over the fender of the Galaxie. The hood was open above him, and he was going to town with a spark plug wrench. He had on a black bowling shirt with a print of a teetering pin wearing a crown and the words *King Pins* across the back. He'd rolled the short sleeves tight on his biceps. From where I was lying, all I could see of my father, who stood on the other side of the Galaxie, was his hand on top of that fender. His long, narrow hand. The face of his Timex watch seemed enormous on his slender wrist. A brown leather band wrapped around that wrist with plenty of length to spare. I knew he'd had to punch an extra hole in it so the watchband wouldn't be too loose.

"Dammit, R.T." Bill banged the spark plug wrench against a motor mount. "You need to put a stop to that monkey business. For Roger's sake if for no other reason."

My name came to me through the window and caught me by surprise, as if my father and Bill knew I was eavesdropping, even though I was sure they didn't. My father's hand pulled away from the fender, and I imagined him, outside my view, fuming.

The leaves on the maple rattled together. It was August, the start of the dog days, and we were grateful for every stir of air. Next door at the Timms's house, a radio was playing. The curtain at the window lifted and fell back with the breeze. I could hear the faint strains of "Too Late to Turn Back Now," and the chorus—*I believe, I believe, I believe I'm fallin' in love*—annoyed me because I knew it was Connie Timms listening to it, and I was fretting about her because she'd told me after church that she and I were through.

"I can't do this anymore," she said. We were outside on the sidewalk, and people were coming out of the church and down the steps. "I want a boyfriend I can tell the world about. I don't want some . . ." Here she struggled to find the words she wanted, the ones that would describe what she and I had been up to that summer. "I don't want an affair," she finally said.

Now I can almost laugh at the way that word sounded coming from a girl her age. At the time, though, my heart was breaking. I watched Connie run down the sidewalk to her father's Oldsmobile '98, fling the door open, and get inside. I knew she didn't mean for me to come after her. I wanted to, but I didn't have the nerve.

If not for my mother and Mr. Timms, everything between Connie and me might have been fine. Bill and my father weren't saying anything I didn't already know. My mother and Mr. Timms. Like my father, I tried to ignore what was going on between them, but it was impossible.

Earlier that summer, Connie and I began to take note of each other, and as we got cozy, we agreed to keep our hey-baby-hey a secret. What would people think if they knew? *Apples didn't fall far from the tree.* Why did that concern me? I suppose there was a part of me that believed I was betraying my father by throwing in with the daughter of the man who was coming between him and my mother.

How could Connie and I make our affections known when her father and my mother were the subjects of so much gossip? I'd like to say we wanted to be better than that gossip, but I suspect the truth was we were embarrassed. We were afraid the town was watching us, and every time we were together on the sly, I felt guilty. I wanted to think that we'd found each other solely from our two hearts syncing up, but as long as there was the story of my mother and her father, I wasn't sure. Maybe we were just following their lead.

We couldn't have said any of this at the time. At least I couldn't have. I won't presume to speak for Connie. I only know this: no matter what we could say then, or what we knew by instinct, one fact was plain—whatever was happening between the two of us could never be separated from the fact that her father and my mother were lovers.

"We can't let anyone find out," I told Connie early on. "We can't be trashy like them."

"My father's not trashy." She had a pageboy haircut and her bangs were in need of a trim. We were talking over the wire fence that ran between my backyard and hers. She had on Levis and white Keds sneakers and a T-shirt that advertised Boone's Farm, a soda-pop wine popular in those days. She brushed her bangs out of her eyes and stared at me. "He's lonely. He's a very lonely man."

I loved her brown hair and her blue eyes. I loved the smell of her perfume—something called Straw Hat, which was all sweet and woodsy and made me want to press her to me and breathe in that scent. She could have said anything to me at that moment and I would have taken it as gospel. So I let that statement about Mr. Timms's loneliness absolve him, and with my silence—much to my shame now—I allowed my mother to become the wicked one in the story of their affair.

Mr. Timms was a widower. His wife, a nervous, fretful woman, took sick one winter night when a heavy snow was falling. It started around dusk, and before long the streets were covered. The snow kept coming down as night crept in. My father and I went into our living room to watch it out the window. By that time the snow was up to the top of the drainage ditches that ran alongside the street.

"It's like a picture out there," my father said. I was thirteen then. We stood in the dark room and watched the snow coming down past the streetlights. No cars passed by. We could see lights on in the houses around us. Everyone was hunkering down to wait this one out. Over twenty inches by morning, said WAKO radio out of the county seat, Phillipsport. The wind was up, and already the snow was starting to drift against the side of our shed. My father's Galaxie, parked in our driveway, was barely holding its shape as the snow covered it. "Roger, I swear." He put his hand on my shoulder and gave me a squeeze. "It's like we're in a picture," he said, and I've always remembered that, because it was one of the first times he ever said anything that I sensed came from some private place inside him, which he generally kept to himself.

My mother was in the family room behind us with the television playing. It was a Saturday night. I'm sure of that because I remember that *The Carol Burnett Show* was on. My mother laughed at something, and I could hear the television audience laughing too. My father and I turned at the same time, looking back through the French doors that separated the living room from the family room. We saw the lamplight there. He squeezed my shoulder again, and at his touch we headed toward those French doors. Once we opened them, we stepped back into the life that was ours.

"Baby, you should've seen," my mother said to my father. She was kicked back in her Barcalounger, her arm bent at the elbow so it went up at a right angle. She held a Virginia Slims cigarette between her fingers and the smoke curled up into the lamplight. "It was the funniest thing. I was afraid I was going to wet my pants."

She was wearing a pair of black slacks and a black turtleneck sweater. She'd just had her hair done the day before, and her loose blond curls came down over her shoulders. I'd always known she was a pretty woman—prettier than most of my friends' mothers—but she looked particularly glamorous there in the lamplight. Big gold hoop earrings dangled against the sides of her turtleneck.

"We were watching it snow," my father said.

I believe now he must have been uncomfortable with my mother's beauty. He wasn't the kind of man who could enjoy knowing that wherever he went with his wife other men would be looking at her. He was more the type—thoughtful and shy—who preferred to live a private life. If there were pleasures to be had, he'd rather the world not know about them. He was the county tax assessor, and he knew that it was a man looking for trouble who chose to parade his riches and not expect someone to take notice and wish himself into a share of that wealth.

"Everyone has to pay for what he has," he told me once. "That's what I know, Roger. No one gets off scot-free."

He wasn't a looker. Not that he was an unattractive man, but next to my mother he paled. He had sloped shoulders and a long face and a nose that was too big. I expect he spent most of his married life shaking his head over his dumb luck in landing a woman as beautiful as Annie Griggs.

One night at the Uptown Cafe, we walked away from our table, and just before we got to the door I heard a low wolf whistle. I know my father heard it too, because just for an instant his back stiffened, and he gave a quick glance behind him. My mother took his arm, and that claiming gesture must have soothed him, because he opened the door and we stepped out onto the sidewalk. Later, when I was supposed to be sleeping, I heard them talking about what had happened. "Dang it, Annie," my father said, and after a while my mother answered in a quiet voice, "It's not like I ask for it."

What she was asking that winter night, when she told my father about the comedy sketch she'd seen on TV, was for us to sit down with her and be a family—to give her, I imagine now, a reason to be happy with her home and the people in it.

But before any of that could happen, someone knocked on our front door.

"My word," my father said. "Who could that be on a night like this?"

He went into the living room to open the door, and after a while I heard Mr. Timms's voice. It was a loud voice, full of dread and fear. "It's Jean," he said. "She's sick and I don't know what to do about it."

"Sick?" my father said in a way that told me he didn't know what to do about it either.

"She went to bed for a rest after supper, and now I can't get her to wake up."

My mother had already put the footrest down on her Barcalounger. I could feel the cold air around my legs, and I knew my father was holding the front door open as he talked to Mr. Timms.

"Tell him to come in," my mother called to my father. "Harold, come inside," she said.

The ceiling light snapped on in the living room. The front door closed, and I heard Mr. Timms stomping snow from his boots on the rug just inside the door.

I followed my mother into the living room, and there he was, bareheaded, the collar of his black wool coat turned up to his ears. He'd stuffed his trouser legs into the tops of a pair of green rubber boots, from which snow was melting. He wore a pair of glasses with black plastic frames, and those glasses were steamed over now that he'd come in from the cold.

"Annie?" he said, and he sounded so helpless.

"Don't worry, Harold." My mother walked right up to him. She reached up and took his glasses off his face. She used the hem of her sweater to wipe the steam from the lenses. "I'm going to get my coat and boots on," she said. "Then I'm going to come see to her. Everything will be fine."

Mr. Timms reached out and touched my mother lightly on her arm. "Thank you, Annie," he said, and I believe it may have been then, though he surely couldn't have known this, that he started to fall in love with her.

It must have been a feeling that simmered those three years after Mrs. Timms died. She died that night, was dead already, in fact, when Mr. Timms stood in our living room, putting his glasses back on and waiting for my mother to come with him.

"There wasn't a thing I could do," she said later, after the ambulance had finally made its way through the snow and taken Mrs. Timms away. "Poor Jean. She was gone when I got there."

My father and I had eventually put on our own coats and boots and made our way next door. My mother called for the ambulance, which was something, so my father said later, that Mr. Timms should have done instead of coming next door to our house. "He didn't know what to do," my mother said with a sharp bite to her voice. "That poor man. He was lost."

Connie wasn't crying. That would all come later. She sat on the couch in the living room and stared straight ahead, not saying a word. My mother finally sat down beside her and took her up in her arms. "You sweet girl," my mother kept saying, rocking Connie back and forth. "You sweet, sweet girl."

Mr. Timms was in the bedroom with Mrs. Timms, and from time to time I heard a thud and I imagined that he was banging his fist into the wall. "Go see about him," my mother said to my father. After a while I heard his and Mr. Timms's voices coming from the bedroom. "Oh, Jesus," Mr. Timms said, and I heard my father say, "We're right here, Harold."

Then finally my father came out of the room, and without a word he went outside. Soon I heard the scrape of a shovel, and when I looked out the Timms's front window, I saw my father clearing the sidewalk and the steps up onto the porch. He kept at it, digging out the driveway. "The ambulance was coming," he told me once we were back in our own house. "I didn't know what else to do but to clear it a path."

In the weather, it took a good while, but finally the ambulance was there, its swirling red lights flashing over the Timms's house. The paramedics took Mrs. Timms out on a gurney, and later we learned that she'd died because of a bad heart. "Who'd have thought?" my mother said. She told us that it made it plain how quick we could go. "If you want something, you better grab it," she said. "You never know if you'll have another chance."

After Bill and my father finished with the Galaxie that Sunday in August, they decided to go squirrel hunting. Bill called for me, and I got up from the bed and went outside to see what he wanted.

"Grab your .410," he told me. "We're going after bushytails."

I looked toward my father. He was putting down the hood of the

Galaxie, and he said, "How 'bout that, Roger? It's just the three of us here anyway. Just the three bulls. What say we get out and roam around a little? Shoot a few squirrels, have a little boy time."

That summer he'd been trying extra-hard with me, imagining, perhaps, that he and my mother were close to being finished, and once they were, he'd want to have me on his side. The problem was he'd never been the kind of har-de-har-har man that Bill was, and any attempt on my father's part to be friendly with me came across as forced and left me feeling uncomfortable.

We should have been talking about my mother and the fact that our family was on the verge of coming apart. We should have considered what was causing that to happen and what we might be able to do to stop it. Instead my father was puffing himself up, getting all wink-wink, palsy-walsy, pretending there wasn't a thing wrong. It was just a summer Sunday, and we were going hunting. Men out with their shotguns. A part of me thought that if my father were truly a man, this thing between my mother and Mr. Timms wouldn't be going on, and Connie and I would still be sweet on each other. I wouldn't be living in the shadow of my mother's indiscretion and my father's inability to do anything about it. As wrong as it was, I found myself giving him the blame, thinking there was something about him—a lack of heart, or courage, or by-God-you-won't—that made my mother do what she did.

So when he made that big show about the three bulls going off to have some boy time, I got a little fed up with the way he kept acting like we were charmed when really we weren't at all. We were gossip. We were the family folks could feel sorry for or judge. Either way, our lives weren't ours anymore. We belonged to the town and its prying eyes and clucking tongues. I was tired of that. I wanted my father to finally acknowledge that fact.

So I said, "Where'd Mom go?"

She'd slipped out of the house after dinner. We'd gone to services at the First Christian as usual and then come home to the meal she'd prepared. Bill came by and had coconut cream pie and coffee with us. Then he and my father went out to work on the Galaxie. I lay on my bed and heard Mr. Timms fire up his Olds. He honked his horn as he went up the street, and Bill said to my father, "There he goes."

From my bedroom I could hear my mother singing along with the radio from next door. She had a pretty singing voice, and as I listened to her, I couldn't help but think how happy she sounded. Soon I heard our screen door creak open and then slap against the jamb. I sat up and leaned over to look out the window. She had on a red summer dress that had a halter top and a pleated skirt. Her bare shoulders were shiny in the sunlight. She carried a box purse made from woven straw. It had strawberries and white blooms on it, and she held the handle and swung it back and forth as she walked. Her shoes, a pair of strappy sandals, slapped over the side-walk. Her curls bounced against her bare back, and I thought she looked like a girl heading off to somewhere she'd been looking forward to, and despite the fact that I knew that Mr. Timms was most likely waiting, I couldn't help but feel happy for her.

She turned back once and waved at my father and Bill. "Going fishin', boys," she said and then walked on up the street.

Now, as I waited for my father to answer my question, I saw the slightest grimace around his lips.

"She went visiting," he said.

I wouldn't let him off that easily. "Visiting who?"

Bill was wiping off his hands with a red shop rag. "Get your gun, hotshot." He threw the rag into my face and gave me a hard look that told me to shut up and fall into line. "Chop, chop, buddy boy. I mean it. Right now."

It was a quiet ride down into the country. Bill drove his El Camino, and the three of us crowded onto the bench seat. I was crammed in between Bill and my father. Our guns, my .410 and my father's and Bill's twelve-gauges, were cased and stowed behind us in the bed.

"Damned hot," Bill said.

We were on the blacktop south of town, and the fields were flashing by, the corn stunted along the fencerows, the ground cracked from lack of rain.

"No good for the crops," my father said, and it went like that for quite a while. Just a thing said here and there. The windows were down and the hot air was rushing in, and it was hard to carry on a conversation, but I knew, even if we'd been cruising along in air-conditioned quiet, no one would have felt much like talking.

That was unusual for Bill, because he generally had something to say, and he wasn't afraid to say it. He was a different sort of man from my father. He was blustery and hot-tempered, but fun-loving too. He was always pulling a prank on someone and then looking so daggone happy about it that everyone forgave him. He was a trackman on the section gang, and back in the winter his trickster ways had finally caught up with him. He pulled a joke on Mr. Timms, stuffed five cigarette loads into one of his cigars, and when Mr. Timms put a lighter to it, the cigar exploded and frayed at its end. Mr. Timms, startled, jumped back, slipped on the icy rail, and fell onto the slope of the gravel bed.

He was all right, just shaken and bruised a little, but he was pissed off too. "I don't have to ask who did that," he said, staring right at Bill. "Some people are ignorant. That's all that needs to be said about that." What Bill didn't know—or if he'd ever known, had no reason to recall—was that day was the anniversary of Jean Timms's death. "Now how was I to know that?" Bill asked my father later. "He's got it in for me now. You can by God know that for sure." True enough, Bill had spent the rest of winter and on into spring and now summer suffering the brunt of Mr. Timms's anger. "Any shit job you can think of," Bill had said to my father earlier while they were working on the Galaxie. "You can bet I'm the one who'll get it. I've just about had enough." Bill blamed this all on my father. "R.T., if you just told him you know what's what between him and Annie, maybe then he'd ease off." Bill had never been married himself, but he thought he knew how to handle matters of the heart. "Timms wouldn't be so quick to bust my ass if he knew that you were onto him. He's that way. He likes to think he's a decent man. Let him know he's a phony, R.T., and he'll be more humble."

My father wasn't made for such a thing. As we went on down the blacktop in the El Camino, I took note again of that Timex watch he was wearing—the face so big on that delicate wrist—and I found myself thinking, *He doesn't have the heart.* I'm ashamed of that thought now, considering everything that was about to happen that day, things I still can't get straight enough to suit me.

Bill and my father owned eighty acres in Lukin Township just off the County Line Road. The farm had belonged to my grandparents, but that summer my grandfather was dead, and my grandmother was living in a nursing home. She'd deeded the place to Bill and my father, and they leased it out to a tenant farmer. Often on Sunday afternoons they came down to give the place a look-see. The home place, they always called it. Sometimes, like the day I'm recalling, they brought their shotguns.

We uncased our guns and started out. We skirted the old chicken house and the clump of horseweeds taller than the roof.

"Should've brought a hoe to cut those down," Bill said.

"Next time," said my father.

We walked single file along the edge of the field that came up to the chicken house and the patch of ground my grandparents had always used for their vegetable garden. The tenant farmer had plowed up the field and sowed it in soybeans once he'd cut the wheat. The bean plants were already reaching toward knee-high. We had to crowd up into the foxtail growing along the wire fence to keep from tromping the beans. The leaves on the plants in that outer row brushed against my legs.

"Sowing fencerow to fencerow, ain't he?" Bill said.

He was in the lead, and my father was right behind him. "Using all he can," he said. "Getting everything he can get."

A little air stirred the bean plants. A covey of quail got up from the fencerow, their wings a loud whirring and clacking that startled me. Bill got his twelve-gauge to his shoulder, but already the covey was banking over the tree line.

"Damn, I should have been ready," Bill said.

"Out of season," my father reminded him.

"Who would've known?" Bill lowered the twelve-gauge and cradled it. "Just you and me and Roger out here. Far as I can see, there's no one else around."

The sky didn't have a cloud in it, just the contrail from an invisible jet stretching out little by little. I thought about Connie—wondered what she was doing, wondered if she'd really meant it when she told me we were through. Some nights that summer we'd driven down to the farm so we could be alone and out of sight. I had a '63 Impala I'd bought with the money I'd saved working hay crews since I was thirteen and the last two summers on a Christmas tree farm west of Goldengate. Connie sat close on the bench seat when she rode with me, her hand on my thigh. Our routine was she'd go for a walk in the evening. I'd hear her screen door slap shut, and I'd see her going on up the sidewalk. She'd have on a pair of Levis and one of the halter tops she favored that summer, her breasts loose beneath it, a blue or red or white bow tied under her hair at her neck and another sash tied at the small of her back, the tails of that bow trailing down over the waist of her jeans and bouncing with the roll of her hips. She'd walk out Locust Street to the city park at the edge of town and wait for me in one of the dugouts at the baseball field. I always gave my horn a honk when I took the last curve out of town, and when I pulled in behind the concession stand, she'd be there, ready to open the passenger side door and slide across that bench seat and kiss me.

I had a blanket in the trunk of the Impala, and at the farm we spread it out on the grass and lay next to each other and waited for the stars to come out. It got so dark out there in the country, and under all those stars we said the things that were most on our minds, the things we could barely stand to face when they were right there in front of us in the daylight.

Connie said she missed her mother, and sometimes she cried a little, and I held her hand and didn't say a word.

One night she said, "Why doesn't your mother love your father?"

I told her I didn't know, which was the truth. I've had years to think about what the trouble between them might have been, but I've never been able to say it was this or that. Maybe it was my father's caution. Maybe my mother grew tired of the careful way he lived his life. One evening when they were hosting a pinochle party for a few couples they knew from church, my father kept underbidding his hands. Finally my mother said, "Oh, for Pete's sake, R.T. Live a little." Little things like that have come back to me as time has gone on, but I can't say for certain they mean anything.

But one thing I remember keeps me up at night, and that's the moment I told Connie about on the Saturday night before that Sunday when she told me she couldn't see me anymore, and later Bill and my father and I were moving into the woods with our shotguns. It may have been the story that spooked her, that made her believe what we were doing was ill-fated and could never come to a good end.

I said to her, "Last night I heard him beg her to stop."

My mother's and father's talking stirred me from sleep in the middle of the night. I don't know how long they'd been at it, trying to keep their voices low so I wouldn't hear, but by the time I was awake, they were beyond that point. They weren't thinking about anything except what had brought them to where they stood—in the midst of an ugliness they could no longer deny or ignore.

My father said, "Please, Annie. I've always tried my best to give you a good life, to give *us* a good life . . ." His voice trailed off, and then I heard a noise I couldn't at first identify as anything that might come from a human being. A groan, a growl, a whimper at the end. In the silence that followed, I remember thinking, *That's my father.* "Annie," he finally said. "You've got to stop this. If you don't . . ."

His voice left him then—swallowed up, I imagine, by the terror he felt over the prospect of a life lived without her.

"You want a divorce," my mother said after a time. "Is that it?"

My father was weeping now. I could hear that. "Annie," he said in a breathless, shaking voice that could barely make the words come out of his mouth. "I want you to love me."

For a good while there was only the sound of him trying to choke down his sobs and get his breath.

Then my mother said in a gentle voice I've always tried to remember for what it was, the voice of a woman who'd found her way to trouble and didn't know how to get out, "I'm here," she said. "R.T., shh. Listen to me." I like to think that she touched him then—touched his face or his hand, maybe even put her arms around his neck and pressed him to her. "I'm right here," she said again. "That's the most you should wish."

Connie hadn't asked for this piece of information. We'd only been lying on the blanket, looking up at the stars, not saying much of anything, just enjoying being close to each other in the dark, and I'd felt safe telling her that story. I was sixteen. She was my first love. She was the only person I could tell. What did I know then about the ties that bind one person to another?

I had to live through what was waiting for me that Sunday to know anything about love at all.

"My father's the cause of that." Connie sat up on the blanket. She crossed her arms over her stomach and started rocking back and forth. "He should have left your mother alone."

"She made a choice," I said. "It wasn't just him."

For a good while Connie didn't say anything. Then in a whisper she said, "Yes, they both made their choices."

Just then a set of headlights came down the lane. They lit up the gravel roadbed and spread out over the fencerows. They came so far that they shined on the wire fencing around the farmhouse yard. I could hear the engine idling and the faint sound of the car radio. The tires crunched over the gravel as the car rolled forward an inch or two. Then it stopped.

I knew whoever was in that car was looking at the grille of my Impala. Those headlights had caught the chrome. Whoever was in that car knew now they weren't the only ones who'd come down that lane, and they were trying to decide what to do.

Connie was still sitting up on the blanket. We were on the grass to the left of the Impala, about even with the trunk, and just barely out of the glare of the headlights in the lane.

"Roger," she said, and I could tell she was scared.

I reached up and put my hand on the small of her back, felt the heat of her skin. "It's okay," I said. "Everything's okay."

It seemed like the car in the lane would sit there forever, the driver unable to decide whether to keep coming. A drop of sweat slid down Connie's back and onto my hand. Then somewhere nearby a screech owl started its trill, the call that seemed to come from the other side of the living, and I felt my heart pounding in my chest.

"Oh, God," said Connie.

Then the car in the lane started backing up. It backed all the way to the end, where it swung out and pointed itself north. I watched the red taillights, and what I didn't tell Connie, though maybe she knew this on her own, was that those long vertical rows of lights, set wide apart, were the taillights of an Olds '98 like her father's.

"Whoever that was, they're gone," I said.

I let my hand fall to the bow of her halter top. I started to untie it, but she slapped my hand away.

"That was spooky," she said. "That car. C'mon. Let's go."

So in my mind now, the image of the two of us walking toward my Impala and getting in and driving back to town is forever tied up with the picture of me stepping into the woods that Sunday with Bill and my father.

We waited and waited around a stand of hickory trees where we'd seen pieces of husks on the ground, and though from time to time we heard a squirrel chattering in the tree mast high above us, we could never get a clear shot, and after too much time keeping quiet, Bill finally said, "Fuck it. I'm done."

He was all for heading back to town, but my father said, "Let's walk on over to the end of the next field and see if there's any better hunting in Kepper's Woods. We're here. We might as well see what's what over there."

Jean Timms had been a Kepper before she married Mr. Timms, and those woods had been in her family longer than I could imagine. I didn't know any of that on that Sunday—Kepper's Woods was just a name to me, the way Higgins Corner or McVeigh Bottoms was, places marked by the names of families, the history of whom I had no reason to know.

Surely my father knew that about Jean Timms and Kepper's Woods. I wonder now whether he had any thought at all of what he might find there.

"Might as well," Bill said, and off we went.

Marathon Oil had a lease road running through those woods, and that's where we came upon the car—Mr. Timms's Olds '98—nosed deep into the shade offered by the hickories and oaks and ash trees and sweet gums.

A flash of my mother's red sundress caught my eye first—just a quick glimpse of red as she came around the front of the Olds—and then, just like that, the whole picture came into view: the dark green Olds with road dust coating the top of the rear bumper, the gold of Mr. Timms's Ban-Lon pullover shirt, the bright red of my mother's sundress. She walked a few steps behind the car, back down the oil lease road, and that's where Mr. Timms caught up to her. He took her by her arm and turned her around to face him. He put his arms around her, and she put her arms around him, and they held each other there in the woods on that road where they thought no one could see.

"There's Mom," I said, and as soon as I said it, I wished I hadn't.

When I saw her with Mr. Timms, I found the sight to be so strange and yet somehow familiar, mixed up as it was with what I felt about Connie, that I couldn't help but say what I did.

I imagine my father would have eventually spotted them, and what took place next would have still been the thing that happened, but even now I can't stop myself from believing that if I'd kept my mouth shut, perhaps we would have veered away from that oil lease road, and Bill and my father never would have seen my mother and Mr. Timms. I can't keep myself from thinking that maybe there was that one chance that we would have gone on, maybe found some squirrels, maybe not, and then driven back into town, and our lives would have gone on the way they'd been moving all that summer. Maybe there was that one possibility of grace that I cost us because I spoke. *There's Mom,* I said, and Bill and my father stopped.

We were hidden in the woods, maybe fifty yards or so away, and my mother and Mr. Timms had no idea we were there.

My father said to me, in a very quiet, very calm voice, "Go back to the car, Roger."

But I didn't move. I was afraid that if I did, my mother and Mr. Timms would hear my footsteps over the twigs and hickory nut husks on the floor of the woods. The thought of my mother's face turning in my direction, her eyes meeting mine, was more than I could stand to imagine, because what Bill and my father didn't know was that one day that summer my mother said to me, "You like Connie, don't you?"

We were alone in the house. My father was at the courthouse in Phillipsport. It was a hot, still afternoon with storm clouds gathering in the west. Soon there'd be a little breeze kicking up—enough to stir the wind chimes my mother had hanging outside the back door, the ones I'd brought her from my class trip to McCormick's Creek State Park. *They're pine cones,* she said when she saw the chimes. *Little gold pine cones,* she said, and even now, whenever I want to feel kindly toward her, all I have to do is call up the memory of how she held the chimes up and blew on them to set those pine cones to tinkling, how she looked at them, amazed.

I'd just come in from mowing the yard, and when my mother asked me that question about Connie, I was about to take a drink of grape Kool-Aid from the glass I'd poured. I stopped with the glass halfway to my mouth, and then I set it down on the kitchen counter.

Soon the thunder would start, at first a low rumble in the distance, and eventually the lightning would come and the sky would open up, but for the time being it was as if there wasn't a breath of air to be found. My mother was sitting at the kitchen table writing out a grocery list on one of my father's notepads that had his name stamped at the top—*Roger Thomas Jordan, Phillips County Tax Assessor.* She hadn't made much progress. *Eggs,* she'd written. *Milk.* Then she'd stopped and the rest of the note page was covered with her name, written in her beautiful hand again and again. *Annie, Annie, Annie.*

"I mean you really like her," she said. "It's all right to like someone that way, Roger." She looked up at me then, and there was such a sadness in her eyes. I've never been able to get the memory of that moment out of my head. "It's the way I felt about your father," she said, and then she ripped the sheet of paper from the pad and wadded it up in her hand.

Somehow I knew that what she was telling me with all that talk about Connie was that she and Mr. Timms didn't like each other in quite the same way, that what they had going on between them was very different from what had brought her and my father together. I think that she was telling me that if she'd had her druthers, she would have felt that way about Mr. Timms—she would have *liked* him, and he would have *liked* her—but what they had between them was something very different from liking someone. It was something born out of loneliness and desperation. I want to believe that she was trying to tell me that what Connie and I had was special and that she wished it would last.

"You know I'm an old woman, don't you?" she finally said to me.

She was forty-one that summer. If she were alive today, she'd be seventy-nine. I like to think she'd have become an elegant woman, well suited to her age, happy with what she had left in her life, but that Sunday when she clung to Mr. Timms in the woods, no one knew she'd only live ten more years, or that my father, who divorced her, would come to the hospital and sit by her bed and hold her hand as she was dying.

"You're not that old," I told her that day in the kitchen.

She looked at me, shaking her head, her lips turned up in a sad grin. "Oh, honey," she said. "You just wait."

So there we were that Sunday, Bill and my father and me, and my father said again, "Roger, go back to the car."

When I still wouldn't move, he said, "We should all go back. We should go home."

That's when Bill said, "Jesus Christ."

And then he was tromping through the woods toward that lease road where my mother raised her head and pushed away from Mr. Timms and saw that they weren't alone.

"I don't know who you think you are," Bill said when he got to where they were standing. "How can you live with yourself? And you, Annie." Here Bill shook his head, took a long breath and let it out. "I thought you were better than this."

There comes a moment when all that's been denied rises up and leaves you raw and trembling. That's what I was learning that day as I stood there—my father and I hadn't moved—listening to Bill's loud voice ringing with accusation and judgment.

Now I find myself wishing again and again that it would have been possible for me to tell him something that would have made a difference. Something about how broken we were. Something about how a time comes when it's best to just walk away, even if it means leaving behind someone you swore you'd love the rest of your life. Maybe we thought we could save ourselves, but it was too late.

Although I felt all this inside me, I couldn't find anything to say that would matter. Even now I can't put it into words. I can only remember the way it felt in the woods in the moments after Bill shouldered his twelve-gauge, and I knew that all of us were about to move from this world into another one that would hold us the rest of our days.

Bill said to Mr. Timms, "Get into your car. Go home." He motioned to the Olds '98 with the barrel of his twelve-gauge. "You've got a daughter," he said. "Can't you try to be a decent man for her sake? Go on now. This is over. Annie's coming with us."

"Bill, calm down," my mother said. "You should take care."

"Don't tell me that," said Bill. "Not you. Not the way you've been whoring around. R.T. might not know how to handle you, but by God I think I do."

My father was moving then, his long legs striding quickly through the woods to the lease road. I remembered that winter night when he'd put his hand on my shoulder and we'd watched the snow come down. The beauty of it all amazed him. *It's like we're in a picture,* he said. I knew he wasn't made for such ugliness as was upon him now, and I couldn't bear to see him walking toward it. I didn't know anything to do but to follow him.

"Bill, let's go." He rested his hand on my uncle's shoulder just the way he had mine that winter night. "Put that shotgun down."

He was talking in a quiet voice, but I could hear the fear in it. "I mean it, Bill. We need to go."

My mother looked at me then, and she was ashamed. "Oh, Roger," she said. "You hadn't ought to be here."

I thought my father would tell me again to go back to the car, but he was intent on dealing with Bill, who still had that twelve-gauge trained on Mr. Timms.

"Bill," my father said, "listen to me."

"Better do what he says, Jordan." Mr. Timms had his hands in the pockets of his blue-and-red-plaid golf pants, standing there in a way that told me he felt positive my uncle was bluffing. "I can make things plenty rough for you," he said. "I can see to it you lose your job."

"I've put up with enough shit from you, Harold." Bill shook free from my father's hand. "I'm not going to put up with any more of it."

That's when Mr. Timms said to my mother, "Annie, tell him. Tell R.T. what's what."

My mother couldn't speak. She looked at Mr. Timms, and then at my father. From where I stood beside him, I could see that she was afraid. Her eyes were wet, and there was just the slightest tremor at the corner of her mouth.

"Annie?" my father said.

"Go on, Annie," said Mr. Timms. "Tell him what we've decided."

Bill stepped up closer to him. He pressed the barrel of the twelve-gauge into the soft spot beneath his chin, and Mr. Timms tilted his head, trying to get free from the nick of the raised bead sight.

"You're not deciding anything." Bill kept up the pressure with that gun barrel, and he walked Mr. Timms backward, away from my mother along the driver's side of the Olds until they were out of the lease road and off in the woods opposite us. "If anyone's running this show, it's me."

I should tell you that Bill was a violent man, but I can't, because the truth was, prior to that moment in the woods, he wasn't. He was my uncle, my father's younger brother, who had done his stint as a grunt in Vietnam and come home, seemingly no worse for the experience. He had his job with the railroad and that little box house on South Street not far from the Uptown Cafe, where he ate breakfast every morning before heading out to work. He kept a pot of wave petunias on each side of the front steps of his house. Some evenings I'd go driving by, and he'd be outside with his watering can. He'd have on a pair of khaki shorts and his old army shirt with the sleeves cut out. He'd throw up his arm, his fingers in the *V* of a peace sign, and I'd think, *There he is, the happiest man alive.*

What did I know about him except that? Whatever he carried inside him was a secret to me.

"I don't know what got into him," my father would say time and time again as the years went on. "I guess it was like he said. He'd just had enough."

Enough of Harold Timms and the way he shoved him around on the job. Enough of the fact that Mr. Timms thought he could take another man's wife and not have to answer for it. Enough of his gold Ban-Lon shirt that Sunday in the woods, and his flashy plaid golf pants, and that Olds '98. Enough of things we had no way of knowing about as he tried his best to live a regular life in the aftermath of whatever he'd gone through in Vietnam. Enough.

So when Mr. Timms said what he did—"I'm going to tell you something, Jordan. And R.T., I want you to listen to this too"—Bill pulled back on the hammer of that twelve-gauge.

"Don't talk," he said to Mr. Timms. "Don't say another word."

The squirrels were chattering high up in the hickory trees, the sun was splintering through the branches, a mourning dove was off in the distance calling for rain. A little wind had come up, and it was cooler there in the woods. I thought for a moment that everything would be all right. Bill backed away from Mr. Timms, and he let his arms relax, the twelve-gauge now held crosswise at his waist. He came back to the lease road, walking backward until he cleared the Olds and was standing a couple of feet away from its rear end.

Mr. Timms followed him, stopping finally about midway down the side of the car. I could see his head and shoulders above the roof. He said, "R.T., Annie doesn't love you. She loves me, and we aim to have a life together."

"I told you to shut up." Bill's voice was loud and shaking. "I gave you fair warning."

But Mr. Timms went on. "She hasn't loved you in a long time. She's just stayed with you for the sake of the boy." Here he pointed his finger at me. "And I know what you've been doing with my

Connie. I saw you . . . *we* saw you, your mother and me . . . Saturday night, two lovebirds on a blanket over there at your grandparents' farm. I want you to leave Connie alone. She's told you, hasn't she? She's only fifteen, for Christ's sake. She's too young to be laying in the dark with a boy."

"I love her," I said, and though I said it in a quiet voice, I could tell right away I'd spoken with force.

I knew that because for a good while no one said a thing. They were stunned—struck dumb because in the midst of all this ugliness, a boy had spoken his heart and reminded them all of what it was to be young and smitten with the first stirrings of something sweet and pure.

Then my mother said, "Oh, honey."

And my father said, "We should all just leave now before this gets out of hand."

"Hell," said Mr. Timms. He laughed, throwing back his head, his mouth open so wide I could see a single gold molar. "You love her?" he said to me. "You don't know what love is. You just love your pecker."

He took a few steps toward us, and Bill shouldered that twelve-gauge again and said, "You better stop. I swear, Harold. I won't let you drag Roger into this."

"Oh, he's in it all right." Mr. Timms took two more steps—he was at the rear of the Olds now, about to step out into the open. He stopped walking and rested his hand on the trunk. "Well, at least there's one man in your family." He laughed again, only this time there was no joy in it. "Ha, ha," he said. "Ha, ha." Then his eyes narrowed, and he said, "Son, you must have inherited your mother's hot blood."

The blast from the twelve-gauge was sudden and explosive. The back glass of the Olds shattered, blown backward onto the bench seat. For a moment that's all I could take in—how there was a loud crack and then the glass came apart in more little pieces than anyone would ever be able to count.

Then my mother called Mr. Timms's name. "Harold." She was moving past me, toward the Olds. "Harold. Oh, God."

It all came into focus for me then, the entire picture. Mr. Timms was on the ground, his torso hidden alongside the Olds. I could see his shoes—a pair of white leather loafers with gold buckles—and I understood that Bill had shot him.

My father was running after my mother. He caught up to her just as she got to the rear of the Olds. She looked down at Mr. Timms and then put her hands to her face. Her shoulders heaved. My father took her by those shoulders as if to hold them still.

He turned back toward me and his eyes were wild. "Don't come over here." He was shouting, though I was only a few feet away from him. "Whatever you do, don't."

My mother twisted around and pressed her face into the collar of his shirt. She beat against his chest with her fists, and he let her do that until she was all wrung out. Then he wrapped her up in his arms, and as I watched him holding her, I understood that Mr. Timms was dead, that Bill had killed him, and now the world would be a different place for all of us.

My father wanted to pass it off as a hunting accident, but Bill said no, we'd call it exactly what it was.

"I'm not going to ask Roger to carry a lie," he said. "I may not be much, but I know what's right and what's not."

"You?" my mother said. "You don't know anything."

"At least I'll own up to what I've done."

A hickory nut dropped from a tree and hit the top of the Olds with a bang. Then everything was quiet. Just the mourning doves somewhere in the distance and a squirrel chattering and the leaves stirring in the wind.

My father said, "And what did you do, Bill? Do you intend to tell me that you meant to kill him?"

Said Bill, "I just wanted him to shut up."

My mother pushed away from my father and went running off into the woods, trying to get away, I imagine, from what we were all going to have to face. Bill had shot her lover and killed him, and all of this had happened while Connie was listening to the radio at her house, and soon she would have to know about it.

My mother stumbled over a fallen branch and went down on her hands and knees. She fell over onto her side and lay there in the dead leaves and the dirt, and she pulled her knees up toward her chest, as if she were going to sleep—as if she'd never get up from that spot.

"I used to know you," my father said to Bill.

Bill nodded. Then he set his jaw and looked off into the distance for an instant. He swallowed hard. "Well, I'm not that person now." There was a crack in his voice. "And I won't be ever again." He looked at my father again, and his voice got steady. "It wasn't your fault, R.T. It wasn't anyone's fault. My life got taken to hell a long time ago, but I'm by God not about to ruin Roger's."

After that, there was nothing left to do but to pick my mother up from the ground.

"My purse," she said.

She said it was still on the front seat of the Olds, and before my father had a chance to stop me, I went to the car and I opened the passenger side door. The purse, that woven straw box purse with the strawberries and the white blooms on it. I picked it up by its thin handle. I resisted the urge to peer out the driver's side window to see what a man who'd been shot with a twelve-gauge might look like. I didn't want that picture in my head. I was just a kid, but I knew enough about the future to know I didn't need that. So I concentrated on the purse. I carried it to my mother, and then the four of us started back through the woods so we could drive into town and call the sheriff. I rode in the bed of the El Camino, so whatever got said in the cab was outside my hearing. I wasn't concerned with it anyway. I was thinking about Connie, and how she was an orphan now, and how unfair it was for me to know that before she did.

My mother was the one who told her. While Bill was on the phone confessing to the sheriff exactly what he'd done down that oil lease road — *I've killed Harold Timms* — my mother went next door and pounded on the frame of the screen until the radio music stopped and Connie came to see what the fuss was all about.

I watched from the window of my bedroom. My father was sitting on our porch steps. Soon Bill would come out and sit beside him, and after a while I'd hear my father say, "I should have walked out on this a long time ago. Then it wouldn't have been yours to deal with." Bill let a few seconds go by, and then he said in a flat, worn-out voice, "R.T., I think I've been looking for something like this ever since I got out of the army and came back to the world." He'd go on in letters that came first from the county jail and then Vandalia Prison in the months to come about how he'd gotten out of Vietnam, but he hadn't been able to let loose of the rage that filled him. *If it hadn't been Harold Timms,* he wrote, *it would've been* someone else. *I was just pissed off, R.T. I wanted someone to have to pay for something. I guess that's the best I can put it.*

That Sunday I watched my mother reach out her hand to Connie as if she were about to touch her face. The she said, "Honey, can I come inside?"

Connie had on cutoffs with frayed threads dangling down and a white T-shirt. She had cotton balls between her toes. She'd been painting her toenails a bright red, and it made me wonder how she imagined her life being the next day and the next one after that—if she was thinking that she was glad to be rid of me so she could have a boyfriend she wouldn't have to sneak around to see. However she saw her life unfolding, she didn't know that my mother was there to let her know that it was all going to be different now.

"It's about your daddy," my mother said, and then she stepped inside the house, and I couldn't hear any more.

I couldn't watch that silent house and the little shaded porch with the wooden swing bolted to the ceiling. So many nights I'd seen Connie in that swing and heard her singing to herself. All those love songs that were popular then: "Let's Stay Together," "Precious and Few," "Puppy Love." She was a girl without a mother, and I was a boy who felt abandoned, so it was easy for us to love each other. But I knew Connie wanted a boyfriend she could show off, parade around with on Friday and Saturday nights, maybe go to a movie at the Avalon Theater in Phillipsport and later drive out to the Dairy Queen to see who was sitting around on the hoods of their cars before heading to the state park or the gravel pits for that alone time in the car, that baby-oh-baby time, secretly hoping that some of the other kids would happen by, so come Monday there would be talk all over school. That was the sort of gossip she wanted to be part of—the kind that said you were part of the cool crowd—not the kind I could give her, the kind filled with shame.

Soon the sheriff's car pulled into my driveway, and I heard Bill say, "Well, I guess this is it."

I went to the other window of my bedroom, the one that looked out over the front yard, and I saw my father and Bill get up from where they were sitting and walk across the grass to meet the sheriff, a tall, lumbering man with a dark mustache.

"I'm going to have to take you in," I heard the sheriff say to Bill. "I've got deputies headed down to that oil lease road."

"I'm ready," said Bill.

And like that he got into the back seat of the sheriff's car, and then it was just my father and me and my mother and Connie, whom we would watch over until her grandparents could arrive from Indianapolis to see to her.

"Go over and sit with Connie," my mother told me when she came back to our house that afternoon. "I want to talk to your father."

What they said to each other when they were alone, I don't know. I only know that later that night he packed a bag and got into his Galaxie and drove off to find a motel in Phillipsport until he could locate a more satisfactory arrangement. My mother told me all of this later.

"It's going to just be the two of us," she said. She put her arm around my shoulders and squeezed. "Just you and me, Roger. Can you believe that?"

I couldn't believe anything then, and I knew she couldn't either. It was that sort of day, a day that felt like it should belong to someone else, the way so much of my life would seem from that point on. It would be a long, long time before I'd let myself trust anyone who said they loved me.

That night I couldn't say I loved my mother, or Bill, or my father, who had gone without saying a word to me. I could only say that I felt sorry for them—sorry for all the trouble they'd found—and I felt sorry for Connie, who didn't deserve to be on the other side of that trouble. It would be a while before I'd be able to say that I didn't deserve it either.

"You've always been nice to me," Connie said to me that evening when we sat on her bed, not saying much at all, waiting for her grandparents to come.

She wasn't crying, as she'd eventually done on the night her mother died. She was sitting with her legs crossed under her on the bed, rocking back and forth, and she let me put my arm around her waist, and then she laid her head over on my shoulder, and we sat there for the longest time, not saying a word.

The Philco radio sat on the table by her bed, but we didn't turn it on. She had a bulletin board on the wall above her desk, and from where we sat I could see it was covered with things I'd never known had meant that much to her—a wrapper from a Hershey bar I'd bought for her once when we were out and she was hungry, a book of matches that we'd used to light a candle on our blanket at my grandparents' farm, the plastic rings from the candy pacifiers we liked. Just little things like that. Nothing that mattered at all, but they did to her, and now, given what was about to happen, they did to me too.

"They won't let me live here anymore," she said.

I told her Indianapolis was only three hours away. "Not far at all," I said.

"Not too far," she said.

The sun was going down and the light in the room was fading. Through the window I could see lights going on in the houses on down the street. I couldn't see my own house on the other side, and I was glad for that. We sat there in the twilight, not saying a word. She let me hold her, and I smelled the strawberry shampoo in her hair and the fresh nail polish on her toes, and there was nothing really we could say because we were in a world now that wasn't ours. It was run by people like my parents and her grandparents and Bill, who sat in jail waiting for what would come to him.

"You'll come see me?" she finally said.

I told her I would.

"I won't forget you." She tilted her head and kissed my cheek. Then she settled her head back on my shoulder and I felt her eyelashes brush my neck. "And I won't blame you for any of this. Never. Not ever."

Then we sat there, and finally we lay down on the bed. She turned her face to the wall, and I slipped my arm around her and fit my legs up against hers. She let herself cry a little then, and I told her everything would be all right. I'm not sure I believed it, but soon she stopped crying and then she said, "I wish we were the only people in the world right now."

"I wish that too," I told her, and it was true. I did.

We stayed like that a good long while. Maybe we even drifted off to sleep. Then headlights swept across the wall, and we heard a car door slam shut outside and frantic steps on the porch and her grandmother's voice calling, "Connie, oh Connie, oh my precious girl."

"Shh," Connie said. "Don't move."

And we had that instant longer—that instant alone—at the end of a story that was never meant to be ours.

She was in my arms and then she wasn't. Her grandmother was there, and I let her go. Connie Timms.

I walked out of her house and stood on the porch. I looked across the way to my own house, where a single light was on, and I saw my mother's shadow move across the closed drapes. I thought how strange it was that I lived in that house, how strange it was that my uncle had killed a man and my mother and father, as I would soon learn, were at the end.

Connie's grandfather, a short man with a big chest and a blue sport coat, came up the steps.

"Who are you?" he said.

"No one," I told him.

"Young man, I asked you who you were."

I just shook my head, already moving down the steps. There was too much to say, and I didn't know how to say it.

"Come back here," he said.

But I kept moving. I still think I should have had a choice, but I was sixteen. What else could I do? I went home.

JAMES MATHEWS

# Many Dogs Have Died Here

FROM *Iron Horse Literary Review*

ON THE AFTERNOON I met my new neighbor, a woman others in the cul-de-sac would dub "Ramba," I wasn't looking for trouble. In fact, I wasn't looking for anything other than to enter my first full month of retirement with a small military pension and dreams of a hop to Florida or Hawaii once a year until my expiration date arrived. My immediate goal was a peaceful night of sipping Stella Artois, catching up on baseball scores, and making a list of things I needed to do to the lawn the next day.

I had just taken a seat in my favorite club chair when the knocking started. I muted the television and glowered at the clock on the wall. I wondered whether to just wait it out. But the knocking continued and grew more insistent. I finally shot up, galloped across the room, and flung open the door in a way I hoped would signal deep emotional instability, which I imagined to be a staple of retirement.

"I'm your new neighbor," the woman announced through a smile of perfectly aligned and pampered teeth, "and I was wondering if you knew how to change a flat tire?"

I stared with disbelief at the woman, who seemed oblivious to the fact that I was irritated. She was young, upper twenties tops. Her complexion was fever-pale, her red hair pulled back and tied off in a ponytail or braid, and her big, goofy smile was more an event than an expression. She wore faded jeans and an olive-drab T-shirt. The shirt was standard grunt issue, although I would never have associated her with the military except for the way she was standing, at parade rest, hands behind her back, rocking slightly on her heels, waiting for me to answer her idiotic question. Somewhere on the other side of the neighborhood, a lawnmower started up on the first pull.

"Call a mechanic," I told her. And for good measure: "Which is what you should have done when you first got the flat."

"Oh, it's not *my* car," she said. "It's yours."

I blinked a few times and stuttered stupidly, "Excuse me?"

"That's right," she said, and from behind her back she produced a Buck knife the size of a billy club. "It's how I've introduced myself to all the neighbors. So that you each know I'm serious. And that I'm not going anywhere."

Her smile was gone now, traceless on her pale skin, as if it had been wiped from her face by the glimmer of the steel knife. I retreated a step and swallowed hard, fully expecting her to move toward me. Instead she executed a textbook about-face and stalked down the walkway and across the lawn, the blade swinging side to side like a machete hacking through an imaginary jungle.

She'd gotten to my tire all right, one of the $229-a-pop Michelin 3000 Weather Breakers on the right front side of my Ford pickup. I had parked ass-end in, with the grille facing the cul-de-sac, and it appeared as if, on her way up the sidewalk to introduce herself, she'd taken the blade and carved a clean line through the top of the treading. This wasn't going to be a patch job.

Harold Cummings, the neighbor to my right, wasn't as lucky. She had slashed the two rear tires of his Volkswagen Gallant. The Popovs, an older husband-and-wife team, escaped altogether because their car had been in the garage. They rarely went out anyway.

For a long time I stood looking at my tire and then walked a full circle around my truck, inspecting it for additional damage. Every few steps, I would glance over at the house to my left, a simple bungalow design with a shadowy porch and grizzled yard spangled with dirt patches. The only evidence that it might be occupied was a black *POW You Are Not Forgotten* flag hanging dead and heavy outside the brick porch. The FOR SALE sign was still sitting out front, where it had been for the last several months. In all that time I had seen no potential buyers come or go. In fact, Harold and I had even taken turns mowing the grass, since no one else seemed at all interested in doing so. We had always prided ourselves in our quiet little cul-de-sac, a place of calm and reflection, filled with residents whose principal occupation was minding their own damn business.

In the entire four years I had lived there, I think the biggest issue had been a complaint or two about the Popovs' pet dachshunds running loose and dumping on other people's yards. As I looked over at the bungalow, I realized we had moved far beyond the scourge of doggie droppings.

"How goes your day, sergeant?" Harold called from behind me. He was standing at the front of my truck, arms crossed, grinning. Harold was a retired professor of psychology and dressed the part to a T. In fact, if he *were* masquerading as a retired professor, he couldn't have found a better outfit—lightweight, rimless spectacles, a two-toned sweater vest, khakis, Birkenstocks, and a curved alabaster pipe. He looked like he'd just walked off a campus movie set.

The Popovs shuffled up and huddled behind him like a pair of eager students.

"Has anyone called the police?" I asked, fumbling for my cell phone.

"Hold on now," Harold said. "We were just talking about that, and the consensus is that it will only make things worse."

"Please," Anna Popov said. She was clutching one of her two long-haired dachshunds across her chest.

Her husband, Vlad, had the other dachshund tucked under his arm like a newspaper. "Yes, no police," Vlad said. "This is to be no good."

The Popovs were Russian and had moved to the States ten years earlier. Harold was convinced that Vlad had been a member of the KGB who had gambled the wrong way when the spirit of glasnost finally petered out. Their faces were always shiny and suffering, their accents heavy. They butchered English to the point that we wondered just how much they really understood.

"Well, good luck with your consensus," I told them as my thumb hit the 9 and then the 1.

Harold reached out and covered the phone with his hand. "Seriously, we think you should talk to her first."

"Who?"

He gestured toward the bungalow with his pipe. "Her. Ramba."

"And say what, for chrissake?"

"Talk," Vlad said with a nervous grunt. "No police."

"Yes," Anna said. "Please to be talking only."

Harold added, "Try to get her on our side."

"I don't even know what that means," I said.

"Look," Harold said, "I've seen this kind of thing many times before, mostly with new students on campus. Moving into a new environment is one of the biggest stressors in life, and this may have been her way of getting it out of her system. If we just tell her we're nice people who don't want any trouble, then —"

"There's already trouble," I said, jabbing a finger at my Michelin 3000 in desperation. "Jesus Christ, Harold, look at my tire! Look at your tires!"

He maintained a serene demeanor, even raising one eyebrow scoldingly. His expression seemed to say, *In the grand scheme of all that is life, what's a tire?* "She just moved in, and she clearly has issues," he said. "But getting the police involved at this juncture could make things worse. Today, we hold the deescalation card. Tomorrow, she could be cutting our throats."

Vlad winced and Anna gasped and both of the dogs—their names were Foo-foo and Rocky, or Rocko and Fee-fee, I wasn't exactly sure—began to whimper.

"Harold," I said, pleading for reason. But he just stared back at me. I had known him since I moved in. We shared a love of landscaping and exotic beer but beyond that didn't have much in common. I suspected he was a bleeding-heart lib, and he probably thought I was a right-wing warmonger. But since we never knew for sure how the other felt, we generally got along. I admit that for once, his psychobabble was appealing. As I said, I wasn't interested in escalating anything with anyone, least of all a bowie-wielding lunatic.

"It's for the good of us all," Harold said.

I smirked. "Then maybe we should all go up there. We could deescalate together."

Anna gasped again and muttered something in Russian.

Harold was shaking his head. "Too confrontational. Besides, she's got a POW flag, so maybe she's prior military. Tell her you were in the air force. Tell her about Iraq. Connect with her. Above all, don't take an aggressive posture."

"I can't believe this," I said. "I can't believe this, I can't believe this," I repeated, even as I shoved my phone into my shirt pocket and began walking up her driveway.

When I mounted the porch steps, the lawnmower buzzing in the distance hit a patch of rock and stopped dead. The wooden planks of the porch creaked with neglect and resentment beneath my feet. I could feel the eyes of my huddled neighbors watching me. And right before I knocked, I heard Anna's weak, frightened voice utter, "Is he just to be talking, Mister Harold?"

Harold answered her in an unruffled, professorial manner. "That's correct, my dear," he said, teeth clenched on the stem of his pipe. "He will just to be talking."

She opened the door on the first knock. I was prepared for anything, especially hostility, but she was wearing the same tremendous smile she wore when she introduced herself. I made sure to locate her hands. One was on the door, and the other was brushing some dust off the front of her shirt. The features of her face were stark white against the darkness of the hall behind her, her eyes open wide and gleaming, as if the strain of her pulled-back hair had stretched the skin too tight. She looked about as crazy as I'd ever seen a person look, like a mad monk preparing to burn a heretic at the stake.

The effect left me speechless. My mind fluttered between what I wanted to say and, per Harold's suggestion, what I was supposed to say. Was it *I'm here about the tires, you crazy bitch?* Or *Gee, I just love your POW flag, so let's connect?* But I couldn't even open my mouth.

She stood up on her toes and looked past my shoulder at the other neighbors. "Let me guess," she said. "You're not happy I moved here."

I cleared my throat and tried to soften my tone, all the while hearing Harold's droning voice: *Don't take an aggressive posture.* "That's not exactly true," I said, "but I—"

"And you don't know what to do or say because you're not used to having someone—especially a new neighbor—greet you like I did?"

"Well . . ."

"Well what?"

"Well, um, I really love your flag. Were you in the service? The military? I was too, so I thought we could, you know—"

Her response was immediate and electric. She clapped her hands together, and her eyes glistened. "A veteran? Why the hell didn't you say so? Come on in."

And here I retreated a step. I was no fool. I had lived long and bore the scars of many narrow escapes to prove it. But then Harold's voice persisted, like some kind of suburban secretary of state. *Play the deescalation card. Get her on our side.*

"Okay, sure," I said, unsurely. "Thanks."

I stepped across the threshold and paused as my eyes fought to adjust. The fading afternoon light I brought with me did nothing to illuminate the dark interior, although my eyes fixed on a glowing lampshade within. There was some kind of cheap, ridiculous foyer chandelier slung low enough that it grazed my head. It was missing several glass hangings and rattled as if mocking me.

The woman had moved on ahead and disappeared. I managed to follow her voice as it faded deeper into the shadows. "You'll have to excuse the mess," she said. "As you can see, I'm having a wonderful adventure in moving. Shut the door, will you?"

By now my eyes had settled, and the foyer took shape as well as the open living/dining room beyond. The layout wasn't that different from my own house. The couple who had lived here prior were an air force sergeant and his South Korean wife. They'd gotten orders to Minot, North Dakota, and, like everything else headed that way, disappeared in the quiet of night, never to be seen again. Despite our shared service, we had never socialized.

I took a few more cautious steps, navigating around a clutter of cardboard boxes, their lids open in mighty yawns of disgorged packing paper. Rather than an adventure in moving, it looked more like one of exile, a picture of abandonment, as if the moving truck had simply backed up to the front door and dumped its contents through the opening.

I moved past a kitchen area to my left and into the living room, where I found the woman crouched over and rummaging through some boxes. "Make yourself at home," she said. "So you were in the army?"

"Air force."

Something flittered across the ceiling above me, some rodent nesting in the ductwork. I couldn't imagine what she might be looking for in those boxes or how she expected to find it. All the windows were covered by thick sheets or curtains. Although my eyes had adjusted enough to see, the only legitimate light source was from the lamp. Near the back of the house was a sliding glass door, where a brush of sunlight glinted below the hem of the curtain.

More disturbing than the lack of light was the smell. The air inside was overwhelmingly musty, scented with low-grade alcohol or perhaps some kind of cleaning product.

"Let's see. Where is it?" she said. "Ah-ha!" With a flourish, she produced a darkened wine bottle and held it out to me, as if it were a small animal she had shot in the woods and expected me to cook. "This was a wedding gift," she announced. "Although I couldn't tell you what kind it is. My husband was the wine expert in the family."

"Please, no," I said. "Really, I don't want you to go to any trouble."

I shifted closer to the lamp, which was positioned atop a round end table, making sure to keep my back to the front door. In the small circle of light was an eight-by-ten picture, neatly framed and standing amid a jumble of prescription pill bottles. I squinted, but couldn't read the labels.

The photo showed a Marine pilot in flight suit, nestled in the open cockpit of what looked to be an F-18 fighter. He was wearing aviator sunglasses and smiling, one gloved hand extended in a thumbs-up salute. A vast desert landscape fell away behind him, and I knew immediately it was Iraq. It could have been anywhere. Nevada, California, or even Kuwait. But I knew by the cast of the shadows that it was the place I'd spent six miserable months at the height of the insurgency. Just looking at the photo, I could taste the desert dust in my mouth and feel it thicken on my teeth. This recognition was a frequent occurrence, most especially whenever I watched a news report about the war on television. Harold probably would have diagnosed me with PTSD if I'd mentioned it to him, which I wouldn't.

While the woman continued to rummage, I gestured toward the picture. "That your husband?"

She glanced at the photo, then at me, blinking in an almost sleepy gesture. Her shoulders wilted, and the smile was gone again. I felt my heart clench up.

"That's right," she said. "He's in Iraq." She shimmied sideways on her knees to another box, this one tattered and torn at the corners.

*Tell her about Iraq,* Harold broke in. *Connect with her.* "I was over there too," I said. "Back in 2006. I worked in the theater hospital. Administrative stuff mostly."

"Really? You must have seen a lot of death."

I detected a trap in her comment and chose my words carefully. "Actually, we had over a ninety percent save rate once the casualties reached us. It's unusual to have that kind of—"

She cut me off with a grunt and said, "*Save rate?* Is that what you said? Wow, that's funny." Her concentration was now focused entirely on the tattered box. She had set the bottle down and started removing small items one by one, each individually wrapped in newspaper. I noted well the size and shape of each package. I didn't want her emerging from the cardboard with a loaded AK-47.

I inched forward again, waving a hand to get her attention. "Please, please, you don't have to go to any trouble."

"There you guys are," she said to something in the box. She produced a bundle cocooned in newspaper. She sat back on her haunches and unwrapped two wineglasses, delicately setting each one down on the floor beside the wine bottle.

Harold started to whisper into my ear again, but I cut him off. "Listen," I said, reverting to my gruff sergeant's voice. "We should really talk about the tires. You've got to understand."

"So you say you were in Iraq?" she said, still not looking up.

I sighed, feeling the weariness of the entire exercise. I said, "I don't think you understand how serious what you did was. I wanted to call the police."

"Why didn't you?"

"Because I thought we could talk first."

"So let's talk. Over some wine."

"I'm really not in the mood to drink wine."

"That's good. Because I never intended you to drink it." She reached back behind her head with both hands and yanked at her ponytail, tightening the hair even further, as if girding herself for battle. Then she grabbed the neck of the bottle, rose up to her feet with the quick grace of a lioness, and hopped over the box toward me.

"Okay, look," I said calmly, and then watched in utter disbelief as she reared back and swung for the fences. I could still feel my mouth forming the words *I really think you need to* when the bottle collided with my skull.

I staggered backward, arms flailing. The bottle, which did not break, felt like it was filled with concrete. The point of impact burned, and my vision boomeranged from focused to double to triple. Some glass or porcelain knickknack, perhaps even a precious memento of her marriage, crackled beneath my sneaker.

I shook my head fiercely and managed to restore my vision. Still, my brain refused to process what had happened. I could feel blood trickling down the side of my head, but I was very much aware and conscious. Somewhere in my brain's circuitry, deep and falling fast away, was Harold's voice saying, *Get her on our side.*

My new neighbor had by now set the unbroken concrete bottle aside and stooped to retrieve something from another box. My heart clutched again, and I thought for certain that her hand would soon be holding the Buck knife. But it was a frying pan. One of those heavy jobs, with a titanium nonstick surface.

Then she was crouching, shoulders back, hips tight, and with a yelp she charged at me, the cookware held high like a caveman's club.

I said, "Wait—listen—you can't—" as if my mind was stuck in reason mode, still looking for a way to talk myself out of it. She swung before I could get my hands up. I took the flat, hard metal of the pan to the left side of my face. Something gave and rattled. It wasn't the skillet.

I was thrown back again, this time into the foyer. I heard the pan drop and hit the floor, another weapon used and discarded. The next few seconds were a blur of bulging eyes, gritted teeth, ringless knuckles. She punched, kicked, elbowed, and pushed, backing me toward the front door. Throughout the attack she huffed and yipped like a redheaded ninja.

Although her blows were not as painful as the bottle or pan, she was much too quick for me and seemed to anticipate every defense I attempted. When I parried low, she head-butted high. When I blocked high, she kneed low. She took my polo-shirt collar in both fists and pogo-sticked me down the tight foyer, up and over the boxes, my head crashing into the chandelier, which sent about a dozen glass hangings smashing down in our violent wake.

She snatched the doorknob and then kicked open the door. She yanked and pulled me across the threshold by my shirt. I almost tumbled over, but she reined back and kept me upright as I floundered across the porch. Finally, using the momentum of my attempt to flee, she sent me airborne diagonally over the steps and the hedge. I landed directly on a patch of hard, grassless dirt.

But before I struck the ground, while I was hurtling through the air, a strange thing happened. Everything slowed, as if I had been plunged underwater. There was even an underwater glow to the early evening light. And I realized at that moment that I had never—in a long life of visiting shady bars the world over—been in a bar fight. I had certainly never been thrown from a bar. I had been asked to leave once while stationed in Turkey, after a friend and I got into an altercation with some Dutch airmen on joint military maneuvers. But there had been no blows, no international incident to answer for. We were insulted, but also outnumbered and still sober enough to be easily persuaded.

Now, as I whispered through the air toward the hardest part of my new neighbor's lawn, my eyes catching the unmoving POW flag, I thought, This is what it's like. This is what it's like to get your ass kicked in a bar fight and then thrown ingloriously out into the street.

I had been lucky until this day. But I would soon look back—to the moment right before she knocked on my door—and realize just how lucky I had truly been.

At the emergency room, business was booming. I hoped they'd see me right away, but once I stepped through the automatic sliding glass doors that opened with a *whoosh* and into the grip of the room, I knew it was hopeless. The place reeked of sickness and injury, and I was right in the middle of it, just another victim. Take a number; have a seat. The oddest thing was the hush of the crowded waiting room. Nothing but muted shuffles and whispers, the faint ringing of phones, and an occasional mewl of pain.

Despite the assortment of faces everywhere, no one seemed to be looking at anyone else, as if doing so would only confirm a dark prognosis. There was one exception, a small boy in a Florida Marlins baseball cap, who sat across from me. He gawked relentlessly at my face with all the wide-eyed, slack-jawed fascination of his first peek at a centerfold. I can't say I blamed him. I was pressing a dripping baggie of ice onto my swollen jaw. Down the front of my shirt was a smattering of fresh blood. I must have looked like a roughed-up zombie.

"What are you in for?" I mumbled to the boy, trying to be humorous but probably only managing to be terrifying.

The boy turned away and yawned.

Harold hustled over from the reception area, deftly sidestepping a gurney being wheeled recklessly past him. He was holding a clipboard and, after taking a seat beside me, began to scribble in my name and address.

"Did they say how long?" I asked him.

He answered by smacking his lips and shrugging. "There was some kind of accident involving a bus, so it could be a while. Good thing you're not so bad off." This more or less matched his medical assessment from the moment he had collected me off the lawn and stuffed me into Vlad's Fiat Strada, which was the only car in the cul-de-sac not disabled and which Vlad enthusiastically suggested we take because, as he said, "I am not to be involved."

All the way to the hospital, Harold alternated between complaints about the battered car—"I guess this passes for luxury in Russia"—and a near obsessive insistence that I was going to be okay. His efforts to calm me only added to my concern. The more he said, "Really, you're going to be fine," the more I became convinced that I was as good as dead.

I removed the icepack from the side of my head and gestured toward the boy, whose eyes had migrated back to me. "I have a feeling he doesn't think I'm going to be okay."

Harold concentrated on the form. "You're almost certainly not as bad as you feel."

"Really? Because I *feel* like shit. Like every-bone-in-my-face-is-broken shit."

"I'm really sorry. I should have expected some resentment on her part, but violence? Very strange."

"I take it none of your homesick students assaulted anyone after moving onto campus."

"You'd be surprised. I've seen many difficult patients in my day. In fact, the difficult ones were my specialty. There are several cases I'm consulting on now that—"

"Seriously, I think my jaw might be broken."

He laughed. "You wouldn't be talking if it were."

I patted my pockets and realized I had lost my phone during the attack. "Did you call the police yet?"

"Let's wait until the doctor sees you. My guess is you're not as bad as you feel."

"You've said that twenty times already."

"You know—"

A woman screamed. The sound burst mournfully through the whooshing emergency room entrance and was loud enough that everyone in the waiting room collectively jumped. A gurney carrying a small child was wheeled through by two attendants. Running alongside was a woman in shorts, a bikini top, and flip-flops, who appeared to be limping slightly. "Please, someone, please!" she shouted. She was waving her arms and pointing, as if trying to direct the two attendants. All of them were swallowed up by another set of double doors. The waiting room resumed its hushed suffering.

It was the same everywhere, I thought. One of the starkest memories I had of Iraq occurred while I was attached to the medical group at the theater hospital. During a lull in American and British casualties, the local clinic transferred to us a girl of about ten who had been caught in crossfire and had suffered a mortal head wound. The doctors who patched her up said she wouldn't live through the night. But she hung on for more than a week. Each day her mother was escorted in under guard and had to be told repeatedly that outbursts of any kind were forbidden. Yet whenever she laid her eyes on her daughter, she would scream and chant and pound the mattress for the child to wake.

I remember one night, late in the evening, as I made my rounds through the area, gathering up soiled sheets and scrubs, I paused beside the little girl's bed. Around her head lay a halo of about a dozen stuffed animals, which a few nurses had left behind. I remember being flooded with yearning. I had never been married and had only dated one woman seriously and for only about six months. I never wanted children and even got a vasectomy when I was twenty-one. This act, I was later convinced, had greatly limited my ability to attract the opposite sex. Even when I stopped telling women about the elective operation, they still weren't interested in any long-term relationship. The one woman I wanted to be free of, the one whom I had dated seriously for six months, shrugged when I told her I was unable to procreate the species and then asked me to pass the salt.

The taste of blood in my mouth snapped me back to the present. Harold was droning on beside me, and it wasn't until he said the word *rape* that I perked up. I asked him to repeat what he just said.

"I said, 'She'll probably cry rape if you go to the authorities.' Something to consider. Especially if your injuries aren't too bad. Which they don't appear to be. To be honest, contacting the police over this matter is probably exactly what she wants."

I leaned over and whispered, "Harold, can you hear what I'm saying right now?"

"Of course."

"Good. I'm going to make sure she's arrested; then I'm going to sue the fuck out of her."

I winced, my tongue having flopped over the bloody gap in my mouth where I had lost a tooth. I groaned as I thought about that tooth. How it had traveled with me on many journeys. Over fifty years it had been in my mouth, and now it was—where? In my stomach? On the floor of her house with my phone, the porcelain, and other assorted debris?

Harold sighed. "A shame you'll have to take such drastic actions against a fellow war veteran."

"She's not a vet. Her husband is. He's deployed, and if it makes you feel any better, I have no plans on having *him* arrested."

He began to scribble on the hospital form again, but stopped. "We never talked about the war."

"Why would we?"

"You might be surprised how I feel."

"Maybe we'd both be surprised. Or maybe neither of us would give a shit how the other one feels."

"Perhaps." He set the pen down and adjusted his glasses nervously.

And that's when it struck me, with the crystal clarity of a long-hidden truth suddenly revealed. "You know her, don't you? You sonofabitch."

He grimaced and shook his head. "It's more complicated than that. Please don't be upset."

"I'm not upset. I'm just exhausted and missing a tooth, and my face is broken in about ten places. I mean, what's there to be upset about? Now what the hell is going on?"

Harold sighed again and told me what he knew, which was a lot more than I did. The woman was a patient of a colleague, a former student of his. She was the widow of a vet—yes, her husband had been killed while deployed—but he didn't know the details. She had been moved off base and didn't have anywhere to stay. It was Harold who had volunteered the empty house and helped arrange for her to move in temporarily.

"Can you imagine if your significant other was lost forever?" he asked. "Especially in such a cruel and senseless war. Can you imagine such a thing? And then having nowhere to turn?"

"No," I said, still struggling to control my anger and pain, "but maybe we should just stop talking about this."

"Of course. But really, I had no idea she would react this way. In fact, I thought just the opposite."

I wasn't seen until late in the evening, having been triaged to the lowest rung of the injury ladder. The bus accident had been serious, but no fatalities. The doctor who examined me was wearing a white coat with a splotch of blood above his nametag that resembled the state of New Jersey. He apologized profusely for the long wait until he found out that I was not in fact one of the bus crash victims. He turned indignant and dismissive, telling me that my wounds were superficial, and offered vague instructions about what to do if I developed symptoms of a concussion.

When I told him I had lost my tooth, he confirmed what I already knew by peering halfheartedly into my mouth. "You bet you did," he said. "You'll need to have an oral surgeon look at that. Just don't let them talk you into a porcelain bridge for any back teeth. Go with metal, and you'll thank me later."

After filling a prescription for Tylenol 3, Harold and I were back in the Popovs' Strada and headed home. "What did I tell you?" he said, as if he'd won a bet. "In and out, good as new."

"Like it never happened," I said, trying to lay on the sarcasm.

But he didn't catch on. Instead he grunted and fought the gearshift, grinding it mercilessly. "Who owns a Fiat these days?" he said. "Honestly."

"At least the tires work," I said.

*

For the next few weeks I simmered, I watched, and occasionally I felt better. I also steered clear of Harold, even though he called frequently and left updates on my answering machine about our neighbor or, as he called her, "my student's patient." She was improving, he assured me. She had not missed a single session. What's more, although she'd clearly become more reclusive, she hadn't bothered anyone.

I agreed with the reclusive part. Only once since I returned from the hospital had I seen her, and that was just a glimpse of her shadow, staring out the front bay window of the bungalow, watching the comings and goings in the cul-de-sac as though it were the entire world in micro and she its sentinel. And although her features were lost behind the glass, I couldn't imagine her face with anything other than that huge psychotic grin.

I myself made a few inquiries about her background, calling a flight surgeon friend who turned out to be quite aware of the unfortunate demise of the Marine in question. In fact, he was the last U.S. military pilot shot down over Iraq. The pilot's call sign was "Buster," and as the name would suggest, he was a wholesome, stand-up guy and a worthwhile Marine. He had been shot down near Balad while laying down covering fire for a squad of Army Rangers. Before anyone could get to his body, insurgents had swarmed over the wreckage and spirited away most of what remained. The Defense Department had identified him by DNA left at the crash site — mostly blood and shreds of his flight suit.

"What about his wife?" I asked my friend.

He paused thoughtfully on the phone. "Didn't know he had one."

"She's my neighbor." I almost added, *She beat me up*, but assumed it would invite a whole new series of questions.

"It's sad," he said, and his voice turned bitter. "He never had a chance to punch out. Pararescue had boots on-site within twenty miles of the crash. Those fucking *hajis* were just a little quicker. What the PJs could get back wasn't much, but it was enough to tell he was KIA."

"Jesus Christ."

"Yep. That's the guy to talk to about it."

After the call, the picture of a somber funeral with a near-empty coffin stayed with me and cooled my resentment of the woman. I even felt a bit guilty.

That is, until a day later, when one of the Popovs' dogs turned up missing. Anna arrived at my door in a state, shaking and runny-eyed, her hands clasped together. In broken English, she explained that she had let her dachshunds out into the front yard to do their business. Only one was there when she went to call them back inside. "They are never leaving the yard, never!" Then she shivered and sheepishly extended a torn sheet of paper in my direction. "Please to tell me," she said. "What does these message mean?"

Scrawled on the paper, in black capital letters, were the words *MANY DOGS HAVE DIED HERE.*

"It came in mailbox," Anna said.

"Anyone could have put it there," I said, realizing I sounded just like Harold, which prompted me to add, "Even *Harold*. Have you seen the way he drives?"

Still, the look on my face must have given Anna the answer she was looking for. She spun around and ran back across the lot toward her house, whimpering in Russian.

I left a message on Harold's cell phone to call me.

He showed up on my doorstep the next morning, a Saturday, with two cups of Dunkin' Donuts coffee. I stepped out just in time to see Vlad and Anna climbing into the cab of a U-Haul truck, their surviving mutt yelping from a carrier between them. The day was overcast and windless, which spoke of a coming storm the local stations had been talking up all week. The trees in the yards and at the entrance of the cul-de-sac looked subdued in the gloom.

"What the hell's going on?" I asked.

"Tropical storm. They say the coast is really going to catch hell."

"I'm talking about the Popovs."

"Oh," he said, shaking his head. "I've already tried talking them out of it. They apparently spent the whole night packing up. Vlad wouldn't say anything else except that they're going to stay with relatives in Jersey." He sighed and sipped his coffee. "I can only guess that the recent unpleasantness must remind them of God only knows how many KGB horrors."

We both watched as the truck drove off. I thought about the ragged note. "Which one was it?" I asked.

"Which one was what?"

"The one that disappeared. Was it Rocko or Fee-Fee?"

"I couldn't say. Foo-Foo, I think."

"This is crazy. Somebody's got to call the cops."

"And tell them what? Who's to say the animal didn't just run off?"

"Gee, I don't know. Maybe the cryptic note in the mailbox?"

He huffed and shook his head. "We are just talking about a dog, you know."

"That's right. Just a dog. So do you think maybe she's got it out of her system yet, professor? Or will it take one more incident? Like maybe one of us spitted and basted over a giant grill in her basement?"

"Look, I've already called my former student. I've told him my concerns and feelings, which mirror yours."

"You sure about that? Maybe you'd be surprised how I feel."

He gingerly removed the lid from his coffee and poured the contents into the brush beside my porch steps. I still had not taken a drink from the cup he had handed me. "So hard to anticipate this kind of thing," he said with resignation. "But I suppose we should have. There are people all over the country right now living the nightmare she's living." He looked up at me, his eyes as gray and remorseless as the thickening clouds stretched out above the trees. "The terrible reach of this sickening war on so-called terror is quite evident, don't you think?"

"I saw a few things over there that would make your pipe explode. You don't see me running around slashing tires and offing the neighborhood pooches."

He turned away. "Hmmm," was all he said.

I retreated back into the house and stared at him through the screen door. The wind had picked up a bit, and the shock of white hair on either side of his head put me in mind of a contemplative Albert Einstein, dreaming about the potential of a split atom. "When this half-assed psycho relocation program of yours gets out," I said, "you might find yourself answering a whole lot of questions."

"Perhaps that's the least of our worries."

"What do you mean?"

His features drooped, and now he reminded me of a depressed Albert Einstein after having watched the first atom bomb explode. "My former student tells me that she's developed a bit of an unhealthy interest. In you."

"Me?"

"Hmmm. You really upset her the other day."

"You mean the other day when she assaulted me? *That* other day?"

"I told you not to take an aggressive stance."

"That's a load of—. What else did your friend say?"

"Not much. Except . . ."

"Except?"

"Except that you might want to purchase a gun. I told him you were prior military, so you probably already had one. That is correct, right? You do own a gun?"

"Sonofabitch," I said, meaning *he* was a sonofabitch.

But Harold didn't hear me. He simply sighed again and made a sweeping gesture at the darkening horizon and stirring trees. "I just hope this isn't as bad as last year's big one. We were without power for a week, remember? It was like being stranded on a deserted island."

I locked every door and window of the house, even the narrow casements in the cellar that were surely impossible for any adult to crawl through. When I was finished, I retraced my steps and checked each lock again. The act of barricading myself in was therapeutic. I found a quiet relief surging over me. The feeling continued as I gathered candles, batteries, and a flashlight from the kitchen drawers and cupboards. I kept telling myself it was all for the coming storm and potential power outage and not for the purpose of defending against a home invasion by a psychotic neighbor who was now fixated on me as—what? The cause of her husband's demise? A participant in what Harold called a cruel and senseless war? The collapse of the real estate market? Shit, who knew? But there was no denying my purpose when I retrieved a .22-caliber Marlin 39A rifle from beneath my bed, removed the bolt, cleaned the chamber, and methodically loaded it.

I had not recovered my cell phone, so I kept the landline within easy reach, positioned on the kitchen table amid a scatter of batteries and extra ammo. Harold would have a clinical name for my preparations. And I suppose he would be right. I surveyed my spartan dwelling and wondered why I was satisfied—if I was in fact satisfied. I had lived my entire life alone, in the bachelor dorms for over twenty years in the military and now in an empty house.

Never married, never in love. No family, or even close friends for that matter. Even the friends I had made in the air force were mostly relationships of convenience, none of them standing out enough to mark and identify as special, as worthy of the name *brotherhood*. The one tangible remnant of my time in service was a shadowbox of "gimme" medals that I kept on the wall in the foyer. I contemplated it now as if it represented a stolen identity.

And then it struck me: all I had—all I ever really had—were neighbors. All of them utterly forgettable. Save one.

The realization bestowed a sudden and empowering effect on me. In a bitter huff, I stormed through the house and unlocked every door and window. Of course I kept the gun loaded.

No sooner had I unlatched the last window than it began to rain, huge drops going *phut, phut, phut* on the rooftop. I sat at the kitchen table and listened to the shower begin to increase, the wind whistling now, shaking the doors and window frames.

The phone rang. I barely heard it over the hiss of wind. The caller ID showed Harold's name and cell phone number. Somewhat reluctantly I answered, but the line was dead.

From the kitchen window I could just see his house through the bent and swaying trees in my front lawn. The rain was now hammering down at a sharp angle, creating a blurred effect through the glass. I redialed his number but got a busy signal. *The lines must be down,* I thought.

Thunder cracked overhead, followed by a flash of lightning that revealed a hazy figure racing across the rim of the cul-de-sac. I grabbed clumsily at the barrel of the gun. Almost immediately, as if in diabolical collaboration with my unease, the power went out.

I snatched up the flashlight, threw on my slicker, and stepped out onto the porch. The screen door slapped savagely shut behind me, and the gutters gurgled and strained in the torrent. From the porch I could see the whole of Harold's house. His front door was wide open.

"Terrific," I muttered, and the fear in my voice startled me. Harold would probably have a name for that too. I hefted the rifle and adjusted my hold on the flashlight. The note declaring the death of dogs flashed into my thoughts.

After a slight bounce, I pushed off, clambered down the steps, and dashed down my driveway and through the rain. By the time

I reached his house, I was completely soaked. I yelled Harold's name through the open doorway, then stepped inside. Hearing nothing, I closed the door behind me with some effort. Rainwater had pooled around my sodden shoes, and I called out again. A muffled ticking of a clock and the scent of pipe smoke were the only signs of life.

Then I saw it. Lying atop a foyer table was a frayed dog collar decorated with glassy studs, some of them broken. A small metal tag identified the collar as belonging to Fee-Fee Popov.

I held my breath and listened again. Nothing but the spasm of the storm. I left the scene as I found it, although I did make sure the front door was shut tight. By now the wind and rain were beyond raging. I could barely see as I struggled back toward my house. Once inside, I sucked and gulped at the air as if I had been underwater, which I suppose I had been. Once again I listened for any sound beneath the raging din.

And I knew—I don't know how, but the knowledge was absolute—that she was there.

I flipped on the flashlight, and it glimmered across the shadowbox and bookcases, television, couch, and my favorite club chair. I moved the circle of light onto the floor leading into the living room, looking for wet tracks. I swept the light through the kitchen door, and my eye caught something on the table there. It was my cell phone, placed neatly where it had not been just a few moments earlier.

As I approached it, the phone began to vibrate, its display glowing a white-blue color. The number was Harold's cell. I didn't pick up. Instead I turned back toward the entrance to the kitchen and peeked around the corner into the living room. I imagined her using Harold's phone to call me from behind my club chair. Waiting for me to pick up, only to fall on me in a fury of assorted blunt weapons.

Ten seconds ticked by. Twenty seconds. Then the phone burped twice, signifying the arrival of a text message. Keeping one eye and the flashlight beam on the open kitchen doorway, I picked up the phone and read, *I'm down in Silver Lake with my mother. Just checking to see if all is well. Hope you've battened down the hatches.*

I licked my lips and considered typing a response. But the creak of wicker sounded behind me. I spun around. She was sitting in a small chair tucked beside the refrigerator, staring at me.

"What are you doing here?" I said in a shudder, struggling to level the rifle at her with one hand while trying to hold the cell phone and flashlight with the other. The flashlight's beam shined unsteadily in her eyes. She never flinched. My heart beat upward into my throat, but I concentrated on forcing the fear from my voice. "I said, what are you doing in my house?"

"Do you like it?" she said, her voice soft and almost childlike. Her red hair was untethered and smeared wet and flat around her pale face. Water dripped from her nose and chin.

"What?"

"This. Living alone."

"I've got a gun."

"That's funny."

"Not really, no," I said.

"I'm not going to hurt you."

"You mean, *again*, don't you? You're not going to hurt me *again*."

"The dog was already dead when I found it. Your friend, the professor, backed over it the other day. He threw it into the trunk and drove off, but he forgot the little collar and tag."

"I don't believe that."

"It's the truth."

"So why the note? Because maybe it's funny?"

"It was a warning. I didn't want that poor couple to lose another dog."

"Okay," I said, somehow convincing myself to feel convinced. "So how did the collar end up in his house?"

"I put it there. I want him to know that I know. That I have power over his cowardice. That there are consequences for daring to forget."

The rifle in my hand felt as heavy as a dumbbell. Yet I still didn't move for fear she would see me shaking. I said, "I'm going to call the police, and you're going to be arrested."

Her response was softer still, almost maddening and out of breath. "When my husband said goodbye to me, I knew he was going to die. I don't know how, but I knew. And yet"—her features twisted up in pain—"and yet I also expected him to come back home. Safe and the same as when he left. And then we would laugh together at my silly premonition."

"I can't do anything about that," I said. "I wish it didn't have to be this way."

"Do you know what they put in his coffin? Do you know what they put there instead of his body?"

"Look—"

"You saw body bags in Iraq. You saw those that were full and those that only held pieces. You must know."

I started to respond but stopped. I stopped because suddenly I believed her. Every word. Especially about what happened to the dog. But even more important than that, I suddenly felt her grief, arrayed around her, an instinctive defense mechanism that emitted its own warning signal. The sense of it was almost pious in its depth, like a religious ceremony, all of which made her pitiful, deflated appearance seem all the more heroic.

The woman straightened her back and stood up.

"Stop," I said.

"Stop what?"

The cell phone finally slipped from my grip and clacked onto the linoleum floor of the kitchen. I settled the stock of the rifle across my forearm and steadied the light on her face. My fear was gone. Even the strain of holding the gun level had dissipated to numbness. I said, "I really don't think I can help you."

"I don't either." She edged closer.

Smoothly, I flicked the safety off, hoping the sound would deter her. "I'll shoot," I told her.

"I know," she said. She walked forward but quickly veered to my left, toward the open kitchen doorway. I stepped aside, my finger loose against the trigger. Then she was past me and in the foyer. Without pausing, she opened the front door. The force of the wind threw it back against the wall, shaking the house. She had to lean forward to push herself out of the screen and into the wind.

As I watched her stumble out and down the porch steps, I felt it. Relief, certainly, but also something else. Something meaningful and harsh, like a wave of fever. It was something—or rather a mix of something, gunked together in a stew of senses—that I had not experienced before and would probably never experience again. It was the taste of sorrow, the wreckage of war, the feeble cries of the dead and dying, the silence of children—all of it culminating in a barren loneliness that we had fought for and so dearly deserved.

I ran forward, shouldering my way through the screen and onto the porch. I stopped there and called out to her. "Don't! Wait!"

I yelled. But she might as well have been walking into a roaring waterfall. In an instant she was gone, lost in the mighty pull of the storm, her dim impression sealed over.

I wanted to pursue her, to embrace her, to comfort her and share my feeling with her. I wanted to do all of that. I really did. But I could not move.

THOMAS McGUANE

# Motherlode

FROM *The New Yorker*

LOOKING IN THE hotel mirror, David Jenkins adjusted the Stetson he disliked and pulled on a windbreaker with a cattle-vaccine
logo. He worked for a syndicate of cattle geneticists in Oklahoma,
though he'd never met his employers—he had earned his credentials through an online agricultural portal, much the way that
people became ministers. He was still in his twenties, a very bright
young man, but astonishingly uneducated in every other way. He
had spent the night in Jordan at the Garfield Hotel, which was an
ideal location for meeting his ranch clients in the area. He had wo-
ken early enough to be the first customer at the café. On the front
step, an old dog slept with a canceled first-class stamp stuck to its
butt. By the time David had ordered breakfast, older ranchers occupied several of the tables, waving to him familiarly. Then a man
from Utah, whom he'd met at the hotel, appeared in the doorway
and stopped, looking around the room. The man, who'd told David that he'd come to Jordan to watch the comets, was small and
intense, middle-aged, wearing pants with an elastic waistband and
flashy sneakers. Several of the ranchers were staring at him. David
had asked the hotel desk clerk, an elderly man, about the comets. The clerk said, "I don't know what he's talking about and I've
lived here all my life. He doesn't even have a car." David studied
the menu to keep from being noticed, but it was too late. The
man was at his table, laughing, his eyes shrinking to points and
his gums showing. "Stop worrying! I'll get my own table," he said,
drumming his fingers on the back of David's chair. David felt that
in some odd way he was being assessed.

The door to the café, which had annoying bells on a string, kept clattering open and shut to admit a broad sample of the community. David enjoyed all the comradely greetings and gentle needling from the ranchers, and felt himself to be connected to the scene, if lightly. Only the fellow from Utah, sitting alone, seemed entirely apart. The cook pushed dish after dish across her tall counter while the waitress sped to keep up. She had a lot to do, but it lent her a star quality among the diners, who teased her with mock personal questions or air-pinched as her bottom went past.

David made notes about this and that on a pad he took from his shirt pocket, until the waitress, a yellow pencil stuck in her chignon, arrived with his bacon and eggs. He turned a welcoming smile to her, hoping that when he looked back the man would be gone, but he was still at his table, giving David an odd military salute and then holding his nose. David didn't understand these gestures and was disquieted by the implication that he knew the man. He ate quickly, then went to the counter to pay. The waitress came out of the kitchen, wiping her hands on a dishcloth, looked the cash register up and down, and said, "Everything okay, Dave?"

"Yes, very good, thanks."

"Put it away in an awful hurry. Out to Larsen's?"

"No, I was there yesterday. Bred heifers. They held everything back."

"They're big on next year. I wonder if it'll do them any good."

"They're still here, ain't they? I'm headed for Jorgensen's. Big day."

Two of the ranchers had finished eating, and, Stetsons on the back of their heads, chairs tilted, they picked their teeth with the corners of their menus. As David put his wallet in his pocket and headed for the door, he realized he was being followed. He didn't turn until he was halfway across the parking lot. When he did, the gun was in his stomach and his new friend was smiling at him. "Name's Ray. Where's your outfit?"

Ray had a long, narrow face and tightly marcelled dirty-blond hair that fell low on his forehead.

"Are you robbing me?"

"I need a ride."

Ray got in the front seat of David's car, tucked the gun in his pants, and pulled his shirt over the top of it, a blue terry-cloth shirt with a large breast pocket that contained a pocket liner and a number of ballpoint pens. The flap of the pocket liner said *Powell Savings, Modesto, CA.*

"Nice car. What're all the files in back for?"

"Breeding records—cattle-breeding records."

"Mind?" He picked up David's cell phone and, without waiting for an answer, tapped in a number. In a moment his voice changed to an intimate murmur. "I'm there, or almost there—" Covering the mouthpiece, he pointed to the intersection. "Take that one right there." David turned east. "I got it wrote down someplace, East 200, North 13, but give it to me again, my angel. Or I can call you as we get closer. Okay, a friend's giving me a lift." He covered the mouthpiece. "Your name?"

"David."

"David from?"

"Reed Point."

"Yeah, great guy I knew back in Reed Place."

"Reed Point."

"I mean Reed Point. Left the Beamer for an oil change, and Dave said he was headed this way. Wouldn't even let me split the gas. So, okay, just leaving Jordan. How much longer, Morsel? Two hours! Are you fucking kidding? Okay, okay, two hours. I'm just anxious to see you, baby, not being short with you at all."

Lifting his eyes to the empty miles of sagebrush, Ray snapped the cell phone shut and said, sighing, "Two fucking hours." If it weren't for the gun in his pants, he could have been any other aging lovebird. He turned the radio on briefly. "Swap Shop" was on the air: "Broken refrigerator suitable for a smoker." Babies bawling in the background. He turned it off. David was trying to guess who Ray might really be—that is, if he was a fugitive from the law, someone he could bring to justice, in exchange for fame or some kind of reward, something good for business. He had tried everything he could to enhance his cattle-insemination business, even refrigerator magnets with his face on them that said, "Don't go bust shipping dries."

He asked, "Ray, do you feel like telling me what this is all about?"

"Sure, Dave. It's all about you doing as you're told."

"I see. And I'm taking you somewhere, am I?"

"Uh-huh, and staying as needed. Jesus Christ, if this isn't the ugliest country I ever seen."

"How did you pick me?"

"I picked your car. You were a throw-in. I hadn't took you along you'd've reported your car stolen. This way you still got it. It's a win-win. The lucky thing for you is you're my partner now. And you wanna pick up the tempo here? You're driving like my grandma."

"This isn't a great road. Deer jump out on it all the time. My cousin had one come through the windshield on him."

"Fuckin' pin it or I'll drive it like I did steal it."

David sped up slightly. This seemed to placate Ray and he slumped by the window and stared at the landscape going by. They passed an old pickup truck traveling in the opposite direction, a dead animal in the back with one upright leg trailing an American flag.

After they'd driven for nearly two hours, mostly in silence, a light tail-dragger aircraft with red-and-white-banded wings flew just overhead and landed on the road in front of them. The pilot climbed out and shuffled toward the car. David rolled down his window, and a lean, weathered face under a sweat-stained cowboy hat looked in. "You missed your turn," the man said. "Mile back, turn north on the two-track." Ray seemed to be trying to send a greeting that showed all his teeth, but he was ignored by the pilot. "Nice little Piper J-3 Cub," Ray said.

The pilot strode back to the plane, taxied down the road, got airborne, and banked sharply over a five-strand barbed wire, startling seven cows and their calves, which ran off into the sage, scattering meadowlarks and clouds of pollen. David turned the car around.

Ray said, "Old fellow back at the hotel said there's supposed to be dinosaurs around here." He gazed at the pale light of a gas well on a far ridge.

"That's what they say."

"What d'you suppose one of them is worth? Like a whole Tyrannosaurus rex?"

David just looked at Ray. Here was the turn, a two-track that was barely manageable in an ordinary sedan, and David couldn't imagine how it was negotiated in winter or spring, when the notorious local gumbo turned to mud. He'd delivered a Charolais bull near here one fall, and it was bad enough then. Plus the bull had torn up his trailer and he'd lost money on the deal.

"So, Dave, we're about to arrive and I should tell you what the

gun is for. I'm here to meet a girl, but I don't know how it's gonna
turn out. I may need to bail and you're my lift. The story is, my car
is in for repair. You stay until we see how this goes and carry me
out of here, if necessary. My friend here says you're onboard."

"I guess I understand, but what does this all depend on?"

"It depends on whether I like the girl or not, whether we're
compatible and want to start a family business. I have a lot I'd like
to pass on to the next generation."

The next bend revealed the house, a two-story ranch building
with little of its paint left. Ray gazed at the Piper Cub, which was
now parked in a field by the house, and at the Montana state flag
popping on the iron flagpole. *"Oro y plata,"* he said, chuckling.
"Perfect. Now, Davey, I need you to bone up on the situation here.
This is the Weldon Case cattle ranch, and it runs from here right
up to the Bakken oil field, forty miles away, which is where all the
*oro y plata* is at the moment. I'm guessing that was Weldon in the
airplane. I met Weldon's daughter, Morsel, through a dating service. Well, we haven't actually met in real time, but we're about to.
Morsel thinks she loves me, and we're just gonna have to see about
that. All you have to know is that Morsel thinks I'm an Audi dealer
from Simi Valley, California. She's going on one photograph of
me standing in front of an Audi flagship that did not belong to
me. You decide you want to help, and you may see more walkin'-
around money than you're used to. If you don't, well, you've seen
how I put my wishes into effect." He patted the bulge under his
shirt. "I just whistle a happy tune and start shooting."

David pulled up under the gaze of Weldon Case, who had
emerged from the plane. When he rolled down the window to
greet the old man again, Case just stared, then turned to call out
to the house. "It's the cowboy way," Ray muttered through an insincere smile. "Or else he's retarded. Dave, ask him if he remembers falling out of his high chair."

As they got out of the car, Morsel appeared on the front step
and inquired, in a penetrating contralto, "Which one is it?" Ray
raised his hands and tilted his head to one side, as though modestly
questioning himself. David noted that the gun was inadequately
concealed and turned quickly to shake Weldon Case's hand. It was
like seizing a plank.

"You're looking at him," Ray called out to Morsel.

"Oh, Christ," she yelled. "Is this what I get?" It was hard to say whether this was a positive response or not. Morsel was a scale model of her father, wind-weathered and, if anything, less feminine. Her view of the situation was quickly clarified as she raced forward to embrace Ray, whose look of suave detachment was briefly interrupted by fear. A tooth was missing, as well as a small piece of her ear. "Oh, Ray!"

Weldon looked at David with a sour expression, then spoke, in a lusterless tone: "Morsel has made some peach cobbler. It was her ma's recipe. Her ma is dead." Ray put on a ghastly look of sympathy, which seemed to fool Morsel, who squeezed his arm and said, "Started in her liver and just took off."

A small trash pile next to the porch featured a couple of played-out Odor-Eaters. David wondered where the walkin'-around money Ray had alluded to was supposed to come from. "Place is kind of a mess," Morsel warned. "We don't collect but we never get rid of."

As they went into the house, Weldon asked David if he enjoyed shooting coyotes. He replied, "I just drive Ray around"—Ray turned to listen—"and whatever Ray wants I guess is what we do . . . whatever he's into." David kept to himself that he enjoyed popping coyotes out his car window with the .25-06 with a Redfield range-finder scope and a tripod that he'd got from Hill Country Customs. David lived with his mother and had a habit of telling her about the great shots he'd made—like the five-hundred-yarder on Tin Can Hill with only the hood for a rest, no sandbags, no tripod. David's Uncle Maury had told him a long time ago, "It don't shoot flat, throw the fuckin' thing away."

David, who enjoyed brutally fattening food, thought Morsel was a good cook, but Ray ate only the salad, discreetly lifting each leaf until the dressing ran off. Weldon watched Ray and hardly said a word as Morsel grew more manic, jiggling with laughter and enthusiasm at each lighthearted remark. In fact, it was necessary to lower the temperature of the subjects—to heart attacks, highway wrecks, cancer—in order to get her to stop guffawing. Weldon planted his hands flat on the table, rose partway, and announced that he'd use the tractor to pull the plane around back. David was preoccupied with the mountain of tuna casserole between him and the peach cobbler and hardly heard him. Ray, small and disoriented next to Morsel, shot his eyes around the table, looking for something he could eat.

"Daddy don't say much," Morsel said.

"*I* can't say much," Ray said, "with *him* here. Dave, could you cut us a little slack?"

"Sure, Ray, of course." David got up, still chewing.

"See you in the room," Ray said sharply, twisting his chin toward the door.

Weldon had shown them their room by walking past it and flicking the door open without a word. It contained two iron bedsteads and a dresser, atop which were David's and Ray's belongings, the latter's consisting of a JanSport backpack with the straps cut off. David was better organized, with an actual overnight bag and a Dopp kit. He had left the cattle receipts and breeding documents in the car. He flopped on the bed, hands behind his head, then got up abruptly and went to the door. He looked out and listened for a long moment, eased it closed, and shot to the dresser, where he began rooting through Ray's belongings: rolls of money in rubber bands, generic Viagra from India, California lottery tickets, a passport identifying Raymond Coelho, a woman's aqua-colored wallet, with a debit card in the name of Eleanor Coelho from Food Processors Credit Union of Modesto, Turlock grocery receipts, a bag of trail mix, and the gun. David lifted the gun carefully with the tips of his fingers. He was startled by its lightness. Turning it over in his hand, he was compelled to acknowledge that there was no hole in the barrel. It was a toy. He returned it to the pack, fluffed the sides, and sped to his bed to begin feigning sleep.

It wasn't long before Ray came in, singing "Now Is the Hour" in a flat and aggressive tone that hardly suited the lyrics: "Sunset glow fades in the west, night o'er the valley is creeping! Birds cuddle down in their nest, soon all the world will be sleeping. But not you, Dave. You're awake, I can tell. I hope you enjoyed the song. It's Hugo Winterhalter. Morsel sang it to me. She's very nice, and she needs a man."

"Looks like you got the job."

"Do what? Hey, here's what's going on with me: I'm starving."

"I'm sure you are, Ray. You ate like a bird."

"I had no choice. That kind of food gathers around the chambers of the heart like an octopus. But right behind the house they got a vegetable garden, and my plan for you is to slip out and bring me some vegetables. I've been told to stay out of the garden. Don't touch the tomatoes—they're not ripe."

"What else is there?"

"Greens and root vegetables."

"I'm not going out there."

"Oh, yes, you are."

"What makes you think so?"

Ray went to his pack and got out the gun.

"This makes me think so. This will really stick to your ribs, get it?"

"I'm not picking vegetables for you, or, technically speaking, stealing them for you. Forget it."

"Wow. Is this a mood swing?"

"Call it what you want. Otherwise, it's shoot or shut up."

"Okay, but not for the reason you think. I prefer not to wake up the whole house."

"And the body'd be a problem for you, as a house guest and new fiancé."

"Very well, very well. This time." Ray put the gun back in his pack. "You don't know how close you came."

"Whatever."

David rolled over to sleep, but he couldn't stop his thoughts. He should have spent the day at Jorgensen's with his arm up a cow's ass. He had a living to make, and if it hadn't been for his inappropriate curiosity about Ray and Morsel, he'd already be back in Jordan, looking to grab a room for the night. But the roll of money in Ray's pack and the hints of more to come had made him wonder how anxious he was to get back to work. There was opportunity in the air, and he wanted to see how it would all play out.

"Ray, you awake?"

"I can be. What d'you want, asshole?"

"I just have something I want to get off my chest."

"Make it quick. I need my Z's."

"Sure, Ray, try this one on for size: the gun's a toy."

"The gun's a what?"

"A toy."

"You think a gun's a toy?"

"No, Ray, I think *your* gun's a toy. It's a fake. And looks like you are too."

"Where's the fuckin' light switch? I'm not taking this shit."

"Stub your toe jumping off the bed like that."

"Might be time to clip your wings, sonny."

"Ray, I'm here for you. Just take a moment to look at the barrel of your so-called gun, and then let's talk."

Ray found the lamp and paced the squeaking floorboards. "Taking a leak off the porch. Be right back," he said. Through the open bedroom door, David could see him silhouetted in the moonlight, a silver arc splashing onto the dirt, his head thrown back in what David took to be a plausible posture of despair.

By the time Ray walked back in he was already talking: ". . . an appraiser in Modesto, California, where I grew up. I did some community theater there, played Prince Oh So True in a children's production and thought I was going places, then *Twelve Angry Men*—I was one of them, which is where the pistol came from. I was the hangman in *Motherlode*. Got married, had a baby girl, lost my job, got another one, went to Hawaii as a steward on a yacht belonging to a movie star, who was working at a snow-cone stand a year before the yacht, the coke, the babes, and the wine. I had to sign a nondisclosure agreement, but then I got into a fight with the movie star and got kicked off the boat at Diamond Head. They just rowed me to shore in a dinghy and dumped me off. I hiked all the way to the crater and used the restroom to clean up, then took the tour bus into Honolulu. I tried to sell the celebrity drug-use story to a local paper, but it went nowhere because of the confidentiality agreement. Everything I *sign* costs me money. About this time, my wife's uncle's walnut farm was failing. He took a loan out on the real estate, and I sold my car, which was a mint, rust-free '78 Trans Am, handling package, W-72 performance motor, Solar Gold with a Martinique Blue interior. We bought a bunch of FEMA trailers from the Katrina deal and hauled them to California. We lost our asses. The uncle gases himself in his garage, and my wife throws me out. I moved into a hotel for migrant workers, and started using the computers at the Stanislaus County Library and sleeping at the McHenry Mansion. One of the tour guides was someone I used to fuck in high school and she slipped me into one of the rooms for naps. I met Morsel online. I told her I was on hard times. She told me she was coining it, selling bootleg Oxycontin in the Bakken oil field, but she was lonely. It was a long shot. Montana. Fresh start. New me. Bus to Billings and hit the road. I made it to Jordan, and I had nothing left. The clerk at that fleabag barely let me have a room. I told him I was there for the comets. I don't know where I come up with that. Breakfast at the café was my last dime and no tip. I had to make a move. So what happens now? You bust me with Morsel? You turn me in? Or you join us?"

"You pretty sure on the business end of this thing?" David asked, with a coldness that surprised him.

"A hundred percent, but Morsel's got issues with other folks already in it. There's some risk, but when isn't there, with stakes like this? Think about it, Dave. If you're at all interested in getting rich, you tell me."

Ray was soon snoring. David was intrigued that all these revelations failed to disturb his sleep. He himself was wide awake, brooding over how colorless his own life was in comparison with Ray's. Ray was a con man and a failure, but what had *he* ever done? Finish high school? High school had been anguish, persecution, and suffering, but even in that he was unexceptional. He'd never had sex with a mansion tour guide. He'd had sex with a fat girl he disliked. Then the National Guard. Fort Harrison in the winter. Cleaning billets. Inventorying ammunition. Unskilled maintenance on UH-60 Blackhawks. Praying for deployment against worldwide towel heads. A commanding officer who told the recruits that the president of the United States was "a pencil-wristed twat." Girlfriend fatter every time he went home. He still lived with his mother. Was still buying his dope from the same guy at the body shop he'd got it from in the eighth grade.

Perhaps it was surprising he'd come up with anything at all, but he had: Bovine Deluxe, LLC, a crash course in artificially inseminating cattle. David took to it like a duck to water: driving around the countryside detecting and synchronizing estrus, handling frozen semen, keeping breeding records—all easily learnable, but David brought art to it, and he had no idea where that art had come from. He was a genius preg-tester. Whether he was straight or stoned, his rate of accuracy, as proven in spring calves, was renowned. Actually, David *preferred* preg-testing stoned. Grass gave him a greater ability to visualize the progress of his arm up the cow's rectum. His excitement began as soon as he donned his coveralls, pulled on his glove, lubed it with OB goo, and stepped up to the cow stuck in the chute. Holding the tail high overhead with his left hand, he got his right hand all the way in, against the cow's attempt to expel it, shoveled out the manure to clear the way past the cervix, and finally, nearly up to his shoulder, grasped the uterus. David could nail a pregnancy at two months, when the calf was smaller than a mouse. He never missed, and no cow that should have been culled turned up without a calf in the spring. He could tell the rancher how far along the cow was by his informal gradations: mouse, rat, Chihuahua, cat, fat cat, raccoon, beagle. Go through the herd, or until his arm was exhausted. Throw the glove away, write up the invoice, strip the coveralls, look for food and a room.

Perfect. Except for the dough.

He'd once dreamed of owning jewels, especially rubies, and that dream was coming back. Maybe glue one on his forehead like a Hindu. It'd go over big on his ranch calls.

Morsel made breakfast for her father, David, and Ray—eggs, biscuits, and gravy. David was thinking about Ray's "last dime" back in Jordan versus the rolls of bills in his pack and watching Weldon watch Ray as breakfast was served. Morsel just leaned against the stove while the men ate. "Anyone want to go to Billings today to see the cage fights?" she asked. David looked up and smiled, but no one answered her. Ray was probing around his food with his fork, pushing the gravy away from the biscuits, and Weldon was flinching. Weldon wore his black Stetson with the salt-encrusted sweat stain halfway up the crown. David thought it was downright unappetizing, not the sort of thing a customer for top-drawer bull semen would wear. At last Weldon spoke at top volume, as though calling out to his livestock.

"What'd you say your name was?"

"Ray."

"Well, Ray, why don't you stick that fork all the way in and eat like a man?"

"I'm doing my best, Mr. Case, but I will eat nothing with a central nervous system."

"Daddy, leave Ray alone. You'll have time to get to know each other and find out what Ray enjoys eating."

When Morsel brought Ray some canned pineapple slices, he looked up at her with what David took to be genuine affection.

She turned to David and said, "It's all you can eat around here," but the moment he stuck his fork back in his food she put a hand in his face and said, "That's all you can eat!" and laughed. David noticed her cold blue eyes and thought he was beginning to understand her.

To Weldon, she said, "Daddy, you feel like showing Ray 'n' 'im the trick?"

Weldon stopped his rhythmic lip-pursing. "Oh, Morsel," he said coyly.

"C'mon, Daddy. Give you a dollar."

"Okay, Mor, put on the music," he said with a sigh of good-humored defeat. Morsel went over to a low cupboard next to the pie safe and pulled out a small plastic record player and a 45-rpm record, which proved to be a scratchy version of "Cool Water," by the Sons of the Pioneers. Weldon swayed to the mournful tune and then seemed to come to life as Morsel placed a peanut in front of him and the lyrics began: "Keep a-movin', Dan,/Don't you listen to him, Dan./He's a devil not a man." Weldon took off his hat and set it upside down beside him, revealing the thinnest combover across a snow-white pate. Then he picked up the peanut and, with sinuous movements, balanced it on his nose. It remained there until near the end of the record—"Dan, can you see,/That big green tree,/Where the water's runnin' free"—when the peanut fell to the table and Weldon's chin dropped to stare at it. When the record ended, he replaced his hat, stood without a word, and left the room. For a moment it was quiet, and then came the sound of Weldon's plane cranking up.

"Daddy's pretty hard on himself when he don't make it to the end of the record," Morsel said glumly as she cleared the dishes. Heading for the living room, she added, "Me and Ray thought you ought to see what dementia looks like. It don't look good and it's expensive."

David had taken care to copy out the information from Ray's passport onto the back of a matchbook cover, which he tore off, rolled into a cylinder, and put inside a bottle of aspirin. And there it stayed until Ray and Morsel headed off to the cage fights. David used his cell phone and 411 Connect to call Ray's home in Modesto and chat with his wife or, as she claimed to be, his widow. It took two calls, a couple of hours apart. The first try, he got her answering machine: "You know the drill: leave it at the beep." On the second try, he got Ray's wife. David identified himself as an account assistant with the Internal Revenue Service and Ray's wife listened only briefly before stating in a firm, clear, and seemingly ungrieving voice that Ray was dead: "That's what I told the last guy

and that's what I'm telling you." She said that he had been embez-
zling from a credit union, left a suicide note, and disappeared.

"I'm doing home health care. Whatever he stole he kept. Killing himself was the one good idea he come up with in the last
thirty years. At least it's kept the government from garnisheeing
my wages, what little they are. I been through all this with the
other guy that called, and we have to wait for his death to be confirmed before I get no benefits. If I know Ray, he's on the bottom of the Tuolumne River, just to fuck with my head. I wish I
could have seen him one more time to tell him I gave his water
skis and croquet set to Goodwill. If the bank hadn't taken back his
airplane, I would have lost my house and been sleeping in my car.
Too bad you didn't meet Ray. He was an A-to-Z crumb bum."

"I'm terribly sorry to hear about your husband," David said me-
chanically.

"I don't think the government is 'terribly sorry' to hear about
anything. You reading this off a card?"

"No, this is just a follow-up to make sure your file stays intact
until you receive the benefits you're entitled to."

"I already have the big one: picturing Ray in hell with his ass *en
fuego*."

"Ah, you speak a bit of Spanish, Mrs. Coelho?"

"Everybody in Modesto 'speaks a bit of Spanish.' Where you
been all your life?"

"Washington, D.C.," David said indignantly.

"That explains it," Mrs. Coelho said, and hung up.

Of course he had no car when we met, David thought. No need
to leave a paper trail by renting cars or buying tickets on airplanes.
He'd got done all he needed to get done on the Modesto library
computers, where he and Morsel, two crooks, had found each
other and gone into business without ever laying eyes on each
other.

Before heading to Billings, Morsel had told David how to get to
the Indian smallpox burial ground to look for beads. Otherwise,
there was nothing to do around here. He wasn't interested until
he discovered the liquor cabinet and by then it was early evening.
He found a bottle marked Hoopoe Schnapps, with a picture of a
bird on its label, and gave it a try: "Bottoms up." It went straight to
his head. After several swigs, he was unable to identify the bird but

he was very happy. The label said that the drink contained "mira-belles," and David thought, Hey, I'm totally into mirabelles.

As he headed for the burial ground, David was tottering a bit. Rounding the equipment shed, he nearly ran into Weldon Case, who walked by without speaking or apparently seeing him. Behind the ranch buildings, a cow trail led into the prairie, then wound toward a hillside spring that didn't quite reach the surface, visible only by the greenery above it. Just below that was the place that Morsel had told him about, pockmarked with anthills. The ants, Morsel claimed, carried the beads to the surface, but you had to hunt for them.

David sat down among the mounds and was soon bitten through his pants. He jumped to his feet and swept the ants away, then crouched, peering and picking at the anthills. His thighs soon ached from squatting, but then he found a speck of sky blue in the dirt, a bead. He clasped it tightly in one hand while stirring with the other and flicking away ants. He didn't think about the bod-ies in the ground beneath him. By the time it was too dark to see, his palm was filled with Indian beads and he felt elevated and still drunk.

As he passed the equipment shed, he made out first the silhou-ette of Weldon Case's Stetson and then, very close, the face of Wel-don himself, who gazed at him before speaking in a low voice. "You been in the graves, ain't you?"

"Yes, to look for beads."

"You ought not to have done that, feller."

"Oh? But Morsel said—"

"Look up there at the stars."

"I don't understand."

Weldon reached high over his head. "That's the crow riding the water snake," he said, and turned back into the dark.

David was frightened. He went to the house and got into bed as quickly as he could, anxious for the alcohol to fade. He pulled the blanket up under his chin, despite the warmth of the night, and watched a moth batting against an image of the moon in the win-dow. When he was nearly asleep, he saw Morsel's headlights wheel across the ceiling, then turn off. He listened for the car doors, but it was nearly ten minutes before they opened and closed. He rolled close to the wall and pretended to be asleep, while the front door

opened quietly. Once the reverberation of the screen-door spring
had died down, there was whispering that came into the bedroom.
He felt a shadow cross his face as someone peered down at him.
Soon the sound of muffled copulation filled the room, stopped for
the time it took to raise a window, then resumed. David listened
more and more intently, until Ray said, in a clear voice, "Dave, you
want some of this?"

David stuck to his feigned sleep until Morsel laughed, got up,
and walked out with her clothes under her arm. "Night, Ray. Sweet
dreams."

The door shut, and after a moment Ray spoke. "What could I
do, Dave? She was after my weenie like a chicken after a June bug."
Snorts and, soon after, snoring.

Morsel stood in the doorway of the house, taking in the early sun
and smoking a cigarette. She wore an old flannel shirt over what
looked like a body stocking that revealed a lazily winking camel
toe. Her eyes followed her father as he crossed the yard very slowly.
"Look," she said, as David stepped up. "He's wetting his pants.
When he ain't wetting his pants, he walks pretty fast. It's just something he enjoys."

Weldon came up and looked at David, trying to remember him.
He said, "This ain't much of a place to live. My folks moved us out
here. We had a nice little ranch at Coal Bank Landing, on the Missouri, but one day it fell in the river. Morsel, I'm uncomfortable."

"Go inside, Daddy. I'll get you a change of clothes."

Once the door had shut behind him, David said, "Why in the
world do you let him fly that airplane?"

"It's all he knows. He flew in the war and dusted crops. He'll
probably kill himself in the damn thing."

"What's he do up there?"

"Looks for his cows."

"I didn't know he had cows."

"He don't. They all got sold years ago. But he'll look for them
long as he's got fuel."

Morsel turned back to David on her way inside. "I can't make
heads or tails of your friend Ray," she said. "He was coming on to
me the whole time at the cage fights, then he takes out a picture
of his wife and tells me she's the greatest piece of ass he ever had."

"Huh. What'd you say to that?"

"I said, 'Ray, she must've had a snappin' pussy, because she's got a face that would stop a clock.' He didn't like that too much. So I punched him in the shoulder and told him he hadn't seen nothing yet. What'd you say your name was?"

"I'm David."

"Well, Dave, Ray says you mean to throw in with us. Is that a fact?"

"I'm sure giving it some thought."

David was being less than candid. He would have slipped away the day before if he hadn't felt opportunity headed his way on silver wings.

"You look like a team player to me. I guess that bitch he's married to will help out on that end. Long as I never have to see her."

David had an unhappy conversation with his mother, but at least it was on the phone, so she couldn't throw stuff.

"The phone is ringing off the hook! Your ranchers are calling constantly, wanting to know when you'll get there."

"Ma, I know, but I got tied up. Tell them not to get their panties in a wad. I'll be there."

"David!" she screeched. "This is not an answering service!"

"Ma, listen to me. Ma, I got tied up. I'm sparing you the details, but relax."

"How can I relax with the phone going off every ten seconds?"

"Ma, I'm under pressure. Pull the fucking thing out of the wall."

"Pressure? You've never been under pressure in your life!"

He hung up on her. He couldn't live with her anymore. She needed to take her pacemaker and get a room.

That week Morsel was able to get a custodial order in Miles City, based on the danger to the community presented by Weldon and his airplane. Ray had so much trouble muscling Weldon into Morsel's sedan for the ride to assisted living that big strong David had to pitch in and help Ray tie him up. Weldon tossed off some frightful curses before collapsing in defeat and crying. But the God he called down on them didn't hold much water anymore, and they made short work of the old fellow. At dinner that night, Morsel was a little blue. The trio's somewhat obscure toasts were to the future. David looked on with a smile; he felt happy and accepted and believed he was going somewhere. His inquiring looks were met by giddy winks from Morsel and Ray. They told him that he was now a "courier," and Ray unwound one of his bundles of cash. He was going to California.

"Drive the speed limit," Ray said. "I'm going to get to know the airplane. Take it down to the oil fields. It's important to know your customers."

"Do you know how to fly it?" This was an insincere question, since David had learned from the so-called widow about Ray's re-possessed plane.

"How's thirteen thousand hours sound to you?"

"I'll keep the home fires burning," Morsel said, without taking the cigarette out of her mouth.

David had a perfectly good idea of what he was going to California for, but he didn't ask. He knew the value of preserving his ignorance. If he could keep his status as a simple courier, he was no guiltier than the United States Postal Service. "Your Honor, I had no idea what was in the trunk, and I am prepared to say that under oath or take a lie-detector test, at your discretion," he rehearsed.

He drove straight through, or nearly so. He stopped briefly in Idaho, Utah, and Nevada to walk among cows. His manner with cattle was so familiar that they didn't run from him but gathered around in benign expectation. David sighed and jumped back in the car. He declined to pursue this feeling of regret.

It was late when he got into Modesto, and he was tired. He checked into a Super 8 and woke up when the hot light of a California morning shone through the window onto his face. He ate in the lobby and checked out. The directions Ray had given him proved exact: within ten minutes, he was pulling around the house into the side drive and backing into the open garage.

A woman came out of the house in a bathrobe and walked past his window without a word. He popped the trunk and sat quietly as she loaded it, then closed it. She stopped at his window, pulling the bathrobe up close around her throat. She wasn't hard to look at, but David could see you wouldn't want to argue with her. "Tell Ray I said be careful. I've heard from two IRS guys already." David said nothing at all.

He was so cautious that the trip back took longer. He stayed overnight at the Garfield again, so as to arrive in daylight, and got up twice during the night to check on the car. In the morning he skipped eating at the café for fear he might encounter some of his rancher clients. Plus he knew that Morsel would take care of his empty stomach. He was so close now that he worried about everything, from misreading the gas gauge to flat tires. He even imagined the trunk flying open for no reason. Now he drove past fields of cattle with hardly a glance.

He had imagined a hearty greeting, an enthusiastic homecoming, but the place was silent. A hawk sat on the wire that ran from the house to the bunkhouse, as though it had the place to itself. It flew off reluctantly when David got out of the car. Inside, there were soiled plates on the dining-room table. Light from the television flickered without sound from the living room. David walked in and saw the television first—it was on the shopping network, a closeup of a hand dangling a gold bracelet. Then he saw Morsel on the floor with the channel changer in her hand. She'd been shot.

David felt an icy calm. Ray must have done this. He checked the car keys in his pocket and walked out of the house, stopping on the porch to survey everything in front of him. Then he went around to the equipment shed. Where the airplane had been parked in its two shallow ruts lay Ray, also shot, a pool of blood extending from his mouth like a speech balloon without words. He'd lost a shoe. The plane was gone.

David felt as if he were trapped between the two bodies, with no safe way back to the car. When he got to it, a man was waiting for him. "I must have overslept. How long have you been here?" He was David's age, thin and precise in clean khakis and a Shale Services ball cap. He touched his teeth with his thumbnail as he spoke.

"Oh, just a few minutes."

"Keys."

"Yes, I have them here." David patted his pocket.

"Get the trunk for me, please." David tried to hand him the keys. "No, you."

"Not a problem."

David bent to insert the key, but his hand was shaking and at first he missed the slot. The lid rose to reveal the contents of the trunk. David didn't feel a thing.

KYLE MINOR

# A Kidnapping in Koulèv-Ville

FROM *The Normal School*

THE TOP FLOOR of the Beirut Supermarket was a fur shop—fox, rabbit, mink, beaver, otter, sable, seal, coyote, and chinchilla. Other racks displayed cowboy hats, suede jackets, thigh-high leather boots, knee boots, harness boots, stacked heels, stiletto heels, kitten heels, pumps, platforms, mules, and sling-backs. The middle floor was a children's boutique, with shelves filled to the ceiling with the kinds of toys you never saw anyplace else in Haiti—Star Wars TIE fighters and programmable Lego robots, Barbie dolls and Nerf guns, a five-foot-tall princess play castle and a diesel-powered go-kart with a driver's seat sized for a six-year-old. Things for rich ladies, rich children. Money things.

All the real action was at ground level, on the grocery floor, which was as well stocked as any food store anywhere, a credit to the Nasser family, and especially to Samir Nasser, chief proprietor, who had inherited two tiny storefront operations from his father and grandfather and turned them into a twelve-store import-and-retail operation spanning from Cap-Haïtien to Jacmel, of which the Beirut was the crown jewel. The fruit came through the port in Saint-Marc if it wasn't local. Husky tangerines, golden kiwi, Cavendish bananas, freestone nectarines, bunches of grapes. Purple grapes, green grapes, black grapes. Other sweets too. Chocolates and red velvet cakes and baklavas and taffies and ice creams and sherbets. And dry goods in packages lettered in French, Spanish, English, Dutch, and Arabic. In the back of the store, the vodkas, rums, and whiskeys lived in a dark anteroom, the backlit shelves glowing like Amsterdam in a phosphorescent bluish white. Past the liquor area, another dark room, this one carpeted in Persian rugs and ringed in black-and-white frescoes after the manner of the woodcuts in Frankétienne's *Dezafi,* and where, more than once, I saw Samir's fingers brush the edges of the iron bars that guarded the money-changing station.

The rest of what I knew about Samir Nasser could fit in a paragraph. He was rich. He was fit. He was short and handsome. He was well regarded in the community. He was married. His one daughter, beloved Anna, was a senior at the Baptist high school in Koulèv-Ville. They belonged to a large extended family of Maronite Christians who had emigrated from Lebanon in the late nineteenth century. The rumor is that one brother impregnated the fiancée of another and boarded a ship and fled for Marseille, but that's how the Lebanese are sometimes slandered. More likely the founding Nassers sailed from France in hope of selling silk in some American port—New York or Boston or Baltimore or New Orleans—but they never made it past Port-au-Prince. Maybe something went wrong—news arrived of immigration hassles or violence on the American side, or a silk deal went bad and the family was stranded without money. Or maybe something went right. Maybe one of the Nassers fell in love on the island and wanted to marry. Maybe they found a thriving marketplace at the port and saw an opportunity to make a lucrative living as middlemen. Maybe it was simply the Caribbean sky that I miss so much now that I no longer get to live beneath it—a quality of light so embracing, so flattering, that it is impossible for a person to be ugly.

It seems right to speak now of ugliness and beauty. There's Anna Nasser, seventeen years old, standing in her white dress on the balcony of the Beirut Supermarket. I was the photographer who snapped the famous picture. That's her face, lit by three hundred vigil candles. There's the priest from Bel Air. There are the people, marchers rich and poor, standing in solidarity against the kidnappings, against the gangs of *chimères,* against every variety of violence and extortion. There's Samir, weeping openly in the company of all of them, warning against mob violence, saying, *Anna's kidnappers must be brought to justice in the courts, not the streets. The law must be honored. It is a new day in Haiti. But today, we celebrate. My daughter was lost and now she is found.*

Then he gave the signal, and the produce salesmen passed baskets of fruit throughout the crowd, and the fur salesmen launched the fireworks from the roof of the Beirut. Skyrockets and Roman candles and enormous fire fountains that sprayed thirty feet into the air. I took a tangerine in my mouth, and then a nectarine, and bit, and tasted their cold juices. A massive Catherine wheel, powered by a hundred fuse-lit explosives, spun blue wires of sparks in circles that many later claimed could be seen from space. Certainly they could be seen throughout the city and beyond, from the low-lying slums of La Saline and Cité Soleil to the high places at the edge of the mountains north, south, and east.

We joined hands, and the *mizik rasin* band began with the drums and the guitars and the horns and the singers. It seemed to me that all the world was being emptied of its ugliness. In the streets people began to dance, and I was dancing, and even a few days later, when it was discovered that we had been marching and weeping and dancing in the service of an elaborate lie, I still could taste the nectarine in my mouth, the brown wet ridges of the pit on my tongue.

Around the Baptist school at Koulèv-Ville, some of the teachers say Samir Nasser pushed his daughter too hard. Unlike almost every other Nasser father, he wanted her to go away and stay gone. He tutored her in math until the math got beyond him, around the trigonometry stage, which she had reached by the second semester of the ninth grade, and he tutored her in science until the science got away from him, which was around the first semester of the tenth. His idea was that she'd become a brain surgeon, and every morning before school he lectured her about the entrance test for medical school, the MCAT, which wasn't as far away, he reminded her, as she might think. He believed that the finest undergraduate education in the world could be found only in Providence, Rhode Island, at Brown University, where, as he had read in a business magazine, Ted Turner had come into the maverick genius that had enabled him to invent cable television and buy up half the available grazing land in the American West. Let me tell you how long life is, Samir told Anna, and then he'd blink or snap his fingers. He demanded straight A's; he hired tutors from among the Baptist school faculty and from the university. He punished her severely for any A-minus or B-plus: No cell phone. No occasional beering. No dancing with friends at the teen club. He didn't hit her, but she'd rather have been hit. Some say she got enjoyment from being hit in other ways, but that's not for me to say.

They never let me into the teen club, but many times I have imagined it. Bodies glistening and glitter and crepe paper and the thumping that travels from the speakers to the floor to the blood your heart hustles. Flushed flesh and eye makeup, even on the boys, a phenomenon you shouldn't pillory until you've tried wearing it around town after a *Diwali* party. You walk into a drugstore in Lincoln, Nebraska, at two in the morning, and you're dangerous, a feeling worth chasing, and surely Anna Nasser had it in her same as you and me, that seeking after shadows, that dark desire. I want to make an argument on behalf of prurience. Go home tonight and pick up a book or turn on your television when nobody's watching you. What are you watching? If it's a cooking show, imagine something goes wrong. The chef burns himself, and it's live TV, and there's a brown streak the length of his forearm, and now there's the cameramen you usually never see, running into the frame, carrying buckets of ice or salves or whatever in advance of the medical people. Or maybe there's a fire. Maybe it's a NASCAR race, and you're waiting for the crash. Maybe it's a documentary on Hiroshima and Nagasaki. Maybe it's a *loup-garou,* fur and fangs, or spirits, ghosts, vampires, rabid hoot owls, children raised by wolves, women without faces. Your attention is perked up, and mine is too. Forget bearing witness, forget concern for the pain of others, forget every noble justification. Mortality is in view, families might soon be splintered, bodies are fragile, the king lives in a castle on the hill and commands a sizable army, the president can call down drone planes to strike tent cities like lightning from the sky.

So she's there. It's a Friday night. She's dancing. She likes to grind, and so do the boys, and so do the other girls. It's an international scene, beyond bourgeois; some of these kids will one day sit on a couch in the White House and negotiate treaties that put navy bases ten miles from their greatest port cities. The linguae francae are English, French, and Spanish, but there's a fair amount of fashionable slumming in Kreyòl, especially when it comes to the Dutch and the Germans. Her father's threat hangs like a guillotine over her head, and if that sounds dramatic, try to remember your veins full of the chemicals of adolescence. As it happens, there is a crucial calculus exam the next morning that she's hidden from her father, the AP Calculus BC exam, which will demonstrate to the bigots at Brown that she's not just some girl from a Third World backwater, that she can hang with the kids from prep schools or Paris. There was a time she knew this stuff cold, but because of her advanced standing, it's been a while. It's been busy at the Beirut—otherwise, her father would be on top of the dates the way he has been most of her life. All she needs is a few hours to brush up on parametric equations, polar and vector functions, plus maybe a little jogging of the mind where polynomial approximations and series are concerned, especially Taylor series, Maclaurin, all that $\sum_{n=0}^{\infty} \frac{f^{(n)}(a)}{n!}(x-a)^n$ nonsense.

She has to get home, but there's this beautiful boy from Miami. At first she thinks he's Haitian, but he says no, his father is an attorney and a representative in the Florida statehouse, and his mother is a chemistry professor at St. Thomas. He's not Haitian, only his grandmother is, and he's here with her and his mother, visiting ignorant relatives. It's a drag. Under other circumstances she'd push back against this kind of talk, but he's older, he's built, he's got teeth like Denzel Washington. Then he says he's a med student. University of Miami. He tells her about the cadaver work, and he likes it when she doesn't recoil. You're real cool, he says, and she likes this too, more than she could have imagined. I have to get home, she says. She tells him about the calculus exam, and he says, What? Integrals? Derivatives? That's nothing. I could get you there in an hour. He talks smart for five minutes about anti-differentiation, and she has never met a boy like this. Providence, Rhode Island, is probably crawling with them, but who's to say? Come home with me, he says, so she calls her mother and tells her she's staying at a girlfriend's house, and she makes all the necessary arrangements of deception with the girlfriend, like she's done plenty of times before.

Then they're off. He drives a rented Mercedes with bulletproof windows. He's got the Wyclef Jean suite at the Hôtel Montana. The rest of his family is in his great-aunt's gingerbread house, but he refuses to stay there, and his mother indulges him. She says he's selfish and small-minded, but secretly she's proud she's raised such an American. She wishes him the distance from here to the moon, and the money to get the liquid fuel and build the steel cylinder.

In the suite he kisses her face and kisses her neck and kisses her collarbone, and he says, Do you want to? and she says yes, and she's done it before, but not like this, not with someone who knows what he's doing. She's just beginning to know her own body too, that's important, and because she hardly knows him, she can run her own show. He's a version of himself he will never be for another person in the sixty years he has left to live. Idealized and utmost. The sum total of the available love and lust in the Northern Hemisphere. She fixates on his one cracked fingernail.

It's not yet morning when they're good and exhausted, and she's complaining: I can't keep my eyes open. I can barely lift my pencil hand. She kisses his chest and says, The bad people sent you to keep me from Brown. She kisses his forehead and says, I hate you. She kisses his mouth and says, You've ruined everything.

He reaches into a bag beside the bed. He props himself up on one elbow. He unscrews a plastic safety lid. I'm not the bad people, he says. He takes a strand of her hair between his fingers.

Try this, he says.

I have taken a few 30-milligram slugs of amphetamine salts in my time. They arrive in yellow pharmaceutical capsules dosed at 60 milligrams. You take a sheet of wax paper and cut two three-inch squares, open the capsule, and pour it out onto one of the squares. Then you take a razor blade and separate the salts into two piles of equal size. Then you put one of the wax paper sheets under the other one and push one of the piles onto the lower sheet. Carefully, so you can avoid wasting any of the precious salts. Then you chew the head off a Gummi Bear, fold the wax paper into a kind of funnel, channel the salts into one side of the yellow capsule, and cap it with the Gummi Bear head. That's supply enough for two days. Then you pour a big glass of water and swallow one of the half-capsules. Then you wait half an hour. Then the angel of bliss and joy and every earthly pleasure pierces your crown with the tip of her wing. Right there in the center of your brain—a place where you don't otherwise feel anything—you can feel the squirt of a cold pleasant liquid. It fills your head and then you can feel a lifting throughout your body, and there is no touch, no kiss, no orgasm in the world to rival it. You are flying, but you are clearheaded. Sleep is no longer at issue. You deeply love whoever is imprinted on you by the fact of their presence. For twelve or fifteen hours you can contemplate a fixed point fifteen feet in front of you, or you can become the most productive person in the history of human beings.

The high is directly proportional to the complexity of the brain work you bring to it. More than once I've filed for Reuters or IPS this way, and I've tried other things—composing on the piano, reading Proust, playing chess with Ben Fountain—but imagine her synapses on speed and calculus. Lit up like the Main Street Electrical Parade, Pete's Dragon, and twelve Mary Poppins chimney sweeps in tight black shirts, dancing to Kraftwerk, a pharmacological miracle that ends in a wooden desk chair in a concrete kindergarten in Port-au-Prince, under the stern eye of a Jamaican proctor named Madame Roosevelt, who wears her glasses on a chain around her neck and watches Anna Nasser's pencil fly through graph analyses, asymptotic and unbounded behavior, every near-quantification of infinity.

She'd been awake for thirty hours when she went back for more of the salts and more of the boy, and when they swam in the pool this was love, she'd do anything, forget Providence, she'd never seen snow and there was no reason she ever needed to see snow. They both opened their eyes underwater. Their noses were less than an inch apart, and when they surfaced, he said, I've never met anyone like you, in all my life, swear to God, and it felt so good to believe him. Her body had become a magical forest, and somewhere in the center there was a wizened old lady with a stove and a lantern, and later, in the bathtub, he said he liked those stories too, anything creaky with yellow pages and British diction, anything partially in Elvish.

He flew home, but he flew back. He studied on the airplane. He cut classes here and there to squeeze out two-day visits in the Wyclef suite, three or four a month. In the hotel, he studied, and she studied alongside him. All they did was sex and swim and study, and there was no way of knowing which was better. She told her parents she'd joined a ballet class, strictly amateur stuff, but as fitness goes it was better than tennis or cross-country. She got bold, showed her mother how toned her glutes had become. She was taking the cut capsules all the time now, and though her energy was extraordinary, she found that she needed very little food. Her face became angular in a way that almost everyone attributed to good health. At the late spring parent-teacher conference, all the

American schoolmarms raved. She imagined them in their sad, thin blouses and frumpy haircuts, waving the Anna flag, and then she imagined what such a flag would look like. It would be the periodic table of elements on a lipstick-red field the shape of a swallowtail, fixed above the mainsail of a luxury yacht. Yes, her father told her teachers. We are very proud of our Anna.

The third week of April, he said, Do you love me? Yes, she said. How much do you love me? The most. What if I told you I was in trouble? Anything, she said. Would you punch a hundred priests in the face? Anything, she said, I'd kick my grandmother in the knees. He quoted two French psychoanalysts, both dead, on the subject of bicycle horns and how it's the triangle's job to vibrate, to resonate, under the pressure of what it retains as much as what it thrusts aside. He spoke of the orchid and the wasp, the lateral spread of bamboo and other grasses through subterranean rhizomes. He said he'd lost a lot of money at a cockfight at the edge of the Everglades, and though he'd had a lot of money, it was mostly gone now. The people he owed had made threats, not only against his neck and knees, but also against his mother's and his father's. My father wants to be a congressman one day, he said.

Be quiet, I love you, I'll do it, she said. What do you want me to do?

There is so much we will never know. Maybe she was conflicted about her choices. Maybe she rationalized: What is $200,000 to my parents? Maybe she bargained: I will pay them back silently one day. I will hire a lawyer to set up a blind trust in the Bahamas. I'll be making neurosurgery money. I'm good for it. Or maybe her motives were darker, maybe she had simmering resentments, and the thought of his beautiful knees broken tipped the pot. Perhaps whatever second thoughts she might have had couldn't match the power of the promise she had made without knowing what it was she was promising: Be quiet, I love you, I'll do it. I need you to tell me, he said: Who is the most terrible person you know? It has to be a truly despicable person, the worst person, a person other people would believe capable of the craziest, the most vulgar, the most violent things otherwise beyond imagining.

Her answer was the same as anyone's answer would have been, under the circumstances: Charles Leblanc, nineteen years old, the son of Canadian missionaries who ran an orphanage in Delmas.

He'd been kicked out of the Baptist school for carrying a knife, then reinstated despite massive faculty resistance the following year. He'd been seen driving around town with the gang that called themselves the Dominoes, waving a Glock out the passenger side window. It was said he wore white sneakers he had stolen from a fifteen-year-old Polish boy at gunpoint. He liked to brag about his connections with several of the kidnap gangs, the *chimères,* those lost boys who had been raised out of the slums of La Saline and Cité Soleil. Even their name a secret: *chimères,* specters invisible of body, ghosts. Don't call me Charles Leblanc, he'd been saying. That's my slave name. I'm giving up my Canadian passport. I was born in Pétion-Ville. I'm as Haitian as anybody. I'm as revolutionary as anybody. I'm as badass as anybody.

He wanted to be known instead, far and wide, as the white *chimère.* He said one day he'd be the richest man in Haiti. One day, he said, he would handpick the president with his money. He'd have the country's mineral wealth privatized, buy it for a pittance, sell it to the Russians on the open market, build a national network of trains to link his factories to seaports, die wealthy as a Carnegie or a Rockefeller. The bourgeois kids scoffed at this boasting— *Watch out, ladies, here comes the white chimère!*—but after a classmate, a fellow Canadian, shorthanded it to Casper, as in the Friendly Ghost, this classmate was accosted outside his house one day and pistol-whipped, and he would never say by whom, so you knew, everyone knew, and Leblanc got what he wanted from the whole affair: a little respect, a little deference, a little fear.

Tell Leblanc you have been thinking about him, the boyfriend said. Ask him if he'd like to hang out for a little while after school. Tell him you aren't one hundred percent sure you want to fuck him. Tell him you are only ninety-six percent sure. Tell him you'll decide on the road to Boutilliers. Tell him you'll ride with him, no problem. Make sure twenty or thirty people see you get in his truck.

So she did. She told him that morning, and Leblanc spent the rest of the day bragging to the other boys. I'm going to bag the Beirut princess, he said. He pantomimed a little tiara on her head. At lunch he stared at her across the cafeteria, and she smiled sweetly at him. She told the other girls at her table he'd invited her over to help him study, but she had a bad feeling about the whole thing. Something was off by a degree and a half. Don't go, they said. Maybe I won't, she said. But then, after school was over, she made a show of dropping her books in the parking lot dirt, and a few people came over to help her pick them up, and when they were safely in her arms, she got into Leblanc's truck. First, Boutilliers, she said, and they drove away, down one set of mountains, through the city, in the direction of another. Somewhere in between—no one has been able to establish with any certainty where—she asked him to make a quick unscheduled stop, and that was when they both disappeared for a few days.

When I was downtown, I liked to ride the tap-taps to hear the local versions of the news I was supposed to be reporting, and that's where I was when I first heard about the disappearance of Anna Nasser. I was among people I mostly knew, at whose tables I had taken meals. Ghislaine said the ransom note was written in blood on paper made from the skin of babies. Yves said the ransom note was sewed inside a pouch full of poison. Yvette said the ransom note was sent by text message from a Digicel phone near the smaller airport in Port-au-Prince. Serge said the ransom note was hand-delivered by three masked men in a red truck. Prudeut said there was no ransom note, just a raspy voice on the phone and a lot of heavy breathing: Two hundred thousand dollars for the rich girl.

Not all of these things turned out to be true, but there was a text message from the smaller airport, and there was a raspy voice. Smallpox doesn't spread any faster than gossip, and there's always a little bit of the devastating and true stowed away like an urchin child among the more ostentatious baggage, the steamer trunk wardrobes and the suitcases with the leopard-print slipcovers.

When her father gets the phone call, he is in bed with a woman who is not his wife. She is a good woman, and his wife is a good woman, which makes him believe that, in this moment, he is a bad man. Or maybe it doesn't. Maybe by now he's come to think of these liberties as due compensation for the low-to-the-ground life he's lived in service to the futures of others, all those long days in the store or at the port, all those late hours hunched over the accounting books, the imported bottle of Glenlivet untouched at the edge of the desk for the sake of clarity with the all-important numbers. Her leg is thrown over him, this woman he believes to be truly beautiful, whose aesthetic interests align with his, her good taste in music, her sense with fashion, her ease at talking. He loves her voice; he loves the smell of her; he steals what hours he can to sit with her in the evenings and talk and listen to records. He can imagine a future with her, but it is an unlikely future. More often his fantasies run in the other direction, toward a past where he met her as a young man, and the world and time spread unknown before them, perhaps in an easier country, perhaps in a Costa Rican villa, perhaps in an oceanside house in Belize, not far from Francis Ford Coppola's, California wine in the evening, sophisticated conversation, movie actors, cigarettes.

Two hundred thousand dollars for the rich girl. First the phone call, then the text message. Come alone. Bring $10,000 in $100 bills. Have exactly $190,000 in a new account, and bring the account numbers. Don't tell your wife. Don't call the police. For all you know, this might be the police. Believe, now and forever, that you are speaking with the police. Be ready at all hours. Keep the phone near your head. We came for her, didn't we, like a thief in the night? We came, didn't we, on blood horses in the sky? We came, didn't we, with knives and automatic rifles? In the fullness of time we'll call. We'll tell you when and where. Take off your shirt, get in your car, drive to the place. Keep her safe. Don't make her unsafe because of your bad behavior. The time is now to start making good choices. Listen to the sound of my voice. I'm your best friend, Samir Nasser. You have no better friend in the world.

Twelve hours passed. He put on his good suit. He made quiet inquiries with friends whose children had been kidnapped and ransomed, but they all had American passports. They had the FBI. There would be no FBI for Samir Nasser. He went to the banks and did his business, and his bankers thought nothing of what he'd asked. He'd asked for more in the past, quickly, and anyway it was not a country where bankers felt it prudent to ask too many questions of businessmen.

When the call came, he was ready. He took the money. He took off his shirt. Delmas 73, the voice said, and he drove there and waited. The parking lot of the police station, the voice said, and he drove there and waited. Do you have the money? Yes. Good. Drive to the Lesly Center near the cathedral and wait. He did. Do you want to see your daughter alive? Yes. Good.

Drive to the Marché Hyppolite and park on the street and wait. Do you see that man on the street in the white shirt? Do you see that woman selling lettuce? We have eyes by the hundreds. You must be humble. Have you been humble in your life, Samir Nasser? Are we good friends? Touch the bag with the money. Take off your pants. Fold them. Set them in the passenger seat. Put them back on. You can't walk out into the street, a rich man without pants. Walk in the direction of the palace. See that tree? Set the money there. Don't worry. We are watching the tree. Walk away. Get in the car. Drive toward home. You will await further instructions. It's not yours to know when. You've done well, Samir Nasser. Tonight you may drink for pleasure. Kiss your banker for me.

It was three days before he saw his daughter again. He went on the radio to make his plea. I've paid the money. I've done all you've asked. Be honorable, he said.

There was a general buzzing throughout the province. Everyone agreed that the *chimères* had taken her because her parents owned the Beirut. People argued about the nature of the Lebanese: All Lebanese are thieves. Is it wrong to steal from thieves? Fewer Lebanese are thieves than Haitians are thieves. Everything in Haiti belongs to Haitians, not to the Lebanese. All the children of the world belong to their parents. All the children of Lebanon belong in Lebanon. She was born in Haiti. Her mother and father were born in Haiti, and their mothers and fathers. She is a Haitian citizen. She travels with a Haitian passport. She is *blan*. She is Haitian. She is bourgeois. She is a human being. She is a parasite in the intestine.

Samir washed his face three times daily. He rubbed his wife's shoulders. The house filled with relatives he was expected to feed at all hours, and Samir told his wife not to tell anybody anything. Maybe there's a spy among us, he said. He told the relatives in the house that they must be strong. In the bathroom, beneath the Levantine crucifix, he pissed blood. He had a vision of Lake Pontchartrain, a body of water he'd once crossed by bridge in the company of a woman from Boston. He was upset by the unnecessary word *chimère*. These were young men, not ghosts. But what was more disturbing, the taking of his daughter by young men or ghosts? The beating of his daughter by young men or ghosts? The sexual assault of his daughter by young men or ghosts? Young men had bodies. Young men could torment bodies with bodies. Ghosts could only torment the mind, the spirit. Ghosts could slip into the invisible night, flee on a carriage of warm air, ride some passing storm, stir it into a hurricane, but young men could be hunted down and killed, and Samir felt capable of killing. He felt the ferocity of a father, the skull inkwell from which he'd pen the fated names the moment he learned them.

Then it was three o'clock in the morning. He was sitting on the front porch with the night watchman when the buzzer rang from the gate, where she stood wrapped in a sheet she said she had stolen from a laundry line, and the owner of the sheet had chased her through the streets for half a kilometer. We must pay her for the sheet, she said, and he picked her up, cradled like a child, and carried her into the house, and kissed her cheek and her forehead, and didn't even tell anyone she was home, and rocked her in her mother's gliding chair, and pressed her cheek to his cheek, and together they wept until they woke her mother, and then the room was full of people, and he sent them out into the yard, and told the night watchman to turn on the yard lights, and told the cook to bring out the food and set it on picnic tables, and they went into the bedroom, the three of them, and got into the bed, under the covers, husband and wife and daughter in the middle, the way they had when she was a newborn baby, and they cooed without embarrassment, made all the same sounds they had made when she was a newborn baby, and touched her face, and her back, and stroked her hair the same way they had when she was a newborn baby, and the whole room filled with the rank, unwashed smell of her, and her mother drew her a bath, and her father set her in it, and he left the room as her mother washed her.

On the radio, the priest from Bel Air said enough is enough. Is this not our country? he said. We must claim it for decency. All children are ours. I will provide the candles, and we will raise them to the sky, and all the saints will be reflected in the flames, and all our ancestors.

The procession wound through the city, the marchers and their candles, and others joined them as they marched. When she appears on the balcony, her mother said, she must be wearing a white dress like a baptismal dress, and they summoned the tailor, and quickly, while she had the curlers in her hair, the dress was made ready.

Here again: ugliness and beauty. What was it like for her to look at herself in the mirror in the supermarket fur shop, her hair in dark ringlets to her shoulders, the white dress, the waiting crowd, the grieving and rejoicing parents, the boyfriend on his way to the airport with the bag of cash, the preparation of the fireworks, the secret knowledge opening a void inside her. You are a woman, and I have treated you like a child, her father said. He put his hands on her shoulders. When you get to Rhode Island, don't come back. Don't write for a while. Don't call. Put this place behind you. But before you go, if you can bear it, tell me the faces, tell me the names, whatever you know, I will put an end to their comfort.

What did it feel like, for her, to say Leblanc? At that moment, he was holed up in a dank house in Carrefour, smoking opium for the fourth day in a row. Charles Leblanc, she said. He said he needed help studying. He tricked me. He stowed me with his street friends. They put me in a house with a rooster stenciled above the door.

Already her father was on the phone. An hour later a contingent of Chilean soldiers attached to a UN peacekeeping mission took a battering ram to the flimsy front door of the opium den in Carrefour, and when Leblanc reached for his Glock, they shot him in the arm, and it dangles limp to this day. On the radio, the police said it was not yet time to rest easy. We have apprehended the white *chimère*, but he is not the only *chimère*. We will not rest until all *chimères*, black and white, have been apprehended. On the balcony, Samir spoke of justice and the rule of law, but on the phone with the magistrate, he said, Put him in the malarial cell, the tubercular cell, stick him with eleven murderers in a cell made for two or four, and the magistrate said, You know as well as I do that I can't do that. He's white. He's Canadian. He gets books and magazines and as many meals as his mother and father want to bring him. I might bring him a television myself.

At the smaller airport the Miami boyfriend had chartered a plane for the Cayman Islands, and there was something suspicious in it. The customs agent hinted around about a bribe, but the boyfriend couldn't read the tea leaves, offered a $10 bill where it would have taken a couple hundred, at minimum, to suffice. The customs agent dropped the $10 bill on the ground, declared his indignation, asked what the American had to hide. Nothing, the boyfriend said, you can search me, my bags, whatever you'd like, don't target me with your bigotry. It was a big bluff, disastrous when the customs agent called it. When he found $10,000 among the luggage, he thought, This is it, the big one, my career is made. But when he called his supervisor, he was told to impound the money but let the boyfriend get on the plane and let the charter take off. Why? the customs agent said. Why do birds sing? the supervisor said. Why do senators keep me on speed-dial? Why do snakes eat babies?

In full view of everyone in the supermarket, the police came inside and talked to Samir Nasser. They went into the back room, and then Samir went into the room beside the customer-service counter and got Anna and brought her into the back room. They stayed there for a long time, the father and the daughter and the police. Then the police left, and the store closed early, only a half hour after the police left, and six hours before it was scheduled to close. The girl and her father did not leave the back room until after the store closed.

Leblanc's father went on the radio. My son is innocent, he said. He does not have even the money to hire a lawyer. If he was not innocent he would have the money to hire the best lawyer in Haiti. You see who has the money. It is the boyfriend of the kidnapped girl. I ask you, why was he allowed to get on an airplane to Miami and safely leave the country? Why was he allowed to go free while my son rots in a terrible prison? Why do I have to bring my son food every day while this man's son eats in the finest restaurants in Miami? How did the boyfriend of the kidnapped girl end up with the ransom money her parents paid?

Samir Nasser went on the radio. The facts are not all in, he said. We do not know all the facts. But this American was not a person known to our family. My daughter did not know this American. We will not know the truth until the facts are all in, but we have reason to believe that this American was part of a kidnapping ring with the Canadian Leblanc. We hope the American government will send this man back to Haiti so he may be questioned by the police.

I knew a woman whose niece was a cook for the Canadian missionaries. She said one night during this time, Leblanc's father drove to the Nasser house. Leblanc's father stood outside the gate and knocked for a long time. Then he started yelling. Two security guards with sawed-off shotguns pushed Leblanc's father and told him to leave the property. But Leblanc's father would not leave. He was shouting and crying, and he said, You can shoot me if you want. What do I care? You have already taken my son from me for no reason. You should know what it feels like for someone to take your child for no reason. The security guards began to push him, roughly, in the direction of the property next door, where his truck was parked, and when he had been pushed to the property line, he yelled for the girl: Aren't you ashamed? I know what you have done. Everyone knows. Then he drove away.

It's not what happens next that interests me. Leblanc spent thirteen months, without charges, in a jail cell before the Canadian foreign ministry made one phone call and sprang him, and he got on an airplane for Quebec, where he's living still. The boyfriend finished medical school, did his residency in obstetrics, and makes a comfortable living delivering babies in Boca Raton. The Beirut lost no business to the grumbling, although the Nassers erected a twelve-foot wall around the parking lot, and topped it with broken glass and concertina razor wire. What interests me is Samir Nasser, a few evenings later, sitting with the information he hadn't yet processed into knowledge, of his daughter and her certain betrayal, her deception, his shame. His daughter for whom he had wished to fashion wings so she might flap them north to Providence.

He wanted to annihilate himself with drink, and took the bottle of Glenlivet that sat full on his office desk, and went to his lover's house, and drank it until she couldn't bear watching him drinking it, and then he went into the bedroom alone, and she knocked on the door and said, Come out. Don't be alone in there. Go home to your family.

He left her house but wouldn't leave her porch until he finished the bottle, and then, although he felt it wasn't safe, or perhaps because he thought it wasn't safe, he walked the streets of the city, walked and walked, and sometime past midnight he was lost, even though he was less than five blocks from his home. He began to call people on his cell phone, people in New York and San Francisco and Pétion-Ville and Port-au-Prince, but no one would answer the phone. Finally he called the woman he wished he could have loved, and when she answered, she answered with great kindness. Tell me what you see where you are, she said, and he described the kindergarten across the street, the green and yellow cartoon characters, the X-shaped patterns in the balcony concrete, and she said two blocks in the direction of the moon, then the buzzer, the guard at the gate, the night watchman, the door, your bed.

By the time he arrived, he had decided. She was his daughter, and until the end of the world he would believe that she had not done it, that Leblanc had engineered even this terrible frame-up out of a great intelligence he had underestimated. Leblanc had undone everything, had brought to bear the greatest slander, but for two centuries the Nassers had overcome greater slanders, and one day Anna would own a whole country of supermarkets, would count the money, and, on her deathbed, divide it among her children. Until then, for as long as he lived, he would keep her close. I will trust you forever, he would say. I will put you in charge of the money-changing station. So he installed bulletproof glass in the back room of the Beirut, behind the iron bars, and he installed her there, behind the bulletproof glass. I have seen her there, through the glass, her and her father growing old in chairs behind the iron bars.

JOYCE CAROL OATES

# The Home at Craigmillnar

FROM *High Crime Area*

EARLY SHIFT IS 6:30 A.M., which was when I arrived at the elder
care facility at Eau Claire where I have been an orderly for two
years. Maybe thirty minutes after that, when the elderly nun's body
was discovered in her bed.

In fact I'd gotten to work a few minutes before my shift began
as I usually do, in nasty weather especially (as it was that morning: pelting rain, dark-as-night, first week of November), out of
a concern for being late. For jobs are not easy to come by, in our
economy. And in Oybwa County, Wisconsin, where I have lived
all my life except for three and a half years "deployed" in Iraq as
a medical worker. I am a conscientious orderly, with a very good
reputation at the facility.

If I am interviewed by the county medical examiner I will explain to him: it is a wrongly phrased description — *Body discovered
in bed*. For when I entered Sister Mary Alphonsus's room in Unit
D, my assumption was that the sister was alive, and the "discovery" was that she was not alive, or in any case not obviously alive.
I did not "discover" a "body" in the bed but was shocked to see
Sister Mary Alphonsus unmoving, and unbreathing, with a gauzy
fabric like muslin wrapped around her head (like a nun's veil or
wimple), so that her face was obscured.

She was unresponsive to me. Yet even at this, I did not "discover" a "body"—it was natural for me to believe that the elderly
woman might have lapsed into a coma.

(Not that death is so unusual in an elder care facility like
ours — hardly! All of our patients die, eventually; Unit E is our hos-

pice wing. But the death of the resident in Room 22 of Unit D was not expected so soon.)

In my Iraqi deployment my instinct for things *not-right* became very sharp. Out of ordinary situations there might arise — suddenly — as in a nightmare — an explosion that could tear off your legs. You had to be alert — and yet, how is it possible to be always alert? — it is not possible. And so, you develop a kind of sixth sense.

And so as soon as I entered the room after knocking — twice — at the door, I saw that things were *not-right,* and the hairs at the nape of my neck stirred. There was no light in the room and Sister Mary Alphonsus was still in bed — this was *not-right.* For Sister Mary Alphonsus was always "up" before the early shift arrived, as if pride demanded it. The nun was one of those older persons in our care who *does not accept that she is elderly,* and will turn nasty with you if you behave as if she is.

Sister? — in a lowered and respectful voice I spoke. Always I addressed Sister Mary Alphonsus with courtesy, for the old woman was easily offended by a wrong intonation of voice. Like a bloodhound keen for scent, this one was sharp to detect mockery where there was none.

Not a good sign, Sister Mary Alphonsus wasn't yet awake. Very strange, the light above her bed hadn't been switched on.

And a strong smell of urine in the room. Unexpected, in Sister Mary Alphonsus's room, whose occupant wasn't incontinent, and who was usually fussy about cleanliness.

When I switched on the overhead light the fluorescent bulb flickered like an eye blinking open.

The shock of it, then: seeing the elderly nun in her bed only a few feet away, on her back, not-moving; and wrapped around her head some sort of gauzy white fabric like a curtain, so her face was hidden. And inside the gauze the sister's eyes shut, or open — you could not tell.

*Died in her sleep. Cardiac arrest.*

By the time of our senior consulting physician's arrival at the facility, at about 9 A.M., it was clear that elderly Sister Mary Alphonsus was not likely in a coma but had died. The strip of gauzy material had been unwound from the woman's head by the first nurse who'd arrived at the bedside, and dropped heedlessly onto the floor.

I am not a "medic": I am an "orderly." In all medical matters orderlies defer to the medical staff. I had not tried to revive Sister Mary Alphonsus nor even to unwind the cloth from her head, which did not appear to be tightly tied. So far as I knew, the patient might have been alive following a stroke or heart attack.

A legal pronouncement of death can only be made by a physician.

In a senior care facility like ours, Death strikes suddenly, often overnight. Often, within an hour. Cardiac arrest, pulmonary embolism, stroke—like strikes of lightning. If an elderly resident becomes seriously ill, with pneumonia for instance, or is stricken with cancer, he or she is transported to Eau Claire General for specialized treatment; but most of our residents have long-standing medical conditions, of which the most insidious is *old age.*

In the matter of Death, when a living body becomes "dead," there are legal procedures that must be followed. Our senior consultant was required to sign the death certificate and the county medical examiner's office had to be informed. If the deceased had listed next of kin in her file, this individual or individuals would now be notified and arrangements would be made for removal of the body from the facility and for burial.

About this I knew nothing, and would know very little—though I would learn, inadvertently, that the elderly nun had died *intestate.*

(*Intestate:* a fancy word for dying without a will! A kind of nasty ring to this word *intestate,* makes you think of *testicles,* worse yet in this facility of old men *testicular cancer.* Not a welcome thought.)

Next time I came into contact with Sister Mary Alphonsus was after Dr. Bromwalder's examination, when the body was covered with a white sheet. With another orderly, I lifted it onto a gurney to push quickly and as unobtrusively as possible to the facility's morgue in the basement—*Man, she heavy for an old lady!*

I couldn't resist peeking under the sheet: Sister Mary Alphonsus's face was mottled red, a coarse-skinned face you could not have identified as female. The thin-lashed eyes were shut and the mouth that had resembled a pike's wide mouth in life hung loosely open.

*She anybody you knew, Francis?*

*No.*

There'd never been any doubt in Dr. Bromwalder's mind that the eighty-four-year-old woman had died of cardiac arrest, in her sleep. She'd been a cardiac patient: she'd had a chronic condition. It had not seemed to be life-threatening, but all signs suggested heart failure and not a stroke; under these circumstances, an autopsy was not warranted.

The gauze wrapped around the nun's head was certainly too flimsy to have caused suffocation. It had seemed to the senior consulting physician but mildly mysterious—"eccentric"—but many "eccentric" things happen in elder care facilities, among patients who may be mentally as well as physically ill, and so not much was made of the gauzy fabric except by some of the nursing staff of Unit D, who were puzzled, curious— *Why would the woman do such a thing? What does it mean?*

The fabric was believed to have been taken out of the sister's belongings, some of which were kept in a small bureau in the room. It did appear to be a curtain, or part of a curtain—white, dotted swiss, somewhat soiled, a cheap material.

*Maybe she was confused, in her sleep. Wrapped a curtain around her head thinking it was a nun's wimple!*

*Maybe she knew she was dying. It was some kind of religious thing, like after a Catholic confesses her sins to a priest—penance?*

Among the staff of Unit D, Sister Mary Alphonsus had not been a favorite. To her face the nurses called her *Sister,* behind her back *the old nun.*

Or, *the old nun who'd run that terrible orphanage at Craigmillnar.*

It would be noted that Sister Mary Alphonsus was discovered to be unresponsive in her bed by the Unit D orderly, Francis Gough, who'd immediately notified the nursing staff. Time: 7:08 A.M.

Less certainly, it was determined that Sister Mary Alphonsus had died several hours earlier—Dr. Bromwalder's estimate was between 3 A.M. and 6 A.M. This was a reasonable estimate judging by the temperature of the corpse when it was first examined by the doctor, in the absence of a pathologist. In the pitch-black of the early morning, hours before dawn, patients are most likely to "pass away," for these are the hours of Death.

*There was a death here today. Old woman in her eighties, in my unit. She was found dead in her bed—died in her sleep, they think.*

*Oh Francis! That's so sad. I hope it wasn't you who found her.*

*It's okay, Mom. It wasn't me.*

Most mornings when the early staff began their rounds we

would find Sister Mary Alphonsus fully awake and sitting in the chair beside her bed, a blanket over her knees and a missal opened in her hands, though after near seventy years of the Catholic missal, you would not think that the nun required an actual book to help her with prayers; or Sister might have her rosary of wooden beads twined in her fingers as she waited for an orderly to help her into her wheelchair. Her gaze would be vacant until you appeared—and like a raptor's eyes the vague old-woman eyes would come sharply into focus.

If you greeted her with a friendly smile—*Good morning, Sister!*—she was likely to frown, and to make no reply, as if you'd disturbed her in prayer, or in some private and precious drift of her mind. And so I'd learned to say nothing to her, much of the time. What would be rude behavior with other patients had come to seem, to me, expected behavior with Sister Mary Alphonsus.

Sister Mary Alphonsus was one of those residents at Eau Claire who ate meals in the patients' dining hall, not one whose meals were brought to her room. Despite the difficulty involved in delivering her to the dining hall, which was sometimes considerable, depending upon her medical ailment of the moment, Sister Mary Alphonsus insisted upon this.

In her former life, before "retirement," she'd been a prominent figure in her religious order—for more than two decades, director of the Craigmillnar Home for Children. This was a Catholic-run orphanage about sixteen miles north and east of Eau Claire, at its fullest occupancy containing more than three hundred children.

In the dining hall, Sister Mary Alphonsus asked to be seated at a table with several elderly women whom she might have considered "friends"—of whom two were, like herself, retired Sisters of Charity of St. Vincent de Paul who'd also been at Craigmillnar.

You would think that the Sisters of Charity would speak of their shared past at Craigmillnar, but they hardly spoke at all except to comment on the food. Like elderly sisters who'd seen too much of one another over the decades, and who had come to dislike one another, yet clung together out of a fear of loneliness.

Though it was difficult to imagine Sister Mary Alphonsus as one susceptible to *loneliness.*

Few relatives came to visit the elderly nuns. They'd had no children—that was their mistake. Beyond a certain age, an elderly resident will receive visits only from her (adult) children and, if she's fortunate, grandchildren. Others of their generation have died out, or are committed to health-care facilities themselves. So virtually no one came to see these elderly nuns, who with other Catholic residents of the facility attended mass together once a week in the chapel.

Their priest too was elderly. Very few young men were entering the priesthood any longer, as even fewer young women were entering convents.

Though I'm not Catholic, often I observed the mass from the rear of the little chapel. "Father Cullough"—who made no effort to learn the nuns' names—recited the mass in a harried and put-upon voice, in record time—scarcely thirty minutes. Once, the mass was said in Latin, as I know from having seen old prayer books in my family, that had been published in Scotland and brought to this country; now the mass is said in English, and sounds like a story for simpleminded children.

In the front row of the chapel the elderly nuns tried to keep awake. Even Sister Mary Alphonsus, the sharpest-witted of these, was likely to nod off during the familiar recitation. When the priest gave communion, however, at the altar rail, the old women's tongues lapped eagerly at the little white wafer, the size of a quarter. My gaze shifted sharply aside, for this was not a pretty sight.

Once, when I was wheeling Sister Mary Alphonsus back to her room after mass, the wheelchair caught in a ridge of carpet in the floor, and Sister Mary Alphonsus was jostled in her seat, and lashed out at me— *Clumsy! Watch what you're doing.*

*Sister, sorry.*

*You did that on purpose, didn't you! I know your kind.*

*Sister, I did not. Sorry.*

*You will be sorry! I will report you.*

Many of the patients threaten to report us, often for trivial reasons. We are trained not to argue with them and to defer politely to them as much as possible.

*Think I don't know YOU. I know YOU.*

*Yes, Sister.*

"*Yes, Sister*"—the elderly woman's croaking voice rose in mockery—*we will see about that!*

I made no reply. My heart might have leapt with a thrill of sheer dislike of the old woman, but I would never have said anything to goad her further. It was said of the former mother superior at Craigmillnar, by the nurses' aides who were obliged to take intimate care of her aged body—*Bad enough she has to live with herself. That's punishment enough.*

Yet by the time Sister Mary Alphonsus was back in her room, her interest in reporting me to my supervisor had usually faded. She'd been distracted by someone or something else that annoyed or offended her. She'd have forgotten Francis Gough entirely, as one of little worth.

Not that she knew my name: she did not. While others called me *Francis,* Sister Mary Alphonsus could barely manage to mutter, with a look of disdain—*You.*

She did know the names of the medical staffers, to a degree. She knew Dr. Bromwalder. She knew Head Nurse Claire McGuinn, if but to quarrel with her.

A care facility like a hospital is a hierarchy. At the top are physicians—"consultants." Nurse-practitioners, nurses and nurses' aides, orderlies—these are the staff. An orderly is at hand to help with strenuous tasks like lifting and maneuvering patients, including patients' lifeless bodies; changing beds, taking away soiled laundry, washing laundry; pushing food carts, and taking away the debris of mealtimes; sweeping and mopping floors; taking trash outside to the dumpsters. (Trash is carefully deployed: there is ordinary waste, and there is "clinical waste.") My original training (at age nineteen) was on-the-job at Racine Medical Center plus a weeklong course in "restraint and control."

There were few violent patients at Eau Claire, but I was well prepared for any I might be called upon to "restrain and control." You need two other orderlies at least if you need to force a patient onto the floor. How it's done is you force him down onto his stomach, an orderly gripping each arm and an orderly securing the legs. It's going to be a struggle most times—even the old and feeble will put up a considerable fight, in such a situation; the danger is in getting kicked. (When you're the youngest you are assigned the legs.) In this position—which looks cruel when observed—the patient's back is relatively free so he can breathe, and he's prevented from injuring himself.

Unlike cops, who are allowed "pain" as an element in restraint and control, medical workers are not allowed "pain" and may be legally censured if patients are injured.

Despite my training, there have been injuries of patients I'd been obliged to restrain and control, both in U.S. care facilities and in the medical units in Iraq.

None of these were my fault. And yet, there were injuries.

The nurses were gossiping: Sister Mary Alphonsus had no close next of kin.

Or, if there were relatives of the deceased woman, they were distant relatives who had no wish to come forward to identify themselves.

Maybe no wish to associate themselves with the individual who'd been director of the Craigmillnar Home for Children, which had been shut down in 1977 by Oybwa County health authorities and the State of Wisconsin.

Just recently too, Craigmillnar was back in the headlines.

A full week after her death on November 11, no one from the Oybwa County medical examiner had contacted the facility. So it appeared Dr. Bromwalder's death certificate had not been questioned.

The gauzy strip of "curtain"—unless it was some kind of nun's "veil" or "wimple"—had disappeared from the premises. All of Sister Mary Alphonsus's things had been packed up and removed from Room 22 and a new, unsuspecting arrival, also an elderly woman, had been moved in.

Yet the subject of the mysterious "head covering" continued to come up in Unit D. It seemed strange to me—I said so—that I appeared to be the only person to have seen Sister Mary Alphonsus fix something like a "head-shroud" over her head several times in the past. Some kind of cloth—might've been a towel (I didn't remember it as white)—she'd drawn like a hood over her head, for whatever reason. I hadn't asked the sister what she was doing, of course. She'd have been offended at such *familiarity*.

One day our young consulting physician Dr. Godai asked me about this, for he'd overheard some of us talking.

*So you'd seen the sister putting some kind of "cloth" on her head, or around her head, Francis? When was this, d'you remember?*

*Might've been a few weeks ago, doctor. Maybe two months.*

*How often did you see the sister putting this "cloth" on her head?*

*Maybe three times, doctor. I never thought anything of it, you know how old people are sometimes.*

Dr. Godai laughed. He was the newest consultant on our staff, from the University of Minnesota Medical School. He had a burnished-skinned Paki look, dark-eyed, sharp-witted. Knowing that certain of the elderly patients and certain of the medical staff did not feel comfortable with him, as nonwhite, Dr. Godai was what you'd call forceful-friendly, engaging you with his startling-white eyes and smile sharp as a knife blade. Between Dr. Godai and me there flashed a kind of understanding, as if the elderly nun was in the room with us, helpless, yet furious, glaring at us in disdain and in hurt, that she could not lash out at us to punish.

*Eccentric* is the word, Francis. A kindly word. For you wouldn't want to say demented, deranged, senile—eh?

Dr. Godai and I laughed together. I wasn't naive enough to think that Dr. Godai could ever be my friend, though we are about the same age.

I told Dr. Godai that each time I'd seen Sister Mary Alphonsus behaving in this way, putting a "shroud" on her head, I'd made no comment, of course. I didn't even ask her if she was cold, or needed an extra blanket. Nor did Sister Mary Alphonsus encourage conversation with me or with others on the staff. In my memory it had seemed to me that the woman was just slightly embarrassed, and annoyed, by my having seen her with the "cloths." And so out of courtesy I turned away from her, as if I hadn't seen.

*It's a strange life, isn't it, Francis?—I mean, the religious orders. Poverty, chastity, service, obedience these nuns swore to.*

To this I made no reply. Dr. Godai was speaking bemusedly, and may have been thinking out loud.

*Of course, I don't understand the Catholics, maybe. Are you Catholic, Francis?*

*No, Dr. Godai. I am not.*

*You are an arrogant young man. I will report you.*

*I know YOU. YOU will not get away with this.*

There are two categories of geriatric patient. Those who persist in behaving as if they aren't elderly; or as if their current condition, inability to walk, for instance, is a temporary one; individuals who shuffle slowly, in obvious pain, leaning against walls, against the backs of chairs, out of pride. And there are those who have conceded that they are not "one hundred percent" but must use a cane, a walker, a wheelchair. (It's possible to think that a wheelchair isn't really "permanent"—it is always expedient, helpful more for the staff.) Each step you think is temporary and you will soon return to your real self, but that's not how it goes.

Sister Mary Alphonsus had been in the second category. She may have been elderly but not *old-elderly;* and she would resent bitterly your behaving as if she were. Her hearing, like her vision, was impaired, but Sister Mary Alphonsus was more likely to blame you for not speaking clearly, or loud enough, than she would blame herself. In fact, Sister Mary Alphonsus would never blame herself.

If she spilled food, or dropped something, and you were present—somehow, the fault lay with *you.* At first I'd thought this was a sign of dementia, but later I came to realize it was the woman's perception of *what is:* blame must be assigned, only just not with her.

Unlike most of the elderly women in the facility, Sister Mary Alphonsus hadn't been what you'd call frail. Her body was thick, waistless; her skin was leathery; her eyes were suspicious and close-set; her legs remained heavy, especially her thighs, which strained against the polyester stretch pants she sometimes wore. Her most characteristic expression was a peevish frown.

Sometimes Sister Mary Alphonsus seemed annoyed by rain outside her window, as if it had been sent to provoke *her.* For there was a small courtyard into which we could wheel patients, in good weather.

Once, I'd wheeled Sister Mary Alphonsus outside into this courtyard and had to go away on an errand, and by the time I returned it was raining hard, and Sister Mary Alphonsus had managed to wheel herself beneath an overhang, by an effort of both hands.

*You did that on purpose! You are mocking me.*

No one considered that it might have been poison that Sister Mary Alphonsus had taken. *Poison* that was her own soul.

It was general knowledge in Eau Claire: in recent months the children's home at Craigmillnar, which had acquired a "controversial" reputation since it had been shut down by state health authorities in 1977, had resurfaced in the news.

Now, interest in Craigmillnar was part of a broad investigation into Catholic-run charity homes, hospitals, and organizations following a flood of disclosures of sexual misconduct by priests in the United States, with the complicity of the Catholic hierarchy. A militant group of former residents of the home at Craigmillnar, which called itself Survivors of Craigmillnar, had been picketing the archbishop's residence in Milwaukee, demanding acknowledgment of what they charged had been "widespread neglect and abuse" at Craigmillnar. The state attorney general was considering criminal charges against some former staff members who, the former residents claimed, had been responsible for a number of deaths at Craigmillnar in the 1950s and 1960s.

At the very least, the Survivors were demanding financial settlements, and a public apology from the Catholic Church.

*Public apology!*—my father laughed, bitterly. *The Church will apologize when hell freezes over.*

Both my mother's and my father's families had been Catholic—they'd emigrated to Wisconsin from Glasgow in the 1920s—but no longer. My father and his older brother Denis had expressed disgust with the Church for as long as I could remember, and when I was asked my religion on a form I checked *None*.

In Scotland there are many Catholics. People think that Scotland is all Protestant—this is not so. But lately, since the scandals of the pedophile priests and cover-ups by the Church, there has been a drop in the number of Catholics in Scotland, as in Ireland.

When allegations of abuse and negligence were first made against the Craigmillnar nuns, the diocese had defended the Sisters of Charity. There were Church-retained lawyers, threats of countercharges. The archbishop, who'd been a bishop in Boston at the time of Craigmillnar's worst abuses, had issued a public statement regretting the "unprofessionalism" of the orphanage, but absolving his predecessor archbishop, now deceased, from any blame associated with its administration. It was leaked to the media that Church officials believed that the Craigmillnar Sisters of Charity were "not representative" of the order; that there'd been in fact a "very small minority" of Sisters of Charity of St. Vincent de Paul who'd been involved in this "unprofessional" behavior. Those nuns still living had been "retired" from the order.

In the Eau Claire elder care facility such subjects were not usually discussed. At least not openly.

The former lives of our patients are not our concern unless our patients want to talk about them, as sometimes they do; for it's important to some of the elderly that their caretakers have some sense of who they once were. For most of them, showing photos of grandchildren and boasting of careers will suffice.

Sister Mary Alphonsus, who'd been a resident at Eau Claire for the past eight years, had never spoken of her former life as mother superior at Craigmillnar — of course. Some time before I'd come to Eau Claire to work as an orderly, there'd been a coalition of investigators who'd sought to interview the elderly nuns in the facility, predominantly Sister Mary Alphonsus, but an attorney hired by the diocese had rebuffed their efforts with the argument that the nuns had long been retired and were not in good health.

In 1997, in the wake of the slow-smoldering scandal, the name of the nuns' order was legally changed from the Sisters of Charity of St. Vincent de Paul to the Daughters of Charity of St. Vincent de Paul.

Still, there was a lingering wonderment not only in Unit D but elsewhere in the facility regarding the sudden death of the former mother superior of the home at Craigmillnar. As if the staff didn't want to surrender their most notorious resident quite so quickly.

Maybe (some were saying) Sister Mary Alphonsus had had a hand in her own death.

Since there'd been no autopsy, you could conjecture such things, which were not likely to be disproven.

(For what did Dr. Bromwalder know, or care? The senior consultant's hours at Eau Claire were the very minimum, if not less.)

Managed somehow to cease breathing. And her heart to cease beating.

The gauzy soiled "veil" or "wimple" wound around her head, hiding her face, had to be deliberate — didn't it?

*Could be, Sister Mary Alphonsus felt remorse. For the children she'd had a hand in torturing and letting die of disease.*

*Could be, Sister Mary Alphonsus's death was a penance.*

*Put herself out of her misery?*

Speculations wafted about me. But I was too busy working — pushing trolleys, gurneys, wheelchairs — sweeping and mopping floors, disinfecting toilets, hauling away trash to the dumpsters out back — to be distracted.

Honorably discharged from the U.S. Army with the rank of corporal first class when I was twenty-six, four years ago this January.

Because of my training I'd been assigned to the medical unit. The work was tiring but exciting, always unpredictable. You were made to feel *For the grace of God, this could be me.* It makes you humble, and grateful. It's a feeling that will never fade. The first time a soldier died in my arms it happened in a way to leave me stunned, I could not talk about it for weeks. I have never talked about it even with my father. I'd thought, *Is this what it is? Dying? So easy?*

There is nothing so precious as life, you come to know. Firsthand you know this. And a sick feeling, a feeling of rage, that some people treat the lives of others so carelessly, or worse.

My first work back in the States was in Racine, where I trained; my second job was Balsam Lake Nursing Home, twenty miles north of St. Croix, where my family lives. My third job has been here at the Eau Claire elder care facility, where I am currently employed.

When we were growing up in the family my father never spoke of his own childhood. I knew that he'd had a younger brother—who would have been one of my uncles—who'd died when he was a child. But I didn't know anything more.

Anything *of the past* was forbidden. We did not ask, but we did not think to ask. My mother had warned us— *Your father isn't a man for looking back. That can be a good thing.*

*Francis! Come home this weekend, Denis and I have to speak with you.*

It was a weeknight in early November. At this time, Sister Mary Alphonsus had not yet passed away in her sleep.

Such urgency in my father's voice I had never heard before, not even when I'd left for Iraq.

In an exalted mood my father and my uncle Denis brought me with them to the Sign of the Ram, which was their favorite pub, to a booth at the rear of the taproom behind the high-pitched din of the TV above the bar. Leaning our elbows on the scarred table, hunching inward. My father and my uncle Denis on one side of the table, and me on the other.

I felt a mounting unease. The thrill of such intimacy with my father and my uncle was *not-right.*

In fierce lowered voices they revealed to me their long-kept secret, which no one else knew: not my mother, and not my aunt who was Denis's wife. Not anyone in the family at the present time, for those who'd known had died, and had taken their knowledge of the secret with them, in shame.

Here was the situation. My father spoke, and my uncle interrupted to complete his sentences. Then, my father interrupted.
Then, my uncle. These are not men accustomed to speaking in
such a way in lowered voices and with an air of commingled shame
and rage. For it seemed articles in the local papers had stirred in
them memories of Craigmillnar. TV interviews with "survivors" of
the home whose faces were blurred to protect their identities. One
night Denis had called his brother during one of these interviews
on the local station—*Jesus God, I think I know who that is. And you
do too.*

As boys, Denis, Douglas, and their young brother Patrick had
been committed to the Craigmillnar Home for Children. Their
father had died in an accident at the St. Croix stone quarry when
he was thirty-three. Their mother, only twenty-six when Patrick was
born, had had a mental breakdown and could no longer take care
of herself and her sons; she began to drink heavily, she fed medica-
tions to the boys "to keep them from crying," she died in 1951 of
a drug overdose. One day an uncle came for them to take them to
the orphanage, saying there was "no place" for them now—but he
would come to get them again soon, in a few months perhaps. In
time for Christmas, he'd promised.

Christmas 1951! It would be Christmas 1957 by the time they
were freed of Craigmillnar, and their little brother Patrick dead.

In raw indignant voices the men said to me, *God damn these jokes
about nuns, stupid TV shows about nuns, on TV a nun is meant to be a
comic figure but in life there was nothing funny about these women.* They
were like Nazis—they followed orders. What the mother superior
instructed them, they fulfilled. Some of them were like beasts,
mentally impaired. The convent had done that to them, you had
to surmise. There was a kind of madness in them—you could see
in their eyes, which were always darting about, seeking out dis-
obedience. The mother superior had been the cruelest. For the
woman had been intelligent, you could see. And her intelligence
had all turned to hatred, and to evil.

How the sisters groveled, like all in the Church when confronted with a superior! The ordinary nun groveled to her superior, the mother superior groveled to the bishop, the bishop to the
archbishop, and to the cardinal, and to the pope—a vast staircase,
you are meant to think, ascending to God the Father.

It was strange, when you thought about it—years later. That

the orphanage at Craigmillnar had been theirs to "administer." By the standards of the present day, was any one of the nuns qualified for such work? Did the director—this woman identified as Sister Mary Alphonsus—have any training in such administration? Were the "nurse nuns" trained nurses? Were the "teacher nuns" trained teachers? Had any of the nuns been educated beyond high school? (That is, parochial high school taught by nuns.) Very likely, many of the Sisters of Charity at Craigmillnar had barely graduated from middle school.

The brothers had vowed to protect Patrick, who was so small, and always terrified. Yet, at Craigmillnar, at once the brothers were separated and made to sleep in separate dormitories according to age.

The orphanage was overcrowded, drafty, and dirty. Often two children shared a single narrow bed. You were—often—marched from one place to another through high-ceilinged corridors. There were mealtimes—school times—prayer times—bedtimes. There were "outdoor times"—these were irregular, and brief. You were not allowed to speak except at certain times and then you dared not raise your voice. Laughter was rare, and likely to be a mistake. Prolonged coughing was a mistake. Sharp-nosed as bloodhounds, the sisters were alert to the smallest infractions of law. The sisters could detect a squirming bad child amid a room of huddled children.

Most frantic were the sisters about *bed-wetting*. The children were wakened several times a night to check their beds. Bed-wetters were singled out for terrible beatings, children as young as two and three. They were made to drape their soiled sheets around themselves and to stand in the cold for hours until they collapsed. You were punished for being unable to eat by being force-fed through feeding tubes wielded by the sisters.

There were degrees of "discipline"—"punishment." One of them was "restraint"—the child's arms were bound by towels, tightly knotted, like a straitjacket. Circulation was cut off, there was likely to be swelling, and terrible pain. A child might be bound, water thrown over him or her, so that the binding was allowed to dry, and to shrink. (This had been done, more than once, to both Douglas and Denis. To this day, the men carried the physical memories of such punishments in their arthritic joints and jabs of pain in their muscles unpredictable as lightning strikes.) There were beatings with the nuns' leather belts. There were beatings with pokers. There were slaps, blows with fists, kicks. Striking a child's head with a rolled-up newspaper—this was surprisingly painful. Husky shot-eyed Sister Mary Agatha beat children with a mop handle. Shut Patrick in a cupboard, saying the "little devil" coughed and wheezed "for spite" and kept other children awake.

We were all beaten, we were made to go without proper food, we were made to sleep in cockroach-ridden beds, bed-bug infestations, and no one gave a damn. Neighbors in Craigmillnar must have known—something. The officials of the Church must have known. All those years! The Sisters of Charity could not have been so crude and so cruel at the start. The younger nuns—they were hardly more than girls—must have been shocked, and frightened. Just entering the convent—and being sent to Craigmillnar. Yet, at Craigmillnar, they became crude, cruel women. "Brides of Christ"—what a joke! Their order of nuns was a service order—service to the poor. Saint Alphonsus was one of their patron saints—he'd founded communities for the poor in slums in Rome. They'd vowed for themselves a life of sacrifice—celibacy, poverty, service, obedience. The catch was, the sisters hadn't had to vow to love their charges, only to serve God through them. Soon, then, they came to hate and despise their charges. A young child must be difficult to hate and despise, yet the sisters of Craigmillnar hated and despised. They were quick to flare into anger, and into rage. They shouted, they screamed. They kicked and they struck us with rods. The teaching nuns struck us with the rods used to pull down maps over the blackboards. In their fury at our fear of them they threw pieces of chalk at us. They knocked us to the floor. They locked us in closets—"solitary confinement"—no food, and lying in our own shit. We did not know what we did wrong. There were crimes called "insolence"—"arrogance." A ten-year-old girl in the desk next to mine was struck in the face by our teacher, and her nose bled terribly. Her clothing was soaked in blood. She was forced then to remove her clothing, to stand naked and to wash her stained clothing in disinfectant. The bleach, the lye, was such that our hands burned. Our skins were so chafed, they bled easily. We worked in the kitchen, we helped serve up the maggoty food, and we washed the dishes after meals in scalding water, with such meager soap there were scarcely any bubbles.

Everything was covered in a fine film of grease that could never be scrubbed away. We worked in the laundry, in the stinking lavatories we were made to clean the toilets and the floors. We cleaned the nuns' rooms and their stinking lavatories and bathrooms. Their stained tubs and toilets. We worked as grounds crews. We hauled trash, we mowed the rocky lawn. Denis ran away once, twice—how many times!—always brought back by county authorities, sometimes beaten, for he'd "resisted arrest." Douglas ran away once, and was brought back to the home in a police van, like a captured criminal.

We believed that we would die in the home at Craigmillnar, as Patrick had died, and so many others. We had lost all hope of ever leaving. We were made to pray on our knees, on the bare floor—the prayer I remember was *Christ have mercy! Christ have mercy! Christ have mercy!*

It was a custom of the Craigmillnar staff to punish children for being ill by refusing to treat their illnesses or medical conditions—rheumatic heart, asthma, pneumonia, diabetes, influenza; contagious sicknesses like chickenpox, measles, and mumps, even diphtheria, swept through the drafty filthy dormitories. Catholic physician-consultants who were allegedly on the Craigmillnar staff failed to come to the home or, if they did, spent most of their time chatting with the mother superior and did not meet with sick children.

Children who died were often buried before their relatives were notified, in unmarked graves at the rear of St. Simon's churchyard a few miles away.

We never knew if any child had actually been killed outright, in the years we were there. There were rumors of such murders in the past. It was more likely a child might die of injuries eventually, or was let to die of illness. There were many "accidents"—falling down stairs, scalding yourself in the kitchen. Patrick was always hurting himself, and being "disciplined." He'd had asthma before Craigmillnar that had not been treated. He got sick, he was never well but always coughing, puking. He coughed so hard, his ribs cracked. We begged the nuns to help him, to take him to a hospital, we thought that we could take him ourselves if we were allowed, we knew that pneumonia had to be treated with "oxygen," but the nuns laughed at us, and screamed at us to shut up. Mother

Superior Mary Alphonsus knew of such things, and did not care. She had her own TV in her room. She ate well, she favored sweets. She had a heavy woolen coat and good leather boots for our terrible winters.

He died in January 1953. We had last seen him in the drafty, dank place called the Infirmary. He could scarcely breathe. There was a terrible wheezing in his lungs. It sounded like a wheezing of air from another part of the room—we kept looking up at the windows, which were so high, and ill-fitting. Patrick was shivering, yet his skin was burning hot. His eyes were enormous in his face. His teeth chattered. He could not speak to us—he was too sick. Yet he clutched at us—his hands clutching ours.

*He was let to die. They killed him. Asthma and pneumonia, poor Patrick couldn't breathe. Suffocated and none of them cared. And his body buried in the paupers' cemetery with the others.*

*They hadn't even let us know, when he died. A few days passed before we were allowed to know.*

In St. Simon's churchyard, the nuns and the priests of Craigmillnar are properly buried, with marble headstones. Facts of their birth dates and death dates are inscribed in stone. But the children's bodies, at the back of the cemetery—there are only little crosses to mark them, crowded together. Dozens of cheap little rotted-wood crosses, each at an angle in the earth. And Patrick, who would have been your youngest uncle, among them.

All their bones mixed together. As if their child-lives had been of no worth.

*She* had not commented, when the inquiries had first begun a few years ago. The pedophile priests had been protected by their bishop also. But investigators for the county and the state began listening to complaints and charges against the Craigmillnar staff. A younger generation of prosecutors and health officials, taking the lead of investigators in other parts of the country. Journalists who weren't intimidated by the Church because they weren't Roman Catholics.

Yet, *she* held her ground. She hid behind a lawyer, the Church provided a lawyer to protect her, because of her position and rank. She had refused to give testimony. She had not been arrested, as some others had been in situations like hers. She'd been served a subpoena to speak before a grand jury in Oybwa County, but had suffered a "collapse"—and so had a medical excuse. With the excuse of being "elderly"—in her late seventies—the woman was spared further "harassment" by the state.

Journalists referred to Sister Mary Alphonsus as the "Angel of Death of Craigmillnar," since so many children had died in the home during her years as director: the estimate was as many as one hundred.

Sister Mary Alphonsus was reported to have asked, how one hundred was *too many*? They were poor children, from ignorant families, they'd been abandoned by their parents, or by their (unwed) mothers—they were the kind of children who made themselves sick, eating too much, stuffing their bellies, refusing to wash their hands, playing in filth, fighting with one another, falling down stairs, running outdoors—that they would get sick was hardly a surprise, yes and sometimes one of them died. Over twenty-six years it came out to only three or four a year who died, out of the 350 children at the home: how was that *too many*?

In the Sign of the Ram we'd been drinking for more than two hours. The men's voices were low-pitched, trembling with rage. I had scarcely spoken except to murmur *My God* and *Yes.* For I was shocked and sickened by what the men had told me—and yet, not so surprised. As my mother would be shocked and sickened and yet—not so surprised. *Your father isn't a man for looking back.*

Leaving the pub with my father and my uncle, seeing the men older than I'd recalled, each of them walking unsteadily as in fear of pain. And I realized I'd been seeing my father and my uncle walking this way all of my life. Big men, men for whom the physical life is the primary life, men-who-don't-complain, men who laugh at discomfort, these were men who'd been deeply wounded as boys, the memory of pain in their tissues, joints, and bones, pain of which they would not ever speak, for to speak in such a way was to betray weakness, and a man does not ever betray weakness. And I felt a son's rage, and a sick fear that I would not be equal to this rage. For I thought, Why have they told me this? Why now?

My car was at my parents' house. My father drove me back, with Denis. Wasn't I going to stay the night? my father asked. Laying his hand on my arm. And my mother too asked, wasn't I going to stay the night, my bed was all made up. Seeing in the men's flushed faces that something had been revealed, she could not share. I told them no, I wasn't staying. Not tonight. I had to get back to Eau Claire that night.

My father walked me back outside, to my car in the driveway. And he did not say, *She is at that place you work—is she. She is in your "care."*

That November morning, the morning of the *discovery of the body*, I was the first of the early shift to arrive.

In the pitch-dark pelting rain making my way to the side entrance of the facility. At this early hour the building was but partially lighted, with a warm look inside. No one? No one to see me? Quickly and stealthily I made my way to Unit D, which was near-deserted at this hour. Soon the facility would come awake: the nursing staff and the orderlies would begin their rounds, the patients would be "up" for their interminable day. But not just yet, for it was 5:46 A.M.

From a closet I removed a single pillowcase. In the pocket of my waterproof parka was a three-foot strip of gauzy curtain I'd found in a trash can. I'd snatched it out of the trash—not sure why. A smile had twisted my mouth— *What's this?* I thought I would find a purpose for it.

I have learned to trust such instincts. I have learned not to question my motives.

Quietly then I pushed open the door to Sister Mary Aphonsus's room, which was at the end of a corridor. I did not breathe, my rubber-soled sneakers made no sound. Yet the elderly nun was part awakened by my presence.

I shut the door behind me. Without hesitating, as if I'd practiced this maneuver many times, I stooped over her bed, gripped her shoulder with one hand to hold her still, with the other yanked the pillow out from beneath her head, and pressed it over her face. So swiftly and unerringly I'd moved, Sister Mary Alphonsus had no time to comprehend what was happening, still less to cry out for help. Now in the throes of death she struggled like a maddened animal, her fingers clawing at my wrists.

I was wearing gloves. Her nails would not lacerate my bare skin.

In this struggle of several minutes I crouched over the figure in the bed, the head and face obscured by the pillow. I was panting, my heart beat quickly but calmly. I did not utter a word.

I thought of my father Douglas, and of my uncle Denis. I

thought of my uncle Patrick as a child, whom I had never seen. Buried in a pauper's grave, and his bones scattered and lost. But I did not speak. I did not accuse the evil woman, for what was there to say? You soon come to the end of speech as you come to the end of cultivated land, and stare out into the wilderness in which there are no names for things, as there are no familiar things. For what words would be adequate at this time, so long after the fact? — *God damn your soul to hell. Disgusting old bitch, this is not the punishment you deserve.*

Her hands tried to grip my wrists, to push away the pillow. But her hands grew feeble. I smelled urine. I did not flinch. A pillow held tight over the face of an elderly cardiac patient will snuff out her life within minutes, if you do not flinch.

When I was sure that it was over, I removed the pillow. The pillowcase was soaked with the woman's saliva, tears. Her body, which was surprisingly heavy, with a hard round stomach like an inverted bowl, lay limp and unresisting now. The face like a bulldog's face, contorted in death. I heard a harsh panting sound—my breathing. Hers had ceased, abruptly.

When death is only a matter of seconds, you think that it might be revoked. Life might be called back, if one had the skill.

But no. Once the match is shaken out, the flame is gone.

Without haste, with the precision of a veteran orderly, I removed the pillow from the soiled pillowcase, and pushed it snugly inside a fresh pillowcase. I took time to shake the pillow well down into the pillowcase. This action so frequently performed by me, in my role as orderly, like clockwork I executed it within seconds.

The bedclothes were badly rumpled as if churned. These I tidied deftly, tucking in bed sheets as you learn to do in the U.S. Army as well.

There is pleasure in executing small perfect things. One, two, three—completed! On to the next.

(The soiled pillowcase I might have tossed into the laundry. No one would have thought to look for it there—for the death of the eighty-four-year-old nun would not be considered a "suspicious" death. Yet, I was cautious, taking time to fold the pillowcase neatly to slide it into my backpack, to be disposed of when I left work.)

I lifted Sister Mary Alphonsus's limp head, to wind the strip of cheap gauzy curtain around it, and to hide her flushed and contorted face. *Bride of Christ! Here is your wedding veil.*

Why did I take time to do this?—why, to risk suspicion where there would be no suspicion?

I've thought of it, often. But I don't know why.

A smile comes over my face at such times—a strange slow smile. Am I happy, is that why I am smiling? Or—is the smile involuntary, a kind of grimace?

I could not have explained any of this. Not even to my father. It seemed the "right" thing to do, at the time. It would be my secret forever.

"Dorothy Milgrum" had left no will, it would be revealed. And so the deceased woman's modest estate would be appropriated by the State of Wisconsin.

How much did "Dorothy Milgrum" accumulate, in her years as chief administrator of Craigmillnar? It could not have been much. It was whispered among the staff that there was barely enough money for a decent headstone in the St. Simon's churchyard at Craigmillnar, where Sister Mary Alphonsus had secured a plot for herself years before.

I was the orderly charged with emptying, cleaning, and preparing the room for the next resident.

In the bureau in Sister Mary Alphonsus's room, amid her old-woman undergarments, stockings, and woolen socks, there was a packet of letters. I appropriated these, for there was no one to prevent me. It was a surprise to see so many handwritten letters, dated 1950s. Who'd written to the mother superior at Craigmillnar so often? And why had the mother superior kept these letters? The return address was Cincinnati, Ohio. The stationery was a pale rose color. The salutation was *Dear Dotty*. The signature was faded maroon ink—it looked like *Irene*. I tried to read a few lines, but could not decipher the curlicue handwriting. Another nun? A dear friend? There was also a packet of snapshots, yellow and curling. In these, Sister Mary Alphonsus was a young woman in her thirties—with sharp shining eyes, bulldog face, wide glistening smile. She wore her nun's dark robes with a certain swagger, as a young priest might wear such attire. The wimple was tight around her face, dazzling white. Her face looked cruelly and yet sensuously pinched, as in a vise.

In several snapshots the youthful Sister Mary Alphonsus was

standing close beside another nun, a stocky broad-shouldered middle-aged woman with a moon face and very white skin. Both women smiled radiantly at the camera. The older woman had flung off her nun's hood, her hair was close-cropped, gray. The older woman was taller than Sister Mary Alphonsus by an inch or so.

In the background was a lakeside scene—a rowboat at shore, fishing poles.

In the last of the snapshots the women were again standing close together, now both bareheaded, arms around each other's waist. These were thick arms and thick waists—these were husky women. Then I saw—it was a shock to see—that both women were barefoot in the grass, at the edge of a pebbly lakeside shore.

I thought—*They took these pictures with a time exposure. It was a new idea then.*

The snapshots and the letters covered in faded-maroon ink I burnt as I'd burnt the pillowcase soaked with a dead woman's saliva. If it had been in my power I would have burnt all trace of Sister Mary Alphonsus on this earth, but the truth is, some smudge of the woman's sick soul will endure, multiplied how many hundreds of times, in the memories of others.

I would say nothing—not ever—to my father or to my uncle Denis, but a certain long level look passed between us, a look of understanding, yet a look too of yearning, for what was concealed, that could not be revealed. When I next saw them, and the subject of the nun's death arose. My father had kept a newspaper to show me, the front-page headlines, though I didn't need to see the headlines, knowing what they were. In a hoarse voice Dad said— *Good riddance to bad rubbage.*

By which Dad meant *rubbish*. But I would not correct him.

Now that months have passed there is not much likelihood of a formal inquiry into the death of Sister Mary Alphonsus aka "Dorothy Milgrum." The Oybwa County medical examiner has never contacted us. Dr. Godai has left Eau Claire to return to Minneapolis, it has been announced. (Many, including me, were disappointed to hear that Dr. Godai is leaving us so soon, though it isn't surprising that a vigorous young doctor like Dr. Godai would prefer to live and work in Minneapolis, and not Eau Claire.) Yet, I have prepared my statement for the medical examiner. I have not written out this statement, for such a statement might seem incriminating if written out, but I have memorized the opening.

*Early shift is 6:30 A.M. which was when I arrived at the elder care facility at Eau Claire where I have been an orderly for two years. Maybe thirty minutes after that, when the elderly nun's body was discovered in her bed.*

ERIC RUTTER

# The Shot

FROM *Alfred Hitchcock's Mystery Magazine*

BARBARA PAUSED WITH her hand on the doorknob, clearing her head. Sometimes she could learn something from her first glimpse of a patient. On the other hand, it was all too easy to project onto them preconceived notions she already had. Not that she truly had patients in this job. A patient was someone you saw more than once. Most of the people she dealt with here were suspects who'd been arrested and the people they'd victimized — that is, *allegedly* victimized. In an odd sort of way the members of the police department were more like real patients, or they would be if she wound up working here a few years.

She opened the door to the waiting room. He was sitting in the chair by the far wall, legs crossed, not reading anything. He might have been staring at her receptionist, Maggie, the moment before, but somehow she doubted it. He looked too at ease, content just to sit there thinking his own thoughts. His eyes met hers and in them she saw no trace of uncertainty or dread, which did indeed tell her something about him.

She smiled and said, "Officer O'Donnell? I'm Dr. Neal."

He smiled faintly. "Hello."

"Come in."

As he stood up and crossed to her, she studied him without seeming to. In his gait she saw calm self-assurance. A man whose career was on the line wasn't supposed to walk that way.

She stepped out of the doorway to let him into her office, then closed the door behind him. "Please sit down," she said, gesturing to the patient's chair.

He took it. She took the one opposite, noting how he looked the room over. She'd already learned that police officers seemed to notice everything. If she asked him, he could probably tell her how many framed diplomas were hanging on the wall behind him. From the way his eyes lingered on the box of tissues sitting on the cabinet beside his chair, she surmised he'd never visited a psychologist before.

She said, "Is it all right if I call you Keith?"

"Yes."

"My name's Barbara." When he nodded once, she added, "I don't think we've actually spoken before. I haven't been with the department that long."

"No, we haven't."

"Well, it's nice to meet you."

"You too."

There was a second's pause. During it Barbara thought, So this is a police sniper. Captain Smith had said they were a different breed. Her first impression of Keith was that he was quite a bit more restrained than the average person. No, *restrained* was the wrong word. That implied he was keeping his emotions in check. He didn't seem to be. He just seemed . . . cool.

She said, "Do you understand why you're here?"

"Yes."

"Good. I don't want you to worry. I'm not here to judge you. I just want to find out what happened. See if we can figure out where the trouble started."

"I know just when it started."

"Really? When?"

"Back in March. The hostage situation on Seventh Avenue."

Barbara remembered it. She would have even if she hadn't read the official reports of that incident earlier this morning in preparation for this session. Hostage crises didn't happen every day in Miami.

But she said, "Tell me about it."

I filed a report about it. If you really want all the facts you should probably read that. But I guess you want to hear it from me, right?

Okay. That incident was a workplace shooting. A guy named Guinness had a problem with his boss, so he went to work one day with a gun in his pocket. He took it out and started yelling.

Probably just wanted to scare his boss, but somehow or other he got carried away and shot him. Then he wouldn't let anyone leave. I mean the people who hadn't snuck out when he first pulled the gun. He had nine hostages in there with him, plus the boss, who was dead.

I got there with the team—the Special Response Team. When we got there the street was cordoned off and the building had been evacuated. I set up in a building across the street, in an office on the fourth floor. We'd evacuated that too. I had a nice view of the whole office Guinness was in. It was a row of rooms with big windows facing me and he hadn't thought to close the blinds. I set up first. Dean—Dean Farleigh. You know him? He's the other sniper on the team—we trade off on two-hour shifts. I took the first one.

So I was watching Guinness through the scope. He was twitchy, pacing back and forth. You could see he was trying to think. He was in over his head and he knew it. I was only like sixty yards away, and from there a sniper scope gives you a real close look. I could see the beads of sweat on his forehead. I could see his eyes darting around, looking for a way out of there. But he never looked my way. He stayed away from the windows, so I guess he was clear-headed enough to be afraid of getting shot by someone down in the street. But he never glanced at my window, which he might have done, since I had it cracked open. I was set up a little ways back from it, lying prone on some desks we'd pushed together. And we had the lights off. So he didn't know I was there. I could see him but he couldn't see me.

I could see the other people in the office too. The hostages. Most of the time I've got a better view of the scene than anyone else so I do surveillance, especially early on, before I have a green light and when it seems like there's still a chance we might be able to wrap things up peacefully. That's how it was those first two hours. Guinness was still talking to Barry then. Barry the negotiator. I was making reports through my headset to Sergeant Erb. He was the supervisor on the scene. I was checking out the hostages, to see if any of them were wounded or anything. That's when I saw her.

I mean I saw her a couple of times, put my eyes on her and moved on. But then I started to notice her—how beautiful she was. She had dark hair. It was brown but a brown that's so dark it looks black. And it had this shine to it. The light shone off it like light shines off the curve of a waterfall, you know what I mean? Her eyes were brown too. I don't know how to describe the color of them, or the shape of her nose and her mouth or anything like that, but she was beautiful. My eyes kept coming back to her.

That's a big deal. I mean I had a good excuse. Guinness was still pacing around, and sometimes he'd walk past her and out of sight into some dead space behind an interior wall. I had to keep my scope where I last saw him and she was right there, sitting on the floor with the other hostages. But she was breaking my concentration. Sometimes even when Guinness was in sight at the other end of the room I'd be thinking about her, wanting to look at her again.

She looked scared. She must have been crying before I got there because her makeup was smeared and her nose was red. You know in a situation like that she must have been afraid she was going to die. I didn't want that to happen. That's a big deal too. That's not how you're supposed to think. You're supposed to keep your eyes on the bad guy, watch what he does, and if he does something actionable, get ready for the green light, because when you get it you have to take him out before he can do anything else. But you're not supposed to, you know . . . *relate* to the hostages.

Guinness didn't do anything during my shift. When Dean set up at another window I got up to stretch and move around. I went downstairs to talk to Sergeant Erb.

I asked him how it looked. He said, "I don't know. He's still talking, but it's all Barry can do to keep him calm."

I said, "Did he say anything about having a grudge against anybody else in there?"

"No," Sergeant Erb said.

I was relieved. I was thinking about that woman.

Instead of walking around some more and getting loose, I went back up to my post again right away. Dean had a pair of binoculars up there that he'd been using while I was on station, so I got them and stood watching Guinness and the woman. She was starting to calm down a little. Actually it wasn't calm — she was starting to go numb. Shock was kicking in. She leaned her head back against the wall and closed her eyes partway. If you didn't know any better you'd think she was about to fall asleep. But it was shock. I kept watching her, and Guinness, but her more and more. When she pulled up her legs and wrapped her arms around them, my eyes kept going to the fourth finger of her left hand. You know, I was making sure I'd seen right, that she didn't have a wedding ring on.

I knew this wasn't right, so I tried to stop watching. I put down the binoculars, but then after just a minute or two I brought them up again. I did that a couple of times. Then I put them down and started pacing the room. Dean told me to knock it off, I was distracting him. So I went out in the hallway.

I was only out there a few minutes when Dean's voice cut through the chatter in my headset. "Suspect's down," he said.

I hurried back inside. "What happened?"

"Suspect ate his gun."

I picked up the binoculars. People were running around in the office, most of them toward the door but not all of them. Some were panicked, running every which way. A few of them weren't moving at all.

I said, "Did he shoot anyone else first?"

"No," Dean said.

I was relieved when I saw he was right. The hostages who were sitting still were just too exhausted or relieved to move. One of them was the woman. As I watched she started crying, softly. She covered her face with her hands and her shoulders moved with her sobs.

Dean and I kept our positions while the team went in to secure the room. Dean kept his sights on Guinness, just in case. But he was dead. All the hostages got out okay.

Dean and I got word then to pack up. I got this feeling, like a panic, when I realized we were going to go back to headquarters and I might never see the woman again. I mean, we'd get her name and all for the reports, but we'd get all their names and if I didn't know which name was hers that would be it. So I hurried and got my equipment packed and went downstairs ahead of Dean.

I went to the big office on the ground floor we were using as a command center. It was still full of people, department personnel mostly, but the hostages had been brought there too. The woman was sitting in a chair with a blanket wrapped around her shoulders. She was talking to an EMT. I hung back, watching, while the other hostages talked to EMTs or police officers or each other. The place was buzzing. I just stood there, staring at her.

The EMT who was standing over her finally moved off. I walked up to her then. I didn't really decide to, it's like my legs just sort of took me there on their own.

I said, "Miss?"

She looked up at me.

I said, "Are you all right?"

She said, "Yes."

I stood there staring at her for another long moment, like an idiot, my rifle case in one hand and a duffel bag in the other, while all the other people in the room moved and talked around us. She sat there looking up at me, her face kind of blank. She was still in shock.

I said, "My name's Keith O'Donnell."

She said, "Mine's April Ozga."

I smiled at her and nodded and turned and walked away. I can't even tell you how glad I felt, knowing her name.

When it was clear he'd finished talking, Barbara said, "Has that ever happened to you before? Getting distracted by a pretty woman while you're working?"

"No. Never. They train you to focus. But they hardly even had to with me. I've gone hunting ever since I was a kid. You learn how to keep your eyes on the target while you're hunting. You don't get a second shot most of the time."

Barbara nodded. That fit with what little she knew about snipers—all of which she'd learned in the last twenty-four hours. When the military looked for soldiers to train as snipers, they liked to pick men who'd been hunting since they were old enough to carry a rifle. In fact they preferred those who'd killed deer, or some other animal that was bigger than a man. Apparently killing something that size required you to cross a critical psychological threshold.

According to Keith's service record, he had crossed that threshold many times. He joined the Marine Corps at the age of eighteen and after a couple years of service enrolled in their sniper school in Quantico. He passed with flying colors, which was quite an accomplishment, since only the best Marines were allowed in and fewer than 40 percent passed. Keith was subsequently deployed to Iraq, where in two years he tallied twenty-four confirmed kills. Barbara really wasn't sure what *confirmed* meant in that context, but she thought it meant Keith had killed considerably more than twenty-four people.

But he hadn't killed any since he joined the Miami Metro-Dade Special Response Team. He'd never been given "the green light." Except for once.

She said, "If you had been told to shoot Mr. Guinness that day, could you have done it?"

Keith answered without hesitation. "Yes."

She could see he believed it.

She said, "So this woman, April Ozga . . . Did you ever see her again?"

Yes. I went to her house a couple days later. That was as long as I could make myself wait. I knew it was wrong. Maybe not against department policy, technically, since with Guinness dead the case was closed, so I didn't have to worry about tainting a witness or anything like that. But I knew going to see her was . . . just wrong. But I couldn't help myself.

The address she'd given us was in Bay Heights. I went there on a Saturday, figuring she'd be home, but when I found the address I started to worry. It was a house, not an apartment. A nice house too, way nicer than a woman in her mid-twenties should be able to afford. I started to worry that maybe she was married even though she didn't wear a ring. I realized then I didn't actually know anything about her. She could be a lesbian, for God's sake. If she wasn't, she pretty much had to have a boyfriend, as beautiful as she was. But I got out of my car anyway and walked up to the door. It seemed to take forever for someone to answer when I rang the bell.

The man who did looked old enough to be her father. He said, "Yes?"

I said, "Hi. I'm Officer O'Donnell, Metro-Dade Police. Is April Ozga here?"

"Oh. Sure. Come in. Is everything all right?"

"Yes," I said, stepping in. The living room was filled with furniture that looked like it was pretty old. That is to say, it wasn't new and expensive stuff like a young person with money might buy, or really beat-up hand-me-downs like you'd expect for a young person who blew everything they had on the mortgage. I saw some family photos on the walls. They included pictures of this guy who'd let me in, looking younger, and a couple of dark-haired girls. One of them looked like she might have been April at about ten or twelve years old.

The man said, "You're here about Thursday."

I said, "Yes."

"Thank God she's all right."

"Yes."

"Sit down. I'll go get her."

I nodded, although I wasn't going to sit down—I was too nervous. But a woman came in just as the man turned to leave the room. She had to be his wife, April's mother. He explained to her who I was, then went as far as the bottom of the steps to yell April's name up them. It was so much like I remembered from when I was a teenager, going to pick up dates, I almost laughed. Her mother came over to me and gripped my hand. She didn't shake it, she just held it with both of hers and gazed into my eyes with a look that said my being there reminded her of how scared she'd been on Thursday.

She said, "Nothing's wrong, is it?"

I said, "No. Everything's fine."

She offered me something to eat or drink. In between the words I heard footsteps on the stairs. I turned toward them and watched April come into the room. Watched her pause, recognizing me.

Her father said, "This policeman's here to see you."

I said, "Keith O'Donnell."

April said, "Yes, I remember." She came toward me slowly, stopped a fair distance away.

Her parents turned to look at me then. Everybody stood there, waiting for me to say something.

I said, "How have you been?"

April said, "Fine. All right, I guess."

"I wanted to . . . see how you're doing."

There was a moment's pause. Then her mother said, "That's nice. It's nice to see the police know she might be, you know, *affected* by what she went through."

Her father said, "Sit down. You two can talk."

April said, "Let's talk outside. We can go for a walk."

She headed for the door. Her mother made these cooing noises, encouraging us to stay, but her father said, "No, no. It's all right. Give her some privacy."

I nodded and smiled to them both and followed April outside.

She started up the sidewalk and I fell into step beside her, not knowing what to say. After a moment she said, "They mean well but . . ."

"They're your parents?"

"Yeah. I had to move back in with them. I had an apartment, but my roommate lost her job. She couldn't pay the rent, so she moved out. I couldn't manage on my own, so I had to move back here."

"Well, maybe it's for the best. This way you weren't living alone when Thursday happened. It's good to be able to go home to someone who cares about you after something like that. Even a boyfriend wouldn't have been the same if you don't live with him."

"I don't have a boyfriend right now."

I didn't say anything, pleased as hell with myself for getting that information out of her so cleverly.

She made a sound. I looked over and saw she was crying.

"Oh!" I said. "I'm sorry. I should have been more sensitive. You know the department has victim's advocates you could talk to. They could help you work through this."

She looked over at me, wiping her eyes. "I thought that's what you were."

"No, I'm a police sniper. I was there that day. I saw you through my rifle scope."

At the time I couldn't read her expression, but now I see that was the moment she realized what I was doing there.

I said, "Does that make you feel any better? To know I was watching over you?"

She didn't answer for a moment. Finally she said, "That day is the scaredest I've ever been. I actually peed myself."

"I've done that lots of times."

She looked at me again, trying to see if I was kidding.

"Seriously. When I was in the Marines. You get set up on a target and sometimes you can't move. I mean you can't move at all or someone will shoot you. If you really gotta go, you just go."

We walked in silence for a while.

Then she said, "Did you see the whole thing? Thursday?"

"Not the beginning. We got there at nine-ten."

"But you saw the end?"

"No. The other sniper was on station then. I'd just stepped out into the hall."

"I saw him do it. Kill himself, I mean. I didn't see him shoot Martin but I saw him put the gun in his mouth and pull the trigger. All that blood. I was looking at him then. I saw the look in his eyes right before he did it. He realized he didn't have a choice."

"He had a choice. Lots of choices. He made a couple of bad ones."

She didn't say anything.

I said, "I'm glad you're all right."

She said, "Thanks."

"We don't have to talk about it if you don't want to."

"What should we talk about?"

"Anything you want."

Again, I didn't think of it then, but right there she could have turned around and gone home. She could have told me to get lost, told me what a scumbag I was for coming around like this, so soon after what happened. But she didn't. We kept walking, and talking. We walked around the block five times.

"We started dating."

From his expression and his tone of voice, Barbara knew the answer to her next question. But she asked it anyway. "Are you still seeing each other?"

"No."

"When did you stop?"

"A couple weeks ago."

She nodded, watching him. The sadness in his eyes was the first real emotion she'd seen from him. It wasn't much, at that, but he obviously wasn't very expressive. Most people fidgeted at least a little bit when describing stressful situations they'd been through, maybe tapping one foot or wringing their hands, but Keith had just sat there so far. Captain Smith said snipers needed to be able to remain perfectly still for long periods of time. They also had to be intelligent and observant and extraordinarily patient. Keith seemed to have all those attributes.

She said, "So around this time, did you keep having trouble concentrating at work?"

"Yes. Sort of."

"What do you mean?"

"I, uh, I started seeing targets differently."

*

My first sniping assignment after the Guinness case was providing cover for an undercover narcotics officer. He was going to make a buy off a drug dealer in West Miami, back in this industrial area. I was set up on the third floor of an old factory 175 yards away. This was like eleven o'clock at night. Dean was there with me, sweeping the area with night-vision binoculars, but I had my regular scope. The buy was supposed to happen in an open space that was lit with streetlights. I could see just fine. I could see the dealer. He was there before our guy, standing there waiting around. Dean and I joked about that. This guy was supposed to be a big shot, that's why Narcotics targeted him, but big shots don't show up early and then stand around waiting. They sure don't stand around lit up like that, so anyone can see them. We figured this guy was either a small fry who'd been sent there by his boss or he'd just recently jumped up the ranks. If he'd been promoted, at this rate he wasn't going to stay on top very long.

Dean and I both had headsets on. We were listening to the task force we'd been loaned to arguing about whether they could send their guy out to meet the dealer early without looking suspicious. It was while I was waiting for them to make up their minds that I started noticing things about the dealer. He didn't look nervous exactly, but he looked, you know . . . uncertain. Like he really was some low-level guy who wasn't sure what he was doing yet. I could see his expression clear as day. It made me think of April and the look on her face a couple weeks before.

It bothered me. It *worried* me. I felt like I could feel how vulnerable this guy was, standing there not knowing I had him in my sights. Snipers can't afford to do that. They make sure you don't think that way when you're in school. That's why they have you put your sights on real people sometimes, not just bull's-eyes. I never had a problem with it before. In Iraq most of the targets I took out didn't know I was there, and some of them were unarmed. I watched some of them for a long time, hours maybe, waiting to get the right shot. I watched one guy for days. That whole time, with all of them, they looked like they were so close I might have been standing right next to them. You get to know somebody's habits when you watch them like that. You see their mannerisms, you get to know their personalities to some degree. And the whole time you have their life in your hands, right up until the moment when you take it. But it never bothered me.

It was bothering me now. I watched the dealer look up and down the road between the buildings, cross his arms and uncross them, lick his lips and then lick them again like his mouth was dry. I told myself to get over it. This guy was a criminal. He was there to sell drugs. He probably had a gun tucked in his waistband under his shirt. But it didn't matter. I could feel the power I had over him and it gave me a weird sort of itch between my shoulder blades.

Maybe it didn't help that the task force was arguing about whether this might be a trap. The dealer looked so clueless, they thought he might be some pissant whose bosses sent him out there as bait. Dean was checking every alley mouth and window for signs of an ambush, but he didn't see any. Still, we agreed I had to be ready to drop this guy in a heartbeat.

So I kept the crosshairs trained on him. The task force finally decided to send their man out, so I listened to the supervisor giving him last-minute instructions. I listened with half an ear, since now I was thinking about April's parents, the look in her mother's eyes when the sight of me made her remember how scared she'd been for April. I wondered if somebody somewhere was worrying about this dealer. I wondered if he had any kids. When I tried to imagine pulling the trigger on him, it made me feel sort of weak and sick.

It turns out I never had to take the shot. The undercover went out there and made the buy and there wasn't any trouble. The dealer never pulled a gun and no one else ever came out of the shadows. And we got the whole conversation on tape. The task force was happy. I wasn't. I was relieved I didn't have to shoot the guy, and when I realized that, I was scared.

Over the next six months, I had I don't know how many other sniping assignments. I don't get that many. It must have been June before I had someone in my sights again. During that time I was mostly providing cover for raids on crack houses, watching the windows while the team went in the front door. A couple of times I saw suspects come out windows and make a break for it, but none of them started shooting at the team, so I didn't have to take them out. I could have done it, though. I'm sure of that. I'd worry about it while I was sitting there staring at the house—I'd worry that I would start to worry, and that would get me going—but when someone popped out a window I snapped into focus. I'm sure I wouldn't have hesitated if any of them had pulled a gun.

I'm sure of it now and I was sure of it then too, and that made me feel better, since I started to think that if it was a different story shooting someone who was shooting at my guys, then I probably could have shot that dealer after all, since that's the only reason I would have been told to. At least that's how I figured it. After a while I changed my mind, or realized I was wrong in the first place. The problem wasn't that I couldn't shoot a target unless they were dangerous, it was watching their every move that bothered me, getting to know them, and then putting a bullet through their head.

By September I wasn't sure I could do that anymore.

Barbara said, "Did you tell anyone?"

"No."

"Why not?"

Keith shifted uncomfortably in his seat. Finally, some sign they were getting somewhere.

"Well," he said, "like I said, I didn't really think it was a problem until September. Probably late September. That's only, what, five, six weeks ago."

"But those were five or six weeks you weren't sure you could do your job."

"Well, I only got like three assignments during that time."

"Still, what if you'd found yourself in a situation where you were told to take the shot? Did you have a plan for that?"

"No."

"So what happened yesterday . . ."

"That wasn't planned."

She didn't say anything, watching him.

Eventually the silence became too much for him. He said, "Most of those weeks were when things were going bad with April. That's part of this. I don't know how, but . . ."

He trailed off.

For a moment Barbara didn't respond. She wasn't sure what April had to do with this, but he obviously needed to talk about her.

So she said, "Tell me about your relationship with her."

She moved in four weeks after our first date. So I guess you could say things were going good. I guess she wouldn't have moved in if she hadn't been living at home, but there weren't any problems once she did. We still got along great. She cooked every night I was home and insisted on chipping in with the bills even though I said she didn't have to. She never complained about my hours and she didn't worry about me getting shot, or if she did she didn't show it. Living with her was easy. I loved it.

I loved her.

That lasted . . . oh, I don't know how long. When I look back now, I'm not sure when the trouble started. I think of times when she seemed happy and I wonder if she really was. But I think what happened is, the trouble started when I met her friend Cory.

We met him and his wife for dinner at a restaurant. I got the feeling he didn't like me right away. There was something in his eyes when April introduced us. I don't know if he has some secret crush on her, or maybe it's a protective older-brother kind of thing; he's like fifteen years older than her. He was in the army, although I didn't know that till he said so. Maybe he knew I was a Marine and that was the reason he acted like he did.

Actually, the way he acted, April might have told him I was a sniper in Iraq. When he asked if I was there, and what I did, he didn't look surprised when I told him.

He said, "I was there too, back in 'ninety-one. Twenty-fourth Infantry. Right out in front."

And then he just sort of looked at me, glaring at me.

I said, "Hot as hell there."

He said, "You got that right."

There was some more silence.

The girls seemed to get that something was going on between us. Cory's wife, Jessica, broke in and said to me, "You're a policeman now, right? That's how you two met."

I said, "Yes."

April smiled and said, "He fell in love with me through his rifle scope."

Jessica rolled her eyes and smiled, loving it. "Oh my God. I've heard of love at first sight, but that's awesome!"

Cory said, "I can't believe there's a lot of work for a police sniper."

I said, "There isn't. I'm on regular patrol most of the time."

He nodded, looking like he had something else to say but he was keeping it to himself. I knew exactly what he had to say. That sort of made me regret answering his question. It felt like I'd tried to defend myself, even though I knew I hadn't.

He and I didn't talk to each other much during dinner. The girls chattered the whole time, acting like there weren't any hard feelings between Cory and me. But afterward, when we were driving home, April asked me about it right away.

She said, "Was that an army thing? That vibe between you and Cory?"

I said, "Maybe. Sometimes guys who were in different branches of the service sort of look down their noses at each other. A rivalry kind of thing. But Cory's deal probably has more to do with me being a sniper in Iraq."

"Why?"

"Because he was general infantry. 'Right out in front,' you heard him say. That was a dig at snipers. We aren't out in front, so we don't get shot at as much."

"You don't?"

"Not like them. We stay hidden. That's the whole point of sniping—not being seen. Taking out the target and no one even knowing where the bullet came from."

April was confused. "So . . . what? He thinks he's braver than you?"

"I don't know if that's it. It's more like general infantry thinks it's not fair that we don't take the same risks as them. We take other risks, but they don't think about that. And they think it's wrong somehow, the way we sneak up on the enemy and take them out. It's not sporting."

"That's crazy."

"It's how they think."

She didn't ask me about it again for . . . it must have been a month. Then one night we were lying in bed and she said out of the blue, "What was it like being a sniper in Iraq?"

I said, "I already told you about that." Meaning the little bit I'd said driving home from the restaurant that night. We hadn't talked about it before or since.

She said, "You weren't very specific."

"Well, it's sort of like hunting."

"Only hunting people."

"Yeah."

She fell quiet. I lay there in the dark, wondering if she was going to ask for more details. I hoped she wouldn't.

Then she said, "Were they shooting at you, the people you shot?"

"Some of them."

"But not all."

"They all would have, if they could have."

"The ones who couldn't . . . is it because they didn't have guns?"

I turned my head toward her in the darkness. "Why do you want to know about this stuff?"

"I just want to understand what it was like for you there."

"It was hot. And dirty. And dangerous. A lot of people died. But the media didn't get it right. The Iraqis didn't hate us as much as the news made it sound."

"So you were shooting regular soldiers?"

"There weren't any regular soldiers. Not like you're thinking of, guys with colored uniforms that are easy to spot. These were insurgents. And yes, most of my targets had guns. Once in a blue moon we'd go out looking for a high-value target, some big terrorist leader. I got a couple of those. They didn't have guns in their hands when I got them, but they probably had a pistol on them somewhere, and if they didn't you can be sure they had an AK-47 in the next room."

"Is it hard shooting someone like that? I mean when you have time to think about it, not just in the heat of the moment?"

Right then I knew where these questions were coming from. She'd been talking to Cory. He'd laid out the rank and file's opinion of snipers for her.

I said, "You mean am I a cold-blooded bastard?"

"I didn't say that."

I wasn't going to say anything more. But then I realized if I didn't, she'd think a cold-blooded bastard was exactly what I was.

So I said, "All the worst things soldiers do happen in the heat of battle. Taking time to think is good, when you have time to do it. It keeps innocent people from getting killed."

"So police snipers . . . Is doing it for the police the same as doing it in Iraq?"

"It's easier. And not as many people have a problem with it. Criminals are the only people who get shot by police snipers. People don't mind that so much. Especially since I'm never going to shoot anybody unless they're an imminent danger to someone else."

She stayed quiet, but I felt compelled to add, "Anyway, I've never had to shoot anyone yet. Hostage situations are so rare. Most of what I do is surveillance, watching the team do raids and providing security for visiting ambassadors, stuff like that."

She never asked me about it again. But from then on I thought about it, that conversation, whenever she seemed a little quiet. I'd wonder if she was thinking about what I do and what kind of person it makes me. I'd wonder if Cory was talking to her about it, bad-mouthing me behind my back.

Then her grandmother died. It wasn't quick. She was in the hospital for a while. So there were trips to see her, and visits to April's parents' house. And then the last trip to the hospital, and the funeral and everything. I went with April to all of them. Well, I guess I missed a few, because of work, but I went along when I could. And I was there for her at home. I held her a couple of times when she cried. I was extra-nice to her, like you are with people who just lost someone. I thought I did a good job. I thought I was being supportive.

But then, a few days after the funeral, April started crying again, so I tried to hug her, but she pushed me away.

She said, "Don't."

I said, "What's wrong?"

She wouldn't answer me.

I said, "Are you mad at me or something?"

Again, she wouldn't answer. She wouldn't even look at me.

I had to ask a couple more times, but finally she said, "You can't help me with this."

I said, "Well, I guess that's right. Nobody can help, really. Only time will make it better."

She said, "No, I mean *you* can't help."

"Why not?"

"You don't know how this feels."

I wasn't sure what she meant. I didn't know exactly what kind of relationship she'd had with her grandmother, but I've lost grandparents too, and other relatives. I tried to tell her that, carefully, trying hard not to be insensitive.

But she said, "No, I mean no one who kills people for a living can really know how this feels."

I was floored. "What are you talking about?"

"If you'd ever felt this way, you wouldn't be able to do your job."

It was everything I'd been afraid of. And somehow it made me mad.

I said, "So you think I'm a robot? I never grieved for anyone? I'm not capable of it?"

She just looked at me and said, "I don't know what you feel. But it can't be like normal people."

I couldn't talk after that. I couldn't make words come out. The worst of it was, she wasn't mad. She was just sort of cold. Closed off.

We talked about it some more later that night, a little bit, but I don't remember anything I said. I don't think I made any sense, I was so upset. I know I didn't say anything that had any effect on her. Nothing made a dent.

She moved out four days after that. Not back to her parents' house. She already had an apartment lined up.

Barbara said, "Did she give you a reason?"

"Lots of them. She had a whole list. We were two different people, that's the main one I remember."

The look in his eyes showed that he was in fact capable of feeling grief. Barbara said, "I'm sorry. Did you ever live with a girlfriend before her?"

"No."

Barbara wasn't surprised. His personnel file included his results from the Meyers-Briggs Personality Type Inventory, which he'd been required to take when he joined the force. It showed he was introverted, cerebral, and extremely self-reliant. Just the qualities you wanted in a sniper, but not necessarily in a romantic partner. It would have been only natural if he'd had trouble getting along with his first live-in girlfriend.

She said, "Well, how did you cope with your relationship ending?"

"I don't know. I just tried to work. Tried not to think about it. But in the end I couldn't do either one."

Gently Barbara said, "Tell me about what happened yesterday."

I got the call while I was out on patrol. I got to the scene first, before Dean, so I picked a spot to set up in. It was in one of the offices of a car dealership across the street from the suspect. I had a clear shot out the window from there, straight at the side of the car the suspect was sitting in. It was only fifty yards away. The scope brought him so close I could see the pores on his face.

His name was Clarence Schappell. I remember thinking you wouldn't expect someone named Clarence to ever do anything violent. His girlfriend's name was Valerie. She was sitting in the front seat on the passenger side and he was sitting behind her, both of them facing front. Most of the time he kept the gun pointed at the back of her headrest, but sometimes he'd put it down. It was a heavy gun, a Smith & Wesson 686. That's the big .357 Magnum, stainless steel with a six-inch barrel. It holds seven rounds, but one would be enough to kill Valerie, no question.

I got set up. It took Dean a long time to get there. I was on my own for probably an hour. And that whole time I'm worrying, the same old thoughts running through my head. But now it's worse, because now I feel like I have answers to a lot of the old questions. I feel like I really do know this guy because of what he's going through. You see, before I got there he was already on the phone with Barry. He told Barry he's just trying to work some things out with his girlfriend. I can sure relate to that. I mean he's gone way overboard, but I know just how he feels. A week or two ago I had moments when I fantasized about cornering April in a room somewhere, locking the door, and not letting her leave until she told me whether or not she ever really loved me, and why she did what she did. I didn't do it, of course, but I felt like I knew what drove Clarence to do this.

And now there I am, and I'm going to have to shoot the guy. I can see it. He's even more squirrelly than Guinness was. Whatever answers he was hoping to get from Valerie, she's not giving them to him. Sergeant Erb can see it too, and everybody else. I can hear through my headset, people warning each other this guy's going to lose it.

About five minutes after Dean gets there, Sergeant Erb asks me for a status report. He wants to know my state of readiness. That's him giving me a heads-up, letting me know the next thing I get from him is going to be the green light.

So now I'm trying hard to find a way out. Which is ironic, because you can see Clarence isn't even thinking about that, he's so wrapped up in his conversation with Valerie. He's looking more and more upset. I can't think what to do. Things are getting so tense, Sergeant Erb tells Dean to go on station along with me. As Dean finishes unpacking his gear, I hear Sergeant Erb put the team on standby. Time is running out, fast.

Clarence is crying now. I watch him lift up the gun. He had it down out of sight, in his lap. Now he puts it to the back of Valerie's headrest and cocks it with his thumb.

Sergeant Erb says, "O'Donnell, green light."

I break out in a cold sweat. I've got one second to make a decision here. If I don't shoot Clarence he's going to kill Valerie, but I'm still hesitating. If I can't shoot this guy in this situation, who can I shoot? But I still can't make myself do it. But I can't let Valerie die.

Clarence is holding the gun perfectly still, pressing it hard against the back of the headrest. I adjust my aim and squeeze the trigger.

My focus was too tight to see what happened. I just saw the gun jump out of my field of view. Or the hammer, to be more accurate. I back out my focus a little and I can see Clarence through the broken window. He's staring down toward his lap. I didn't know it in that moment but he still had the gun in his hand. When I shot the hammer off it, I didn't knock the gun out of his hand. And by some stroke of luck he was clearheaded enough to see what I did and realize that meant the gun was useless. It's a good thing, otherwise he might have pointed it at the team. They were rushing at him right then, with their own guns raised. They would have shot him in a heartbeat.

Barbara said, "Department policy is to shoot the suspect in that situation, not the gun."

"I know it is."

"Do you know why that's the policy?"

"Because the objective is to eliminate the threat posed by the suspect. The only sure way to do that is to kill him, and kill him instantly. Just wounding him might make him pull the trigger out of reflex, or anger. And trying to shoot the gun out of his hand might make it go off too."

Barbara nodded, straight-faced, as if she'd known any of that herself twenty-four hours ago. She couldn't admit it, but her first reaction yesterday had been delight when she heard what Keith had done. Captain Smith needed to explain to her that disarming a suspect is the goal when the suspect is suicidal, but when they're homicidal it's a different story.

Keith said, "I just couldn't put a bullet through his head."

"From what I understand that was a tough shot, shooting the hammer. A small target, behind glass?"

"The bullets we use are big enough to go through glass without breaking up or changing trajectory. And there was no chance I'd miss. I'm too good a shot. If I can't make that shot from fifty yards, I don't have any business being a sniper."

His lips twisted into a grimace. "Well," he added, "I guess I don't have any business being a sniper regardless. If you can't take that shot . . ." He waved vaguely, then ran that hand through his hair, a gesture of helpless frustration. "Well, at least you can tell the brass I wasn't hot-dogging it. I'm sure they'll wish I was."

"Do you still want to be a sniper?"

"No, I guess I don't."

"Do you still want to be a police officer?"

Desperation flashed in his eyes. "Yes! But—Jesus! What if . . . what if I can't take *any* shot? What if somebody pulls a gun, points it at my partner—or at me!—and I can't shoot him?"

Barbara said soothingly, "We can examine that. I'm going to recommend we keep on meeting while you're on suspension. We should meet two or three times a week. During those sessions we're bound to get some idea what you're capable of. If I think you can still fulfill all your responsibilities as a patrol officer, I'll recommend you be returned to active duty—once the investigation into yesterday is finished. But understand, not everyone is capable of shooting a person. A lot of people couldn't do it even if their life depended on it. And that's not necessarily a bad thing."

"How can it change?" he cried, frustrated and angry. "For God's sake, all the people I shot before! Why would it change now?"

"People change."

She wanted to say more. She wanted to tell him there was a reason why the military preferred eighteen-year-old recruits, boys who were so young they didn't yet have fully developed consciences and higher reasoning faculties. But like so many other revelations, it would be better if her patient came to that realization himself.

Still, she could offer Keith some consolation.

She said, "Think of it this way. Whatever else happens, you saved Clarence's life. And Valerie's. You saved them both."

He nodded, relaxing visibly.

Then he said, "You know, it's like she cast a spell on me. April."

"She might have been the catalyst for change, but she didn't force change upon you. Remember, you worried about shooting that drug dealer before you and April ever talked about your job. Before you met Cory."

Keith nodded, relaxing some more. He sighed. "Still, if I'm going to have all this trouble—if I'm going to lose my career and everything—you'd think I should at least get the girl."

Barbara smiled wanly. *You'll get another one,* she almost said. *When you're ready.*

But she didn't think hearing that would help him right now, so she didn't say it.

# Contributors' Notes

# Other Distinguished Mystery Stories of 2014

# Contributors' Notes

The author of eight novels and more than 120 short stories, **Doug Allyn** has been published internationally in English, German, French, and Japanese. More than two dozen of his tales have been optioned for development as feature films and television.

Allyn studied creative writing and criminal psychology at the University of Michigan while moonlighting as a guitarist in the rock group Devil's Triangle and reviewing books for the *Flint Journal*. His background includes Chinese-language studies at Indiana University and extended duty in USAF Intelligence in Southeast Asia during the Vietnam War.

Career highlights? Sipping champagne with Mickey Spillane and waltzing with Mary Higgins Clark.

His first published story won the Robert L. Fish Award from Mystery Writers of America, and subsequent critical response has been equally remarkable. He has won the coveted Edgar Allan Poe Award twice, five Derringer Awards for novellas, and the Ellery Queen Readers' Award an unprecedented twelve times.

▪ A few years ago, in my hometown, a judge's widow and two elderly lady friends shared a convivial lunch at a local steak house. On their way home, they rear-ended a car hauler. No one was hurt. The widow was cited for driving under the influence and released.

The story made a splash in the papers and on TV, but the small-town buzz it created was totally sympathetic to the three ladies. What purpose had been served by their public humiliation?

The phrase I heard constantly repeated was, *"In the old days, this never could have happened."* They were right. In the old days, in our small town, the story would have been quietly suppressed. No harm, no foul.

In those days our town was run by an old-boy network, a loose circle of

398

*Contributors' Notes*

friends (lawyers, judges, doctors, cops) who golfed and hunted and partied together. Policy decisions that affected the entire county were often made by a few friends over drinks at the Yacht Club.

A conspiracy? In a way it was, but I'm not complaining. My own youthful misdeeds, from DUIs to street scuffles, were glossed over and dismissed because I came from a "good" family. If those exceptions hadn't been made, I and many of my friends might be living very different lives now. And wearing ankle bracelets.

Still, those days weren't all Hallmark card moments. I know mistakes were made, some of them pretty egregious, which gave rise to this story. What if the old-boy network, with the best of intentions, made a fatal mistake?

God, I love this game.

**Andrew Bourelle**'s fiction has been published in *Hobart, Kestrel, Jabberwock Review, Prime Number Magazine, Red Rock Review, Thin Air, Weave, Whitefish Review,* and other journals and anthologies. He is an assistant professor of English at the University of New Mexico. He lives in Albuquerque with his wife, Tiffany, and son, Benjamin.

- I wrote this story several years ago, when I was a graduate student at the University of Nevada, Reno. I had been interested in writing a modern-day western for a while, and after reading Cormac McCarthy's *No Country for Old Men,* I decided to go for it. I wanted to write a fast-paced story where I could put my foot on the gas and not let up. I also tried to take common western themes and subvert them. Instead of riding off into the sunset at the end of the story, Jack is riding toward the sunrise. He has his whole life ahead of him, a life where he'll never be able to outrun what he's done.

I'm indebted to my former professor Christopher Coake, who gave me excellent advice for revising the story. I'm also thankful to Amy Locklin for first publishing the story in the anthology *Law and Disorder.*

**Tomiko M. Breland** is just beginning her literary career. Her short fiction has won the *Ploughshares* Emerging Writer's Award and placed in the *Writer's Digest* Popular Fiction Contest. She runs a small editing, manuscript review, and graphic design business out of her home in Monterey, California, where she lives with her husband and two sons, and is completing her first novel. "Rosalee Carrasco" was her first published piece of fiction.

- According to Stephen King, original stories occur when "two previously unrelated ideas come together and make something new under the sun." I think that's the best way to describe what happened with this story. I had this idea that I wanted to write a short story that cheated—that accomplished what a novel accomplishes (telling the past, present, and future of a cast of three-dimensional characters) in a very short space. I came up with my form, and then tinkered with a number of story ideas, all terrible, for several weeks. And then I read an article about a horrific social media bullying incident—and there was my second idea.

I began with a Stephen King quote because I think that Rosalee has the bones of King's *Carrie*: she is a sympathetic outcast, her "becoming a woman" is witnessed by others, and we even have the backdrop of a girls' locker room. But what happens when that girl's "becoming a woman" is witnessed in the age of Facebook, Twitter, and Instagram? When bullying becomes viral and untraceable, public and exponential? Nothing good. My second idea—Rosalee and her tragic but not unbelievable circumstances—poured itself into my first idea with the smoothness and liquidity of juice into a glass carafe, taking shape the way you always hope your stories will when you start out. To ensure that I really, *really* stuck to the short story form, I challenged myself to keep each character—past and future—to just one typed page, and that resulted in a dense little story that packed some punch, and I found that I had written "something new under the sun."

Previously a law student, theater technician, television director, and union organizer, **Lee Child** is now the globally best-selling author of the Jack Reacher series.

▪ I was asked to contribute to *Belfast Noir* on the basis of my father being a Belfast man, which meant I had spent time there both before and during the Troubles and was familiar with the culture that had led in that tragic direction.

Family legend has it that when my grandparents moved in the 1940s, they sold their house to a couple named Morrison, whose first child, Ivan, went on to become the musician Van Morrison. I was interested in the idea of foreign fans seeking out his birthplace, but in the end opted for an imaginary writer instead of the real-life singer. (But the story's title, *Wet with Rain,* is a common line in Van Morrison's lyrics—as well as a perpetually reliable description of Belfast's weather.)

I was also interested in the idea that although Belfast's rifts were relentless and implacable to the point of psychosis, there must have been participants who on occasion opted for restraint, and *Wet with Rain* is about one of them.

**Michael Connelly** is the author of twenty-seven novels and one book of nonfiction. Ten of his novels—featuring the characters LAPD detective Harry Bosch, defense attorney Mickey Haller, and journalist Jack McEvoy—have hit the number-one spot on the *New York Times* bestseller list. His books *Blood Work* and *The Lincoln Lawyer* were produced as films starring Clint Eastwood and Matthew McConaughey. He is executive producer of the streaming television show *Bosch,* based upon his long-running series of books. He lives in Florida and California.

▪ The task faced by Dennis Lehane and Michael Connelly was figuring out how to legitimately bring together two characters who live and work on opposite coasts of the United States. Harry Bosch is an LAPD detective and Patrick Kenzie is a Boston private eye, and it would seem never the twain should meet. But it was decided by the authors that the most believable way to pull this off was to have Harry Bosch follow a lead on a cold case to Boston. And so Connelly wrote the setup. Evidence in the cold case leads to identifying a solid suspect in Boston. He gets on a plane and lands in Boston. From there he stumbles into Kenzie and the story goes from there. Since Boston is Lehane's turf, he sort of met Bosch at the airport and took it from there.

**Joseph D'Agnese** is a journalist, author, and editor who has written for adults and children alike. His nonfiction has appeared in *The Best American Science Writing* two years in a row. His crime fiction has appeared or will appear in *Shotgun Honey, Plots with Guns, Beat to a Pulp, Alfred Hitchcock's Mystery Magazine, Ellery Queen's Mystery Magazine,* and *Sherlock Holmes Mystery Magazine.* One of his short stories was a finalist for the 2014 Derringer Award. He's the author of three popular history titles, a children's picture book on the Fibonacci sequence, and some novels. He lives in North Carolina with his wife, the author Denise Kiernan (*The Girls of Atomic City*).

▪ The seeds of my story "Harm and Hammer" were planted the day I visited the Biltmore Estate in Asheville, where I live, and encountered a blacksmith who entertained tourists by playing his anvil as a musical instrument. The sound of hammers on steel struck me as so beautiful, so clear, so pure, and so unlike any instrument I've ever heard that it lodged in my mind and never left. I'm not religious, but I am still strongly moved by hymns. Two of my favorites have always been "Amazing Grace" and "Jerusalem," probably because the lyrics hint at their composers' inner struggles. Years after I'd first seen that smithy's anvil performance, I began to find the notion of combining these two disparate elements—the anvil and the hymns—in one story nearly irresistible. I just needed a protagonist. That got me thinking about the sort of person who might be drawn to obsessively play the anvil as a form of expiation. Before long I envisioned a young woman consumed with guilt, her anvil perhaps offering a somewhat healthier form of self-flagellation. Naturally, because of the way my mind works, it wasn't enough to have one crime in the story. The deceit and violence, like the music itself, had to ripple outward.

A former journalist, folksinger, and attorney, **Jeffery Deaver** is an international number-one bestselling author. His novels have appeared on bestseller lists around the world, including the *New York Times,* the *Times* of London, Italy's *Corriere della Sera,* the *Sydney Morning Herald,* and the *Los Angeles Times.* His books are sold in 150 countries and translated into twenty-five languages.

The author of thirty-five novels, three collections of short stories, and a nonfiction law book, and a lyricist of a country-western album, Deaver has received or been shortlisted for dozens of awards. His *The Bodies Left Behind* was named Novel of the Year by the International Thriller Writers, and his Lincoln Rhyme thriller *The Broken Window* and a stand-alone, *Edge,* were also nominated for that prize. He has been awarded the Steel Dagger and the Short Story Dagger from the British Crime Writers' Association, as well as the Nero Wolfe Award, and he is a three-time recipient of the Ellery Queen Readers Award for Best Short Story of the Year and a winner of the British Thumping Good Read Award. *The Cold Moon* was recently named the Book of the Year by the Mystery Writers of Japan, as well as by *Kono Mystery Wa Sugoi!* magazine. In addition, the Japanese Adventure Fiction Association awarded *The Cold Moon* and *Carte Blanche* their annual Grand Prix. His book *The Kill Room* was awarded the Political/Adventure/Espionage Thriller of 2014 by Killer Nashville.

Deaver has been honored with the Lifetime Achievement Award by the Bouchercon World Mystery Convention. He also recently received another lifetime achievement honor in Italy, the prestigious Raymond Chandler Award. He contributed to the anthology *Books to Die For,* which won the Agatha Award and the Anthony Award. Deaver has been nominated for seven Edgar Awards from the Mystery Writers of America, an Anthony, a Shamus, and a Gumshoe. He was recently shortlisted for the ITV3 Crime Thriller Award for Best International Author. *Roadside Crosses* was on the shortlist for the Prix Polar International 2013.

His most recent novels are *The October List,* a thriller told in reverse; *The Skin Collector* and *The Kill Room,* Lincoln Rhyme novels, and *XO,* a Kathryn Dance thriller, for which he wrote an album of country-western songs, available on iTunes and as a CD; and *Carte Blanche,* the latest James Bond continuation novel, a number-one international bestseller.

His book *A Maiden's Grave* was made into an HBO movie starring James Garner and Marlee Matlin, and his novel *The Bone Collector* was a feature release from Universal Pictures, starring Denzel Washington and Angelina Jolie. And yes, the rumors are true: he did appear as a corrupt reporter on his favorite soap opera, *As the World Turns.* He was born outside Chicago and has a bachelor of journalism degree from the University of Missouri and a law degree from Fordham University. Readers can visit his website at www.jefferydeaver.com.

▪ I was, to put it mildly, bookish as a child. I read constantly. (It didn't hurt that I had absolutely no talent for sports whatsoever; fiction was a safer—and less shameful—way to while away the hours.) Two authors stand out in the well-populated pantheon of my young reader's experience: J.R.R. Tolkien and Arthur Conan Doyle.

I can't tell you how many times I read *The Hobbit* and *The Lord of the Rings* (I can still recite a poem in Elvish, but please don't tell anyone). Nor could I tally up the hours I spent, yes, in the company of Sherlock. I appreciated then, and still do, an intellectual protagonist: someone who had to out-think the villain and, ideally, prevail in a wholly unexpected way. (Aren't we all tired of heroes who win simply because they shoot straighter or karate-kick higher?) Add a dash of exotic location, a different era, quirky characters, police procedure, and I'm on that tale in a London minute. Doyle delivered exactly what my story-hungry heart longed for.

When asked what were the inspirations for my own series protagonist Lincoln Rhyme, I answer not *Ironside* or Jimmy Stewart in *Rear Window* (Rhyme is a quadriplegic) but Sherlock Holmes. Rhyme is a forensic scientist and criminalist who uses his brain to track down the perps, since he obviously can't outshoot anyone. He's also a curmudgeon, reclusive, and substance-dependent (Scotch). Oh, I gave him a Watson too, though Amelia Sachs is a touch different from John: she's a former fashion model turned NYPD detective who drives a muscle car and shoots like nobody's business.

When I was asked to be in *In the Company of Sherlock Holmes,* I did a lot of thinking about the direction to take, rereading many of the original stories, since I knew mine would be among those of so many fine writers—and some with a far better grounding in the Holmes catalog than I possessed. At some point during this research I decided that Doyle seemed to share a trait with me: I delight in creating my villains, and no one created better bad guys than Sir Arthur.

*Ping.* There was the answer. I would imagine an antagonist in my story worthy of the rarely seen but undeniably evil and enigmatic Moriarty.

The result was "The Adventure of the Laughing Fisherman," a fairly typical story of mine, in which nothing is quite what it seems to be at first blush.

**Brendan DuBois** is the award-winning author of seventeen novels and more than 135 short stories. His latest novel, *Blood Foam,* was published in May.

His short fiction has appeared in *Playboy, Ellery Queen's Mystery Magazine, Alfred Hitchcock's Mystery Magazine,* and numerous anthologies, including *The Best American Mystery Stories of the Century,* published in 2000, and *The Best American Noir of the Century,* published in 2010. This is his sixth appearance in the annual *Best American Mystery Stories* anthology. His stories have twice won him the Shamus Award from the Private Eye Writers of America and have earned him three Edgar Allan Poe Award nominations from the MWA. He is also a *Jeopardy!* game show champion.

Visit his website at www.BrendanDuBois.com.

▪ When I saw that the Mystery Writers of America was soliciting short stories for an anthology based on the Cold War (*Ice Cold: Tales of Intrigue from the Cold War*), I knew I was going to submit a story. All right, at the time I didn't have a story, but I knew one would quickly come to me, and I was right.

I was a child of the Cold War, and growing up in Dover, New Hampshire, I was just a few miles away from two key military bases, Pease Air Force Base, the home of a nuclear-armed Strategic Air Force installation, and the Portsmouth Naval Shipyard, where nuclear-powered submarines were constructed and overhauled.

This was a time when FALLOUT SHELTER signs were located at my Catholic elementary school, where "duck and cover" drills had been conducted, and when the roaring sounds of B-52 bombers taking off at night during an exercise would shake the house.

With that background, a story idea immediately came to me, concerning the sinking of the submarine USS *Thresher* on April 10, 1963, with the loss of all hands. This disaster still reverberates among the residents of my home state, and my family has a connection: reactor control officer Lieutenant Raymond McCoole was a neighbor of ours, and survived because he had to take an ill wife to the hospital.

But suppose the *Thresher* wasn't lost because of an accident? Suppose it was sabotage? And that's where "Crush Depth" came from. It was an intriguing yet melancholy story to write, and I'm honored to have it appear in this anthology.

**John M. Floyd**'s short stories and features have appeared in more than two hundred different publications, including *The Strand Magazine, Alfred Hitchcock's Mystery Magazine, Ellery Queen's Mystery Magazine, Woman's World,* and *The Saturday Evening Post.* A former air force captain and IBM systems engineer, Floyd won a Derringer Award in 2007 and was nominated for an Edgar in 2015. He is also the author of five collections of short fiction: *Rainbow's End* (2006), *Midnight* (2008), *Clockwork* (2010), *Deception* (2013), and *Fifty Mysteries* (2014). He and his wife, Carolyn, live in Mississippi.

▪ The idea for my story "Molly's Plan" began years ago, when I was employed with IBM. During most of my career there, I worked with bankers and banking software and spent a lot of time in the lobbies, back rooms, and computer centers of financial institutions. One of these was a big, ugly branch of a regional bank located at the very end of a narrow street that was always jammed with traffic. Its limited access triggered an idea in my devious mind, which was already seriously devious, even back then. My thought was, This bank would be really hard to rob—or at least really hard to escape from after the robbery. It would be so difficult, in fact, that no sane criminal would attempt it. As I later mentioned in the resulting story, "Smart rustlers tend to avoid box canyons." Needless to say, the characters in my story—who consider themselves both smart *and* sane—do attempt it. The story itself was great fun to put together, and the setting is so similar to the one I remembered (my memory bank?) that I felt I was actually there during the writing process. Which makes me wonder, sometimes, about my own sanity . . .

**Scott Grand** is the pseudonym for Zach Basnett, who lives on the California coast with his wife and cat. "A Bottle of Scotch and a Sharp Buck Knife" is his first published work and appeared in *Thuglit*, issue 11. His other short stories, "No Rest for the Wicked" and "Sight," can be found in *Dark Corners Pulp Magazine*, Vol. 1, issues 1 and 2. His science fiction novella, *Proximity*, will be published this year. His other works include the self-published novellas *SPORT*, *3 Day Life*, and *Only Child*.

▪ In many ways, I don't think I will ever have better friends then I did when I was twelve. Maybe it's because we grew up together, learned how to talk shit and fight and set things on fire. I don't really understand it; maybe that is an age before greed and selfishness and jealousy kick in. It could be I was just better back then. I hope to have captured those experiences of adolescence accurately, of friendship and loneliness and loss.

**Steven Heighton**'s short fiction and poetry have appeared in *Best English Short Stories, Best American Poetry, Zoetrope: All-Story, Tin House, Poetry, London Review of Books, New England Review, TLR, Agni,* and five editions of *Best Canadian Stories*. His novel *Afterlands* appeared in a number of countries, was a *New York Times Book Review* Editors' Choice, and was included on best-of-year lists in ten publications in the United States, Canada, and Britain. Heighton has been nominated for the W. H. Smith Award in Britain and has received four gold National Magazine Awards in Canada, where he lives. He was the 2013 Mordecai Richler Writer-in-Residence at McGill University and reviews fiction for the *New York Times Book Review*.

▪ On rereading "Shared Room on Union," I see that the mystery at its core is the mystery of marriage, or at least of marriages that endure for any length of time. Most enduring ones sooner or later include chapters where one or both partners act in cruel, faithless, bizarre, or otherwise unlaudable ways. Unforgiveable things—or at least unforgettable things—get said and done. How does a marriage metabolize such compound calamities and emerge intact, and, often enough, annealed and deepened? I can't seem to answer the question in a pithy way that transcends truism and cliché; maybe that's why I've explored the mystery through fiction, a mode of inquiry more suggestive than conclusive, and hence truer to human relationships.

As for the predicament at the heart of "Shared Room on Union": short story writers can't waste time if they mean to bare the hearts and minds of their characters (and, in this case, the workings of a relationship) within a few pages. Tipping a couple suddenly into an appalling situation seems as good a way as any to get them to show their souls quickly and for all time.

**Janette Turner Hospital** grew up, was educated, and taught high school on the steamy subtropical northeastern coast of Australia. She married a fellow graduate of the University of Queensland, and she and her husband came to the United States as graduate students, not intending to stay; but life, careers, children, and grandchildren intervened. A sabbatical spent in an equatorial village in South India led to a short story, an "Atlantic First," in March 1978. The village sojourn also led to a first novel, *The Ivory Swing*, which won Canada's Seal Award and international publication in 1982. Hospital has published ten novels and four story collections in multiple languages and has won literary awards in Australia, Canada, and the U.K. *Forecast: Turbulence*, her most recent collection of stories, was a finalist for the Prime Minister's Literary Award in Australia in 2013. Her most recent novel, *The Claimant*, was published in Australia last year. Both books are forthcoming in 2015 in the United States. Hospital is Carolina Distinguished Professor Emerita at the University of South Carolina but has also taught at MIT, Boston University, Colgate, and Columbia. She and her husband divide their time between the U.S. and Australia.

Website: www.janetteturnerhospital.com

▪ A few years ago, I was riveted by two brief articles which appeared two days apart in a major national newspaper. The heading of the first one was "Man Claims to Be Boy Taken in 1955: Federal Officials Await DNA Results as Lead Revives NY Kidnap Mystery." The opening paragraph read: "More than 50 years ago, a mother left her stroller outside a Long Island bakery and returned minutes later to find her two-year-old son had vanished." The baby sister was still in the stroller. No trace of the two-year-old had ever been found, and the case had gone cold. The parents divorced a few years later. But now a Michigan man in his fifties was convinced that he was the kidnapped child. He made contact with the woman he believed to be his sister and an emotional bond was formed. They believed they were related. The man said he had "long suspected the couple who raised him were not his biological parents." The FBI was conducting DNA tests. Two days later, a second article indicated that the man was *not* the kidnapped toddler and that the couple who raised him were indeed his biological parents.

This story was so disturbing and tragic and poignant in so many ways that it haunted me and still does. I read these articles a year before my retirement, when I was still teaching an MFA fiction class. I ran off photocopies of the articles and distributed them to the class. I often used what my classes called my "story prompts"—a device that has led to a number of publications for my students. Their assignment was to select a point of view and write a fictional version of the kidnapping/identity confusion from that perspective. As always, I received finely written and nuanced stories, but all from the perspective of one or other of the parents or from the point of view of the man who believed he was the missing child.

As so many writers have noted, there are ideas that will not let you go. They become obsessions. They show up in dreams. What haunted me were the black holes in the account, the permanent absences: the abducted child; the kidnapper/killer; the absence of closure (the never knowing what happened).

By this time I had actually written three novels about psychopaths, the first of these (*Oyster*) prompted by the cult messiah David Koresh and the horrific conflagration at Waco, Texas. I was trying to understand what made so many people willing to submit all to a darkly charismatic figure. I read voraciously in the scholarly literature on psychopathology. I realized it was impossible to portray a psychopath from inside because there *is no inside*. It is like reporting on an earthquake or a tsunami. All the fiction writer can do is chronicle the devastation on all sides and seek to pay tribute to the survival strategies and the stricken inner lives of those left behind. I confess, to my own regret and dismay, that as a fiction writer I have become morbidly obsessed with psychopaths, both violent (cult messiahs, terrorists) and nonviolent (Bernie Madoff, a fictional clone of whom is a major character in *The Claimant*). The kidnapper/killer (?) in this short story is the closest I have been able to come in an attempt to get inside the mind of such a person; though of course that is sleight of hand. The reader is never really inside the mind of the killer but is inside the mind of the man who needs not only to construct an alternative narrative of his own life but to construct his supposed kidnapper and killer.

To me, the greatest mystery is how anyone manages to survive catastrophic loss and trauma, and I am fascinated by the narrative strategies used.

**Richard Lange** is the author of the short story collections *Dead Boys* and *Sweet Nothing* and the novels *This Wicked World* and *Angel Baby,* which won the 2013 Hammett Prize. His stories have appeared in *The Sun, The Southern Review,* and *The Best American Mystery Stories* and as part of the *Atlantic*'s Fiction for Kindle series. He was the recipient of a Guggenheim Fellowship and the Rosenthal Family Foundation Award for Literature from the American Academy of Arts and Letters. He is currently working on a novel.

▪ A number of years ago I started a novel that never got off the ground. One of the characters from that book, a security guard living in a skid-row hotel, stuck with me, and one day I started writing about him again. That story eventually became "Apocrypha." So, in the end, something positive came out of that earlier failure. There's a lesson in there somewhere.

"Apocrypha" is a story about an invisible man engaged in a life-and-death struggle in a place most of us pass through — car doors locked, windows rolled up — as quickly as possible on our way to somewhere else. It's these men and these places that fascinate me and that I keep returning to in my work. In this milieu, people live so close to the edge that the smallest misstep can be ruinous or even fatal. Just thinking about it scares me, and what scares me inspires me. I'm glad that I got to save the lost soul in "Apocrypha." I only wish that I could save them all.

**Dennis Lehane** grew up in Boston. Since his first novel, *A Drink Before the War*, won the Shamus Award, he has published eleven more novels, which have been translated into more than thirty languages and become international bestsellers: *Darkness, Take My Hand; Sacred; Gone, Baby, Gone; Prayers for Rain; Mystic River; Shutter Island; The Given Day; Moonlight Mile; Live by Night; The Drop;* and his most recent book, *World Gone By*. Lehane was a staff writer on the acclaimed HBO series *The Wire* and a writer-producer on HBO's *Boardwalk Empire*.

Three of his novels — *Mystic River; Gone, Baby, Gone;* and *Shutter Island* — have been adapted into award-winning films. In 2014 his first screenplay, *The Drop*, based on his short story "Animal Rescue," was produced as a feature film starring Tom Hardy and James Gandolfini in his final role.

Lehane and his wife, Angie, currently live in Los Angeles with their two children, a fact that never ceases to surprise him.

▪ As I remember it — and a writer's memory is about the last person's you should trust — Michael Connelly and I were approached by Steve Berry about a unique collection of stories he envisioned. We'd take our series protagonists and have them work together, which would mirror Michael and me working together. Michael said he couldn't imagine Patrick Kenzie in L.A., so he thought it best and more believable if Harry Bosch were led to Boston on official business. So Michael took pole position and started the story with Harry arriving on the East Coast. At some point he and Bosch reached the place where Bosch's path crossed with Patrick's, and that's where I jumped in. From there, I can't explain how we decided when and where we'd toss the potato back into the other's hand, but making prose is a lot more like making music than laypeople suspect, and a lot of riffing between successful collaborators happens organically. The whole experience, in retrospect, was a lot more fun than it had any right to be. Maybe the story reflects that. I hope it does, anyway.

**Theresa E. Lehr** is a scuba diver and educator and has published in *Alfred Hitchcock's Mystery Magazine* and in *Texas Magazine* of the *Houston Chronicle*.

▪ Years ago, while six months pregnant and traveling Down Under with my children and husband by camper van, we stopped at a roadside park next to a rushing stream. Within moments a motorcyclist, dressed completely in black leather, pulled up next to us. Once the rider removed her helmet, I realized she was a young woman. Her independent spirit fascinated me, and she was the inspiration for my main character.

I have been a scuba diver for thirty years. Near-drownings, bad air, faulty equipment, and poor decision-making have given me a mighty respect for the power of the sea. However, nothing can keep me from exploring the wonders of the ocean whenever possible. After watching a show about the pearling industry in Western Australia, I knew I had to write this story.

Family dynamics can be such a complicated universe. Having three brothers, I found it only natural to make sibling rivalry and competition a main component of "Staircase to the Moon." I chose estranged twin sisters for a dark twist. The twins are of Japanese descent to connect them to the immigrant Japanese who brought pearl diving to Australia. Writing about the tensions between the family members gave me the opportunity to explore jealousy, resentment, forgiveness, and reparation without having to interact with any of my own family. Great fun.

And last, pearls and Japan? I was born in Japan and have always coveted my mother's strand of cultured pearls she bought in 1955.

**Lee Martin** is the author of the novels *The Bright Forever*, a finalist for the 2006 Pulitzer Prize in Fiction, *River of Heaven, Quakertown*, and *Break the Skin*. He has also published three memoirs, *From Our House, Turning Bones*, and *Such a Life*. His first book was the short story collection *The Least You Need to Know*. He is the winner of the Mary McCarthy Prize in Short Fiction and fellowships from the National Endowment for the Arts and the Ohio Arts Council. He teaches in the MFA Program at Ohio State University, where he is a College of Arts and Sciences Distinguished Professor of English and a past winner of the Alumni Award for Distinguished Teaching.

▪ "A Man Looking for Trouble" began, as my stories sometimes do, with a narrator's voice that I heard one day while I was out for my morning run. I remember hearing the line "My uncle was a man named Bill Jordan." Immediately I wondered who was speaking and why his uncle's presence made it urgent that he tell this story. I often write from a point of curiosity. I try to complicate that curiosity while moving the story forward but never quite answering all the questions that are there to be answered. In that way, I'm like the reader with anticipations and expectations and a reason to keep moving forward. When I got home from my run, I wrote the sentence "My uncle was a man named Bill Jordan, and in 1972, when I was sixteen, he came home from Vietnam, rented a small box house on the corner of South and Christy, and went to work on a section gang with the B & O Railroad." Later, after the story's interests had announced themselves to me in the first draft, I added the second sentence, about the narrator's mother's romance with Harold Timms, and just like that I had two threads to follow. By this point I also knew why this story mattered so much to my narrator. I wanted to place the innocence of his love for Connie alongside the ugliness of the adults' lives. At the end of the story, my narrator knows that he and Connie are now helpless in a world run by the adults. "A Man Looking for Trouble" is a story about what ruins us. Above all, it's a story about those moments when love might save us if only we'd let it.

**James Mathews** grew up in El Paso, Texas, and now lives in Maryland. He is a graduate of the Johns Hopkins University Masters in Arts Program. His fiction has appeared in numerous literary journals, including *Painted Bride Quarterly*, *Iron Horse Literary Review*, *The Florida Review*, *Northwest Review*, *The Wisconsin Review*, *The South Carolina Review*, *Carolina Quarterly*, and many more. His short story collection, *Last Known Position*, received the 2008 Katherine Anne Porter Prize in Short Fiction. He is also a retired air force chief master sergeant who has served overseas numerous times, including two tours in support of Operation Iraqi Freedom (in 2003 and 2006). He is currently at work on a novel.

- As an Iraq war veteran who has depended on the "band of brothers" mentality during hazardous deployments, I have always been intrigued by that rare breed of serviceman who willingly rejects the bonding process and instead isolates himself from comrades. It struck me as a defense mechanism, albeit one that was starkly counterintuitive. "Many Dogs Have Died Here" is my attempt—with a dash of mystery and absurdism—to better understand the self-exiled warrior in a postwar setting who must ultimately account for his isolation and face the grief and loss from which there is no hiding.

**Thomas McGuane** lives in McLeod, Montana. He is the author of numerous novels and short story and essay collections, including *Ninety-Two in the Shade*, *Driving on the Rim*, *Gallatin Canyon*, and *Crow Fair: Stories*. His stories and essays have been collected in *The Best American Short Stories*, *The Best American Essays*, and *The Best American Sports Writing*. He is a regular contributor to *The New Yorker* and a member of the American Academy of Arts and Letters.

- "Motherlode" is a story that suggested itself out of my preoccupation with life in the American West and its collision with the energy industry, often an enemy of the earth with the capacity to generate, besides money, its own publicity and access to government. These are of course generalizations, but I know intimately people like this vulnerable protagonist, and I have seen much of the deterioration of civic life at the behest of oil and its broadly corruptible allies.

**Kyle Minor** is the author of *Praying Drunk,* winner of the 2015 Story Prize Spotlight Award.

- Alice Munro said it better than I can say it:
"Two mysteries, really: Why do they do it? And how do they live with it?"

**Joyce Carol Oates** is the author of many novels of mystery and suspense, including most recently *Ace of Spades, Daddy Love, The Accursed,* and *Mudwoman,* as well as collections of stories, including *Give Me Your Heart, The Corn Maiden and Other Nightmares,* and *Black Dahlia & White Rose.* She is a member of the American Academy of Arts and Letters and was the 2011 recipient of the President's Medal in the Humanities. "So Near Anytime Always" will be included in *Evil Eye: Four Tales of Love Gone Wrong.*

- "The Home at Craigmillnar" was written during a very anxious time in my life, about which I can say only that I survived it!

During this enforced time in Edinburgh at the hospital bedside of my husband, stricken with pneumonia, I had the occasion to read of a breaking scandal involving a Catholic-run orphanage that was truly horrendous — dating back decades and involving generations of abused children. The nuns were as atrocious in life — or more so — as in my story. I found the material extremely upsetting, especially as there seemed to be little remorse among the surviving abusers.

The story of the American-set "Home at Craigmillnar" was my way of converting a personal crisis into something larger and I hope more valuable. It is still very hard for me to reread the story and recall those circumstances spent in a Scottish hospital, though — fortunately! — my husband, Charlie, recovered and we returned home a week after we had planned.

**Eric Rutter**'s first short story appeared in *Alfred Hitchcock's Mystery Magazine* in 2007. Since then he has contributed half a dozen more stories to that magazine, including one that was nominated for a Barry Award. He is a lifelong resident of southeast Pennsylvania.

- My taste in mystery stories has changed over the years. In the beginning I preferred what I think of as the traditional kind, stories of deduction where clues are gathered and a puzzle solved. These days character interests me at least as much as plot. I find the drama more powerful in a story that arises from some personal conflict—someone facing, and then making, a difficult choice. "The Shot" is a good example of this kind of story. The protagonist finds himself in a tough spot, and as the story progresses, the walls close in on him steadily, relentlessly. But he finds his way out.

In terms of this story's origins, the climax came to me first. I did some research to make sure the climactic act was plausible, then some more to learn about snipers in general. Research is always an integral part of my writing process, and this story was no exception. The fascinating details about snipers I uncovered didn't just flesh out the story, they gave it a shape I couldn't have imagined.

# Other Distinguished Mystery Stories of 2014

ABBOTT, PATTI
    Fall Girl. *Needle,* Spring

BECKETT, C. M.
    Silence. *Needle,* Winter

BLOCK, LAWRENCE
    The Ehrengraf Settlement. *Defender of the Innocent: The Casebook of Martin Ehrengraf* (Subterranean)

BREWER, RICHARD
    Last to Die. *Trouble in the Heartland,* ed. Joe Clifford (Gutter Books)

BROWN, TAYLOR
    An Unkindness. *Needle,* Spring

COLLINS, MAX ALLAN, AND MICKEY SPILLANE
    It's in the Book. *Bibliomystery #15* (Mysterious Bookshop)

DEAN, ZOE Z.
    Getaway Girl. *Ellery Queen's Mystery Magazine,* November

DEPOY, PHILLIP
    Mary's Shallow Grave. *Alfred Hitchcock's Mystery Magazine,* July/August

EGAN, KEVIN
    Term Life. *Alfred Hitchcock's Mystery Magazine,* June

FAYE, LYNDSAY
    The Scroll of Sheba. *Bibliomystery #18* (Mysterious Bookshop)

GATES, DAVID EDGERLEY
    Stir Crazy. *Alfred Hitchcock's Mystery Magazine,* July/August

GONZALEZ, J. DAVID
    Ofrenda. *Thuglit,* May/June

HAGELSTEIN, EDWARD
Our Lady of Mercy. *Thuglit,* March/April
HARRIS, CHARLAINE
Sarah Smiles. *Ellery Queen's Mystery Magazine,* September/October
HART, ROB W.
How to Make the Perfect New York Bagel. *Thuglit,* January/February
HAVERTY, CHARLES
The Cherry Wood Heart. *New Orleans Review,* Winter

KREUGER, PAUL
One-Step's Last Meal. *Noir Riot* (Gutter Books)

LEOPOLD, BRIAN
The Card Counter. *M: Mystery and Horror,* November
LOPRESTI, ROBERT
The Accessory. *Ellery Queen's Mystery Magazine,* June
LOUIS, MATTHEW
My Hometown. *Trouble in the Heartland,* ed. Joe Clifford (Gutter Books)

McFADDEN, DENNIS
The Purloined Pigs. *Ellery Queen's Mystery Magazine,* January
McGUIRE, MICHAEL
Three Sisters. *Kenyon Review,* Spring
MINER, MIKE
The Hurt Business. *Thuglit,* July/August
MORROW, BRADFORD
The Nature of My Inheritance. *Bibliomystery #19* (Mysterious Bookshop)

ROBINSON, TODD
We Take Care of Our Own. *Trouble in the Heartland,* ed. Joe Clifford (Gutter Books)

TAYLOR, ART
Precision. *Gargoyle,* September

WARTENBERG, PAUL
Why the Mask. *Mardi Gras Murder,* ed. Sarah E. Glenn (Mystery & Horror)
WASHBURN, MICHAEL
In the Flyover State. *New Orphic Review,* Spring
WILLIAMS, TIM L.
The Last Wrestling Bear in West Kentucky. *Ellery Queen's Mystery Magazine,* September/October
WILSON-FLAHERTY, STEPHANIE
Murder in a Family. *Family Matters,* ed. Anita Page (Glenmere Press)

# THE BEST AMERICAN SERIES®

*FIRST, BEST, AND BEST-SELLING*

The Best American series is the premier annual showcase for the country's finest short fiction and nonfiction. Each volume's series editor selects notable works from hundreds of periodicals. A special guest editor, a leading writer in the field, then chooses the best twenty or so pieces to publish. This unique system has made the Best American series the most respected—and most popular—of its kind.

Look for these best-selling titles in the Best American series:

*The Best American Comics*

*The Best American Essays*

*The Best American Infographics*

*The Best American Mystery Stories*

*The Best American Nonrequired Reading*

*The Best American Science and Nature Writing*

*The Best American Science Fiction and Fantasy*

*The Best American Short Stories*

*The Best American Sports Writing*

*The Best American Travel Writing*

Available in print and e-book wherever books are sold.
Visit our website: *www.hmhco.com/popular-reading/general-interest-books/by-category/best-american*